# Praise for the writing of Rachel Bo

*Strength in Numbers 2: Danger in Discovery*

"Rachel Bo manages to conjugate a great story with profound emotional drama and the most scorching and vivid sex scenes there are. If you are an adventurous erotic reader longing for a great story to go with it, you will not want to miss this one."

—Rocio Rosado, *Coffee Time Romance*

"This book touched me, and made me think. Ms. Bo, thank you for a poignant book that will always have a spot on my keeper shelf and definitely a place in my heart."

—Michelle Naumann, *Just Erotic Romance Reviews*

*Strength in Numbers 3: Branded*

"Rachel Bo has written her best work to date. *Strength In Numbers – Branded* is a dynamic tale of BDSM that will leave you breathless and crying out for more.

—Stacey, *The Romance Studio*

"If you are looking for something to heat up these cold winter nights then look no further than Rachel Bo's *Strength in Numbers 3: Branded...* The relationship between Brandy, Lin and Eric is very intense and erotic..."

—Barb Hicks, *The Best Reviews*

LooseId
ISBN 10: 1-59632-201-2
ISBN 13: 978-1-59632-201-1
**STRENGTH IN NUMBERS**

Cover Art by April Martinez
Edited by: Raven McKnight


Printed in the U.S.A. by
Lightning Source, Inc.
1246 Heil Quaker Blvd
La Vergne TN 37086
www.lightningsource.com

# Contents

# STRENGTH IN NUMBERS 2 : DANGER IN DISCOVERY

## Chapter One: First Steps

David Campbell read the first paragraph of Arthur's deposition for the third time, then realized he still was not absorbing the information and threw down the file in disgust. He ran long, strong fingers through blond hair peppered lightly with silver strands, and sighed. "What the hell's wrong with me?"

David stood and walked over to a large window facing the Gulf of Mexico, watching as seagulls performed aerial acrobatics above white-flocked waves. The trouble was, he knew *exactly* what was wrong—he just didn't know what to do about it. He should be with his grandchildren right now, enjoying the weekend, instead of spending his Saturday at the office working on a nuisance case. But Kendall, his daughter-in-law, had informed him that Joy and Jason would be at the picnic, and David had bailed.

David turned away from the window and flopped down onto the plump-cushioned leather sofa against the wall. Approximately two years earlier, he had seen Joy and Jason again for the first time in many years. Until that moment, he hadn't even realized how much he missed them. How much they both meant to him. The sad part was that he had thought to himself at the time that he would do whatever it took to bring them back into his life—then was too weak-willed to actually do so.

David rubbed his tired eyes and frowned. *Weak.* He hated the word. Hated the feeling. But when it came to these two lovers from his past, he couldn't seem to get beyond the self-imposed exile he'd sentenced himself to so long ago.

*Joy.* A rush of heat flooded his groin as he pictured her two years ago at Kendall's New Year's Eve party. A petite, slender brunette when they first met, he had been surprised to find her plump now, with silver streaks throughout her dark locks. The other surprise was the fact that she had still looked beautiful to him, stirring a desire he had thought long dead. Joy was the only woman he had ever truly cared about. He had considered asking her to marry him, back in college. But he hadn't been able to reconcile his feelings for her with his equally intense feelings for Jason, so he had let her go. At least, that was the official version he gave himself, when he thought about it.

*Jason.* David shifted uncomfortably as his cock began to harden. At a time when homosexuality was the kiss of death—especially for someone like him, heading into law practice with a bunch of hard-nosed, macho Texans with a black-and-white outlook on life—David had been drawn to Jason despite the stigma. Under the guise of helping out a friend, David had invited Jason to move in with him, and it hadn't been long before the relationship became intimate. He'd never really felt as though he was doing anything wrong, all those years ago. He loved Jason, just as he loved Joy, regardless of the fact that Jason was a man.

But David was the product of a stiff-necked, Southern aristocrat in a long line of such men, and he knew that all the help and advantages he enjoyed, courtesy of his father's connections, would evaporate instantly if it was ever suspected that he was gay. So he and Jason lived a lie, hiding their feelings in public, until David felt that he could no longer believably justify the amount of time they spent together and called it off. Or so he had said when he kicked Jason out.

The faint memory of a harsh voice and his father's strong arms restraining him echoed in his mind. David sat up, burying his head in his hands as a wave of intense sadness washed over him. How could one person love two people so much? Then he laughed, shaking his head. Hell, his own son was involved in an openly acknowledged three-way marriage. It might not be a marriage recognized by the law, but no one who spent any time with the three of them could doubt that they loved each other completely—heart, mind, body, and soul.

David had spent years trying to destroy the relationship between Josh and Sutter—a relationship he had inadvertently facilitated when he sponsored a young, disadvantaged boy into the prestigious private school, Whitecliff. He realized now that he had felt responsible not just for bringing Josh into Sutter's life, but for Sutter's "aberration." His homosexuality. Or bisexuality, actually. He had been fighting not only his son's way of life, but the knowledge that, deep down inside, he was the same.

Thank God Kendall had come along. David might have ultimately exiled himself from his son, as well—the only person left that he had cared about. But Kendall was a fighter.

Threatened by his actions, she had done what was necessary to make him face himself, and in the end, he had accepted their alternate lifestyle. For some reason, this did not make it any easier for him to accept those desires in himself.

The tightness at his groin became unbearable, and David unbuttoned his jeans and pulled down the zipper. He pushed his underwear aside and grasped his throbbing cock, watching as a droplet of pre-cum swelled at its tip. He started massaging slowly, his entire body flushed with heat as he imagined Joy kneeling between his legs, taking his hard length into her mouth.

And Jason. If Jason were here… David pictured Joy lying beneath him, drinking from his cock while Jason fucked his ass. The old inhibitions rose in him, making him feel ill, but he couldn't push the image away. A fierce, buzzing need invaded him, his entire body trembling from the intensity.

"Damn!" He pumped vigorously, forbidden images running rapidly through his mind—burying himself in Joy's hot flesh while he took Jason's cock deep in his throat; jacking Jason's cock while he finger-fucked Joy, making them both come on his hands. "God damn!" David arched as intense pleasure flooded his loins and his cum spewed. The orgasm seemed to go on and on, but finally faded, leaving him drained and shaking, shocked at his own reactions.

A high-pitched buzzing jolted him to his feet. David stumbled as he half-walked, half-hopped over to his desk, punched a flashing button, and picked up the phone. "Hello?"

"David? It's Kendall."

He could hear the excitement in her voice. He took a deep breath and willed himself to relax. "Hey, Kendall. What's up?"

"Hayley has something she wants to say to you." There was a bumping sound, and a moment later, David heard his granddaughter breathing heavily into the phone.

"Hayley? It's Grandpa. Are you having fun?" He could hear Kendall in the background, prompting her daughter.

"G'pa?"

David's heart did a somersault, and he spread his lips in a wide grin. "Hayley! Yes, it's Grandpa!"

"G'pa!" There was a clatter, and then Kendall was laughing into the phone.

"So what do you think, Dad? How does it feel, to hear her say 'Grandpa' for the first time?"

David couldn't wipe the grin off his face. "Awesome!"

"So why are you up there?" The teasing note faded from Kendall's voice and she became serious. "You should be here, David. With the people who love you." There was a pause, then she added. "With the people *you* love. All of them."

David hesitated. Kendall knew of his feelings, and she thought he was crazy to continue denying them. Maybe she was right. Most men fantasized about being with two women at the same time. Here he was, jacking off to images of two people he could be spending time with in under an hour. But it was hard to set aside years of self-conditioning. Hard to put aside his pride.

*Pride.* David looked down at himself and burst out laughing. He was standing half-naked in his office on a Saturday morning, covered in ejaculate, while he talked to his daughter-in-law and granddaughter on the phone.

"David? Is something wrong?"

David's suppressed his amusement. "No, Kendall. Everything's fine." He started kicking his pants off. "Tell the kids Grandpa will be there in just a little bit."

Kendall gasped. "Really, Dad?"

It still surprised David sometimes, how good it felt to have Kendall call him Dad. Sutter, too, for that matter. Before Kendall, Sutter's "*Dads*" had been full of bitterness and resentment. Thanks to her, David enjoyed a good relationship with Sutter now, and he was beginning to win over Josh, as well. Kendall was right—it felt good to have people in his life who really cared about him. "Yes, Kendall. Really."

Her breath came out in a rush. "That's great! Hayley, Race—your Grandpa's coming!" Hayley's giggles and Race's happy shout were music to David's ears. "Do you hear?" Kendall asked.

David nodded, then realized she couldn't hear that. "Yes."

Her tone became serious once more. "But…are you sure? I mean, it's been so awkward, the last few times. I don't—" She stopped, seeming at a loss for words.

David knew her well enough to guess that she was probably biting her lip, trying to decide how to tell him that she didn't want him to come if he was going to ruin everything. She would try to tell him nicely, but she *would* tell him. That honesty was one of the things that endeared her to him. "Don't worry," he said softly. "I'm going to talk to them this time. I'm ready to get some things out into the open."

"Really?"

"Yeah."

"I'm glad, David. Really glad." He heard tears in her voice. "It's been so hard—"

"I know how much Joy and Jason have come to mean to the five of you, Kendall. I—" He almost couldn't say the words, and had to swallow hard before continuing. "I care about them, too. And I'm going to let them know that." *Maybe.*

"You can't imagine how happy I am."

David savored the strange mixture of apprehension and anticipation running through his veins. "Actually, I think I can."

* * *

David was surprised to find himself humming with the radio as he raced along in his deep blue, fully restored nineteen-seventy-four Mustang convertible. He had cleaned himself up at the office and changed into jeans and a golf shirt—one of the extra outfits he kept in his closet there. It was as though a great weight had been lifted from his shoulders, and he was free to enjoy life again. He felt as though he had reached a major crossroads in his life, and made the right decision. It definitely beat feeling miserable, and he now realized that he had been feeling miserable for far too long.

David turned his car into the long gravel drive leading up to the house, admiring the view. Sutter and Josh had put together a magnificent building, but Kendall had made it a home, in more ways than one. With the garden that covered the porch in a profusion of bougainvillea, jasmine, and passionflower vines; with her forceful personality, yet accepting, loving nature and the laughter that seemed to follow wherever she went. A wonderful blend of disparate elements, just like her relationship with Sutter and Josh.

David parked and turned off the engine. Suddenly nervous, he sat in the car, wondering if he really was doing the right thing. Then the front door burst open and Race was toddling across the porch, Sutter rushing to grab him just before he reached the steps.

"G'pa!"

David threw open the car door and met his son and grandson at the bottom of the stairs. Taking Race from Sutter's arms, he held him high, whirling in a circle. "Race, m'boy! You, too?"

Race giggled and shouted, "G'pa, G'pa!"

David hugged him tight and grinned at Sutter.

His son chuckled. "You think it's cute now, but wait until he's said it a half-a-million times in thirty minutes."

David shook his head. "I couldn't ever get tired of hearing this."

Sutter smiled and clapped his father on the back as they walked up the stairs. "I'm glad you came, Dad."

David just nodded. It was much easier for him to be emotional around Kendall. She had known his flaws from the beginning, and accepted him in spite of that. He found it much more difficult to be emotionally honest with other people, though. Especially people he knew—he'd been playing a role for so long, it could still be difficult to break character.

"Hi, Dad!" Kendall greeted him at the door, hugging him warmly and kissing his cheek. "Did you bring your swimsuit?"

David shook his head. "I came straight from the office. Didn't even think about it."

Kendall shrugged. "That's okay. I'm sure Sutter has one that you can borrow."

David glanced at his son's slim waist, then frowned down at his own. He wasn't fat, but he was definitely heavier than he'd been in his youth, and his few extra pounds rode firmly around his waist.

Kendall noticed his expression and laughed. "Okay, then. Josh's."

David nodded. Josh was short, with a broad build. Though he was muscular and rock-solid compared to David's middle-aged spread, his trunks would probably fit. "He won't mind?"

Kendall waved a hand in dismissal. "I'll grab a pair for you. Everybody's already on the beach." She jogged lightly up the staircase, while David appreciatively eyed her rounded bottom in its bikini.

Sutter laughed. "Dad!"

David turned innocent eyes to his son. "What?"

Sutter raised his eyebrows and David grinned. "Can't blame a guy for looking."

There was a twinkle in Sutter's eyes as he shook his head. "Can't teach an old dog new tricks."

"Dad-dy!" Race squirmed in David's arms, and he passed the wriggling handful over to his son. "Sim! Sim!"

"Go ahead," David said. "I'll change and be down in a minute."

He watched Sutter push aside the sliding glass door and head out onto the deck. A soft touch on his shoulder made him jump. Kendall handed him a suit. "Here you go." She walked over to the door and stepped out, glancing back after she crossed the threshold. "Are you sure about this?"

David made himself nod. Kendall studied him for a moment more, then nodded and turned away. David went into the hall bathroom and changed into the suit, eyeing himself critically in the mirror. He frowned at his pale skin and the roll of fat hanging over his waistband. His arms and legs were muscular, thanks to his weight bench at the house, but he definitely needed to add some crunches to his daily workout.

Sighing, he turned away from the mirror. With all the insensitive things he had done over the years to the people waiting for him now, his physical appearance was the last thing he needed to be worrying about.

## Chapter Two: Rediscovering Joy

David made his way carefully down the steep steps leading to a private stretch of beach. Even this early in March, the air was warm, the sun shining bright on dark waters. Race and Hayley ran giggling after a ball Kendall rolled toward them. Brandy—Kendall and Sutter's shop manager and Kendall's best friend—sat on a brightly colored blanket, deep in conversation with Joy. Her former professor and mentor was radiant in a hot pink tank suit that David never would have pictured a fiftyish woman wearing. But on her, with her generous curves and golden tan, it looked good. Joy was laughing, head tossed back, silver highlights shining in the sun, her plump breasts bouncing enticingly. She glanced up and met his gaze. After only the briefest of pauses, she smiled and waved.

Heat flooded David's cheeks and he looked away, only to see Jason standing over the barbecue, basting ribs. Jason turned, as though sensing David's presence, and their eyes met. Jason, too, hesitated for a moment. But then he smiled.

For the first time in his life, David experienced the meaning of the phrase "took my breath away." Expecting awkward tension, even anger at first, from these people he had abandoned long ago, he was met with tentative but eager smiles, genuine affection evident in their eyes. David looked away. This was just too hard. What if he was doing the wrong thing? What if he hurt them again? He started to turn, intending to leave, but Kendall was there, thrusting Hayley into his arms.

"G'pa!" Hayley gave him a slobbery kiss.

"She wants to see Joy," Kendall murmured. "Will you take her over there?"

David stared into his daughter-in-law's knowing eyes. She pushed him gently but firmly in the direction of the blanket. "Thank you, David." There was a world of meaning in those simple words.

David couldn't believe how hard it was to turn and walk toward that blanket. He was a defense lawyer, for Christ's sake! He thrived on pressure. But his heart was hammering as he carried a bouncing, wiggling Hayley over to the blanket, wincing as she shouted "G'pa!" into his ears a dozen times along the way.

David sank down on the blanket and deposited Hayley in Joy's lap. "Te-Joy!" Hayley gave Joy a sloppy kiss as well.

"Te-Joy?" David raised his eyebrows in question.

Joy smiled. "Kendall calls me 'Auntie Joy.' They can't quite say it yet." Hayley was tugging at her hand.

"Pay ball, Te-Joy. Pay ball."

Joy's eyes sparkled. "How about it, David? Think you can keep up with us?"

David snorted. "Are you kidding? In my sleep."

Joy eyed him critically as she stood, holding Hayley's hand and taking a step backward. "I don't know…you look a little peak-ed to me." Joy grinned wickedly. Hayley squealed and started running as David jumped up and chased them both across the sand.

* * *

Brandy kept watch over Hayley and Race as they napped on blankets beneath a huge umbrella while Sutter, Josh, and Kendall soundly beat David, Joy, and Jason at volleyball. Then, their energy restored, the twins awoke and kept David busy rolling in the sand and frolicking in the shallows until Jason shouted, "Soup's on!"

As David munched on ribs and potato salad, happy chatter washing over him, he realized that he couldn't remember the last time he'd had so much fun. Even the sand in the potato salad tasted wonderful. Everything seemed more immediate, more vibrant, somehow. Joy kept glancing at him as she ate, beaming when he smiled at her, making him feel welcome. They had slipped easily into the camaraderie of their college days.

Jason was quiet, though. David frowned slightly. He felt so self-conscious regarding Jason. As though everyone were watching them and wondering about their relationship. Which was stupid, because everyone here knew about their college liaison except the twins. He knew what the problem was. His damn self-conditioning. As long as he didn't acknowledge what had happened, he could pretend it never had. But did he really want to spend the rest of his life that way? Excluded from much of this family's life because Jason and Joy were an integral part of it and he just couldn't bring himself to be a man and face his desires?

David could feel himself growing tense, and made a conscious effort to relax. He had promised Kendall, in spirit at least, not to ruin this picnic. Hell, he wasn't sure exactly what he wanted, but he'd never find out this way. Squaring his shoulders, he cleared his throat. "So, Jason. I know you took a job with *Big G* magazine. Are you liking it?"

Jason's eyes widened in surprise. All the other adults emitted silent waves of approval that made David's cheeks burn. Nothing like having a handful of matchmakers working on you.

"Ummm, yeah. I'm loving it, actually."

The truth was that David knew perfectly well Jason's career had skyrocketed since he signed on with the magazine. He had a regular monthly feature now, and David kept a notebook at home filled with clippings of those photo essays—in addition to the one he kept of Joy's professional articles. "That's great." He tried to think of something else to say, but his brain seemed to have shut down.

"How about you?" Jason wiped sauce-laden fingers on his napkin. "I heard you'll never have to work again, after winning the Manchester case."

David started to protest, but then nodded. If he was going to try and mend fences, he needed to start being honest. False modesty wouldn't be appreciated by these people who knew him so well. "I have to admit, that's not far from the truth." He scooped up the last bite of potato and swallowed it, sighing contentedly. "To be honest, I could have retired a few years ago. I toyed with the idea, but there didn't seem to be any point." He looked around the gathering, knowing that they understood what he meant—that there hadn't been anyone in his life that he wanted to spend that time with.

Joy surprised him by meeting his gaze and asking boldly. "How about now?"

David studied this new Joy. This bold, independent Joy whose eyes hid nothing and who challenged him to speak plainly. His heart beat a little faster. He decided he liked this confident, sassy woman even better than the person he'd known in college. "I don't know," he answered honestly. "I'm still trying to decide." He couldn't help glancing at Jason, and an electric tension seemed to build between the three of them.

Kendall interrupted the long silence. "David, you're going to burn to a crisp!" She was pointing at his chest.

David looked down. Indeed, his pale skin had been painted red by the sun. Joy stood, taking his empty plate and tossing it into the trash with hers. "Come on." She held out a hand to him. "I've got something that will help with that."

David grabbed her hand and let her pull him up and lead him over to her bag. Reaching in, she pulled out a bottle of aloe vera gel. "Walk with me." Joy retained her grip on his hand as they meandered across the sand, rounding a pile of boulders that jutted out onto the beach. On the other side, she stopped him. "Sit down."

David obliged, perching on a large rock. Joy moved close, pushing his legs apart to stand between them. David inhaled deeply, savoring her wind-blown, gulf-water scent. Joy squirted a dab of gel into her hands and reached out, gently massaging the cool substance into his forehead, his temples, his cheeks.

David relaxed, closing his eyes as she caressed his jaw line, smoothed his neck, cooled his shoulders. Her fingers were magical, gliding smoothly down his arms and between his fingers. Joy lifted his hand, surrounding each finger with her palm, twisting as she ran it up and down the length of each digit.

David opened his eyes, fervently hoping that she wouldn't notice the bulge at his crotch. Joy met his eyes, then lowered her gaze very deliberately. A smile tugged at the corners of her mouth as she looked back at him. Picking up his other hand, she massaged each finger as she wet her lips with her tongue. David was afraid to speak, afraid she would stop if he said the wrong thing.

Joy placed his hand gently at his side. She squirted a huge mound of the clear gel into her hands, rubbing them together, then placing them on his thighs. David breathed in sharply as she ran her hands up under his trunks.

"David."

His mouth was so dry he had to swallow twice before he could speak. "What?"

Her slick hands were beneath his cock, cradling his balls. "I'm thirsty, David."

"Thirsty?" he croaked. He couldn't quite bring himself to accept that this was happening. Not so soon, though he wanted it badly.

"Yes, David." Joy ran her thumbs up along the thick vein running the length of his cock.

"God." David arched, spreading his legs wide.

"Take them off." Joy removed her hands and stepped back.

David stripped hastily and resumed his seat.

Reaching back, Joy grasped one end of her suit tie and pulled. Her cups slipped down, revealing plump breasts with dark, swollen peaks he ached to taste. In one swift movement,

Joy had pushed her swimsuit off and was stepping out of it. Picking up the bottle again, she squeezed glistening jewels onto her chest, slathering the slippery substance between her breasts.

David groaned in anticipation, and Joy grinned. "I *know* you want to fuck them," she purred. "Don't you, David?" She glided forward, pressing herself into him as she whispered against his lips. "You always loved fucking my breasts."

David moaned and trapped her head against him, ravaging her mouth with his tongue. The swollen pebbles of her nipples grew harder where they pressed against his flesh.

Joy drew back and bent, capturing his cock between her breasts. "I'm thirsty, David," she repeated. "Is there something you can do about that?"

David tangled his hand in her hair, pushing her roughly toward his member as he grasped her shoulder with the other hand, urging her to glide against him. Joy pressed her breasts tight around his shaft as she took the tip of his cock into her warm, hungry mouth.

"Joy." David thrust against her. Joy chuckled, the sensation causing a trickle of pre-cum to escape into her mouth.

"Damn." Though he wanted to, David couldn't wait; couldn't be gentle. It had been too long. He grasped Joy's hands where they were cradled around her breasts and crushed them against him, urging her back and forth, faster and faster.

"Mmm." Her sound of satisfaction vibrated along his cock. David squeezed her ripe orbs mercilessly, and Joy amazed him by chuckling deep in her throat, sucking greedily. She ran her forefinger up beneath her breasts, tickling the base of his cock with her nail.

"Oh, God!" David wrapped his legs around her, spasming as his cock exploded in her mouth. After what seemed an eternity, he was finally empty, staring in astonishment as Joy stood, licking her bruised lips, and said, "God, I've missed that." She brought her lips to his mouth. "You always tasted so good." Her tongue darted between his lips, and the taste of him in her mouth filled his loins with renewed fire.

David drew his hand down her abdomen. Joy cocked her leg as his finger crept into her slit. Liquid warmth dripped down his hand as he slid another finger in, murmuring, "You're so fucking *wet*!"

A shock ran through him as Joy placed a hand between her legs, sliding two fingers down along the back of his hand, to join his inside her. This was *not* the shy, tentative girl he'd initiated in college. She was a vixen, and he wanted to fuck her until she screamed. David grabbed her waist as she raised her leg even higher, resting her heel beside his hip on the rock. Damn flexible, too, for a woman her age.

David looked down, watching their fingers slide in and out of Joy's pussy, coated with her arousal. He was shocked as hell when he felt a twinge in his cock. He'd been pretty randy years ago, but he hadn't come twice in one sitting in a long time. He studied the beautiful woman moaning before him. Joy had closed her eyes, her lashes just kissing the faint pink sunburn on her cheeks. He looked down again, enjoying the way her pussy sucked at their fingers. *I wish Jason were here,* he thought.

Joy's eyelids flew up. "Do you?"

*God, did I say that out loud?*

"Do you, David?" Joy gasped, and he felt her muscles tightening on his fingers. "Because he wants to be."

David's new-found passion drained away abruptly. Confronted with having to admit to someone face-to-face how he felt about Jason, he couldn't do it. "W-what are you talking about?" He pulled his hand away, staring at Joy in denial.

"God, David." She reached for his hand with her free one. "Don't bail on me now!" But David drew away. "Damn it, David." She thrust her own fingers desperately deep inside her cunt. "Did you honestly think I didn't know?" She brought her knee down abruptly, squeezing her thighs tightly together, gasping as a long shudder ran through her short frame. Involuntarily, David reached out to steady her while she came.

When she looked up again, her gaze was hot, and her cheeks were red—whether with anger or embarrassment, he wasn't sure. "For someone who is such a fearless, macho lawyer, you sure are a fucking coward."

Anger, obviously. "Joy, I—"

Joy grabbed her suit up, shaking out the sand. "Don't, David." She stepped into it and pulled it up, turning her back to him. "Tie the damn thing."

Dazed, David did as he was told. Joy bent over again, grabbing his trunks and tossing them at his chest. "Why are you so angry?" he asked.

Joy stared in disbelief. She opened her mouth, closed it, then opened it again. "Because I thought you had finally, after all these years, matured to the point where you could be open and honest about who and what you are. About how you feel. Obviously, I was wrong." She shook her head as he opened his mouth to speak. "I can't talk to you about this right now. Just get dressed so we can go. They're waiting for us."

David pulled on his suit, and Joy led the way back to the others, head held high but radiating a sad disappointment that shook David to his core. How had things gone from hopeful to hopeless in just a few short minutes?

## Chapter Three: At the Movies

David tossed his keys onto the mantel and sank into a deep armchair in his study. He rubbed his eyes wearily. Since that day on the beach, he seemed to be falling apart. He had no patience anymore, his temper was on a short fuse, and his attitude in court today had almost earned him a contempt charge. He didn't know what the hell to do.

Emotionally, it had come as a shock when Joy verbally acknowledged his past relationship with Jason, even though he had known she was aware of it. And to realize that she condoned it—was even willing to be a part of it… David shook his head. If Joy could accept it, why couldn't he? But every time he thought about it; every time he reached out to call Joy and apologize, to ask for Jason's number, something inside him balked. "So just stop thinking about it!" he yelled into the empty room. Standing, he walked over to the bar and poured himself two fingers of scotch, then stepped over to his desk and shuffled through the mail.

At the bottom of the stack, he found a plain, brown, padded envelope with no return address. He started to toss it—it could be some kind of hate mail from a disgruntled client, or something even more sinister—but curiosity got the best of him, and he tore the package open. A VHS-C cassette fell out. In large black lettering, the label simply said, "Watch me." David frowned, then walked over to the VCR. Sliding the tape into an adapter, he pushed it into place and pressed 'Play'.

A bedroom popped onto the screen. Midnight blue velvet cover on the bed, dark purple accent pillows nestled against the headboard. A woman moved onscreen, and David nearly choked on his drink. Joy, naked as a baby, tugged Jason into the frame.

"This is a bad idea," Jason was saying.

Joy shook her head and looked straight into the camera. "I know what I'm doing, Jason." She smiled. "Hello, David."

David sat down heavily in the armchair.

"Joy, this is—"

"Shh." Joy put a finger to Jason's lips. "No talking." Her hand slid down to the top button of his shirt. "I love undressing you, Jason," she murmured, releasing each button slowly. "You're incredibly muscular for a man your age, you know."

A smile tugged at the corner of Jason's lips. "You think so?"

"Uh-huh." Joy released the last button and slipped his shirt off. "I *know* so." She ran her hands over his biceps, then trailed her fingers over his tight abdomen. "Mmmm. So *firm*."

*Hell.* David gulped down the rest of his drink and set the glass on the carpet at his feet. Jason looked damn good. David patted his stomach ruefully. He'd added crunches to his daily routine and was beginning to see some results, but Jason was already there. And dark, too. He'd always taken a tan well. He had definitely aged well. He looked better now than he had in college.

"So hard," Joy murmured, glancing at the camera. "Do you remember, David?" Very deliberately, she licked her forefinger and teased one of Jason's nipples, making it stand out, gleaming wetly in the bright lighting.

*Shit.* David's own nipples were fucking *aching.* He pulled off his shirt, hoping the cool air would quench the fierce ache.

"Hmmm, David? Do you remember how he feels?" Joy leaned in and circled Jason's nipple with her tongue, causing Jason to shiver visibly. David noticed a prominent bulge had appeared at Jason's crotch. "How he tastes?" Joy drew her tongue down across Jason's abdomen, dipping into his belly button and following a narrow line of dark hair to the top of his pants. Kneeling, she reached for his waistband.

*Hell, yes.* David remembered. But not just Jason. He watched as Joy removed the rest of Jason's clothing. David remembered how good Joy tasted, as well. Both of the people on this screen had haunted his midnight hours for years. He had tasted them in his dreams, over and over. Almost of their own volition, his hands moved to his crotch. As Joy took Jason's cock into her mouth, his own swelled beneath the smooth fabric of his slacks. David unbuckled his belt and pulled off his pants.

In minutes—minutes filled with the soft sounds of Joy sucking on Jason's cock—David was hard as a rock. He cupped his hands around the steely rod. He hadn't masturbated in years, but now, because of these two, he was doing it for the second time in a few weeks.

Onscreen, Joy was standing. She turned and lay back on the bed, spreading her legs for the camera. David pumped his shaft desperately, wishing he had those warm, wet folds wrapped around his shaft, instead of his cold, rough hands. Joy grabbed something from the bedside table. "Come here, Jason," she purred.

Jason pounced onto the bed. He seemed to have forgotten the camera, completely natural and unselfconscious as he gathered Joy in his arms, giving her a long, very thorough kiss. In his head, David was fighting to push away an image of himself, there on the bed with them, participating in their lovemaking. But in his heart, he wanted them. Wanted them both. Wanted to be sandwiched between them, his cock buried in Joy's pussy, Jason's cock filling his ass.

"Fuck me." Joy's voice startled him out of his vision. He'd been lost in his fantasy rather than absorbing what was going on in front of him. Joy's buttocks were now gleaming with oil, and she was rubbing the same substance onto Jason's long, gorgeous cock." She set aside the bottle and looked directly into the camera. "Fuck me, Jason. Fuck me the same way you fucked David." Reaching down, she pulled her legs back and held them.

Jason glanced at the camera, grinning, then spread her cheeks wide with his lean brown hands. "Oh, yes." Jason's words ended on a moan of pleasure as he slid his cock between her cheeks.

David was sweating now, aching for release. Then the screen went blank, and static filled the room. "Fuck!" David tried desperately to release the tight ball of pressure in his loins, but his body wouldn't cooperate. His cock wanted warm, wet flesh, not hard, frantic fingers. Groaning, David gave up, lying back against the cushions to stare up at the ceiling. Damn the woman. What was Joy trying to do to him?

The phone rang, but David ignored it. *Let the machine get it,* he thought. A moment later, there was a beep, and Joy's throaty purr floated into the room. "David? What are you doing, David?"

David sat up and grabbed the phone. "Joy?"

He could hear the triumph in her voice. "Are you watching us, David?" Her sultry tones fired his blood, setting his pulse racing. "Are you touching yourself?" David wanted to speak, but he couldn't seem to find his voice. "You know," she murmured, her voice sweet and low and incredibly sexy, "You can join us any time." After a throaty chuckle and a click, the dial tone rang in his ear.

David slammed the phone into its cradle, pulled on his pants—not even bothering to find his underwear—and grabbed his keys. At the doorway, he realized he didn't have his shirt and turned back, picking it up and pulling it on as he strode out to the garage, climbed into his car, and tore out down the driveway.

## Chapter Four: When it's Right

Joy stared at the phone she had just placed back in its cradle, then covered her face with her hands. "I can't believe I just did that!"

Jason laughed, wrapping his arms around her from behind, his stiff cock pressing into her backbone. "I can. You're a Texas tornado, Joy." He nibbled her ear, sending shivers down her spine. "And this is one storm I'm sure as hell gonna stick around and ride out."

Joy turned and rested her cheek against his chest. "You don't think we're pushing him too hard, do you?"

Jason sighed, running his hands through her brown-gold hair. "I don't know, Joy. On the one hand, David's the kind of guy you have to hit over the head with a brick to make him even consider changing his mind. But on the other hand, if we *do* push him too far..." Jason shook his head. "Well, let's just say we both know he's got a hell of a temper and a bit of a mean streak."

Joy nodded her head thoughtfully, recalling the elaborate lengths to which he'd resorted when trying to get Joshua out of Sutter and Kendall's lives. At least he had changed his mind about that. Then again, if he hadn't tried to frame Josh, she and Jason never would have connected, and she'd still be a sad, lonely woman. "It's just a defense mechanism, you know. Deep down, David is a very good person." After all, he had sponsored Joshua at Whitecliff, even after he became uncomfortable with Josh and Sutter's friendship. And he doted on the twins.

Jason raised his eyebrows. "Sorry, Joy. I'm not as sure of that as you are. Hell, I'm not even sure why either one of us still loves the man."

Joy cupped his cheek with her palm. "Because we've both seen that good in him. However briefly, we got a glimpse of the man deep inside, and he's a man worth loving."

"I don't think he'll ever be able to accept me again, Joy. He's worked too hard over the years to deny that part of himself. He still feels it's *wrong.*"

"He *will* accept you, Jason. I know he will. He was trying, that day at the picnic, really trying. He just… I don't know…"

"Freaked."

Joy's expression became stern. "I love you, Jason. Which gives me a unique insight when it comes to discerning how *other* people feel about you. David loves you, and he will eventually admit it. We just have to make him understand that this is a package deal."

"Do you really think this is meant to be?"

"Yes, I do. I know I've never come close to feeling complete until now, at the prospect of having a loving relationship with *both* of you. And I'm positive David's never felt complete. Or even remotely happy, for that matter. He seemed almost happy, when we were together in college, but even then, something was missing."

Jason nodded. "For me, too. Only I never imagined what it could be, until I saw you again after all those years. When I saw you for the first time in so long, at Kendall's New Year's party..." He looked into her eyes with sudden, burning intensity. "My heart did a flip, even though we had never even spoken much back in college."

"That's because David was working so hard to hide how he felt, from both of us. You know, whenever he and I would be out on a date back then and run into you, David fairly *hummed* with tension. It never occurred to me what the reason for that was until Kendall came to me with her questions. Then it all kind of clicked into place. I'll bet he was scared to death that if we spent enough time together, I'd figure out what was going on!"

Jason let out a long sigh. "Which brings me, again, to the question of why we're trying to drag him into this, despite the kicking and screaming."

"Because it's right, Jason. I feel it. He loves us both. He's just afraid of being different." Joy gripped Jason's upper arms tightly. "Don't you want to be complete?"

Jason's bright green eyes seemed clouded by a deep sorrow. "It hurt, Joy. I went into the relationship knowing he wouldn't be able to commit, but it still hurt. And... I feel stupid saying this to you, I know he hurt you, too. But, I just don't want to go through it again. Isn't what we have enough?"

Joy stared into his eyes. "I don't know, Jason. Is it? Do you not even want to try?"

It seemed an eternity before he finally answered. "Yes, damn it. I want to try."

Joy watched him with a worried expression. "Give him time. It's not his fault he's so anal. His dad was a—"

"Hard-assed bastard. I know." Jason pushed her hair back from her temples and kissed her softly on the forehead. "Don't worry. I'm in this until the end, whatever happens, as long as I know *you're* not going anywhere."

His tone was light, but Joy noted a hint of uncertainty still lingering in his eyes. "I'll never let you go, Jason."

The roar of an engine interrupted their moment, followed by an abrupt silence and then the sound of a car door slamming.

"Oh, God." Joy hurried over to the front window and peeked out between the blinds. "He's here." She'd been so sure of this plan two days ago, when she'd talked Jason into helping her make the tape. She'd still been confident when she slipped the package into David's mailbox earlier that afternoon, and when she and Jason had stripped down just before she made the phone call to David. But now, her hands were trembling.

*Bang, bang, bang.*

"Joy!"

*Bang, bang, bang.*

"Open the fucking door, Joy."

Joy looked at Jason with wide eyes. "What should I do?"

"You have to open the door."

Joy nodded. Taking a deep breath to calm her nerves, she stepped over and pulled it open.

David stood there, hair disheveled, shirt unbuttoned and hanging loose. His face was a thundercloud. "What the hell are you trying to do, Joy?" he demanded.

A hundred flippant replies danced on the tip of her tongue, but Joy settled for the simple truth. "Love you."

David's anger seemed to evaporate. He opened his mouth to speak, then closed it.

Joy reached out, catching the edges of his open shirt in her hands. She stepped back into the house, pulling him with her.

She felt a delicious tingle as his gaze roamed over her form, absorbing the fact that she was naked. With a groan, he kicked the door shut behind him.

Joy smiled. She pushed his shirt off his shoulders and onto the floor, then stepped forward and wrapped her arms around him. David's flesh was hot against hers, warming her chilled, taut nipples.

"Joy, I—"

Joy pressed her lips to his, coaxing his mouth open with her tongue. David groaned again, his arms encircling her waist, his tongue eager and demanding against hers. The hard bulge at his crotch pressed into her stomach. Joy ran her hands up David's back, into the closely-cropped, stiff hair at the nape of his neck. For long moments, she savored the taste and feel of him.

Finally, he broke away, stepping back to hold her at the waist and stare into her eyes. "God, I've missed you."

Joy caressed his cheek. "I've missed you, too." She had promised herself she wouldn't cry, but she couldn't stop the tears that tumbled down her cheeks.

David raised one of his hands, brushing away her tears with his thumb. "I'm sorry," he rasped, his voice thick with emotion.

Joy glanced to the side, and David's gaze followed hers. Jason was watching them, looking awkward and uncomfortable, just out of reach.

"What about Jason?" Joy asked. "Can we stop pretending you don't want him as well?"

David's eyes met hers. Full of desire, yet uncertain. His muscles tensed beneath her hands, and she sensed that he was fighting with himself. Finally, he nodded once.

Jason stepped forward immediately and stood behind David. As Jason ran his fingers down David's back, David's hands crept up her sides, and Joy shivered when his thumbs began circling her nipples, bringing them to taut, hard peaks.

His fingers trembled against her as Jason's hands found his waistband. Embracing him from behind, Jason unzipped David's pants and pushed them down, freeing his swollen cock.

David froze, his fingers digging painfully into Joy's sides.

"He loves you, David. I do, too." Joy searched his face for a hint as to what he might be feeling. "Can you accept that? Can you accept that we want to be with you? Both of us?"

For a long moment, he wavered. Joy could read the indecision in his eyes. But then, with a shiver, he turned abruptly and claimed Jason's mouth with his.

Jason moaned, his hands shaking as he reached down and traced the outline of David's cock with his fingers. "God, Jason," David whispered against his mouth.

Joy watched as Jason knelt before him, staring up at David as he licked his lips. David groaned. "Hell."

Jason leaned close to David's cock, waiting. Joy slipped her arms around David from behind, not saying anything, simply offering her silent support.

David was like a deer caught in the headlights, uncertain which way to turn. Then, his hand moved, and he was cupping Jason's head, pushing his cock up against the waiting lips.

Joy peeked around David's side, an electric thrill pulsing through her abdomen at the sight of Jason running his tongue along David's ripe staff, his fingers squeezing David's heavy balls at the same time. David moaned, tilting his head back and closing his eyes.

Joy's nipples were throbbing, and her pussy became wetter with each passing minute. She nibbled at David's neck and was rewarded with a sigh of pure pleasure. Then the sigh turned into a gasp as Jason took David's cock into his mouth.

"Fuck!" David arched. "Hell, yes."

Joy was awed at how deeply Jason could take him. She watched in fascination, pleasantly surprised at the look of enjoyment on Jason's face as David's cock filled him. She wondered if she looked so content when she went down on Jason. She hoped so. Reaching down, she began rubbing her clit with an eager finger.

"Suck it," David groaned. "Suck it, Jason."

Jason got up on his knees, sucking noisily as David's hands held his head tightly, urging him on. "Oh, yeah!"

Joy's pussy was demanding attention. She dropped to her knees. Pushing David's legs apart gently, she lay on the floor, scooting between them, placing her own legs to either side of Jason's thighs.

Without missing a beat, Jason's hands were there, lifting her hips. Joy grasped David's ankles and wrapped her legs around Jason's waist as he drove his cock into her. "Oh, yes!"

David bent slightly, grabbing her beneath the knees. He straightened. His grip tight, he spread her legs wide, supporting her as Jason's cock pierced her deeper than ever before. "Oh, God. Yes." Her cunt spasmed, and Joy moaned.

David rocked his hips urgently above her. "Suck, Jason," he commanded. "Suck!"

Jason's thrusts quickened, his cock pounding deep into her pussy as he sucked David's dick. Joy shuddered as a hot core of pleasure began to build. "Oh, God. Yes. Yes!" Joy arched, screaming as the orgasm ripped through her. David's hips froze above her, and she dimly heard Jason swallowing rapidly, drinking David's cum as his own hot seed poured into Joy's pussy.

"Yeah!" David yelled. "Hell, yeah!"

Joy experienced a long moment of fierce pleasure, followed by several jolting aftershocks. Then David was easing her legs down to the floor. Joy lay there panting, drenched in sweat, as Jason reluctantly released David's cock.

To her pleasure, David ran a gentle hand over Jason's head, caressing him. She began to think that everything would be all right. Such moments of unexpected tenderness were one of the fleeting ways David revealed the caring person inside him.

David helped Jason to stand, then they both reached out to Joy, pulling her up from the floor. For a moment, the three of them eyed each other shyly.

"What now?" Jason finally asked.

David ran a hand through his bristly hair. "Can we talk?"

Jason and Joy nodded. Joy took David's hand and led him to an easy chair, then she and Jason sat on the couch, waiting.

"How did you...how did *this* happen?" He waved his hand, indicating the two of them.

Joy and Jason shared a look. "Well," Joy began, "Jason and I had corresponded occasionally ever since college." Her cheeks grew faintly hot. "He always asked about you. I didn't realize why, at the time. I always thought it was a little odd that he kept in touch, since we never got to know each other that well." She glanced over at Jason, taking his hand in hers. "But, when Kendall came to me about what was going on between you and Sutter and Josh, it kind of clicked into place."

She shrugged. "Thing was, I wasn't that surprised when Kendall confirmed what Brandy thought might have happened. It felt like something I'd always known, deep down inside." Joy took a deep breath. "Anyway, when Jason and I renewed our acquaintance at that first New Year's Eve party, we discovered that we felt something for each other."

Jason nodded. "It was the first time I'd ever felt attracted to a woman." He smiled into her eyes. "She's so easy to talk to. She accepted what she knew about us without judgment. We had a lot of common interests." His gaze flicked briefly to David.

"We started calling each other, first just a couple of times a week, then nearly every day. I was shocked as hell when I hung up the phone one night and realized I had a raging hard-on. We had just been talking about work, nothing sexual. But I was stiff as a rod."

Jason grinned widely and gave Joy's hand a squeeze. "I was sitting there, wondering what the hell to do about it, when this woman calls me back and asks in that sexy voice of hers if I'm as horny as she is." Jason closed his eyes, apparently savoring the memory. "Mmmm. She whispered things...she had me doing things to myself, saying things…" He met David's gaze. "I highly recommend it."

David stared at the two of them, shaking his head.

"What?" Joy asked, her tone defensive.

"It's just…a lot of things have changed since college."

Joy could guess what he was thinking. She'd been a shy, quiet mouse of a girl when they started dating, and not very experienced in the sexual department. Their encounters had been intense, but awkward, though now she suspected there was more to that than just her own inexperience. She straightened abruptly, scooting to the edge of the cushion.

"Some things haven't changed, though." She raised her eyebrows. "How about it, David? How do you feel about us?"

David swallowed hard. He stayed silent for a long while, staring into space above their heads. Eventually, he cleared his throat. "I know I'm attracted to both of you. I don't know whether I love you." He met Joy's pained gaze. "Not yet." He looked down at the hands clasped together in his lap. "At this particular moment, all I can say is that I want to see more of you."

"Both of us?" Joy asked.

David nodded. "Is that enough?"

Joy and Jason exchanged a look. "For now," she said.

David moved his hands, grinning crookedly. "Then, do you think you could help me with *this*?"

Their gazes came to rest on his renewed erection. Joy wiggled her eyebrows and grinned. "You're pretty frisky for an old man." She jumped off the couch and ran into the bedroom as David exploded from the chair and raced after her.

"Old, huh? I'll show you, you little vixen!"

Jason followed them into the bedroom, joining them on the bed, where David tickled Joy mercilessly.

When David's hand inadvertently brushed against Jason's cock, David heard the quiet gasp, quickly stilled. Wickedly, perversely, David did it twice more on purpose, relishing the tingle of pleasure that lanced his groin with each response. His cock burned with need, and he remembered the fantasizing he had done recently, featuring the two people on the bed with him now. He rolled over, trapping Jason beneath him.

A jolt of desire pierced his belly as he rubbed his cock against Jason's. Jason looked up at him, his eyes dark with desire, an uncertain frown creasing his forehead.

"I have such an itch," David growled.

Jason tilted his head. "Is that an itch *I* can scratch?"

Joy rested her head on the pillow, watching the byplay with interest.

David lowered his head, catching Jason's bottom lip between his teeth and sucking lightly. "I want to fuck you," he murmured against Jason's lips. "I want your tight ass sucking my dick while you fuck Joy."

Jason's breathing quickened. Joy leaned over and kissed Jason's cheek. "Mmmm. I like the sound of that." She moved closer, and suddenly they were all tasting, teasing, touching with their tongues.

David shivered, their combined touch twisting his desire tight. "Now, Jason."

David pushed himself up. Joy opened a drawer in the bedside table. "Here." She handed David a tube of lubricant.

David waited while Joy positioned herself on the bed, opening her legs invitingly. Jason move to cover her.

"Wait." David pushed Jason gently aside and lay on his stomach in front of Joy's glistening pussy. Looking up at her, he ran his tongue from the back of her dark slit up to her clit, inhaling deeply. "Mmmm. That tastes good." Joy's legs trembled and her cunt spasmed.

David laved her lips, then slid his tongue into her dark warmth, rewarded by a gasp as her powerful muscles tightened against his tongue. David nuzzled his nose against her clit, inhaling deeply again, savoring the scent and feel and taste of her. His heart ached when he thought of the time they could have spent together. Did that mean he loved her?

David pushed away those thoughts. He wasn't going to try and unravel his feelings right now. He was just going to enjoy this moment.

He delved deeper with his tongue, his explorations accompanied by a chorus of quiet noises of pleasure from Joy. He grinned as she began moving her hips to meet his thrusts.

He felt Jason's hands on his ass, parting his cheeks, and something cold teased his anus. He drew in a sharp breath, rising up on his knees, thrusting his ass out to offer Jason better access. He glanced up at Joy and saw her watching Jason, her eyes open wide.

He looked back, watched as Jason slid a short, slender butt plug into his ass. David groaned, closing his eyes. It had been so long. He'd denied himself for years, not even using toys to relieve his desires. It was sheer pleasure to have his ass filled again. He opened his eyes to find Jason eyeing him anxiously. "Feels good," David murmured, reassuring him.

Jason grinned, then nudged him playfully. "Move over. My turn now."

David moved aside, and Jason knelt between Joy's legs. "Mmmm." Jason slipped his third and fourth finger into her pussy and began circling her clit with his thumb. "Your pussy's so *hot*, baby." Joy moaned and wriggled.

David's groin tightened as he watched Jason's slick fingers plunge in and out of Joy's cunt. His ass tightened on the toy; his cock felt as though it were on fire. David grabbed the tube of lubricant and pulled off the lid, shivering as the cool fluid coated his straining cock. He reached out and grasped Jason's hips, guiding him up onto his knees. Joy arched and gasped as Jason leaned over her, sucking a ripe nipple as he slid his cock between her wet folds.

Jason moved his hips slowly, Joy tossing her head back and forth as he stroked in and out. David rubbed lube onto Jason's taut buttocks, working his way to the tight pucker he so wanted to penetrate.

Holding Jason's cheeks wide, David watched for his lover's reaction as he pushed his forefinger past the rim.

Jason arched and froze.

"Talk to me, Jason," David murmured.

Jason groaned. "Damn, David. You feel so good inside me."

David wiggled the tip of his finger just inside Jason's anus. Jason gasped. "You like this?" David teased.

"Deeper," Jason growled.

David slid his finger in a little further. "Here?"

Jason groaned again and leaned down, wrapping his arms tight around Joy as he began thrusting again. "Deeper," he demanded.

David pushed his finger in even deeper. Glancing up, he noticed Joy watching him over Jason's shoulder. "Faster," she urged. David wasn't sure if she was talking to him or to Jason, or both, but when he began sliding his finger rapidly in and out, she closed her eyes and hugged Jason tight as his rhythm increased also.

David turned his finger and began stroking Jason's prostate.

"Fuck!" Jason arched and reached back, grabbing David's wrist. "Not yet," he panted. "I don't want to come yet."

"What *do* you want?"

"Fuck me, David." Jason let go, and David withdrew his finger. He parted Jason's cheeks and drizzled more lube into the crack, then rubbed the head of his cock against the gleaming pucker. "How do you want it?"

Jason turned back to Joy, looking into her eyes. "How do we want it, baby?"

Joy wiggled. "Fast and hard."

Jason grinned, then glanced back at David. "You heard the lady."

David worked two fingers into Jason's anus. Parting them slightly, he turned his hand, twisting his fingers, stretching the tight orifice until he could slip the head of his cock inside.

"Yes!" Jason leaned down and wrapped Joy tightly in his arms again.

A ripple of pleasure shot through David's body. Jason's ass was so tight, pressing urgently against David's bulging head. The sides contracted, and David gasped. Growling, he thrust, hard and quick. Jason moaned and pushed his cock deep inside Joy as David pulled back for another thrust. They developed a counter-rhythm, David's cock penetrating Jason's ass as he pulled back, meeting David's thrust, then Jason's cock penetrating Joy deeply as David's cock retreated.

Joy's eyes watched him as he penetrated Jason again and again. Her eyes glazed with desire, her breathing becoming ragged. "Yes," she groaned. "Oh, yes."

David felt pressure building in his loins, a fire raging out of control. Grabbing the lube, he squirted it onto his cock, plunging into Jason's slick, tight canal more and more urgently. The plug in his ass slipped in and out slightly with each thrust, intensifying his pleasure.

"Yes, fuck me." Joy moaned. "Both of you." She thrust her hips up. "Harder!"

David responded, driving himself into Jason, hard and fast. Jason's buttocks pounded against his sweat-slicked groin. Joy let out a sharp cry and brought her legs up as she arched.

David grabbed her calves, holding them tight against his hips as he and Jason both buried themselves deep and froze. Then Jason shuddered, his anus spasming as his seed pumped into Joy's pussy. A wave of fiery pleasure washed over David's body as his own cock emptied, spilling his hot seed into Jason's ass. For a moment, he felt as if they were all suspended in a glass bubble, riding upon the crest of a wave of sheer pleasure. Then the wave collapsed, and so did they, lying weak-limbed and trembling across the bed.

## Chapter Five: After the Lovin'

David opened his eyes, then winced, shielding them with one hand from the bright sunlight invading the room. For a moment, he couldn't remember where he was; then the memory of the night before came back.

His body cradled Joy's, her plump buttocks nestled in the crook formed by his abdomen and bent legs. His arm rested lightly around her torso, just below her breasts.

Jason's body warmed him from the other side. The man's firm chest was melded to his back, his limp cock tucked just between David's buttocks, one of Jason's legs thrown across both David and Joy's calves.

David absorbed the moment, memorizing the feeling of being surrounded by warmth and contentment, languishing in...love? Maybe. Maybe this threesome thing could work. Maybe he could—his gaze came to rest on the clock at Joy's bedside. "Shit!"

David bolted upright. "Is that clock right?"

Joy stirred sleepily, opening her eyes. "Huh?" She ran a hand through her tousled hair.

"That clock. Is it right?"

"Uh, yeah," Joy mumbled. "It's right."

"Shit, shit, shit!" David squirmed awkwardly out from between their warm bodies and stood at the foot of the bed. "Where are my pants?"

Joy stretched, obviously not understanding the gravity of the situation. Beside her, Jason rolled onto his back, yawning as he opened his eyes.

"Joy!"

"Oh, uh… I think you left them in the foyer."

David turned and strode into the living room, grabbing his socks from near the couch, then snagging his shirt and pants from the floor by the front door. Joy came in and perched on the edge of the couch, watching as he struggled into his slacks and pulled on his shirt. "What's wrong?"

"I was supposed to be in court at nine o'clock, that's what's wrong." David patted his pocket. "I can't believe Abby didn't—" He found his cell phone, pulled it out, and groaned. "She did call me. She's been calling every fifteen minutes for the past hour."

Even as he spoke, the phone began to buzz. David punched a button and brought it up to his ear. "Abby."

"Hey, boss. Are you okay? I've been—"

"I'm fine. Just overslept."

There was a long pause. "Uh…overslept?"

"Yes, Abby. Now, call Gerald Finn's cell and tell him not to worry, that his court date's been postponed until next week."

"Right."

"I'll call Maxfield and explain things. I'll be at the office within the hour."

"All right, boss."

David hung up and began buttoning his shirt. He tucked it into his pants as he walked over to an overstuffed chair and sat, punching buttons on his cell phone with one hand as he pulled on a sock with the other.

"Where the hell are you, Campbell?" Judge Winston Maxfield's voice boomed in David's ear.

"Sorry, Max." David switched the phone to his other ear, pulled on the other sock, and stood, looking around for his shoes as he talked.

"I granted you a continuance until next Thursday," Max grumbled. "But I didn't appreciate this. What happened, man?"

David found his shoes under the coffee table and jammed his feet into them. "Sorry, Max. I overslept."

"Overslept!" Max hollered. "What the hell?"

"Yeah, Max. I fucked the living daylights out of someone last night, and I overslept."

Max's hearty laughter rang out so loud that David had to hold the phone away from his ear for a moment. "Did you? Well, that's all right, then. We still on for golf Friday?"

"You bet."

"See you then," Max said, still chuckling.

David slapped his phone shut and looked up to find that Joy had put on a robe, Jason had pulled on shorts, and they were both watching him with sour expressions. "What?" he asked.

"That good-ol'-boy network is quite the lifesaver," Joy observed curtly.

"You're not mad because I told him the truth, are you?"

"Oh, come on, David. We both know you left him thinking you had boinked some hot young thing."

David started to deny it, but then nodded. "Sure, and what's wrong with that? Is it necessary for him to know who I slept with?" He didn't understand her irritation.

Joy sighed. "No, it's not. My point is that it wasn't necessary for him to know you slept with anyone at all. I don't like the idea of being used as an excuse."

David looked from one to the other of them, bewildered. "Okay. I'm sorry. I won't do that again." He glanced at his watch. "Look, I've got to go. I'll call you later, all right?"

Joy nodded. David grabbed her by the shoulders and gave her a quick peck on the cheek, waved casually at Jason, and rushed out the door.

* * *

Joy stared at the front door for several minutes after David left. Jason's hands on her waist brought her out of her reverie.

"What's wrong?" His breath was warm on her ear.

"I just..." Joy shook her head. "I don't know if we got through to him, I guess. Last night, I thought he was coming around, but now...it feels like a one-night stand."

"Did you think he was going to be all sweetness and light this morning? Canceling his appointments? Staying for breakfast?"

Joy smiled slightly. "No."

Jason gently turned her around to face him. He quirked an eyebrow. "No?'

Joy grinned in earnest. "All right. Yes. The romantic in me hoped it might play out that way."

Jason pulled her close and she closed her eyes. Resting her cheek against his chest, she basked in his tender affection, his warmth. "He'll come around," Joy whispered. "He has to."

She felt Jason nodding, his chin brushing the top of her head, but she didn't look up. She knew there would be doubt in his eyes, and she couldn't stand to see it. Especially when she was beginning to question David's feelings herself.

* * *

David pushed the speed limit on the way home. In the shower, he realized he still had the butt plug in his ass. He tried to suppress the sudden urge to masturbate, but couldn't, and stood there pushing the plug in and out of his ass as his cock hardened and finally exploded.

He put on clean clothes, then headed for the office. Abby gave him a strange look, which he ignored. At his desk, he sat and looked over his notes for the trial he'd missed that morning. Next, he started reviewing the files for a couple of upcoming cases.

One moment he was reading. The next, he was leaning on one hand, staring into space as he pictured Joy's face, flushed and happy, smiling up at him over Jason's shoulder. David shook himself and dragged his attention back to the stale report on his desk. After another few moments, he realized he was staring into space again, remembering how it had been to wake up sandwiched between the two people he cared the most about, outside of his family.

Frustrated, David stood and began pacing. A part of him wanted to cancel his afternoon appointments and rush back to the cottage. Another part was horrified at what had gone on the night before.

An image of himself, with his cock buried in Jason's ass, ran through his mind, accompanied by the stinging sounds of a switch striking flesh and his grandfather's harsh, bitter voice. David shut his eyes, hands clenched, pushing the memory and the voice away. Abruptly, he turned and opened the office door. "I'm going to lunch, Abby. I'll be back around two."

Abby raised her eyebrows. "Okay, boss." He could feel her watching him as he crossed to the lobby and opened the door. "Anything wrong?"

David shook his head, not looking back as the door shut behind him.

One steak lunch, three margaritas, and two hours later, David felt ready to face the day again. When he got back to the office, he went into the bathroom and carefully removed the plug he'd put back after his shower. He washed it off, stuck it in a plastic bag, and stuffed it into his briefcase. Last night had been fun, but he wasn't a homosexual. He just wasn't. It was an experiment, that's all. Physical pleasure, nothing more. It wouldn't happen again. He wouldn't let it.

David strode over to his desk and threw himself into his work with a vengeance, ignoring the twinges of a new ache—a feeling as though something very important were missing from his life.

## Chapter Six: Two is the Loneliest Number

Joy lounged in a reclining lawn chair, shading her eyes as she watched Jason make his last pass across the back yard with the mower. In the far corner, he cut the engine. Pulling off his tank top, he mopped at his face. Sunlight glinted on the sweat coating his biceps, and Joy smiled appreciatively as his muscles rippled. Jason had the body of a man in his middle thirties, rather than someone the age of fifty-four. It was a nice view.

Joy glanced thoughtfully at her own body. A couple of years ago, she would have been mortified at the thought of wearing a swimsuit, let alone a bright pink one, in public. Now, not only did she wear it, she felt comfortable and even attractive doing so. She watched the man coming toward her, a rush of gratitude flooding her chest with heat. It was Jason's doing, this new-found confidence. Despite his initial shyness, he had sparked emotions and desires in her that Joy had thought she would never feel for anyone other than David. She had sensed his interest from the moment they met again, but had soon realized that he would never make the first move. So she'd taken a deep breath and plunged right on in, being uncharacteristically bold and brash, and damned if the water hadn't been...almost perfect.

The object of Joy's thoughts squatted next to her, reaching out to pick up the glass of lemonade she had waiting for him. He tilted his head, swallowing rapidly. "Mmm." Jason set the glass back on the short table between their chairs and grinned. "That hit the spot."

Unexpectedly overcome by a wave of tender affection, Joy reached out and cradled his head with her hand, drawing him to her. She kissed him, sliding her tongue between his parted lips, savoring the sweat-tangy taste of him.

When she finally drew away, Jason eyed her shrewdly. "What was that for?"

Joy caressed his cheek. "For being such a kind, wonderful man."

Jason smiled and kissed her palm, but his eyes still searched hers. "You're still upset, aren't you? Because we haven't heard from David in six weeks."

"David doesn't have anything to do with how much I love *you*," she protested.

"I know, but..." Jason faltered, looking away. When he turned back, it made her heart ache to see the hurt in his expression. "Do we really need him, Joy? Can't we make a life without him? We did it before, both of us, for years."

Joy took a deep breath. She almost regretted the things she'd done trying to bring the three of them together. Almost. "I don't know, Jason." She stared into his eyes, seeing the torment he'd been hiding so desperately these past few weeks. Instead of mourning David's silence openly, like she had, Jason pushed his pain deep inside, trying to hide it beneath wry wit and a quick smile. "I'm not ready to give up yet. Are you?"

Jason opened his mouth to speak, but a shrill buzz from the portable phone interrupted. Irritated, Joy grabbed for it and jabbed a button. "Hello?"

"Joy?"

Her heart did a flip. "David?"

"Hi." There was silence for a moment, but when Joy didn't say anything, David spoke again. "Umm…I was wondering if…you and Jason, uh, might want to…drive out to New Orleans with me tomorrow?"

Joy raised her eyebrows. "New Orleans?"

Jason whispered, "Who is it?"

"David," Joy mouthed back silently.

Jason's eyes widened.

"Uh, yeah," David was saying. I thought we could visit the casino, have dinner out. A weekend away." He cleared his throat. "I mean, I was hoping…if you both want to… I was thinking we could spend the night." The last words came out in a rush, as though David were afraid if he didn't say them fast, he wouldn't say them at all.

"Hold on a minute." Joy covered the mouthpiece. "He wants to take us to New Orleans."

"Really?" Jason's features were a mixture of surprise and doubt. "Both of us?"

Joy nodded. "He wants to spend the night."

Jason swallowed hard.

"It's up to you," Joy said. "I know this has been difficult for you. If you're ready to stop—"

Jason shook his head. "No. This is...definitely a step in the right direction." He grinned sheepishly. "I guess I'm not ready to give up, after all."

Joy gave him a quick kiss, then spoke into the phone. "That sounds nice. Should we meet you somewhere?"

"No, I'll swing by and pick you guys up." His words were casual, but Joy sensed the tightly reined tension in his voice. He wasn't sure about this, not really, but at least he was making the effort. "Can you be ready at seven in the morning?"

"Sure." Joy strained to keep the excitement from her voice, chiding herself for feeling like an overeager puppy.

"Okay." There was another awkward silence. "Um, I guess I'll see you in the morning, then."

"All right. Goodbye, David." The dial tone rang in her ear, and Joy hung up. Jason was watching her with a worried expression, chewing on his bottom lip. "What's wrong?"

"I'm just surprised. Seems sudden."

Joy grabbed his shoulders and pulled him close, staring into his eyes. "You know how he is, Jason. He does things abruptly. Takes a while to make up his mind sometimes, but then, wham!" She trailed one hand along Jason's shoulder and up, tracing his jaw with her fingers. "Don't look so worried," she whispered. "*He* called *us*, right?"

Joy caught one of his hands in hers and brought it up to her breast, guiding his fingers to her already prominent nipple. Together, they stroked until it was a hot pink bulge beneath her swimsuit. Jason brought his head down, and Joy drew in a sharp breath as he nipped her peak through the fabric.

His hand glided over the mound of her belly, slipped between her legs. Joy spread them slightly. A frisson of pleasure raced through her as Jason's lean, strong fingers pushed back her suit, finding her wet slit.

He teased her, watching her face as he pushed the very tips of his fingers just inside her waiting folds. Joy grabbed his wrist, held him tight as she pushed her hips up, driving him deep inside her.

Jason pushed down his shorts. Joy watched, thankful that they had installed privacy fencing at the beginning of the summer, as he began stroking his cock. Jason's fingers danced inside her, touching all the magical places they had discovered together over the past year.

Joy pumped her hips more and more desperately. She watched and waited until Jason stiffened abruptly, the setting sun gilding him like a bronze Adonis. Joy leaned over quickly and captured his cock in her mouth, bringing her thighs together to trap his hand. She sucked the fruit of his loins greedily as her own orgasm rippled through her.

One last shudder, and then Jason was joining her on the lounge chair. Joy settled her head against his shoulder with a contented sigh. His fingers toyed with her hair. The release had relaxed him somewhat, but Joy still sensed a thread of tension running through him. She didn't think talking would help, so she just held onto him, willing her love to flow into him—to give him the strength and confidence that he had given her.

## Chapter Seven: One Wild Ride

David rang Joy's doorbell at six fifty-eight the next morning. Joy answered, looking radiant in a pale yellow top embroidered with butterflies, and crisp, white walking shorts. Both were colors that showed off her summer tan. He felt a rush of warm affection as her open, trusting face smiled up at him.

"You guys ready?" David tried not to jiggle the keys in his hands, knowing that would betray his nervousness.

"You bet."

David drank in the sight of her. She really was even more beautiful than she'd been when they were young—all soft, round curves and a breezy confidence she hadn't exhibited back then.

Jason sauntered into the entryway, carrying a couple of gym bags. David's gaze took in his tousled hair, his half-lidded, sleepy eyes. Bedroom eyes. David's cock twitched. *Down, boy. We've got a bit of a drive ahead of us.*

"Let me take one of those." David reached out, and Jason handed him one of the bags. "Anything else?" Jason and Joy shook their heads. "All right, let's go."

The guys stowed the bags in the trunk while Joy locked up the house. Jason opened the front passenger door and waved Joy into the car, then took a seat in the back.

Twenty minutes later, they were speeding down I-10 in David's convertible. He felt almost like a kid again, driving along with Jason humming and Joy outright singing to songs on the radio. He'd been pleasantly surprised that they both liked the current alternative rock as much as he did.

"You have a beautiful voice."

Joy stopped singing. "Oh, thank you."

"I don't remember you ever singing when we dated back in college."

Joy shrugged. "I was too self-conscious back then. I didn't think I had a good voice." She laughed. "Now, I don't care whether I have a good voice or not; I just love to sing."

David grinned. "I'm glad. It's nice."

Joy reached out and laid her hand on his where it rested on the gear shift. "Thanks." She glanced into the back seat. "Jason's got a great voice, too, but he won't sing."

David quirked his eyebrows at Jason in the rear view mirror. Jason shrugged. "I'd rather listen to Joy."

"He plays the guitar, too."

David frowned. "Really. Why didn't I know that?"

"It's something I got into later in life."

David nodded. They rode in silence for a while, David mulling over the fact that he really didn't know that much about Jason any more. Or Joy, for that matter. He had watched their careers, but hadn't delved into their personal lives. By virtue of living in the same town and having mutual friends, he knew that Joy had never been married, but he had no idea whether there had been anyone significant in her life after college. From a couple of bios in magazine articles, he knew that Jason, also, had never married; but again, he had no idea whether he'd ever been in another serious relationship with anyone. Suddenly, it seemed important to find out.

After a short while, he asked, "Will you play for me some time, Jason?"

The shock on Jason's face was almost comical. "Uh…sure."

David started to let it pass, but he had to know. "Why did that surprise you so much?"

"What, that you would want to hear me play?"

"Yeah."

David watched him in the rear view mirror. Jason's expression was that of someone who couldn't decide how honest he should be. Finally, he said, "Well, to be honest, David, you're not usually a 'what's-up-with-you' kinda guy." He met David's gaze in the mirror. "It's usually about what *you're* doing. What *you* want."

David felt a flash of anger, but he forced himself to really consider the comment. He had to admit it was true. He'd been totally driven, totally focused, on his career for so long that he hadn't even realized he was driving his own son away. He nodded. "You're right." David glanced back at Jason briefly. "But I'm trying to change that." Their gazes locked, and for a moment, it was as though they were back in college, when a single look could convey a host of meanings.

David dragged his eyes back to the road, and the moment passed.

Three hours later, they pulled into a deserted rest stop, and David passed out the fried chicken and potato salad his cook had prepared.

"Does Mrs. Thomas still do your cooking?" Joy asked. "This tastes just the way I remember her chicken." Jason nodded agreement.

"Yep. She's in her seventies now, but she's still going strong." David put a big scoop of potato salad on his plate. "I don't bring her in every day, though. She comes on Monday and does up a couple of casseroles, or a casserole and a roast. Something I can heat up the rest of the week, when I'm not eating out. And I bring her in on special occasions. Her daughter has a catering business now, and Anita does a lot of the cooking for that, I think."

Jason licked his fingers. "She definitely has not lost her touch."

Oil and salt glistened on Jason's bottom lip. The desire to kiss him was so strong, David couldn't resist. Instinctively, he glanced around, even though he knew no cars had pulled up since they stopped. Then he leaned over and ran his tongue lazily along Jason's bottom lip. Jason swallowed hard, searching his eyes. David slipped his tongue into Jason's mouth, savoring his salty flavor.

Jason shifted restlessly on the bench. David reached down and ran his hand along the hard bulge at Jason's crotch. "I can't wait until tonight," David murmured, stroking Jason slowly through the stiff fabric of his jeans shorts.

Jason pulled back. "Really?" The desire in his eyes was tempered by skepticism.

David leaned forward. "I'm going to suck you dry," he promised, then kissed Jason again, hard and deep.

When David broke away, Joy was watching them with a faint smile playing about her lips. "Come here." David beckoned her over, patting his lap. Joy stood and walked to him. He drew her into his lap, her legs spread to straddle him. He slipped his fingers up under her shorts, and his already-hard cock began to ache when he discovered she had nothing on underneath. He watched her eyes as he penetrated her slit. "And you," he murmured. "I brought a surprise for you."

Joy brought her lips to his, the potato salad giving her kiss a sweet-tart taste, just like her personality. Groaning, David pulled his hand out. "We'd better stop this."

Joy grabbed his hand. She glanced at Jason, and then they were each taking a finger, holding David's gaze as they sucked off her juices. "God," David croaked.

Joy grinned wickedly, swirling her tongue around his finger one last time before she climbed off his lap. "Just think how good it will be, tonight."

It was David's turn to swallow hard.

They finished eating quickly, fueled by a new sense of urgency. David's crotch ached. How in the hell was he going to wait until that night? But he thought of the conversation, the tender moments the three of them had shared in just these few hours, and that was sweeter than any sex they'd ever had. The sex was great, but the connection between them—that was what he missed the most.

They cleaned up after themselves and climbed back into the car. Joy insisted that Jason sit in the front. Soon they were flying down I-10 again.

After about half an hour, Joy became quiet, and David peeked back and saw that she had dozed off. He grinned at Jason and tilted his head toward her. Jason smiled. “I don’t think she slept much last night.”

“Really? Why?”

Jason snorted. “Umm, nervous maybe?”

“Oh.” David looked away. “I really am clueless sometimes, aren’t I?”

Jason touched his arm. “Hey. You’re trying, David. I hope you know how much that means, to both of us.” Jason shifted in his seat.

David let his glance flicker to Jason’s hard-on. “Let me see it.”

Jason’s jaw dropped.

“Please. Let me see it.”

Jason hesitated, but then unsnapped his shorts and pulled down the zipper. He pushed his underwear down so that David could see him.

“Mmm.” David feathered his fingers across Jason’s hot flesh. “You were always so long. I loved that, that you could fuck me so deep.”

Jason groaned. “David—”

David wrapped Jason’s hard rod with his hand. “I’ve missed you, Jason.” He began running his hand roughly up and down Jason’s cock.

Jason’s gaze flew to the cars on the road. “David—” he said again in a warning tone.

“What?” David ran the tip of one finger over the head of Jason’s cock, then brought the finger up to his mouth and licked the pre-cum from it. "They can't see. I want to make you come, Jason."

"You will," Jason said in a strangled tone. "Tonight." He pulled up his underwear and zipped his pants.

David sighed. "All right." He glanced down at the dash, saw that he was going almost ninety, and eased up.

After a few more miles, David cleared his throat. "Was there…ever anyone else?"

He felt Jason looking at him, but refused to meet his eyes. He wasn't sure he wanted Jason to know how important the answer was.

Just when David had decided that Jason wasn't going to answer him, Jason spoke. "There were…a couple of one-night stands. And…one guy that was really just a friend, but he was in a similar situation, and we…relieved the pressure for each other regularly for about five years. It was a lot safer that way, with HIV and everything out there."

"Similar situation?"

"You know." Jason's tone was bitter. "In love with someone who wasn't in love with him."

"Have you been, all this time? In love with me?"

Jason groaned. "Do we have to do this now?"

David finally looked at him. "I want…no, I *need* to know."

"It's not fair for you to ask, when you won't—"

"I know."

A short silence, then, "Yeah. All this time. I've been in love with you."

A wave of happiness and relief swept over David, so intense that it brought tears to his eyes. "That's...thank you, Jason. For telling me."

Jason didn't answer. David glanced over at him and saw that he was looking out over the passing scenery, his jaw tight. David stared out at the road before him. There was too much unresolved, between him and Jason, and between him and Joy. Problems David couldn't begin to deal with right at this moment, but there was an unfamiliar pain in his chest. For the first time, he began to realize how devastated he, himself, was going to be if things didn't work out between the three of them this time around.

## Chapter Eight: Playing Games

Joy woke up shortly before they arrived at the hotel, and her light, easy banter lifted the tension somewhat. David turned the car over to a valet, with strict instructions on how to drive it and where to park. Then, the three of them headed in to register.

"Separate rooms?" the clerk asked.

Joy and Jason started to nod, but David said, "No. I believe you have a suite for three?" His pulse raced at the brilliant smile Joy rewarded him with.

"We do. And how many nights will you be staying?"

"Just tonight."

"Very well." The clerk gave him his total and scanned his credit card, then a concierge took them up to the suite, waiting to see that everything was to their liking before taking his leave.

"Are we going to the casino right away, or—"

"Hell, no!" David walked over to the bed and began stripping. "If I don't take you both right now, I'm going to explode." He sat on the edge of the bed, naked, looking at them with a desperate gleam in his eyes.

Joy's smile was a slow, sensuous creature that crawled down inside him and curled around his loins. She pulled off her shorts and walked over to him, straddling his lap. As his cock slid between her slick folds, she sighed. "Oh, I've been looking forward to this," she whispered in his ear.

David couldn't answer. His throat was tight. She felt so wonderful, so right, wrapped around him. He closed his eyes and reveled in the moist warmth enfolding him. He didn't want to move, just wanted to sit here, surrounded by her.

A shifting of the bed made him open his eyes. Jason was naked, lying on his side across the bed, watching them. A translucent drop gleamed at the tip of his engorged penis. David glanced at Joy. Very deliberately, she reached down and slipped a finger into her pussy alongside his cock. "God, Joy. What—" She brought the finger out, began rubbing the juices on her right nipple. Her tantalizing scent wafted to his nostrils. "Oh, shit."

David lay back on the bed. This time, Joy rose up, letting his cock slip out as she put two fingers of first one hand, then the other, into her pussy, capturing her juices. Her cunt surrounded him again as she began swirling the tips of her fingers over her breasts, coating the nipples with her pungent scent. A shaft of pure lust lanced through David's core. Moaning, he arched, tossing his head back and forth as Joy rode him.

His gaze came to rest on Jason's beautiful cock. He reached out, surrounding it with one urgent hand. Tugging, he brought Jason up to his knees, urged the man to straddle him. He swirled his tongue around Jason's bulging head, cupping his balls and massaging them gently. "Oh, yes," Jason breathed. He leaned forward, giving David better access. David reached around Jason's thighs, began kneading his buttocks to the rhythm of Joy's thrusts.

Jason drove his cock deep into David's throat. David hummed a low note, remembering how that used to drive Jason wild. "Oh, God, David. Yeah!"

David felt Joy's hands on his. Following her guidance, he pulled Jason's butt cheeks apart, beginning to suck Jason's cock gently as he did so. Jason shuddered. "Oh, yeah. Suck me, David." His voice was harsh, demanding. "Suck me dry!"

David pressed Jason's hips against his face, taking him deep, sucking so hard his throat began to ache.

"Oh, yeah! Yes!"

Joy was bucking frantically, taking David fast and deep. David moaned, flicking his tongue across the bottom of Jason's dick. He felt Joy lean forward, felt her hands on his, then Jason began pumping frantically, driving deep and hard into David's mouth. "Joy!" Jason hollered. "Oh, damn, yes. Fuck my ass, baby. Fuck it with that tongue!"

David realized what Joy must be doing. The image that sprang to his mind, of Joy's sweet face buried in Jason's ass, her pink tongue dipping into his hole, was so torrid that his cock exploded, flooding Joy's magnificent pussy. At the same time, Jason erupted, his delicious cum pouring down David's throat, easing his hunger. David sucked greedily, dazed by the sensory input—Jason holding David's head tight in both hands, groaning as his dick pulsed. Joy moaning as her cunt spasmed over and over again, milking David's cock. Fierce waves of pleasure swamped his body from head to toe.

David sucked Jason's cock dry, just like he'd promised, while Joy's hungry pussy sucked his. Finally, the three of them collapsed on the bed, breathing heavily. "Oh, hell." David ran a shaking hand over his head. "That was…fucking phenomenal!"

"Yeah, it was." Jason rolled over and ran a hand down David's abdomen, sending a shiver up his spine. "Worth waiting for, right?" He cocked an eyebrow at David.

David grinned, remembering the car ride. "Yeah. Definitely worth waiting for." Beside them, Joy stretched. "What about you, beautiful? Was it good for you?"

Joy turned and caressed David's chest, then ran her hand up along Jason's arm to the nape of his neck, tousling his hair. "Fantastic." She propped herself up on one arm, favoring them both with a sinfully decadent look. David couldn't believe it when his cock twitched. How did they do it? How could they make him so horny?

Joy noticed his body's reaction and laughed as she sat up. "I think we should clean up a bit, then head to the casino." She bent down, planting little kisses along the length of David's shaft, which hardened even more. "But there's something for you to think about, while we're placing our bets." She reached out and caressed Jason's cock, smiling with satisfaction as he began to swell, also. "Who said men are at their prime in their early twenties?"

"Honey, you could make a rubber band hard as a rock," Jason said, capturing her hand in his and wrapping it tight around him.

"I do my best." She grinned impishly, freeing her hand from his grasp. "Now, get dressed, you two. We need to go play, then eat." She licked her lips and ran a sultry gaze over every inch of their bodies, until David's whole body flushed with the heat of desire. "Then play some more."

* * *

Joy had more fun that night at the casino than she had experienced in a long time. She and David played blackjack. She bet on roulette with Jason. They all three played the slots for a while, but David quickly became bored, so they returned to the gaming room, closing the night out at the craps table. Afterward, they headed out for thick, juicy steaks and loaded baked potatoes accompanied by a delicious house wine at a restaurant David suggested. By the time they got back to the hotel, it was after midnight.

Joy had been tired on the trip back from the casino, but she felt her energy returning as she contemplated what they might do when they got back to the suite. It was just the three of them when they got in the elevator. Joy hesitated for a moment, knowing there might very well be cameras in there, or the car might stop for someone. But not for someone going *up* from another floor, probably, so she threw caution to the wind. The guys were standing behind her. She reached up and quickly undid her silk blouse, popping her breasts out from the shelf bra she was wearing. Turning, she was rewarded by their startled gasps, and then the look of hot desire in their eyes fanned from embers into flames as she held one breast to her mouth and sucked the tender peak.

"Mmmm. Suck the other one, baby," Jason murmured.

Joy switched, suckling noisily as they both watched. David and Jason reached out simultaneously, each beginning to caress the other's crotch. Joy stepped forward, joining them, running her hands over theirs, cupping both their erections through their tight slacks. When the elevator stopped, she didn't even cover herself—simply grabbed their hands and tugged them to the room, waiting impatiently while David fumbled with the key-card.

Once inside, she pushed David up against the door, pressing her trembling body against his. He groaned, pulling off his shirt, then pulling off hers. "Suck them again, baby. I want to watch."

Joy took one breast in her mouth, watching him as his breathing quickened. He unzipped his pants and pulled them off, then began stroking his cock. Joy felt Jason's hands at her waist, and then he was pushing her skirt down, to fall around her ankles. A soft kiss on her left buttock sent a pulse of need spiraling into her pussy. Joy let the fingers of one hand travel down below her belly, to rub her clit as Jason feathered more kisses across her ass. David took her hand.

"Come here." He led her to the bed. "Lie down on your stomach."

Joy did. David pulled her down a bit, so that her pussy was off the bed. David crawled onto the bed, leaning across her back, facing her feet. She had no idea where Jason was.

"Oh!" Joy shivered as a soft, warm tongue teased her clit. Jason's tongue wiggled and danced, flicking back and forth across her clit, across her swollen labia, dipping into her pussy unexpectedly for a taste. "Oh, God!"

David was rubbing her buttocks, moving both cheeks in a spiral motion, creating an incredible hot itch in her anus. "Mmmm," she moaned. "Will you fuck me, David? The way you fucked Jason?"

She felt him spreading her cheeks wide, and then his tongue was tormenting her tight hole, swirling all around it, flicking back and forth across it, but not inside, where she wanted it. "Here?" He murmured. "Is this where you want my cock?"

"Oh, yes." Joy squirmed as the tip of his tongue finally delved into her. Jason's tongue was probing her pussy, investigating her slick folds. Her cunt was dripping wet.

David's tongue crept deeper, wiggling inside her. Joy gasped with pleasure. "Please, David."

He raised his head. "Uh-uh."

"What?"

He brought his head close to hers, his breath hot on her ear. "Uh-uh. I brought you a present. I want you to see it first."

He rose from the bed, and Joy moaned as Jason's tongue began darting rapidly in and out of her pussy. "Oh, Jason. Yes!" Joy spread her legs wider, pushing herself a little farther off the bed, taking him deeper. With an inarticulate cry, she clutched the covers of the bed as her body convulsed, caught in the grip of a powerful orgasm. She began to relax as it faded, then cried out again as Jason parted her lips and held them wide, slipping his forefingers inside her, seeking her sweet spots with the tips of his fingers as his tongue plunged into her over and over and over.

Joy buried her face in the covers, muffling her scream as desire twisted tight within her, then exploded outward. Through a haze of lust, she heard David murmur, "That's it, baby. Let it go." And then his fingers were inside her, too, alongside Jason's. Their four fingers filled her, caressing her slippery folds, fondling her, carrying her to one overwhelming peak after another, until she lay limp across the bed, trembling and incredibly sated.

David and Jason lay to either side of her, caressing her gently while she caught her breath. Joy was astonished when her nipples began to harden anew, her pussy to tingle. She pushed their hands away. "Please."

Jason wiggled his eyebrows at her. "Please what?"

Joy shook her head. She didn't know. She wanted more, but even though her body might be able to take it, she wasn't sure her mind could.

David set a box on her tummy. "Here, open this."

Joy pushed herself up, sitting cross-legged on the bed as she unwrapped the package. Inside was a white box with no markings. She pulled off the lid and stared at the contraption inside, puzzled. She lifted it out, realizing it was a harness of some sort. "Wh-what's it for?

David looked her in the eye, his gaze more dark and dangerous than she ever remembered, raising goose bumps on her arms. "I want you to fuck me, Joy. Fuck me the way Jason does."

"I-I don't understand. How can I—"

"Stand up, and I'll show you."

Joy scooted off the bed and stood. David sat in front of her and shook out the harness, then he began fastening it around her. One strap went around each leg. There was a rigid, velvet-covered pad with a hole in it attached to the straps. David reached back into the box and brought out a vibrator Joy hadn't noticed when she first opened it. He pushed the vibe through the hole, and lifted the pad so that it rested against her pelvis, the vibrator sticking out like a long, slender cock. A tremor of excitement rushed through her as she realized what this must be.

David must have noticed the change in her expression, because he grinned up at her. "You like?"

"Maybe." Actually, the idea of penetrating him the way he and Jason could penetrate her was making her pussy wet again, making her nipples throb, but she didn't want him to know that. Not yet.

But he had a decidedly knowing smirk on his face as he fastened another strap, this one across her hips, pressing the upper portion of her butt cheeks together as he tightened it. The third strap wrapped snug around her waist.

David tugged at the vibrator experimentally. It stayed put. "Seems stable. How does it feel?" he asked. "Are you comfortable?"

Joy nodded, not trusting herself to speak. This was the most erotic thing that had ever happened to her. Just anticipating the act was making her pussy ripple with mini-orgasms. If this was how a man felt when he became aroused, she could understand their urgency a little better, their tendency to neglect foreplay and go right to the core of the matter, so to speak. Joy giggled a little at her silent analogy, and Jason and David smiled.

David lay back on the bed, scooting up to rest his head on the pillows. "Shouldn't you be..." Joy made the motion of turning over with her hands.

David shook his head. "No. I want to be able to see your face."

Joy took a shaky breath. It was silly to be so nervous, but she was. She climbed up on the bed and knelt between David's legs, completely at a loss as to how to begin.

Jason walked over to his gym bag and opened it. "You'll need this." He tossed a tube of lube onto the bed. Joy took another deep breath, then picked it up.

"Here, let me show you." Jason knelt behind her on the bed. He guided her hands to David's legs, had her lift his calves up and rest them on her shoulders. David scooted down a little, presenting his ass to her. "Now..." Jason cupped her palms, squirted the lube into them. Joy reached down and parted David's cheeks, spreading the oil between them.

As her fingers passed over his anus, he shivered a little. Joy began rubbing him there, enjoying the way he began to grunt and squirm. Jason moved from behind her, lying on his side next to them on the bed, his head and arms near Joy, his feet up by the pillows.

David held out a hand, and without even having to think, Joy squirted lube into it, knowing instinctively what he was going to do. Jason's grin widened as David's hand cupped Jason's balls, bathing them in the smooth oil.

Joy parted David's cheeks again, drizzling lube down between them. She teased the opening of David's anus repeatedly, waiting.

Finally, "Please," he moaned.

"Please what?" Joy murmured huskily, pussy throbbing as his eyes glazed over with desire.

"Fuck me, please. Please, Joy. Fuck me."

A thrill of power went through her with each word. She watched his face as she slipped the tip of one forefinger inside him. "Mmmm," he moaned, his eyes unfocused. She could see the pulse in his neck beating rapidly. She slipped another finger into him, carefully, turning them back and forth and easing them deeper the way Jason had done to her before. David closed his eyes and arched, groaning, and she noticed his hand tightening suddenly on Jason's cock.

Joy ran her other hand over the dildo, glazing it with the lube. She turned her fingers sideways and parted them in David's ass slightly, pressing the tip of the dildo between them.

David opened his eyes and looked up at her, his breath coming in ragged pants. "Yes, Joy." She pressed the tip of the dildo into him, letting her fingers slip out slowly. "Oh, fuck! Yes!"

Joy pushed her hips into him, looking down, parting his cheeks so that she could watch the smooth toy disappear inside him. She moaned herself as raw heat flooded her loins. She held his cheeks apart as she drew her hips back, fascinated by the way his tight anus clung to the dildo despite the lubrication.

David moaned, tossing his head back and forth on the pillow, jerking unevenly at Jason's cock. Jason gasped and arched, covering David's hand with his own, thrusting urgently.

Lust burgeoned in Joy, a primal wave of animal desire. Suddenly, it wasn't enough to take David slowly, watching him writhe beneath her. She wanted to pound into him, hard and fast. Watch him as his climax washed over him. She only regretted that she couldn't feel his hot, tight flesh against hers. Wished for a moment that the toy was real. That she could feel, just once, the same thing he felt when he came inside her. Gasping, she wrapped her hands around David's thighs. Held him still while she pounded into him, deep and fast.

"Oh, hell!" David screamed. "Hell, yeah! Fuck me, Joy. Fuck me!"

Joy plunged the dildo into him over and over, sweat trickling between her breasts, a core of heat coalescing in her groin. Suddenly, she felt she understood what drove a man to be rough, domineering. She experienced the raw power of penetrating a tight pussy or ass, of knowing each thrust was at her discretion, that she controlled the pace, the timing, the moment of release. Even though she herself couldn't feel the tight canal surrounding her toy, she was reveling in the domination. Joy was no longer the passive receptacle, the acceptor. She was the driving force, the penetrator, the taker.

"Deeper," David groaned. "Deeper, Joy."

Joy drove her hips against him. "Yes." David's entire body was trembling, his eyes closed, his hand moving on Jason's cock like a blur. "Oh, yes!"

Joy felt Jason's hand on her butt, ready to push her, help her. She spread David's crack wide and pulled almost all the way out of him, preparing for a huge thrust. Jason reached between them and grasped the top of the pad, depressing a slightly convex rubber button that Joy hadn't noticed.

Joy gasped as the harness began to vibrate, the pulsing beat shivering out along the dildo, shuddering through her pelvis, making her clit throb. The hot ball inside her imploded, her pussy convulsing. Joy grabbed David's calves and pushed his legs back toward his stomach as she drove the dildo in until the pad stopped her. David roared, semen spurting from his cock as Joy writhed against his ass, pressing into the harness in the throes of her own release. Jason arched and moaned, and a fountain of seed spangled David's hand.

Joy pulled back slightly, watching in fascination as David's anus tightened and released, tightened and released, looking for all the world like lips sucking. She knew it had to be even better for a man, able to feel the flesh against him, but damn if it wasn't delicious to know that she had caused that. It was gratifying to watch a man ejaculate, but it was vastly different to watch a hungry part of someone's body taking you in, mouthing you. If she were a man, drinking her.

She wished she could fill David with liquid warmth, as he did her, but she settled for pumping the dildo very quickly, very shallowly, in and out, watching him writhe and moan as his cock continued to pulse. With a final, fierce shudder, he went limp against the bed. Joy pulled out, pushed the button on the harness to still the vibrations, and sat back on the bed, feeling completely drained. When Jason reached out a hand to push her sweat-soaked hair back from her face, Joy was almost irritated. All she wanted to do was to close her eyes and relax.

She widened her eyes at the thought. Another insight. If sex in this role was so draining for her, how must David or Jason feel, after they did the deed for real, emptying their seed into a ravenous body? It had never really been a problem with Jason, but David had sometimes been distant after sex. It had never occurred to her that he might really be exhausted. She resolved to be more understanding the next time he didn't want to cuddle after sex.

Groaning, Jason sat up and nudged David over on the bed, lying down beside him. He held out a hand. Joy took a moment to remove the harness, struggling slightly with one of the catches, but finally it was off. She dropped it beside the bed and grasped Jason's hand, allowing him to draw her up between them. "Did you like my present?" David mumbled sleepily.

"Very much," Joy whispered, kissing the corner of his mouth. He smiled and turned toward her. Reaching out, he twined his fingers in the hand Jason was resting lightly on her tummy. Joy covered their hands with hers. Jason reached over to the side table with his free hand and punched a button on the remote, and the lights went out. Despite her exhaustion, Joy took a long while to get to sleep, wanting to savor their nearness, their warmth, wrapped in a cocoon of happiness, even if only for one night.

## Chapter Nine: Moments of Confusion

Joy woke the next morning to find Jason and David leaning over her, locked in a tender embrace. Watching them, Joy's heart melted. The expression on David's face, in his eyes...she was more convinced than ever that he loved them both. That he was destined to be with them. When they parted, she sighed softly. Jason looked down at her. "Good morning!"

Joy smiled and stretched. "Good morning." Jason leaned over and kissed her belly, a part of their morning ritual. She'd been very self-conscious about her weight the first time he saw her naked, so he had begun kissing her tummy all over, refusing to touch her anywhere else until she agreed that it was the most beautiful thing about her. Now, he kissed it every morning, as a reminder that he loved her just the way she was. Unexpectedly, her eyes filled with tears, and she sat up abruptly.

"I get the shower first," she said.

"I thought we could all take a bath together in that big garden tub," David said hopefully.

Joy shook her head. "Sorry, guys. Ya'll wore me out last night. I need some time to recuperate."

David pouted.

"You'll survive." Joy gave him a quick peck on the cheek. "We've got all the time in the world, don't we?"

David smiled, but Joy thought she caught a hint of wariness in his expression. That was silly, though. He was here, he seemed happy, and he was being openly affectionate with Jason in front of her. She mentally shook off her concern and headed for the shower.

David and Jason shared an amused glance as Joy began humming while she washed. David sat on the loveseat to wait for her to finish, and Jason sat beside him. "So, when did you move back to Galveston?" David asked.

"About a year ago, I think," Jason answered. "It was April, I believe."

David felt a sudden, unexpected stab of envy. They'd had each other for a little over a year now. Intellectually, he knew it was his fault they hadn't connected with him sooner, but emotionally, he hated the idea that he had missed that time with them.

He felt Jason's hand on his neck, kneading. David glanced at him and smiled. He had forgotten how brilliantly blue Jason's eyes were, how they could pierce him to the core. Just like when they were lovers, Jason seemed to sense his moods even before he did. Overwhelmed by a wash of tender affection, he leaned over and kissed Jason gently, passionately. When he drew back, Jason looked up at him in question. "I'm glad you're here," David said.

"So am I." There was still a hint of caution in Jason's voice.

David leaned up against him, resting his head on Jason's chest. After a slight hesitation, Jason wrapped his arms around David, kissing the top of his head and holding him, just holding him, until Joy came out and announced the shower was theirs.

Wordlessly, David stood and held out a hand, helping Jason up off the couch. They went into the bathroom and stood under the shower, bathing each other. Rediscovering familiar, yet different, territory. There wasn't anything erotic about it—simply quiet enjoyment, a reminder of their time together long ago. By the time they were done, and drying each other off with huge, fluffy towels, David was scared. Because he was beginning to realize that what Joy and Jason had been telling him all along was true. He loved them both, but he didn't know how the hell he was going to deal with that.

"What's on the agenda for today?" Joy asked when they had finished dressing.

David shrugged, still a bit dazed at his private admission, and straining to maintain a light tone. "I thought we could go out for a nice, big, leisurely breakfast, then go on and head home, since it's quite a drive."

Jason and Joy nodded. The three of them gathered their things. Joy's cheeks flushed a brilliant red as she picked up the harness. "Wh-what should I do with this?"

David started to shoot off a flippant answer, but then really looked at her expression and realized how nervous she was about what they had done last night. She was embarrassed, for the first time since their renewed intimacy, and it didn't sit well with him. He like the confident, bold Joy. The Joy he'd always suspected lurked behind her reserved exterior in college. He wanted her to know how very much he had enjoyed last night. How very much he wanted to have that experience again.

He went over to her and cupped her face in his hands. "Will you keep it? Please?" The shiver that ran through his body wasn't faked. "Having you fuck me—" He turned her head when she tried to look away, her cheeks even brighter, though that had seemed impossible. "No. Look at me Joy." When her golden brown eyes met his again, he continued. "Having you fuck me last night was heaven. I want you to take me again, Joy. Many times."

Jason had come up behind her, and he murmured in her ear as he met David's eyes. "And you haven't fucked me yet, Joy." David suppressed a stirring of arousal as Jason's tongue traced the curve of Joy's ear. "I want to play with your toy too, Joy. I want you to fuck me the way I've fucked you."

The pulse in Joy's neck was fluttering frantically. "You want to, don't you Joy?" David whispered. He pulled out the waistband of her loose skirt and very deliberately slid his hand down, toying with her clit. "Just talking about it makes you horny, doesn't it?"

Joy moaned, her cheeks still a fiery red, but she parted her legs.

David took the harness from her hand and set it on the bed, pulling her close as his finger massaged her clit. He watched over her shoulder as Jason slipped his hand down the back of her skirt, felt Joy gasp, her hands clutching David's shoulders as Jason's finger slid inside her ass. "Like this, Joy," Jason whispered. "This is how I want you to take me." David moved his hand down to her wet lips, slid a finger inside. Locking gazes with Jason, he pressed in deep, searching. Jason nodded, and then they were capturing her between their fingers. Joy jerked as they discovered one of her sweet spots. "This is how you want to take me, isn't it?" Jason whispered. "Isn't it, Joy?"

Joy's body shuddered between them, her pussy spasming on David's hand. With a look at Jason, David stopped moving his finger, felt Jason stop as well. "That *is* what you want, right?"

Joy moaned. "Please!"

"Will you keep it?" Jason murmured.

Joy tried to move against them, but David caught her waist and held her still. "Will you, Joy? Will you fuck me again, Joy? Will you fuck us both?"

"Yes!" Joy groaned. "God, yes!"

"Yes, what?" Jason murmured.

A desperate sob escaped Joy's throat.

"Yes, what?" David demanded.

"Yes!" Joy screamed. "Yes, I want to fuck you. Both of you. Over and over, until you beg for mercy!"

David grinned wickedly. "Like you, Joy? Are you begging for mercy?"

"Oh, God, yes. Please, David. Please, Jason. Make me come. Please!

David closed his eyes as he and Jason buried their fingers even deeper, massaging that hot, sweet spot until Joy arched and opened her mouth wide in a wordless cry, the walls of her pussy slamming against his fingers, her juices seeping out past her inflamed lips with each violent contraction.

David almost regretted doing this. His cock was hard as a rock now, but he didn't want to have sex with them both again yet. He wanted to spend some quality time with them, getting to know their lives *now* a little better. But no. No regret. He remembered how damn fine it had been last night, after waiting hours with a raging hard-on, and thought that when they did have sex again, it would be so good, he might have a freaking heart attack. But what a way to go!

The tight pulses began to fade, and when they had stopped, Jason and David let her go. "You didn't have to do that, you know. You could have just told me to keep it."

David raised an eyebrow. "Are you complaining?" he teased.

Joy laughed, and David was glad to see the red fading from her cheeks. Glad to see Joy back to her confident, playful self. "Oh, no. Definitely not complaining. You can persuade me to keep this toy as often as you want."

Grinning at each other, David and Jason moved as though to ravish her again. "But not now," she qualified. "If I have one more orgasm, I think I'm going to faint." She grabbed the harness and the box it came in and turned toward the bathroom. "Just let me clean this off and pack it away, and I'll be ready."

David and Jason washed up at the small sink by the suite's bar. When Joy reappeared, the three of them grabbed their bags and headed out.

David began to feel nervous again over breakfast. He, Joy, and Jason were talking in low tones, leaning together as they waited for their food to arrive, when David glanced up and noticed an older man at the next table watching them with what seemed to be a disapproving expression. At first, he told himself the guy must think they were being too loud, but they weren't. They were talking quietly, their heads close. Did they look too intimate to be just friends? Could the man tell that both Joy and Jason were his lovers?

*This is stupid,* David admonished himself. But he couldn't shake the feeling. And it continued after their food arrived. As the three of them chatted, when David would say something witty, and Jason and Joy would laugh, they leaned into him, sometimes touching him in what could be mistaken for a caress by the casual observer. David found himself watching the people around them rather than paying attention to the conversation. By the time the meal ended, he felt as though everyone in the room was looking at them and thinking they were homosexual perverts.

Of course, Jason and Joy picked up on his vibes. As soon as they were in the car, driving down I-10 on their way home, Joy turned in the passenger seat to face him and asked, "What's wrong?"

David could feel her gaze on him, but didn't look over. "Nothing."

Joy shook her head. "Something's wrong. Let's talk about it."

"Really," David said. "It's nothing. I… I've got a tough case going to court this week, and I guess I'm getting back into legal mode, that's all." He couldn't have a serious conversation about this right now. Not when he was feeling so confused. How could something feel so right one morning, and feel so wrong the next?

He felt her staring at him for several moments longer, then she finally said, "Okay." In the back seat, Jason was quiet. David glanced quickly at the rear view mirror. Jason seemed not to have heard their conversation. His head was thrown back against the seat cushion, his eyes closed. David was grateful. Jason seemed almost as skittish about this relationship as David was, although David knew the reason was entirely different. He had the feeling that if Jason sensed his reluctance for much longer, he would decide that he and Joy were better off without David.

*And maybe he'd be right,* David mused. *What do I add to their relationship? They seem perfectly happy together.* But he knew that wasn't true. He felt their longing whenever the three of them were together. Saw the shadows of unhappiness in their eyes. They really did believe their lives wouldn't be complete without him. The problem was that David had been incomplete for so long, he wasn't sure he could function any other way.

He risked a sidelong glance at Joy, found her staring at the road before them, her eyes off-focus. He knew she wasn't buying his explanation, but was glad she'd decided not to push it. He just needed a little more time. Time to decide exactly what he was going to do.

Eventually, Jason stirred and began making small talk. Joy relaxed, and David felt the tension inside him easing somewhat, as well. When they arrived at Joy's house, he was almost completely comfortable again.

"You coming in?" Joy asked as Jason unlocked the door and turned, both of them waiting for his answer.

David wanted to, so badly that he could taste it. But the memory of what had happened the last time he came over was too vivid. He couldn't afford to be late to court again, and he didn't trust himself to get up, even to an alarm clock, if he went inside and did all the things with them that his body was urging him to do.

So he glanced at his watch. "I'd better not. It's getting late, and I really need to look over some things for court tomorrow." He met her shrewd gaze with what he hoped was a calm, open expression. "Rain check?" He glanced at Jason.

Joy cocked her head, still studying him carefully, but Jason nodded. David forced himself to meet Joy's gaze again. "I've got a pretty full schedule for the next three weeks, but I was hoping we could get together that third Friday. I've got to fly up to Dallas to pick up a deposition. Well, I could send Abby, but the attorney I'm visiting is an old colleague of mine." He looked at Jason. "I was thinking maybe, since Jason lived there for a while, that he could show us the sights. You know, make a weekend of it."

"That sounds great!" Jason seemed truly excited, the undercurrent of uncertainty disappearing completely for the first time. "What do you think?"

Joy favored David with one more searching gaze, then looked up at Jason and smiled. "I think that would be fantastic."

David gave Joy a goodbye kiss, then hesitated as Jason leaned forward for one. Only the feeling that Joy was watching him very closely kept him from glancing to see if anyone was around before he kissed Jason lightly on the lips. Jason's smile as he stepped back, however, almost drove away David's self-consciousness. Almost, but not quite.

David waved to them as he drove away. He knew in his heart that Joy was going to confront him about this before long, and he didn't know what he was going to say when she finally cornered him.

## Chapter Ten: Misgivings

Joy watched Jason going through his latest group of photographs, choosing shots for his photo-essay *Nature Gone Wild!*, an examination of the changes that had been wrought across the United States by the invasion of foreign plants and animals brought into the country unwittingly by careless tourists. And sometimes not so unwittingly by pet and plant shop owners. While many articles focused on the negative effects of these imports, Jason had written an unbiased article that balanced the bad news with the good. Joy loved the piece. She had learned so much. She hadn't even known that the introduction of foreign plants and animals had resulted in so many positive effects in certain areas. That was what Jason did best—point out to people things that they couldn't see themselves.

That thought made her sigh. He'd been like an enthusiastic schoolboy for the last week and a half. David's invitation—the knowledge that he intended to continue seeing them, had apparently been thinking about their next encounter even before the New Orleans weekend—seemed to have completely erased the doubts Jason had been plagued with ever since they began this campaign to win David back to them.

The strange thing was that it had produced the exact opposite reaction in Joy. She had felt David's tension in the restaurant when they were eating breakfast and on the porch when they were kissing goodbye. When David let his heart lead him, he did fine. Seemed perfectly at ease with both of them. But when he let his mind intrude, when he started worrying about what other people were seeing, what other people were thinking, she could feel him questioning the entire relationship.

Which would be fine if she were the only one he could hurt. But Joy had dragged Jason into this. Not quite screaming, but definitely kicking. He had been willing for it to be just the two of them. Joy had been the one that had insisted life was too short to continue living unfulfilled, incomplete lives. And she didn't know what she would do if David broke Jason's heart again. Joy would survive, but Jason would be devastated. *Come on, Joy,* she chided herself. *That's not the problem, and you know it.* That was true. Reluctantly, Joy admitted to herself that she didn't want the guilt, if David backed out. If he couldn't finally accept who he was and what he really wanted, she would never be able to look at Jason without feeling guilty for making him vulnerable to being hurt by David again. Jason would survive, too. But her relationship with him would be forever changed, colored by her guilt, and she couldn't stand that thought.

"Oh, yeah." Jason looked up from his worktable. "Did you call David yet?"

Joy shook her head. “No, I was finishing up that story for the *New Yorker.*” She glanced at her watch. “I probably won’t be able to catch him in the office. I’ll call him tonight.”

Jason nodded and returned his attention to his photos. He had suggested to Joy the night before that they invite David over for dinner on Friday or Saturday night. Joy had such an apprehensive feeling about that. She felt sure David was going to say no. But she would call, and she would ask, and she would try very hard not to think that everything was going to fall apart if he said no.

Joy began moving her head in slow circles to release some of the tension building in her neck and abruptly realized that she desperately needed to talk to someone. “Hey, are you going to be busy for a while?”

Jason looked up. “Actually, yes. Why?”

“I thought I’d run out and visit Kendall. “Do you mind?”

“Not at all.” Jason stood up and walked over to her, giving her a kiss. “Call me when you leave to come home, and I’ll start supper.”

Joy smiled and kissed him back. “Okay. See you in a little while.”

Joy went into the bedroom and grabbed her purse, taking her cell phone off the charger. “Bye!” she hollered as she went out the door. Jason waved a hand without looking up from his pictures.

Joy dialed Kendall’s number at the shop before opening the car door and sliding into her seat.

“Lady of the Myths, this is Kendall. May I help you?”

“You sure may,” Joy said.

"Joy, hi! I haven't heard from you and Jason in weeks." Kendall's voice lowered. "How are things going?"

"Actually," Joy said, "that's why I called. I was wondering if you could get away for a while. I need to talk."

"Sure," Kendall said without hesitation. "Brandy's in the office, and Marta's on the register. I was just up here putting out some new jewelry I made. Do you want to meet somewhere in town, or out at the house?"

"Would out at the house be all right?"

"No problem," Kendall said. "I'll head out right now and meet you there."

"Thanks, Kendall. See you."

Joy hung up and started the car. She resolved not to think about anything on the drive out there. She would just enjoy the scenery, and not think about David and Jason any more until she saw her friend.

Kendall was puttering in the front garden, plucking out tiny weeds, when Joy pulled up in front of the house. She stood and walked over to meet her, smiling and sunny in a light cotton dress, embracing Joy as she stepped out of the car. "I've missed you. You look great! So, what's going on?"

Joy laughed. It was just like Kendall to cut right to the chase. "I just need to talk to someone, before I explode. Do you mind?"

Kendall hugged her tight. "Are you kidding? The twins are with Josh. Did you know he and Mason went into business together?"

"I knew they were planning to, but I didn't know if it had actually happened yet."

Kendall nodded. “Yep. And they’re doing great, by the way. And he and Mason have an office space that includes a great room for the kids. Josh takes them to work with him at least once a week.”

Joy smiled as they climbed the stairs to the porch and walked into the house. “God, those guys are so good with the kids. I’ve never seen better fathers.”

Kendall’s expression became thoughtful. “I’m very lucky, aren’t I? Sutter stays home with them on Mondays. His shop is closed that day. So we all have time with them alone, and time to get away. And…” She raised an eyebrow, glancing over at Joy as she led her into the kitchen. “If you can believe it, David’s asked to start babysitting them a couple of nights a month, so Josh and Sutter and I can have some private time.”

“I can believe it. He’s come a long way.”

Kendall grabbed a couple of glasses and filled them with ice, then set them on the table next to a tray that contained a frosty pitcher of tea, sugar, and lemons. Kendall settled into a chair, waiting until Joy sat across from her to say, “But?” She lifted the pitcher and poured tea into their glasses.

Joy sighed. She spooned a couple of mounds of sugar into her tea and squeezed in a lemon, then set the wedge aside. “But…I don’t know.” She stirred her tea with a tall, chilled spoon, then took a sip before continuing. “David wants us, but he doesn’t. He loves us, but he won’t admit it. And in the end, I’m not sure it’s going to be enough to overcome the hell of job he’s done, or society’s done, or whatever, at programming him to be a homophobe.” She laughed, but even she could hear the slight edge of hysteria in the sound. “That’s funny, isn’t it? A homophobic bisexual?”

Kendall placed a reassuring hand on Joy's arm. "It's not so hard to fathom, is it? Society is becoming more accepting, but the male/female bonding pair is still very much the norm. And there are still people out there determined to make life miserable for anyone who is different from them. Why do you think so many people marry, then get divorced later in life and announce that they're homosexual or bisexual or really a woman at heart, not a man? Or vice versa? I think it's because it takes a long time for people to become mature and confident enough with themselves to really explore what their needs are, and even longer to find the courage to act on those needs, despite what society might think." She sat back and sipped her tea thoughtfully. "And there are a lot out there that never find that courage. Who are never able to look at themselves closely enough to even figure out what's missing, much less accept it."

"I know you're right." Joy sighed. "I guess I've been spoiled, seeing the three of you together and so happy. And your circle of friends, they accepted the relationship from the beginning, for the most part."

Kendall chuckled. "And it's kind of ironic that the person who had the most difficulty dealing with it is the topic of conversation, huh?"

"Kind of." Joy stared into her glass, swirling it so that the ice cubes were sucked along by the whirlpool, sort of the way she'd sucked Jason along in her wake. She set the glass down abruptly. "I think I made a mistake, Kendall. Trying to reconnect with David after all this time. Dragging Jason into this with me. It's not going to work." She despised the tremor that had entered her voice, the tears threatening.

"What makes you think that?" Kendall asked.

Joy gave Kendall a long summary of everything that had happened in the last two months, from the tape that she and Jason had made to the premonition she had regarding the dinner invitation. When she finished, Kendall was quiet for a while.

"I don't know what to say, Joy," she finally said. "David is a good man, I know you know that. But the real David is buried deep inside, under who knows what kind of conditioning. Sometimes, I think..." She shook her head.

"Think what?"

"Well, sometimes I get this feeling from him—he *is* Sutter's father, so maybe there's a bit of a psychic connection there, as well—because sometimes I get this fleeting impression that there's more to all of this than your run-of-the-mill, Texas-redneck type of homophobia. Sometimes I think that maybe something happened to him. I get this feeling, every now and then, of pain and embarrassment." She shrugged. "I'm sorry, I'm not explaining very well. Sometimes it's hard to pinpoint these impressions. Hard to put them into words."

"You don't think somebody sexually abused him, do you?" Although that would certainly explain his aversion.

But Kendall was shaking her head. "No...it's something else." She favored Joy with a penetrating look. "Maybe you should ask him.

"Oh, sure. David handles direct questions just fine. I'll just ask him if something happened in his past that made him abhor same-sex relationships even though he had a male lover. I'm sure he'll be glad to tell me, even though he's never mentioned it in all this time."

"Maybe he'll be glad that you picked up on it." Kendall leaned forward. "Sometimes people need a push to get to the core of themselves. Maybe that question will be that push."

Joy found herself shaking her head. "I don't know, Kendall. Asking might make him..."

"What? Break off the relationship? Something you're already suspecting will happen anyway. Wouldn't it be better if you all knew sooner, rather than later?"

Kendall was pushing Joy right now, actually. And Joy hated it, even though she knew Kendall was right. "I'll think about it," she murmured.

"I'm sorry I can't tell you everything's going to be all right," Kendall apologized softly.

"That's okay. I didn't think you'd be able to fix it. I just needed someone to vent to."

"Don't give up on him yet, Joy. I just...he needs the two of you."

"I know that, and you know that, but how do we convince him?"

Kendall didn't answer, but Joy hadn't really expected her to. "Don't worry. I'm not giving up yet. Maybe I will ask him."

They finished their tea in companionable silence, but Joy knew that Kendall could sense the fact that she had absolutely no intention of following through on Kendall's advice.

When Joy finally left Kendall's, after visiting with Josh and Sutter when they came home, and playing with the twins, it was almost seven o'clock. She called Jason to let him know she was leaving. Then, some perverse part of her insisted on swinging by David's, even though it was a bit out of the way. Joy was surprised when she pulled between the open gates and saw his car parked in the driveway. She really hadn't expected him to be home yet.

Joy sat in the drive, car idling, for several moments. She had no idea why she'd even driven over here.

Yes, she did. She had become unsure of David. Unsure of herself, even, and her ability to bring about a successful resolution to their dilemma. She wanted to touch David, to see his face. Joy needed to reassure herself that he would eventually want some type of permanent relationship with them, even if he couldn't—or wouldn't—admit it to himself yet.

The presence of another car finally penetrated her awareness. A little red sports car. Joy experienced a stab of jealousy. It looked like just the sort of vehicle a hot, young legal aide might drive. Was that what David had been so busy with lately? Were she a Jason just a kinky diversion David planned to indulge in every now and then, rather than people he might come to want some kind of life with?

Joy reached up and put her car in reverse just as David stepped out the front door, a young man at his side. Joy's face burned. Could it be? Could David actually be fooling around with another *man*?

Joy rejected the idea almost the same moment she thought it. David's discomfort with that side of himself was real. Wasn't that why she was here—because when it all boiled down, she didn't know if he'd ever be able to totally accept the other male in their trio, and be comfortable enough to have a permanent relationship with them?

Joy took her foot off the brake and started to back out just a moment too late. David had noticed her. He waved, saying something to the man beside him before he started walking toward the car. Joy hit the brake and shifted back into park, then rolled down her window. "I see you're busy. I'll stop by another time."

David leaned casually against the door. "No, we're done. Just a couple more things to say, then he's gone." He reached out and unlocked the door, pulling it open for her, before Joy could protest. Taking a deep breath, Joy turned off the engine, grabbed her purse, and climbed out.

At the foot of the steps, David paused. "Tim, I'd like you to meet Joy Daniels. Joy, Tim Matteo. I just made him a junior partner."

Joy shook the offered hand. "Congratulations."

"Thanks. Nice to meet you."

David waved Joy toward the front door. "Why don't you wait for me in the library?"

Joy went inside and walked down the hall to the library. A flood of memories hit as she pushed open the door and the smell of ink and books and the passing of time hit her. She left the door open and moved to the far wall, settling in a plump leather chair flanked by a floor lamp that cast a warm golden glow over the many titles.

Joy closed her eyes and laid her head back, remembering the first time she had sat in this chair. It was early in her relationship with David. The first time he had touched anything intimately other than her breasts. The first time she had ever experienced an orgasm. Oh, she had engaged in sex with guys before David, but she had never come. Had wondered if something was wrong with her, when other girls talked about sex being so wonderful. Joy shifted, remembering his fingers inside her. How gentle he was, and patient, and the look of pure pleasure on his face when she finally came, clinging to him.

Joy pushed the image from her mind as heat flushed her body from the waist down. Restless, she eyed the books on the shelves nearest her, noticing right away two huge, leather-bound volumes on the bottom shelf. They looked like scrapbooks, but Joy couldn't think of a single soul in David's family who was sentimental enough to put one together. Then again, maybe they were just chronicles of David's career. He wasn't the highest-paid defense attorney south of Austin for nothing. He'd been in the newspapers more times than she could remember.

Idly, Joy grabbed one of the volumes, surprised by its weight, and deposited it in her lap. She opened to a random page and was confronted by the article she'd written in January of nineteen-ninety-eight on literature as national consciousness. Flipping the page, she discovered a clipping from the Journal of American Literature of the same year—a paper on the resurgence of graphic novels in North America. Joy sat up straight and thumbed through a few more pages. All were clippings of her articles, journal papers, research summaries, grant proposals. Everything she'd ever had published, amateur or professional. A chronicle of *her* career, not David's.

Joy leaned down and pulled out the second thick volume. Inside, she found clippings of Jason's photo essays, numerous non-fiction articles on photography and writing, and newspaper, journal, and magazine photos, all attributed to Jason Weir. Joy turned back to the first page and found it to be a newspaper photo, credited to Jason, from the Houston Journal, dated six months after they had all graduated.

Joy closed the book with a snap, her mind reeling. That David had done this—started these scrapbooks and kept them up all these years, accomplished exactly what she'd been vaguely looking for when she swung by here. Renewed Joy's hope. Convinced her anew that David did love them, and that his love for them was every bit as strong as hers and Jason's for him, whether he could accept it or not. Despite his tension, his seeming embarrassment and reluctance, David had never really let them go. Not in his heart.

But that wasn't going to make anything easier. Not really. Actually, Joy was now more concerned than ever. If David's love was this strong, if he'd never gotten over them, then he was fighting the relationship even more than she had realized. If he couldn't freely accept their love in the wake of this kind of longing, would he ever?

Joy restored the books to their place on the shelf and stood, pacing restlessly. She was tired. Tired of trying to figure out how to make this work. She and Jason wanted a lasting, committed relationship with David. One where none of them were afraid to go out in public as a trio and even exchange mild expressions of affection without reservation. Joy was no longer sure that David would ever be capable of that.

When he walked into the library, Joy was standing by the window, browsing the collector's edition of a book billed as the definitive history of dragons, beautifully bound and richly illustrated. She was hyper-aware of him, leaning against the wall and watching her as she finished reading a paragraph and looked up.

"You like it?"

"Very much. I don't know how I missed this. I spend about two hundred dollars a month on books, but I don't remember seeing this one in the stores." She paused for a second, then admitted, "Of course, the books I buy are mostly paperbacks." Joy closed the book and turned to put it up.

David halted her with a gesture. "Take it."

"Oh, no. I couldn't. It's—"

"Don't worry. I wasn't offering to *give* it to you. I know you wouldn't accept. I meant as a loaner. You can bring it back when you're finished.

Joy smiled. "In that case, thank you."

David looked tired, but there was a twinkle in his eye as he said, "You're welcome, ma'am," exaggerating his Southern accent. "And what can this old cowboy do for the lady today?"

Joy said the first thing that came to mind. "Jason and I were wondering if you'd like to come over for dinner Friday night."

A flicker, like a shadow, passed across David's face. "I'm sorry, I can't. I'm swamped this week and next. That's why I made plans with y'all for next weekend."

Joy knew immediately that he was lying. Whenever David lapsed into Southern expressions like *y'all,* he wasn't being honest. "Oh. Okay."

David held her by the shoulders, looking into her eyes. "Are you mad?"

Joy smiled, striving to hide just how upset she was. "Not mad. Disappointed."

"It's just a week and a half, Joy. Then we'll have the whole weekend together."

Joy nodded, tried another smile, but knew she wasn't quite succeeding.

David sighed. "I miss you guys, too. I just have a huge workload right now." Joy might have bought it, if his gaze hadn't strayed. He couldn't look her in the eye. "As a matter of fact, I really need to get busy. I'm in court tomorrow, and I have a hell of a lot to do before I hit the sack tonight."

"Okay." Joy clutched the book to her chest and turned toward the door. "Sorry to bother you." She winced when she realized how petulant she sounded.

David caught her at the door. Wrapped his arms around her from behind and nuzzled her neck. "It's no bother, Joy."

She swallowed hard and managed an airy laugh. "I know, David. Really." Joy closed her eyes and leaned into him, breathing deeply of his scent—a hint of spicy/musk cologne, the second-hand ghost of someone's tobacco smoke on his clothes. Underneath it all, a scent that was uniquely his—part sweat, part David, but one-hundred-percent male. And the only thing she and Jason needed to make life complete.

He nibbled her neck for a moment more, then groaned and gently pushed her away. "You'd better go, before I do something my client will regret in the morning."

Joy did laugh, then. "All right."

David walked with her to the front door, giving her a quick kiss before he opened it.

"You can call us some time, you know. On a lunch break, or before you go to bed. We miss you. It would be nice to hear your voice."

The wind blew a strand of hair across her face, and David pushed it back, trailing his finger across her cheek as he did so. "I will. I promise."

Joy gave him another kiss. She would have enjoyed it, but she was acutely aware of the fact that his gaze was darting about nervously, as though he were scared to death someone might see them. Joy drew away quickly and hurried to her car. David waved to her briefly as she pulled out of the drive, then he was gone.

What was he lying about? That's what Joy pondered all the way home. He couldn't come Friday night, but she felt certain it didn't have anything to do with work. Joy had always had a sixth sense where David was concerned, and she hadn't been wrong yet.

Joy's knuckles began to ache, and she realized that she had a death grip on the steering wheel. She made a conscious effort to push thoughts of David from her mind for the rest of the drive. It was silly to obsess. David had, after all, made plans to see them in a week and a half, plans he seemingly meant to carry out. Joy resolved to bury her suspicions and wait to see how things turned out.

## Chapter Eleven: Trouble in Dallas

Joy was reading in bed when the phone rang the next Thursday night. "Hello?"

"Hi."

"Oh, hello." Joy set her book on the bedside table.

"I'm sorry I didn't call sooner. Like I said, I've been—"

"Swamped lately. Yes, I know." Joy couldn't keep the edge out of her voice.

"You guys are still coming with me tomorrow, aren't you?" He actually sounded worried at the prospect that they might have changed their minds.

Joy was quiet for a moment. Actually, she'd been concerned that he was going to cancel on them, and she didn't trust herself not to squeal for joy if she opened her mouth. "If you still want us to," she finally said.

"Of course! I was calling to let you know that our flight leaves Hobby at six-forty tomorrow evening. Can we meet at the Delta terminal at five-thirty? I'll be coming straight from work."

"Sure." Joy grabbed a pen and jotted the time on a notepad from her bedside table drawer. "Are we coming back Saturday or Sunday?"

"Sunday. If that's all right with you two."

"That's fine."

There was a prolonged silence, during which the phone line seemed to hum with hidden tension. "Um, what are you doing?" David asked.

"Reading."

"Oh."

Another awkward silence, which Joy broke. "Jason's out of town tonight. He's photographing for a convention in Austin."

"He'll be back in time, won't he?"

"Oh, yes. He's driving down in the morning. Should be home by one or two, at the latest."

"Good."

"What are *you* doing?" Joy asked.

"I just came upstairs to shower and hit the sack, but I wanted to call you first. I didn't know if you'd still be up."

"Have you undressed yet?"

"Um, actually, yes."

"Are you naked?"

"Um...well, no."

"What are you wearing?"

David cleared his throat before answering. "Just my briefs."

"Mmmm," Joy smiled to herself. "Is your cock hard?"

After a short silence, David said, "Not yet, but it's getting that way." His tone had changed, his voice deep and a bit husky.

"I wish I was there," Joy murmured. "So I could kneel in front of you, and pull those briefs off. Touch your ripe cock with my hand."

All she could hear was David's breathing.

"Could you do it for me, David? Pull off your briefs and touch yourself? And tell me as you're doing it."

Another short silence, then, "I-I'm pushing down my briefs."

"All the way off, David."

She heard him swallow. "Okay, they're on the floor now."

"Sit on the bed."

A rustle, then, "I'm sitting."

"Now, stroke your cock, soft and slow." David took in a deep shuddering breath she could hear over the phone.

"I'm taking my gown off, now, David." Joy tossed her nightgown to the floor. "I don't have anything on underneath it." David's breath quickened. "You're not trying to come yet, are you? Because that would be a shame. Then I wouldn't have time to tell you how my nipples are so hard, they feel like huge pebbles when I touch them."

"Oh, God, Joy. Are you touching them now?"

"Mmmm." Joy balanced the phone between the crook of her neck and her ear. "Yes, I am. I'm pinching the nipples, right at the tip." She gasped. "Oh. That sends this hot pulse straight down to my pussy."

"Oh, shit. I'm going to come, Joy."

"No. Stop. Put your hands against the bed and just sit there and listen. My pussy's so wet, David. And my nipples are so hot." She waited a moment. "Did you stop?"

"Yes," David answered in a strangled voice.

"My nipples are on fire. I have to cool them off." She reached into her tea glass and pulled out a piece of ice. "I have a piece of ice now, David. Mmmm. I'm circling the very edge of it around my nipple. God, David, you should see how tall and plump it is. Just waiting to be sucked." Joy tossed the ice back into her glass. She moved the phone to one hand, and held her breast up to her mouth with the other. She ran her tongue over the chilled bud. "Mmmm. My warm, wet tongue feels so good on my nipple."

David was breathing deep now, listening hard. "Suck it for me, baby."

Joy chuckled. Taking the firm peak in her mouth, she sucked noisily, holding the phone close so that he could hear her.

"Oh, God. I wish I could see you," David whispered.

"Lick your finger, David, and run it over your own nipple."

David moaned.

"How does it feel?" Joy asked.

"My nipple's getting hard."

"I love how a man's nipple can get just as hard and plump as a woman's. What else, David? How does it *feel*?"

David was breathing hard again. "Shit. Feels good." She heard him fumbling with the phone.

"Are you touching them both now, David?"

"Yes," he groaned.

"Why?"

"Because, it-it sends this spear of…heat down to my cock."

"Use your fingernails, David. Hold them just above your nipples and wiggle just the tips of the nails back and forth, fast."

"Fuck!"

"Tell me, David." Joy trailed her hand down across her belly, burying her fingers in her bush, lightly caressing her clit.

"Pleasure," he gasped. "Just…when I catch them just right, my cock jumps." He groaned again. "Joy, I can't…I've got to—"

"Not yet." Joy gasped as she parted her labia and slipped her middle finger between them. "My pussy's so wet, David. I've got my legs spread so wide. I'm holding my lips open with my thumb and pinky, and my middle finger is inside me. So hot and wet."

David gasped, breathing hard. "I-I'm putting lotion on my dick." His voice shook as he spoke. "I've got to jack off, baby. I've got to."

"Together," Joy gasped. "Let's do it together."

David's only answer was a low moan.

"I'm sliding another finger in, David. Oh, God. Wiggling and touching. Oh, God, that feels so *good.* Listen." She held the phone down by her pussy for several seconds, moving her fingers fast and hard, listening to the moist noises, then brought the phone back to her ear. "I'm so wet. Did you hear, David? Did you hear my pussy sucking on my fingers?

"Oh, damn, yes. I'm fucking my hand, Joy, picturing your pussy. I wish I could be there. I want to see your fingers in that soft, wet pussy."

Joy gasped as a mini-orgasm rippled through her. "Yes, David. I want you to watch me some time. Watch me make myself come for you."

"Yes!"

"David?"

"Yes?"

"Put some lotion on your other hand."

She heard more fumbling, then "Done."

"You like anal sex, don't you David?"

"Oh, shit." His voice shook with desire.

"Don't you?"

"Yes," he groaned.

"I want you to put your finger in your ass, David. I'm there, and I'm stroking your cock, and Jason's there, too. He's putting his long cock in your ass. I've always loved how long his cock is; I can take him so deep. And your cock. So fat. I can't wait until you fuck me in the ass. Are you doing it, David?"

"Oh. Oh, fuck. Yes," he said between gasps.

Joy grabbed another piece of ice, the size of a marble. Her pussy was throbbing, tightening. She was so close. "I-I'm fucking myself with my fingers, David. I'm turning on my side, and I'm putting a piece of ice between my cheeks." She gasped at the cold. "I'm pushing it up against my asshole."

"Yeah, Joy! Yeah!" David's breath came in ragged gasps. "I've got my finger buried in my ass so deep…I'm…oh, hell."

"It's sliding in, David. The ice is…" Joy gasped. "Sliding in and…oh, God!" Joy almost lost the phone as she arched, gasping and writhing. "I'm…coming…so…hard."

David's answer was a series of grunts and gasps. Joy rocked her hips, wiggling her fingers inside both caverns to prolong the sweet ecstasy. "Oh, yes!" she cried.

"Joy! It's...God!"

For long moments, the only sounds were their outcries of mutual pleasure. When the last decadent pulse had faded, Joy sighed.

"Joy?"

"Hmmm?"

"Thank you."

"You're very welcome."

"Did—did you know I was hoping for this to happen?"

"I suspected."

"Do you mind?"

"David, I've just had a fucking tremendous orgasm. Trust me. It's just as hot for me to hear you on the phone, to picture you, as it is for you." She hesitated, then decided to jump in with both feet. "I'd do just about anything for you, David. I love you. I'm very glad you called. I've been wanting to do this ever since Jason mentioned it that first night."

"Mmmm," David murmured. "Me, too. I've gone to bed some nights thinking about it, but I haven't had the guts to call. I usually don't end up sleeping those nights."

"Will you sleep tonight?"

"Mmmm. I'll sleep. Very well."

"Me, too."

After a minute of silence, David chuckled. "I'm dozing off here, but I hate to say goodbye."

Joy smiled. "Me, too. But we'd better get a good night's sleep." She grinned wickedly. "Who knows if we'll get any sleep at all this weekend."

"You're wicked, you know that?"

"Do you mind?"

She could hear the smile in his voice. "Hell, no!"

"I'll see you tomorrow."

"See you tomorrow."

Joy hung up the phone and smiled up at the ceiling. That had been a very unexpected pleasure. She wished Jason could have been there. Joy smacked her forehead, lightly. It had just occurred to her that she should have called Jason as well. She could have put him on the line with them. The next time Jason went out of town, wouldn't that be a nice surprise for him? Three-way phone sex. Hmmm. Joy turned off the bedside lamp and fell asleep with a sly smile on her face.

* * *

Joy got up early the next morning, to pack bags for her and Jason. He walked in around two o'clock, happy but exhausted. Joy took his bag from him. "I'll get your clothes in the wash. You go take a nap."

"That's okay, I can do it."

Joy pushed him toward the bedroom. "Don't be silly. We have to be at the airport at five-thirty. Go rest. I'll wake you up at four."

"But, I have to pack."

"Already done."

Jason hugged her, planting a kiss on her forehead. "You're the best!"

Joy grinned. "I know. Now, go."

Joy filled the washer and started it, and finished cleaning up the kitchen. She hated coming home to a dirty house. When the clothes were dry and she had finished folding and putting them away, she woke Jason. "Time to go."

Jason was in an exceptionally good mood on the drive to the airport. He kept up a running commentary while Joy drove, reciting the latest gossip about Austin's elite, relating a few of the mostly bad jokes he'd overheard. *Please,* Joy thought to herself. *Please let this weekend go smoothly.* Jason was so excited about spending this time with David. Joy fervently hoped that none of the negative premonitions she was experiencing would come to pass.

David made it to the airport by five forty-five, and an hour later, they were winging their way to Dallas. Upon arrival, the hotel had a car waiting for them, per David's request, and by nine o'clock they were ensconced in a very luxurious suite in one of Dallas' finest hotels.

"So." Joy flopped down on the bigger-than-king-size bed. "What's on the agenda?"

"I'm stopping by Flynn's office tomorrow morning. Other than that, the weekend's ours." David turned to Jason. "I was thinking maybe you could suggest someplace to eat tonight, then we could hit the town? I've heard Dallas has some excellent up-and-coming bands."

"If you're in the mood for lobster, I know a little hole-in-the-wall place that has the best lobster you'll ever eat, at the best price."

David nodded. "Sounds great. Lead on."

The restaurant turned out to be small, intimate, and not very crowded. David had the waiter seat them at a secluded table in the back. After they ordered, he looked at Jason and Joy hungrily, devouring them with his eyes. "I missed you two."

"We missed you," Jason replied. He hesitated a moment, then reached out and laid his hand over David's on the table. He smiled in sheer delight as David turned his hand and interlaced his fingers with Jason's. Joy didn't think Jason noticed how David's eyes scanned the room briefly before he responded.

"I read in the paper about your latest client's acquittal," Joy mentioned. "You've been on a roll lately."

David nodded.

"Do you really think he's innocent?"

"I don't know." David shrugged. "The prosecution's case was all circumstantial."

"But, do you—"

"I don't want to talk about work tonight." David reached out and grasped her hand with his free one. "Work kept me away from you guys for three weeks. I want to forget about work this weekend."

"Okay."

David's gaze flickered, and he withdrew his hands from theirs and made a big show of opening his napkin and taking out his silverware. Joy glanced up and wasn't surprised to see the waiter heading their way with drinks and rolls.

"Thank you," she murmured as he deposited everything on the table.

Jason launched into a condensed version of the stories and jokes he'd told her earlier, so Joy sat back, listening with only half an ear, watching David closely. He had chosen to sit in the chair that placed his back to the wall, giving him a view of the room. As he and Jason chatted, he reached out occasionally, touching Jason's arm, running a hand along Jason's thigh. The gestures seemed sincere, but it bothered Joy that he only made them after first checking to make sure no one was watching. At least Jason hadn't noticed.

It had been a long day, and they'd gotten in kind of late, so by the time their food arrived, Joy was starving. She quit thinking about David and how he felt about the three of them, and concentrated on the food.

"What do you think?" Jason asked them.

"Great!" David mumbled around an ear of corn.

Joy finished swallowing a succulent bite of lobster. "Delicious."

Jason beamed, happier than she'd seen him in a long time. Her sense of foreboding, however, would not go away.

All three of them cleaned their plates. "Ready for dessert?" their waiter asked.

Joy shook her head. "No way. I'm stuffed."

"Me, too," Jason agreed. The waiter set their ticket on the table and started taking away plates.

After the bill had been taken care of, David asked, "Where to now?"

"We're really close to club row. We could leave the car here and walk over."

"Let's go."

Joy followed them reluctantly. She really just wanted to go back to the room and talk for a while and eventually make love. She had a bad feeling about the three of them going out in public. David was making a valiant effort to shake off his conditioning, but she didn't think he could hold up under pressure in a very public place.

Jason, however, was exuberant. He and David talked as they walked, heads together, David laughing frequently. *Maybe it will be all right,* Joy thought.

Inside the first club, a rock band was playing, and Jason drew them both out onto the floor. Joy was proud of them all. She'd thought they might look silly, bumping and grinding at their age, but David and Jason were in excellent shape, definitely still had the moves. And no one was staring, so she must be giving a halfway decent account of herself, as well. Joy let the music take her away.

An hour later, the three of them made their way to the bar, having spotted three empty seats side by side. Joy slipped onto a stool and sighed. Jason slid onto the stool to her left and grinned. "Tired?"

Joy nodded, using a napkin to pat away some of the 'glow' dancing had given her face. "I can't keep up with you two!"

David stood between them, one arm draped casually over Joy's shoulder. Jason reached out and put his arm around David's waist, laughing. "Yeah, not bad for old guys, huh?"

Joy felt David tensing beside her as Jason's arm circled him, his gaze darting about the room. Annoyed, Joy leaned into him, wrapping her arm around his waist as well as she grasped Jason's hand, pulling him close for a kiss.

David stepped back abruptly, moving to her right to take a seat. Jason appeared startled, but recovered quickly. Joy turned to the bartender and ordered a soda.

"Soda?" David raised his eyebrows.

Joy nodded without commenting. She had a funny feeling she didn't want to add alcohol to the mix tonight.

David shrugged. He and Jason gave their orders, and the three of them sat there, sipping their drinks. After a second round, Jason stood and grabbed them both by the hand. "Come on, there's another place I want you to see."

David's jaw had tightened, and as they pushed their way through the crowd, he managed to pull his hand from Jason's grasp. Once they were out the door, he moved to Joy's other side, catching her hand in his so that she was between them.

The next club was quieter. The crowd was more eclectic; there were some twenty- and thirty-somethings mixed in, but everyone seemed perfectly at home. Only a few people were on the dance floor. "This is more of a serious music lover's place," Jason explained. "People come here to listen to the best new alternative bands, rather than dance."

David and Joy nodded, and followed him as made his way through the room.

"Hey! Jason!" A shout from one of the guys grouped around a large table caught Jason's attention.

"Mark, hi!" Jason veered over to the group. "How's it going?"

"Good, man!" Mark stood and hugged Jason, a couple of others slapping him on the back over a chorus of "hi"s and "good-to-see-you's. David and Joy hung back.

Jason reached out and grabbed David's arm, pulling them into the group. "I'd like you to meet my friends, Joy and David."

"Hi, Joy. David." Introductions went around the table. Jason and his friend pulled over three more chairs.

"What brings you back to Dallas?" Mark asked.

Jason cocked his head toward David. "David's a lawyer. Had to meet with a guy here. Asked me to show him around."

Mark raised his eyebrows, glancing at David and Joy curiously. Suggestively. "Are you…involved?" He put his arm around the man next to him; Joy thought she remembered his name being Nathan.

David sat up, his back ramrod straight, his arm tightening around Joy's shoulder painfully. Oblivious, Jason nodded, reaching over to stroke David's leg.

Joy could feel David's fury, but he held it in check. For a while. Joy kept trying to catch Jason's eye, to warn him. To suggest that they leave. Even asking him to show her where the bathroom was didn't work, however, as another guy's girlfriend volunteered helpfully, "I'll show you. I need to freshen up, too." As the evening wore on, however, and Jason continued to be openly affectionate toward them both, even going so far as to explain that all three of them were romantically involved, David finally exploded. Jason's hand had strayed close to his crotch, and David suddenly pushed up from the table.

"Fuck, Jason! Can't you keep your hands to yourself?"

The chatter stopped abruptly. Jason stared up at David, face turning pale. "I—"

Joy stood and started pushing David toward the door.

David resisted. "Joy, I—"

"No, David." Joy used her weight, pressing up against him, forcing him to move back. "You need some fresh air."

David glared at Jason a moment more. Then, as he realized that the quiet had begun to spread throughout the room, people staring at him with wary expressions, he turned abruptly and let her escort him out.

"How could he do that?" he said harshly as soon as they stepped out the door. "He knows how uncomfortable it makes me. How?"

Joy eyed him. "Does he?"

"What the hell are you talking about?"

Joy's jaw tightened. "Don't you yell at me, David Campbell."

David continued to glare at her, but kept his mouth shut. Joy held up a hand, ticking points off on her fingers. "You invited us to New Orleans, and fucked his brains out. You invited us to come here, somewhere you know Jason used to live, and asked Jason in particular to show us around. You've been extremely affectionate toward him since we met at the airport. You didn't say anything to him at the restaurant. Hell, you were even instigating things, David. What is he supposed to think?"

David opened his mouth, then shut it, and finally shook his head. "I was trying to be nice."

Joy closed her eyes against a sudden rush of anger. "Be nice? Do you know how patronizing that sounds?"

"I don't know what you want from me!" David was yelling again, but Joy kept a tight rein on her temper, striving to stay calm.

"Yes, you do, David." He opened his mouth, but she wouldn't let him speak. "You know what we want, and you can't do it, but there are things you want, too. So, like always, you're trying to have your cake and eat it, too. Create a situation that benefits *you,* works the way *you* want it to."

Joy took a deep breath. "If everything had gone as planned this weekend—we had a nice night on the town, screwed, another nice night, another screw," she ignored David's wince at her word choice, "—what were you going to do when we got back? Jason's being presented with a lifetime achievement award in a couple of weeks. I was going to call you next week and invite you to the ceremony. But you wouldn't have come, would you? You would have given some excuse, and then invited us out of town again, wouldn't you? That's how it is." She wasn't asking. She knew. "And it's not just Jason. You only want to be with either of us in places where you're not likely to know anyone. You were perfectly willing to have sex over the phone with me, but you were uncomfortable as hell, kissing me goodbye in front of your house the other night." A part of her was praying David would deny this, but deep down inside, Joy knew she was right.

David stared at her wordlessly for a long time, until Joy couldn't stand the silence any more. "It's true, isn't it?"

Finally, David nodded.

Joy was amazed at how quickly the tears came. "Why? What are you so afraid of?" She brushed impatiently at the wetness on her cheeks.

"My work—" David began.

"Work that doesn't make you happy? That's never made you happy?" Joy retorted. "Friends that are no kind of friend, who would just as soon kick you when you're down than help you up?"

"I'm only fifty-five, Joy."

"And perfectly situated to retire and lead the kind of life you really want to live." Joy shook her head. "You might lose some friends, but you'll gain others. And you'd be happy for the first time in your life. I know you would. All those years wasted, David. I know you love us. I *know* it. Why can't you let yourself be happy?"

He looked...defeated. His anger deflated. Looked his age, for the first time in a long while. "It's...complicated," he croaked.

"It doesn't have to be." Joy hated herself for the note of pleading that had entered her voice. "Come back to the hotel. Talk to us. We can work this out."

David stared into her eyes for a long time. "I'm sorry, Joy," he finally whispered. "I can't do this."

He turned and walked away, and Joy stood on the sidewalk, crying. Watching, but she didn't follow. A warm body embraced her. "How much did you hear?" she asked between sobs.

"Everything," Jason rasped.

Joy buried her face in his chest.

"It's my fault," he whispered. "I shouldn't have—"

"No." Joy leaned back, looking up into his eyes. "This is David's problem, not ours. You didn't do anything wrong." *And mine,* she thought to herself. *I'm the one who pushed for trying to bring David back into the relationship.* Despite how much they had both wanted that, Jason had sensed all along that it wasn't going to work. "Right?" Joy waited until Jason nodded, then hugged him tight. They remained that way, clinging to each other, until Mark came to check on them.

Mark gave them a ride back to the hotel. Waited for them while they confirmed that David had checked out. The clerk informed them that he had paid for the room, leaving a message that they should stay, but Jason refused. "Mark said he'd put us up for the night. Is that okay?" Joy nodded. They went upstairs to collect their bags, then went out and climbed back into Mark's car.

## Chapter Twelve: In Doubt

Mark cooked a big breakfast the next morning, making a huge effort to keep the conversation light and constant, but Joy could tell he was dying of curiosity. Eventually, that curiosity got the best of him. "I know it's none of my business, but...what the heck happened last night?"

Jason looked at Joy and she sighed. "It's a long story."

Mark shrugged. "It's Saturday. I don't know about you two, but I don't have anywhere to go."

Joy leaned back in her chair, staring up at the ceiling. "I'll try to condense it. The three of us met in college. David and I dated, and at one point I thought he was going to ask me to marry him, but he backed off. I didn't know why at the time, but a couple of years ago, some things happened that caused me to put two and two together, and I realized that he had been involved with his roommate, as well."

Mark raised his eyebrows at Jason. "You?"

Jason nodded.

"Jason and I reconnected through friends," Joy continued, "and realized that there was an attraction between us, as well."

"The friends happen to be related to David, so we began running into him occasionally, and we both realized that we still wanted him to be a part of our lives," Jason explained.

"I take it the feeling was mutual."

Joy raised her head. "Yes and no. David's definitely attracted to both of us, but—"

"The homosexual element makes him very uncomfortable," Mark guessed.

"Yeah." She shook her head ruefully. "We thought maybe he was coming around, but—" Joy sighed.

"As you saw last night, apparently not," Jason finished for her.

"That's too bad." Mark stood and started cleaning off the table as he talked. "He *did* look like a deer caught in the headlights," he mused. "It's crazy, though. Everyone at that table would have known you three were involved, even if you hadn't said a word and hadn't touched all night."

"Really?" Joy asked.

Mark laughed. "Really. Body language, the way you three look at each other." He paused, meeting her gaze. "Haven't you ever met people that you didn't have any reason to suspect were involved—maybe a couple of co-workers, or people at a party who aren't even standing with each other—and you know, instinctively, that they're together?'

Joy nodded.

"That's the way you three struck me, the minute I saw you. Sometimes, when it's right, it right."

"That's what I keep thinking," Joy said, "but it certainly didn't turn out right this time."

"So, what's his story?"

"What do you mean?"

Mark shrugged. "He didn't strike me as the kind of guy who denies himself many things. So, there's got to be a reason this bugs him so much. Don't you think?"

Joy frowned, exchanging a glance with Jason. "I think it's just that he comes from a long line of ultra-macho Southern bigots who'd rather die than admit they're different from everyone else."

Mark shrugged again. "I guess you'd know better than I would."

After that, the talk turned to more general topics, but Joy found herself considering what he had said and for some reason she simply couldn't get the thought out of her mind.

* * *

David was angry with himself, but that was not unusual. The thing that was different this time was that he was angry for Jason and Joy's sake, not his own. As he sat on the flight back to Hobby, he brooded. He should never have responded to their overtures. David had known from the beginning that he would never be comfortable with that part of him that wanted Jason, and he should have left well enough alone.

David shifted in his seat and rested his chin on his hand, staring out the small window at the stars. He had gone straight from the confrontation with Joy to the hotel, collected his things, and taken care of the financial arrangements, and then proceeded to the airport. He had exchanged his Sunday ticket for the next flight back and called Flynn, telling him that something important had come up and to go ahead and send the affidavit by registered mail.

At first, he had regretted leaving so abruptly. Now, thinking back, he was glad. He owed Jason and Joy a clean break. Leaning back in the seat, David closed his eyes. At least the flight wasn't crowded. Maybe he could get some sleep. But the vision imprinted on his eyelids was that of Joy's tearful gaze, asking one question over and over: "Why?" Groaning, David opened his eyes and reached up, taking his slim briefcase out of the overhead. If he couldn't sleep, he might as well get some work done. An hour later, when the plane landed, David was still staring at the first page of an affidavit, trying to read words that suddenly no longer made sense.

The drive home from the airport seemed to take longer than usual. David shut the front door to the house behind him with a feeling of relief. He headed upstairs, to his bedroom, and dumped his bag and briefcase on the floor, flopping back on the bed. The first fingers of dawn were creeping around the edges of the curtains. Exhausted, David fell into a restless doze. In his dreams, he fought his way through a dense forest in which the saplings seemed to have a life of their own, whipping out to slap his bare legs as he ran.

Around noon, David woke with a sour taste in his mouth and a pounding headache. He pushed himself up from the bed and stumbled into the bathroom. After a shower, he felt marginally better, but as he went through the motions of fixing himself a lunch and taking something for his headache, the huge house seemed emptier than it had since Sutter had moved out when he started college.

For the next hour, David tried to find something he could concentrate on, but the only thing his mind seemed to want to consider was whether Jason and Joy were all right. Whether they were home yet. Whether they would talk to him if he called.

David shook his head. Call? Hell, no! A clean break—that's what he wanted. Right? Frustrated with his own indecision, David grabbed his keys and headed out the door.

He'd had no idea where he was going to go when he climbed into the car, but somehow wasn't surprised when he ended up on the stretch of winding highway that led to Sutter's. When he pulled into the drive, he saw Kendall kneeling by the front garden, the twins squatting by her side.

Kendall stood as David stepped out of the car, her expression pleased but quizzical. "Hi!"

"G'pa!" The twins barreled into him, clinging to his legs as he lifted first one grandchild, then the other, for a fierce hug and sloppy kiss.

"Pu' weez!" Hayley informed him.

It took David a moment to figure out what she was saying. "I'll bet you're good at that," he said, when "weez" clicked as "weeds" in his mind. Hayley and Race both nodded vigorously.

"Want to help?" Kendall asked.

"Sure." David balanced the twins on his hips as he followed Kendall over to the garden. He set the squirming bundles of energy on the ground and sat in the grass beside them. Hayley immediately proceeded to pull up a small begonia. David glanced at Kendall, who shrugged and smiled tolerantly.

David pulled a few weeds, encouraged by his grandchildren, who delighted in showing him which plants were weeds and which were flowers. That they were so often wrong didn't matter in the least. Kendall had a small pile off to the side, of "weeds" they had pulled which were really flowers, and he surmised that she would replant them another day.

David worked alongside his extended family for about twenty minutes, the warm sun beating down on his shoulders. As he worked, he felt a lessening of the tight core of tension he'd been feeling inside for the last few months. Impulsively, he wrapped one arm around Kendall's shoulders, giving her a quick hug.

As usual, her sharp eyes seemed to see much more than his outward appearance. "Is something up?" she asked casually.

David had intended to talk to her about Joy and Jason, but it suddenly occurred to him that this was one problem he needed to solve on his own. He was the only person capable of deciding what he wanted to do with the rest of his life. Again, he had that feeling of standing at a crossroads, on the verge of making one of the most important decisions in his life, and realized that maybe he was just a little bit scared. Kendall was staring at him, waiting for an answer. He shook his head. "No, nothing. I just needed to get away for a while."

Kendall accepted that without comment, though he could sense she was curious.

David spent the remainder of the day at Sutter's, romping with the twins and chatting about inconsequentials with Sutter and Josh after they returned from a trip to town to buy the twins toddler beds.

"Big boy!" Race announced proudly as he swarmed onto his bed once David, Sutter, and Josh had finally gotten it together.

"That's right!" Josh and Sutter beamed as they sat on the floor. Race stood between them with one arm wrapped around each of their necks, pulling their heads close to his chubby cheeks.

The fact that this looked perfectly natural and normal hit David like lightning. Here was a boy with two fathers and a mother, and he was a happy, healthy, well-adjusted child. Loving and loved. David realized why he had chosen to come there. It was because, despite the unconventional arrangement, it was the one place David knew where everyone seemed perfectly content. Where no one judged, accepting people for who and what they were, and loving them even if they weren't perfect.

A lump developed in his throat. David had the sudden, dreadful feeling that he'd made a terrible mistake. Abruptly, he stood. Josh and Sutter stared up at him, startled expressions on their faces. "I'm sorry. I've got to go. I just remembered something important I need to do."

Sutter pushed himself up from the floor. "Okay. We'll walk you out."

When they reached the ground floor, Sutter hollered, "Hayley, Grandpa's leaving!" Hayley rushed into the living room to give him hugs and kisses goodbye. Race started a competition to see who could be the last one to kiss him before he left, and so David carried them out to the car with him, letting them both kiss him—at the same time on opposite cheeks—one last time before he climbed into his car. "I'll see you next weekend," he promised a pouting Race, whose sudden smile was like the sun bursting out from behind a rain-swollen cloud.

"Bye!" David watched the kids in the rear view mirror as he drove away, waving until he couldn't see them any more.

But, typical of his state of mind lately, once he got home, David's sudden conviction flagged once again. He paced his study, silently berating himself for not being strong enough to either end the relationship once and for all or embrace it with open arms. Finally, he picked up the phone and dialed Joy's number. "I just called to see if you two got home all right," he told the answering machine. "Please call me when you get this message."

## Chapter Thirteen: Ultimatum

Joy stared at the answering machine for a long moment, then pressed the 'play' button again. David's voice repeated its message. At the sound of Jason's footsteps on the walk, she pressed the button that would delete it. Joy was the one who had gotten herself and Jason into this mess, and she was the one who would end it, once and for all. She would call David back tomorrow, while Jason was at *Big G's* offices. She turned away and followed Jason into the bedroom to help unpack.

The next morning, as soon as Jason had left, Joy went into the bedroom and sat on the side of the bed, staring at the phone. Finally, she picked it up and dialed David's number with numb fingers.

He answered after the first ring. "Hello?"

Joy couldn't seem to find her voice.

"Hello?"

"David," Joy croaked.

There was a moment of silence, then, "I'm glad you called. I didn't know if you would."

"Neither did I." Joy toyed restlessly with the hem of her shirt.

"We need to talk," David said.

Joy nodded, then realized he couldn't hear that. "Yes, we do."

"Can you meet me for a late lunch tomorrow?"

Joy swallowed hard. "Just me, or…"

After another awkward silence, David said quietly, "Just you, please."

In her heart, Joy had known he was going to say that, but it still hurt, so there was an edge to her voice when she spoke again. "What time?"

"Two o'clock? At the club? I'll leave your name at the door."

Joy just stopped herself from drawing in a quick, audible gasp of surprise. David wanted to meet at his own golf club? Joy didn't know if that was a good thing or a bad. "Okay. Two o'clock."

There was a soft click, and then she was listening to the dial tone while her mind raced, wondering what David wanted to talk about and why he would be willing to meet at a place where they were sure to be seen by people he knew. Shrugging, she stood. No more worrying about David's ulterior motives. Despite intending to keep silent on the subject, Joy had mentioned David to Jason the previous night, not telling him that David had already called, just asking him what they would do if he did contact them again. Unexpectedly, Jason had been willing to give David one last chance, but on *their* terms. She would talk to Jason again that evening, and together they would make some decisions.

* * *

To Joy's surprise, despite the plush décor, the atmosphere in David's exclusive club was casual and friendly. She followed a young host clad in tennis togs to a table in front of a large bank of windows looking out onto the grounds. Joy slipped into the chair the young man pulled out for her and thanked him.

As soon as he took her drink order and left, Joy turned to David. "Before you say a word, I have something to tell you." She paused as their waiter placed her iced tea on the table and retreated. "Jason and I have talked, and we've made some decisions."

Joy held up a hand when David opened his mouth to speak. "Just hear me out, David." He settled back into his chair after a moment, and she continued. "I've said this before, but you need to be made aware of how serious we are about this. Jason and I both feel like we're too old to go through this any more, or to wait much longer for you to make up your mind. We've spent years being lonely and...well, I didn't know I was miserable until Jason came back into my life, but there it is. I was miserable. We both were. Happy with our careers, but lonely and...needing someone. Now, we have each other, and plans, and we'd like you to be a part of them. We're not worried about what other people might think. Life's too short for that, and we're getting a late start."

David started to speak again, but Joy rushed on. "But we're not willing to put up with secret trysts in out-of-the-way places every few weeks. Jason and I want you to be part of our day-today life. Waking up together in the morning. Shopping together. Barbecues in the back yard. Going out in public on a regular basis and not worrying about who sees us all together." She sighed. "I understand that your career is important to you, David. And that a relationship like ours would be frowned upon in the circles you frequent. So, the way we see it, there are only a few options open to us."

Joy took a quick sip of her tea and met David's eyes as she began ticking each proposal off on her fingers. "We could continue as we are now, stealing weekends every now and then, hiding from everyone. But Jason and I aren't willing to do that any more.

"Or, you could continue practicing law, but spend time with Jason and me openly." Joy frowned as she noticed the muscles in David's jaw tightening. "We're not talking about announcing to the world—'Hey, I'm in a ménage relationship with another guy, isn't that great!' We're talking about feeling free to visit each other openly…maybe going to a show or the beach together, the three of us having dinner—maybe even sharing a discreet caress in public without freaking out."

David started. "Discreet? Hey, wait a minute. Jason—"

Joy cut him off. "Jason was only so open with his affection in Dallas because he was in an environment where he knew people accepted that, and you'd been acting as though you were comfortable, too. Face it, David. You were pretty affectionate with him in that restaurant.

"But to get back to my point—yes, maybe you'd lose a few clients. But maybe you'd gain some new ones, people who felt they wouldn't be judged by you as to their guilt or innocence just because of their sexual preference."

David had begun shaking his head. "I don't think I can do that, Joy." He frowned. "It's not just a matter of losing clients. It's about alienating an entire legal and social hierarchy that my family has been a part of for five generations."

Joy nodded, managing to maintain a calm façade even though her heart plummeted to her feet. "That's how I thought you would feel." She sighed. "Well, another option would be retirement. You've said before that you could retire now and live very comfortably." She hoped she didn't sound as desperate as she felt. "What do you think? You could move into my house, or the three of us could relocate to a more rural area, one where there won't be so many people you know."

David groaned. "They'd find out, Joy. People would talk."

"So what?" Joy forgot her apprehension as her irritation grew. "Why would that be such a disaster?" She leaned forward, speaking earnestly. "Exactly what are you trying to preserve, David? The Campbell tradition? For whom? Sutter's certainly not inclined to ever study law, or to even run in that social circle. And I don't think the three of them will raise Hayley and Race to be part of such a hypocritical, narrow-minded group. So what are you trying to preserve?"

Their waiter chose that inopportune moment to see if they were ready to order their meal. David waved him away, then leaned forward, resting his elbows on the table, looking haggard. "I don't know."

"Is it the ménage, or the fact that one of the ménage is a male that bothers you the most? Because I have to say that you've seemed uncomfortable with me, as well. Like the day I came by your house. When you kissed me goodbye, you checked first to see if anyone would see."

David looked at her in surprise. "Did I?"

Joy nodded.

He shook his head. "It's...the same-sex thing. I just...I guess I know that several people are aware that you and Jason are living together, and if they saw us kissing, they'd wonder what was going on."

"But if we were two women, that would be acceptable, wouldn't it? Hell, that would probably even be considered a coup, in your world. But you're afraid people will think you're less of a man if they know about Jason." David didn't respond, but Joy could tell from his expression that her observation had hit the mark. "David," she continued softly, "the only way our relationship can hurt you is if you *believe* them."

David's eyes widened.

"The world has changed. Back when everybody lived in the same small town, or spent most of their lives in one limited section of the city they were born in, maybe it was realistic to think that there might only be one true love for a person in their lifetime, whom they might or might not ever meet.

"But in this day and age, with rapid transit, huge cities, the Internet..." Joy shook her head. "By way of teaching at the university for twenty years, doing the lecture circuit, attending conventions, taking vacations—I, personally, have probably met tens of thousands of people over the course of my life. Is it really so strange to believe that there might be more than one person out there—of whichever sex—that we'll meet in our lives? That we'll care for enough to want to spend the rest of that life with them?"

David's eyes had taken on an unfocused aspect, his mouth drawn into a thin line, wincing as though he were in pain. Joy reached out to touch his arm. "David? Are you all right?"

He jerked as though he'd been slapped, then shook his head. "No. Not really." He looked at her with eyes that were suddenly terrifyingly empty. "What's the bottom line, Joy?"

Joy couldn't keep the tremor out of her voice when she spoke and she hated herself for that. "It's all or nothing for Jason and me. Either the three of us establish some kind of fairly open, committed relationship, or we go our separate ways." She looked away, blinking tears from her lashes. After a moment, she turned back. "Karl Goetz called last night. He asked for help with his archaeological dig down in Mexico."

Joy reached into her purse and pulled out a folded sheet of notebook paper. "This is where we'll be, and my cell phone number. Jason and I are leaving tomorrow." Joy pushed the paper toward him across the table. "We'll be gone for six weeks."

She pulled her purse strap up onto her shoulder and stood. "Jason and I are happy together, but there's always this...sorrow in us. This sense of loss. Our lives aren't complete without you, David."

She shied away when David reached out as though to grab her arm. "We want to be with you, but not if that's something you're ashamed of. If we haven't heard from you by the time we get back, don't call again. It will hurt, but we *will* go on without you, if that's what you choose."

Joy turned and made her way out of the club, managing to keep the tears from flowing until she'd reached her car.

* * *

David drove home from his encounter with Joy in a state of disbelief. How had things become so complicated, so fast?

Thankful that he didn't have any afternoon appointments, he dialed Abby on the car phone and told her he wouldn't be back in. A few minutes later, he was home, ensconced in his chair in the study, brooding over a glass of scotch.

David took another sip of his drink, then made a face and set it aside, shaking his head. Drinking scotch. There was a perfect example of some of the things Joy had said. He didn't care for scotch that much. David laughed suddenly, a wry bark. Didn't care for it? Hell, he *hated* the stuff. Just another thing he did because it was *the* thing to do.

David stood and walked over to the fireplace. He picked up a matchbox from the mantel, lit a couple of matches, and tossed them into the newspaper below the logs. Fireplaces in Galveston. Funny, that. Though they did come in handy on cool winter evenings, they weren't really necessary. But watching a fire calmed David, and he needed that now. Sitting in the leather recliner nearby, he watched the crackling flames, waiting for the brief sense of peace he usually experienced.

But he couldn't get away from his pain. David shut his eyes tightly. The memory had come back to him again, while Joy was talking. The memory of that night so long ago, when his father and grandfather had confronted him about Jason. David had never told anyone about that night. The events of that night were a scar—a deep scar on his soul that he didn't think would ever heal. And until that happened, he could never be with two of the people he loved most in this world.

David stood abruptly as tears threatened. "Aaargh!" He grabbed the scotch glass and threw it, watching it smash against the back wall of the fireplace, flames flaring as the fumes were consumed. Sagging to the floor, David wrapped his arms around his legs and allowed himself to cry for the first time in over twenty years, rocking back and forth like a child.

## Chapter Fourteen: Surprises and Explanations

It took David only two weeks without them—with the knowledge that not only was he not seeing or talking to Jason and Joy, but that they weren't even anywhere near—to convince himself that what had happened to him so long ago wasn't something he could change, but it was definitely something he could finally try to forget.

Looking back, he could see that he had lived his life from that event on as though he hated the world and everyone in it, including his own son. Even sponsoring Josh hadn't been a gift from the heart—just a tax write-off, pure and simple. That, and it had been a request from Joy. One that he could fill without letting her get too close. But there were too many people David cared about now for him to remain the man he had been for so long. Two people in particular that he couldn't bear to lose. Again.

So he spent the third week transferring all his active cases to the care of junior members of his firm, reassuring his clients that they were in good hands. The ones who had him on retainer, he notified that he was retiring and that they would need to begin looking for new counsel. He sold his controlling interest in the firm to his partner, Martin Mitchell. When Marty asked David to remain on the payroll as a consulting attorney, David felt he had to be honest.

Steeling himself for the rejection he was sure was coming, he said, "I'd love to, but I'm not sure that's a good idea."

Marty quirked an eyebrow. "Why?"

"Because I'm...well, I'm involved in a relationship that's...a little unusual." David hated the way he was stumbling over his words, but there was still a part of him screaming in the background, *Don't do this!*

Marty laughed. "If you're talking about Jason, Dave, I already know."

David sat down hard in one of the chairs pulled up to Marty's desk. "How?"

"I knew back in college."

David stared at him, speechless.

"I don't think that many people suspected. But, hey, we spent a lot of time together. We were going to be partners, after all. And I just had this feeling, when I saw the two of you together. And last New Year's Eve, whenever you, Jason, and Joy were in a room at the same time, you could have played drums on the air, the tension was wound so tight. Joy *is* involved, right? I mean, I know Jason's living with her."

He laughed again at David's expression, then leaned forward, sobering. "Seriously. You're the best criminal attorney in Texas. I don't care who you fuck, as long as it doesn't mess with your mind." He sat back. "As a matter of fact, I'm hoping now that you've decided to act on this, you'll be able to settle down and concentrate. Because, frankly, you've been a little out of it the last few months, Dave."

David finally managed to get his voice working. "You knew? And you never said anything?"

Marty shrugged. "Hey, it's not my place to tell you how to live your life."

David experienced a surge of intense relief, tempered with regret. The regret of knowing that maybe he had misjudged some people in thinking that they would judge *him*. The sudden thought that he might have wasted all those years for nothing nearly overwhelmed him, but then it subsided. Marty was a better friend than David had given him credit for, but there were still people who were going to be scandalized by his new lifestyle, whose "friendship" he would forever lose. David pushed that worry out of his mind, where it belonged, and held out his hand. "In that case, I'll be glad to hang around and pull your balls out of the fire every now and then."

Marty grinned and shook his hand. "We never would have made it without your drive, David. I don't think I've ever thanked you."

"That's okay. I knew," David teased. "Seriously, Marty, you're probably the only person who would have put up with my ego. I don't think I ever thanked you for *that*."

Marty rolled his eyes and gave a melodramatic, long-suffering sigh. "That's okay. I knew."

David laughed and pushed himself to his feet. "I hate to cut the male-bonding short, but I have a plane to catch."

Marty stood and walked him to the door, shaking his hand again on the way out. "Call me when you get back, so I know you're available."

"Will do."

* * *

David had been so busy putting his affairs in order that he hadn't really had a chance to let the reality of what he was doing hit him. Now, as he stood on a private airstrip waiting for his chartered plane to pull out, he found himself feeling weak-kneed and apprehensive. What if Jason and Joy had changed their minds? What if they had realized they might be better off without him? He could have uprooted his life for nothing!

David shook his head at himself. No matter how this turned out, it wouldn't have been for nothing. Sure, he was scared, but the fact that he was even able to admit that to himself showed how much he had changed in the past few months. Even if all he got to do was tell them that he loved them, it would all have been worthwhile.

A plane taxied from the hangar, filling the air with its roar. David watched as Jack coasted the Cessna to a stop on the runway. The pilot hopped out and walked over, shaking David's hand. "Hey, Dave!"

"Jack. How are you?"

"A hell of a lot better if you weren't dragging me plumb out to Mexico!" His voice was gruff, but he sported a big grin.

David smiled and picked up his bag. "Ready?"

"Sure 'nuff." Jack spat on the tarmac, lifted his cap and wiped the sweat off his forehead with the back of a hand, then replaced it and started back to the plane.

For a while, David tried to make conversation, but his thoughts were on the ordeal that lay ahead, so he finally gave up and watched the patterns of humanity's presence drift by below them as he worried about what to say when he finally saw Jason and Joy.

Three hundred and fifty billion rattling vibrations later, David breathed a huge sigh of relief as the soles of his shoes contacted terra firma once more. Thankfully, he had enough of a grasp of the Mexican language to be able to arrange fairly quickly for a driver to take him out to the dig.

The closer David got to his destination, the larger the knot in his stomach became. He tried to distract himself by asking questions of the driver in halting Spanish, strove to appreciate the beauty of the wild scenery surrounding them.

The man pulled to a stop at the end of a long stretch of road which was actually just two narrow ruts through crowded vegetation. "We walk from here," he said in heavily accented English.

David nodded and grabbed his bag, following his guide into the jungle. He was immediately glad that he had decided to purchase jeans and some long-sleeved, canvas-type shirts for this trip, as the dense growth they pushed through would have stripped his flesh raw without it.

After what seemed like several hours, but was probably less than one, they stepped abruptly out onto the side of a hill upon which perhaps two dozen people were going about various tasks.

"I come back for you?"

"Um, no." David searched for two familiar faces as he pulled out some cash to pay the man. "I have a ride back." At least, he hoped so.

The man shrugged, took his money, and disappeared back into the jungle without another word. David shouldered his bag and made his way carefully down the rocky hillside.

As he drew closer, a tawny head bobbed up abruptly, accompanied by a disbelieving cry. David's steps quickened as he met Joy's gaze. "David!"

Then she was running, and David dropped his bag to wrap her in his arms as she barreled into him. Joy hugged him fiercely for several minutes, face buried in his chest, wetting his shirt with her tears. David hugged her back, reaching up to run his fingers through the strands of her ponytail, then cradled the nape of her neck as she clung to him. Finally, though, she pulled free and looked up at him uncertainly. "What are you doing here?" Hope and fear battled for control of her gaze, and there was no way David could make her wait for his answer.

"I love you." He glanced around, looking for Jason. "Both of you. I came to tell you that."

Joy waved to her right. "He's across the site, helping Karl in one of the tombs. Are you...does this mean—"

"I'm here to stay, Joy. If you'll both have me." David stepped forward and gathered her in his hungry arms again. Kissed her startled face. "God." His voice broke, and he had to wait a minute before he continued. "I missed you so much." He cupped her face in his hands. "I'm not ever letting go again."

Joy blinked back more tears, relief and wonder beginning to replace the fear in her eyes. "Promise?" she whispered.

"I promise."

She searched his face for an interminable time, during which David's heart leapt into his throat and made it difficult for him to swallow or even to breathe. Finally, she nodded slowly.

"All right." Joy held out her hand. David picked up his bag and allowed her to lead him off to the right, up the slope to a large, flat area that had been cleared for tents. She held the flap of one aside for him as he entered, then followed him in. As David set his bag down, she sat on one of two camp stools within and stared up at him. "I can't believe it." She reached out and touched his arm. "I can't believe you're really here."

David sat on one of the cots. "I'm sorry, Joy. Sorry I've been such a jerk."

A hint of doubt began to creep back into her tiger's-eye gaze. "Are you sure that—"

David leaned forward and grasped both of her hands in his. "I'm sure. I retired, Joy. Marty bought me out. I gave the juniors my active cases, and transferred retainers over to him or the juniors, or they're going to find their own."

Joy gasped. "But, David, I… God. I know that's what we asked you to do, but I never really thought it through." She looked at him thoughtfully, with a new respect in her eyes. "I guess I never really believed you would do it. Are you sure you're going to be okay with this?"

David answered truthfully. "Honestly, I'm a little scared right now. But mostly of the idea that you two might not take me back. Everything else is just not important enough to worry about right now."

Joy closed her eyes and lifted one of his hands, brushing her cheek across the back of it.

"It really is okay, Joy," he assured her softly. "I might have missed the work, but turns out Marty wanted to keep me on as a consultant." He squeezed her hand. "He knows, Joy."

Joy's eyes flew open. "What?!"

David shrugged. "I guess being an asshole can't hide the truth from everyone. Turns out he's a lot more observant than I ever thought. And a much better friend, too."

Joy's eyes lit up. "He doesn't care!"

David shook his head. "Nope. Said he didn't care who I fucked. Actually, seemed to think fucking the two of *you* would do me some good." He wiggled his eyebrows suggestively, and Joy giggled.

She sobered rapidly, however. "David, I don't know about Jason." She pursed her lips and glanced toward the tent opening. "Before we left, he said he was willing to give you one last chance, but he's been pretty cold since we got here. I brought the subject up a couple of times, of what we would say or do if you called, and he was…so bitter."

David tried to swallow the hard lump that settled in his throat. "We'll…I hope we'll work it out. But if he decides he's had enough, I guess I can't blame him. It's—"

They both turned as the tent flap swung aside and Jason stepped through. "I'll grab another roll of film," he called to someone, looking back as he entered. Then he turned his head and froze abruptly as his gaze came to rest on David.

David could have handled anger, resentment, tears. Anything but the blank eyes that stared out at him from a stone-cold visage. "David."

He couldn't move. David told his mouth to open, but it wouldn't obey. Joy's gaze flitted back and forth between them, her face a mask of indecision.

David reminded himself that there was only one thing he would regret when all this was over if it didn't work out, so he opened his mouth and made sure there would be no regrets. "I love you."

It might have been wishful thinking, but David thought Jason's expression wavered for just an instant.

"No."

David surged to his feet. "I do. I love you."

Jason shook his head and started to turn away, but David grabbed his shoulders and looked him in the eyes. "I love you, Jason."

Jason twisted away from him and pushed out of the tent. David followed him into the harsh sunlight, with Joy just a step behind. "I love you, damn it!" David yelled.

Jason's stride faltered. He stopped. David ignored the rush of blood to his face as he registered the sudden silence around them, kept his eyes locked on Jason's back. He told himself fiercely that the people who were now staring didn't matter, not if it meant he would lose Jason, and sure as hell not if Jason stayed. "I love you," he said again.

Jason turned slowly, shaking his head, finally registering disbelief and anger. "Not again, David." His gaze found Joy, now standing beside him. "I'm sorry. I know how much you wanted this."

David took another step forward. "*I* want it, Jase." Jason's gaze flicked back to David. "I do. I know I've been an ass. I have—" David swallowed. He suddenly didn't have to *tell* himself the onlookers didn't matter. They simply *didn't.* David took the one step forward that would bring him to Jason, and dropped to his knees, throwing his arms around Jason's waist. "I'm sorry," he whispered. "I'm *sorry.*"

He knelt there, eyes closed, praying to God that Jason would forgive him. When Jason's hand cradled his head after what seemed an eternity, he couldn't hold back a sob of relief.

"It's all right, David." Jason's hand stroked his hair. "It's all right." His hands reached under David's arms. "Come on."

Jason helped David stand, then glanced around. There was a sudden flurry of activity as everyone occupied themselves with their tasks, trying to pretend they hadn't been watching the whole thing. Jason stared into David's eyes for a long moment. "Come on," he repeated, taking David's hand and turning toward the tent.

David reached out and clasped Joy's fingers in his free hand as Jason pulled them back into the dim shelter. Once inside, Jason gave him a fierce, angry kiss, then stepped back abruptly. David rubbed at his bruised lips. "What does that mean?"

Jason ran a hand through his dark hair. "It means I'm pissed off as hell, but—" His angry façade finally crumbled completely, and then he was holding David tight, running his hands over his back, his arms, through his hair, as though he couldn't quite believe David was really there.

Joy put her arms around them both, and the three of them simply held each other.

Reluctantly, David was the first to break the silence. "I guess I should… I don't know. Introduce myself? Do you think Karl will mind if I stay?"

"Are you kidding? He'll take every bit of help he can get." Joy mopped her face with a shirtsleeve. "It's hot in here, anyway. We should go out and introduce you to everyone." She touched David's arm lightly as his face reddened. "Don't worry. These are good people."

David nodded and let her lead the way.

The last couple of hours before dusk were a blur of faces, names, and dirt. Karl put David to work right away, sifting through rubble dug up by the excavators to retrieve any small objects or bits of pottery that might be hidden within. After only a short while, David was exhausted and dripping with sweat, but it felt good to be doing something with his hands.

As he fished out yet another tiny piece of fired clay from the tray in his lap, Joy walked up. "Time to call it quits."

David set the tray aside, stifling a groan as she helped him stand. "Stiff?" she asked. David nodded. "You'll be fine after a couple of days."

They strolled up to the campsite, their arms around each other's waists. Karl hailed them from near a cook stove. "How'd it go? Think you'll survive?"

David grinned. "It's hot work, but I'll manage somehow." He gave Joy a squeeze and was rewarded with a brilliant smile. "Where's Jason?"

Karl smiled knowingly, and David was pleasantly surprised that it didn't make him feel the least bit embarrassed. "He'll be along shortly. He's taking a couple more shots of the entrance to that tomb. Says the sunset makes for great chiaro-scuro, whatever that means."

David nodded. "I guess it would, at that." When Karl looked at him questioningly, he explained. "Chiaro-scuro. It's the contrast between light and dark. Highlights and shadows."

"Oh!" Karl seemed surprised that David knew. For that matter, Joy was looking at him with a hint of surprise in her face.

David shrugged. "I read."

Karl laughed. "So do I, but I tend to stick to stuffy archaeology journals." He flipped a couple more of the burgers on the grill, nodding toward a water trough beside which a few other people were gathered. "Why don't you go clean up? Sandy and I will have the grub ready pretty quick."

David and Joy rinsed off and exchanged a few pleasantries with their co-workers. A couple of them seemed to find it difficult to meet their eyes, but David decided that was okay. They were still polite and friendly, which was a relief.

By the time they returned to the open-air dining room, there was a plate of hamburgers and a platter of buns set out, with chips and salsa and even an old-fashioned cauldron filled with chili. David had wanted to wait until Jason joined them to fix his plate, but the smell of food reminded him that he hadn't eaten since very early that morning. He fixed a burger and ladled some of the chili on top, forgoing the onions he loved in anticipation of possible intimacies later on. He and Joy found a clear patch of ground and sat with their legs crossed, munching in the fading light.

Jason arrived a couple of minutes later, settling to the ground beside them.

"Did you get your pictures?"

Jason nodded, already getting busy with his burger. The three of them ate quickly. Obviously, this kind of work was good for the appetite. Afterward, they found a shelf of rock that was wide enough for the three of them and sat watching as the sky darkened and stars began to appear.

"There's more stars here," David said.

Jason chuckled. "No, there's just no cities nearby to drown out the stars with their light."

David was sitting between Jason and Joy, and he draped an arm across each of their shoulders. Joy rested her head against him, and Jason reached up and interlaced his fingers with David's.

David felt as though he were adrift, floating gently in a vast empty space, but snug in the warmth of these two people. It was one of the most pleasant experiences he'd ever had. Even the cloud of night insects that gathered around them didn't bother him, at first. After a while, though, Jason stirred. "We should get inside," he murmured. "It's getting late, and it's going to be another hot one tomorrow."

David growled playfully, "Not nearly as hot as it's going to be tonight."

Jason's hand caressed David's crotch briefly. "Damn right." He stood and held out his hands, pulling Joy and David up from their seats.

Back in the tent, which at some point had been outfitted with a third cot, Jason and Joy seated themselves on their stools, looking up at David expectantly. "I want to show you something," he blurted.

He unzipped his bag and reached in, pulling out two thick, leather-bound volumes. "I just… I wanted you to know that I never stopped loving you." He handed one of the portfolios to Jason, one to Joy. "I thought about you every day. Missed you."

Jason opened the book and thumbed lazily through the first few pages, then sat up even straighter and glanced sharply at David. He flipped more quickly through the rest of the book. "This is… I think you've got every article I've ever written. Every picture I ever took—at least for professional use."

"I do."

Jason glanced through the pages again, then looked up. "Thank you. It helps to know that you—" He stopped abruptly, a catch in his voice.

David felt suddenly awkward. "I just wanted you to know."

Joy set her book aside and reached out to take his hand. "Don't talk," she whispered. She brought his hand to her shirt, mute appeal in her eyes.

David stood and took a blanket from one of the cots. Pushing the beds and stools aside as much as possible, he spread the blanket on the floor of the tent. Reaching out, he drew Jason and Joy down to sit before him. His hands trembled as he unbuttoned Joy's shirt, his excitement growing as her golden flesh was revealed.

Jason reached for his own shirt, but David stilled him with a hand. "Let me. You two just sit. Don't do anything."

He released the last button on Joy's shirt and pushed it from her shoulders, slipping it off her arms and tossing it into a corner. Leaning forward, he breathed onto her breast, watching her nipple rise beneath the lace fabric of her bra. Catching the mound lightly between his teeth, he flicked his tongue across its tip until Joy was moaning with pleasure. She grasped his hand, guided it to her back. David released the hooks and pulled the offending garment away. Drawn by the dark promise of her aureoles, he tasted each one, covering her with his mouth.

While he suckled, he loosened Jason's shirt with one hand, pushing it off of him. Jason shook it off and chucked it away, breathing in sharply as David wet one finger and began teasing Jason as well. David turned his head, delighted to watch Jason's nipples harden, the peaks much paler than Joy's, gleaming in the light of two lanterns hanging from a cross-pole.

David switched sides, taking one of Jason's ripe nipples into his mouth as he rolled the tips of Joy's between his finger and thumb. Jason moaned, and Joy squirmed beside him. David let his hands travel to their waists. Finding their snaps. Releasing their zippers. He sat back for a moment, motioning for them to raise their hips while he slipped off their clothing, until they were naked before him, Jason's cock standing tall and stiff in the lamplight, Joy's pussy glimmering wetly between her swollen lips.

David moaned, moving to sit between them. He ran the fingers of his left hand oh-so-lightly over the length of Jason's cock, while the fingers of his right hand circled lazily around the lips of Joy's pussy, moving a tiny bit closer to her damp crevice with each pass.

His two lovers moaned and arched at the same time. David leaned in, tracing the outline of Joy's parted lips, meeting her tongue with his as his fingers slid into her wet slit. He turned away when she gasped, covering Jason's mouth with his own, nipping Jason's lips just a bit roughly with his teeth, the way Jason liked, as his hand surrounded Jason's cock. Jason whimpered and thrust impatiently. "Patience," David whispered against his lips.

David's hands explored their bodies, parting their legs wide, discovering the nooks and crannies, the tiny folds and rills beneath Joy's belly, Jason's balls. "Oh, God, David. Please," Joy breathed.

David guided them back against the blanket, pushing their legs up close to their bodies. "Hold them," he whispered into their ears, wrapping their arms around their knees so that their thighs rested against their bellies.

Their eyes never left his, as he slowly wet one finger, then two, and reached down, exploring their asses until he found that tight hole he liked so well. Moaning with desire, he slid one finger into each of them, rewarded by twin gasps. "Oh, God. Yes," Jason murmured.

David made love to them slowly, sliding his fingers in and out, pressing gently against the sides of each tight canal to loosen them. Then he tested them tentatively, slipping the tip of a second finger into both of their tight tunnels.

Their reply was to reach down, parting their asses further so that his fingers could penetrate deeper. "Faster." David wasn't even sure which one had spoken, his body aching with need, enjoying this slow seduction. He watched his fingers as they slithered in and out, each anus clinging to him eagerly as he drew back, then tightening erratically as he penetrated. "Oh, God. Yes!" Jason was moaning, Joy squirming. David waited until he sensed they were just about to achieve release, then withdrew, moving their hands away, making them relax against the cover.

"Oh, no," Jason groaned.

David chuckled and straddled him. "Oh, yes." He pressed his body against Jason's, a surge of pure erotic pleasure pulsing through his groin as his and Jason's cocks wedded, touching along their entire lengths. Jason groaned and pulled David's head close, biting his earlobe hard, but not hard enough to draw blood, as his hand slipped between them and caressed both feverish erections.

David allowed him a few moments, then sat back. He stood and walked over to his bag, rummaged inside briefly, then returned to his place between them. He squeezed a mound of lube into his hand, then opened the other to reveal two slender bullets attached to cords which led to a remote. David put his hand between Joy's legs, and she presented her ass. He coated her cheeks with the oil, teased the rim of her anus. Joy closed her eyes, anticipating penetration, but David tapped her on the shoulder. When she looked at him, he was lubricating his hands again, then he repeated the process on Jason and on himself. Joy sat up, watching with unrestrained curiosity. Finally, he rubbed a bit of oil onto each bullet, and then began massaging Jason's cock.

When Jason's staff shimmered with oil, David turned and lay back between his lovers. Reaching down, he slipped one of the bullets into his ass. He crooked a finger at Joy. Joy rose, and he guided her onto him, her slick folds encasing his throbbing member with delicious warmth.

No one had spoken, and the silence emphasized each movement. Each brush of skin against skin, each soft slurp of oiled asses, every brief sigh or quiet gasp—an erotic music that had every nerve in David's body tingling. Urgently, he motioned to Jason. Jason's eyes were dark with passion as he rose up behind Joy and parted her cheeks. Joy melded her body to David's, whispering soft, wordless sounds of pleasure in his ear as Jason entered her.

David handed the other bullet to Jason, and Jason inserted it in his own ass, his breath quickening. Slowly, with a synchrony that seemed instinctual, as though the three of them were the joined parts of one organism, they rocked and thrust, their motions quickening as desire mounted.

David gasped. Each time Jason's delicious dick penetrated Joy, it ran up the length of David's own cock, buried deep inside her. Joy moaned. Her nipples were hard pebbles against his chest. David slipped his hand between them, drew one of her generous breasts up to his mouth, sucked gently at the flushed peak.

Joy arched, her cunt contracting tightly. David's cock pulsed, his throbbing anus contracting eagerly against the slender bullet within. David moaned, thumbing the remote in his hand.

He dimly heard Jason's loud gasp as the vibrations started.

"Oh, fuck!" Jason froze for a moment, then closed his eyes, his expression one of ecstasy.

"Oh!" Joy cried out as Jason's fierce, eager thrust drove into her. "Oh, God. Yes."

David moaned, overwhelmed with need. He brought his legs up, pressed his heels into Jason's buttocks, ground his hips against the two bodies above him.

"Oh, God! Oh!" Joy arched and screamed, her pussy clenching his cock like a velvet vise. David groaned, bucking once, twice, three times, a thousand points of pleasure blossoming within his body as his seed exploded into her. Jason arched, his mouth open in a wordless cry, shuddering as he drove himself, over and over, deep into Joy's ass.

Pleasure seared David's nerves, feverish waves that broke over him again and again. Just when he thought he couldn't take any more, the waves receded. Fumbling for the remote, he pressed the button to stop the vibrations. Jason and Joy disentangled themselves, lying exhausted to either side of him.

David rested for several minutes, then sat up and removed the bullets, putting them in a plastic bag to clean later. Joy was sitting up now, and when David went to lie down again, she cradled his head in her lap, running her fingers lightly over his forehead.

"Mmmm. That feels good."

Beside him, Jason propped his head up on one arm, watching David from beneath hooded eyes. David sensed immediately that something was on his mind. He waited, but Jason remained silent. Finally, David said, "Something's bothering you. What is it?"

A flash of the old pain, with an edge of resentment, made itself evident in Jason's face and eyes as he replied. "Why?"

"Why?" David repeated.

"Yes. Why did we have to wait until we were in our fifties for this? Why couldn't we have had all those years together?"

He faced David squarely and said. "Why did you end it?"

David swallowed. He had known this would come. He *wanted* them to know. But now that the moment had arrived, he couldn't seem to force the words out.

Joy's hands were still on his brow. He glanced up and saw her beautiful, loving eyes fixed on him. "We'll understand if it's something you don't want to talk about."

"No. It's—" David faltered as the memory of that night rushed in again. "I want you to know."

He turned his head, staring blindly at the tent walls as he spoke. "I stopped by my father's house one Saturday. You had gone to visit your parents, Joy. And Jason was out taking photos for one of his classes. I was going to hit Mrs. Thomas up for some lunch.

"Grady heard me pull into the drive. He and my father were waiting for me at the foot of the stairs when I walked in. He'd heard a rumor."

David felt Joy stiffen. "Your grandfather? What rumor?"

"He found out that Jason and I weren't just friends."

"How?" Joy's voice was strained. "Hell, I was your girlfriend, and I didn't know. Didn't even suspect, until years later."

David shrugged. "Who knows? Maybe he had me followed. Maybe rumors *were* starting, and he wanted to nip them in the bud. I mean, Marty says he always knew, he just never said anything. Maybe there were others.

"Anyway, he confronted me about it, he and Dad." He laughed ruefully. "You two thought my *dad* was an ass, but you never saw Grady that much. That old man was vicious. He ran the Campbell house with an iron fist in a brick glove." David turned and sat up, burying his head in his hands. "Hell. I was just like Sutter. I didn't even want to be a lawyer. Believe it or not, I wanted to do something with my hands. I wanted to build things. But I didn't have the guts to stand up to my dad and Grady."

David shook his head. "But for some reason, I chose that day to try and grow some balls. Maybe..." He looked up and met Jason's gaze. "Maybe because I loved you. So I said sure, Jason and I were sleeping together, and I liked it, and I wasn't going to stop."

Joy's hands flew to her mouth, and her eyes were open wide, as though she knew what was coming. David looked down at his hands, clenched together tightly in his lap. "His face… I'll never forget that expression. Grady said—" David's voice was thick, and he swallowed a couple of times before continuing. "He told my dad to go get the switch. I thought it was a joke, but when dad came back, he had this long switch in his hand." David looked up again, his gaze traveling from Joy to Jason and back. "The handle was worn so smooth." He shook his head. "My dad's hand was trembling as he held the thing, but he sure did hand it over. I guess I know how Grady punished Dad when he was young."

David took a deep breath. "It seemed so unreal. It didn't even register, what they were going to do, until my dad grabbed me from behind and held me while Grady pulled down my pants."

Joy's eyes brimmed with tears, and she reached out as though to stop him. "David, don't."

David blinked back his own tears and looked at Jason. "I have to. I have to get it *out*."

Joy reached out and clasped one of David's hands. Jason covered their joined hands with his, his gaze never leaving David's face.

"He whipped me with that switch. Over and over. He said he'd make me hurt so much, I'd never want *anyone* to touch me again, much less a man. At first, I wasn't going to let him break me, but I couldn't get *loose*, and it wouldn't stop, and I don't know how long it went on, but in the end, I was begging him to stop." Joy was crying now, and David wished she wouldn't hurt so much for him, but her tears were like a salve, somehow, making it easier for him to finish.

"He whipped me until I promised to kick Jason out and never see him again. Then he whipped me until I promised to break it off with *you*." David reached out with his free hand and caressed Joy's wet cheek. "I loved you, too. I was going to ask you to marry me." He laughed at himself. "I don't know what I thought I was going to do. I never considered telling you about Jason. I think I had this vague idea that you and I would marry and have kids, and Jason and I would have a house, too, and see each other on weekends, or… I don't know. I wasn't thinking it through; I just wanted both of you.

"But Grady said that he had been talking to Sumner, and that I was damn well going to marry Terri, not you. And so I told him what he wanted to hear. And I did everything I promised." He looked at them both, knowing he sounded desperate, but he didn't care. "It's no excuse for hurting you. I should have been stronger. I should have—"

Jason wrapped him in a crushing embrace, shaking his head. "Stop." His voice shook as he held David tight. "It's over."

Joy embraced them both, her cheek cool and damp against David's shoulder. "He was wrong, David. So wrong. But you're here now, and we won't ever let you go."

Hot tears tumbled down David's cheeks, releasing the pain and humiliation of that night. The ones who loved him held him close, sobbing, their tears washing away the last of his doubts. Finally, drained, they clung to each other on the floor. Jason pulled the blanket from another cot and draped it across them. David told them both over and over again how much he cared, and they did the same, whispering the words softly, deep into the night, beginning to heal his scars with their devotion.

## Chapter Fifteen: Harm and Home

When they woke up the next morning, it was raining. A thick sheeting rain that made it impossible to work. The three of them spent the day in the tent. David pulled out their albums again, and listened as Jason and Joy reminisced over the inspirations for certain articles, described trips to attend conventions or obtain photographs.

In addition to getting to know each other's minds more intimately, David memorized every inch of his lovers' bodies, discovering new areas of delight and wonder. They made plans for their future, resting naked in each other's arms as the rain poured down. David felt whole again.

Unfortunately, the rain continued for three days. The tent began to feel too close, and the mingled scent of sweat, sex, and the rain-damp jungle became cloying. By the time the sun showed its face in the late afternoon of the third day, they were all ready for a bath and a break from each other.

Karl's staff had set up cook stoves near the wooden screen behind which everyone bathed, keeping a couple of pots of water heated continuously. After a blissfully wonderful wash with warm water and Joy's carefully hoarded soap, they joined everyone at the tables, enjoying their first hot meal since the rains began. After dinner, Karl went over a list of things he wanted to get accomplished the next day, now that the storms seemed to have passed, and advised everyone to get lots of rest that night so that they could get an early start in the morning.

Jason, Joy, and David visited for a while with the other helpers. Many had worked with Joy and Karl at the university, personal friends whom he had called on. An influx of foreign companies to a neighboring area of Mexico had drawn many previously willing local hands away from the hot, repetitious work involved in excavating an archaeological dig, so Karl had apparently called in a lot of favors. David found himself enjoying the conversation, talking about all the various jobs these people held, their hobbies, their interests. It was a much more relaxed, friendly environment than he was used to. The gatherings of attorneys, judges, legal aides, and high society that he participated in tended to be politically charged events.

People began to drift off, in pairs or alone, to get the rest Karl had mentioned. David and Joy suggested hitting the sack, as well, but Jason was restless. He was an active person, not used to being cooped up. "I think I'm going to wander for a little while. I need to stretch my legs."

"It's pretty dark, Jase." David was frowning up at the star-laden sky.

Jason gave David a quick hug. "Don't worry, I'll be careful." He kissed Joy, then set off toward the eastern edge of the camp.

Jason breathed deeply of the night air. It was good to be out, to walk quickly, get his blood flowing. He headed toward a clump of mounds a little way off from the camp, letting the light of the moon and stars guide him. As he approached, he studied the layout and shapes of the mound, thinking to himself that Karl was probably right, there were probably additional buildings under the dirt and vines deposited here. The fact that there were only a few, and they were laid out in a geometrically precise manner, made him think that it might even be a temple complex.

Jason glanced back, and was surprised to note that he could no longer see the lights marking the perimeter of the camp. He hadn't realized these mounds were so far out. He thought briefly about turning back, but he'd caught a glimpse of something bright reflecting the moonlight at the edge of one squarish heap, and he wanted to check it out.

Sure enough, the recent rains had washed away a small portion of the dirt and viney growths, and the corner of a stone lintel gleamed whitely. Jason stepped back. Unhooking the compact spotlight hanging from his belt, he held it up with one hand. With the other, he depressed the button on the ever-present camera around his neck, adjusting the exposure rate instinctively, and focused in on the carved stone. He flipped on the spotlight, waiting until the momentary blindness caused by the sudden brilliance passed, and snapped a picture.

A shout off to his right startled him, and he dropped the spot. Voices spoke in rapid Spanish from beyond the next hill, too fast for him to figure out what they were saying. Jason walked over to the mound and crept quietly up its side.

Beyond its crest, three men were carrying items out of the partially cleared entrance to what Jason thought might be a temple similar to one found on the west side of the large archaeological site. A fourth man stood watch, his eyes darting here and there among the ruins, a rifle resting on his shoulder.

Relic hunters. Jason had heard of this before. He'd even photographed a dig several years earlier during which looters had come in the night and made off with priceless mementos of the past. But he hadn't been confronted with it alone, on a dark night. Jason backed off the mound as silently as possible, then turned, intending to get help.

A shadow rose before him, and pain blossomed in his left shoulder. Jason turned and ran down the steep slope of the mountainside these ruins clung to, thinking that he could backtrack toward the west once he was out of sight.

But the others had joined the chase, and he heard more noises to his right, so he veered east again. Jason knew this was taking him further into the uninhabited area, but he didn't know what else to do. His mind was finally registering the fact that he'd been shot, and the numbness he'd felt for the first few minutes was passing, bringing with it a throbbing pain.

The slope was getting steeper. Jason found it harder to find purchase without using his arms, and every movement of his right shoulder brought teeth-jarring discomfort. He stopped for a moment, trying to get his bearings.

The silver moonlight revealed that he had entered a deep arroyo. A muddy stream flowed down its middle, runoff from the recent rains. Jason glanced behind him frantically. He could lose his footing, end up slogging through the muddy waters below. Who knew how deep it really was, or what the dark waters hid? He needed to get out of there.

Something whined past his left ear, and a second later there was a small eruption of dirt from the side of the gulch. They were shooting at him again. Seconds later, he could hear them, making strange catcalls into the night, taunting him. His only chance was to keep going, try to stay ahead of them until he could hide, veer back toward civilization, or they tired of the pursuit and went away. Surely they wouldn't continue in the light of day. They would want to get back and stash their stolen treasures.

Jason made his way as quickly as he could along the side of the arroyo, clinging to vines and exposed roots along its face, feeling the saturated soil give way beneath his feet as he passed. But they were gaining on him. He glanced back, and saw that one of them had already reached the arroyo and was following much more swiftly than Jason could move. Two others were close behind. Jason pushed himself harder, ignoring the searing pain in his shoulder. Another whine, and another puff of dirt from the cliffside, a bare two inches from his face. It occurred to him then that they could have killed him already. They were playing with him now, enjoying the chase, but in the end, there was no doubt in his mind that he would be dead.

Fear leant him strength, and he scrambled along the gulch, ignoring the tiny bits of rock and dirt that were now drifting down from above. But—from above? What if one of them had run ahead, and was climbing down now, to intercept him?

Abruptly, the texture of the wall changed. The dirt, roots, and loose rocks became large stone outcroppings. Jason clambered onto one such rock shelf, leaning against the cliff. It was no use. He had to rest for a moment.

Jason hadn't even realized that the other shots had been silent until the rifle report reverberated down the canyon. Jason waited for the bullet's impact, but a sharp ping just below his feet told him they'd missed. He glanced down to see one of the looters standing knee-deep in the muddy water, raising his rifle for another shot.

But the shot's vibrations hadn't faded yet. Instead, they grew louder, became a low, rumbling thunder. Alarmed shouts rang out, and the man below him dropped his rifle, leaving it dangling from the strap across his chest as he turned, splashing to the water's edge, trying desperately to scrabble up the opposite side of the canyon.

Jason looked along his side of the gulch. The three who had been making their way after him were now frantically backtracking. Despite the roaring in his ears, he didn't understand why they were doing that until the wall of mud came sliding down, scouring the two nearest him from the cliffside, and burying the one below.

When the growling thunder stopped, Jason was staring at a new wall not two feet away from his perch upon the rock shelf. One part of his mind realized that the recent rains had undermined the cliff, and the rifle's report had set up a vibration that brought the cliffside down into the arroyo. The only thing that had saved him was the transition from the loose rock and dirt arroyo to the more stable, rocky canyon. The other part of his mind was registering that he was cut off from the camp.

Jason looked up, thinking that he might be able to climb the more stable stone cliff, but the steepness of the sides and lack of light made it seem impossible. It was too bad he had dropped his spot. He might be able to try when the sun rose, but for now, the only thing to do seemed to be to continue along the increasingly wide and treacherous valley. He debated staying where he was, waiting for rescue to arrive. But he had seen five men at the temple, which meant there were still two left, if not more. There could have been others inside the temple that he hadn't seen.

Plus, it finally occurred to him that the first shots had been made with guns equipped with silencers, and the shouting hadn't begun until they were well away from camp. David and Joy would miss him tonight, for sure, but no search would begin until the morning, and even then, they wouldn't know where to look. It seemed like a good idea to keep going until he found a place where he could ascend to the top and make his way back toward the camp.

Jason pushed on through the night, pausing to rest only briefly when he tired, praying that the team would discover the looted temple and have some idea in which direction to begin their search. Though it seemed like he went on for hours, the moon was still high, and the night dark, when he collapsed on a narrow shelf, the cliff spinning above him, and passed out.

* * *

Joy paced back and forth across the tent floor. "He should have been back by now."

David stood at the doorway, the flaps tied back, staring out into the night. "You're right." He grabbed the flashlight from Joy's bag. "I'm going to get Karl."

"I'm coming with you."

Half an hour later, the camp glowed with light, and the entire team was gathered around Karl at the table in the center of camp. "There's no sign of him." The last member to arrive reported. "We've searched the entire complex."

David felt a jolting pain in his heart, and thought for a moment that he was having a heart attack. Then he realized that it was fear—the fear of losing someone you love.

Joy was silent at his side, her hand gripping his so tight that he couldn't feel the tips of his fingers. She looked pale in the spotlights, but her expression was determined. "We have to find him," she said. "We've got to bring in more people, widen the search area."

Karl's voice was thick with sympathy, but firm. "Joy. It will take one of us three hours to reach town." He raised a hand as she started to speak. "I'm going to ask for a volunteer, but I just want you to realize that by the time someone reaches town, gets help, and gets back here, it will be daylight. In the meantime, there's nothing we can do."

"We can keep looking," David insisted. "We've got spotlights, lanterns. We could—"

"I won't risk losing another person. If we start wandering around these slopes at night, whatever happened to Jason could happen to us. We have to stick together until it's light. In the morning, we might be able to find tracks. Figure out which way he was heading, what happened. He might even have been right under our noses at some point tonight, hidden by shadows. We need to wait until morning."

David wanted to protest, but he knew Karl was right. He glanced down at Joy, saw in her face that she knew that, too. "All right," David said. "Who's going to go?"

"Carmen and I will go. My wife knows these hills like the back of her hand and has relatives in town. We'll be better off if we have them speak to the authorities," Derrick Rogers said.

Carmen nodded. "He's right. My uncle is well-liked. He can have many more men here to help in the morning than would come if we went through the local police."

Karl nodded. "Okay. You have a cell phone, right?" Though their use in Mexico's mountainous regions was chancy, at best, it would be some kind of insurance. The two nodded. Karl glanced at his watch. "It's nearly three o'clock. Better get started."

Derrick and Carmen each grabbed one of four powerful halogen flashlights on the table. "We'll be back as quickly as possible," Carmen promised, and the two strode off into the jungle.

The rest of the team offered words of encouragement and hope, then drifted back to their tents to nap while they could. David and Joy knew they wouldn't be able to sleep, and by silent agreement, remained at the table, staring into the shadows.

* * *

Jason woke to the feel of the hot sun on his shoulders. He went to push himself up from the ground, and howled at the pain in his shoulder. More carefully, he pushed up with his right hand, sliding back to lean against the mountain. Just that short task left him feeling dizzy and weak. When his vision cleared, he took his first good look at his shoulder.

The bullet had pierced him about two inches below the top of the shoulder. Slowly, and very gently, Jason eased his arm out of the blood-soaked shirt, careful not to dislodge his camera. There was another ugly hole in the back. Jason guessed that was good. At least the bullet wasn't lodged inside him somewhere. Every slight movement sent jarring pain through the right side of his body. Jason wondered if his clavicle had shattered.

Jason woke to find himself staring at his chest. Apparently, he had passed out again. He shaded his eyes with his good hand and tried to find the sun. From its position in the sky, he guessed it was past noon, maybe two or three o'clock. Groaning, he leaned forward, looking past the lip of his perch to the bottom of the canyon.

It wasn't as far down as he had thought. The flow of water had stopped, presumably dammed by the previous night's rockslide. The hot sun had reduced the stream to a series of puddles in random depressions.

Jason studied the cliff wall. If he slid over to his left, the angle was slightly less steep, and he might be able to make it to the bottom without jarring his arm too badly. He decided to chance it. From the looks of the dried blood on his rock, he had lost quite a bit of that substance, and was probably dehydrated. Even dirty water would be better than no water at all.

Jason scooted carefully to the left. He was afraid to stand because of the dizziness. Every time he moved, the canyon walls spun. Once he was off the solid rock shelf, he spent a moment looking for a loose tree limb, hoping to use it to slow his progress on the way down, but there was nothing close by.

Jason tucked his injured arm in close to his body, biting his lip against the pain. Taking a deep breath, he pushed off with his left arm. Slowly at first, then more quickly as loose bits of dirt and rock began to slide with him, Jason skimmed down the hillside.

His feet hit the bottom with a jolt, and fireworks exploded in the injured shoulder. Jason closed his eyes and forced himself to take deep, slow breaths through his nose until the throbbing faded and his stomach quit threatening to make him review everything he'd eaten the day before.

He tried to stand, but couldn't, the pain and his weakness conspiring against him. Exhausted, he lay back on the ground, then scooted himself around until his head was near enough to one of the puddles for him to roll onto his left side. Unable to effectively scoop water into his mouth with his left hand, he eased his right hand over to the pool. Much of the dirt and silt had settled to the ground, and the top layer of liquid was fairly clear. Jason slurped eagerly, ignoring the pain as cool moisture trickled down his throat.

When the water began looking murky, he stopped and lay back, staring up at the turquoise sky. He could feel his eyelids growing heavy, and wondered when or if he would wake up again.

* * *

David was exhausted, but he forced himself to keep on moving. They had to find Jason. Had to. Failure wasn't an option. He wished Joy was with him, but they had agreed to separate, knowing that the more ground they covered, the better the chances were of finding their lover.

"David!"

David turned toward the voice. Mark Andrews, one of Karl's team, was jogging toward him. When he reached David, he stopped and bent over, his hands on his knees, catching his breath.

"We found something."

"Where?"

Mark motioned for him to follow and started back the way he had come. "Where's Joy?" David asked.

"Claire's looking for her." Mark shook his head. "I guess we should have coordinated this better—nobody really knows where anyone else is. I just happened to have seen which direction you headed earlier." He grunted as he slapped a limb aside.

David pushed through behind him, until they broke past the tree line. Mark led him to the edge of a gully. Sitting down, he pushed off, sliding down the side to the bottom. David imitated him, feet creating a small splash as they contacted the shallow stream of runoff at the bottom. Mark followed the bed of the gulch toward the east, moving up the side when the accumulated water from the rains broadened.

After several minutes, David could see a group of people near what looked like a dead end—a wall of dirt and rock at the gully's end. Two men were yelling, gesticulating wildly. When they got close enough, David could see that one of the men was Karl, and two others were holding him by the shoulders, keeping him off of a man on a stretcher.

David began to run, hoping it was Jason. His heart dropped as he drew closer. He could see that it was a local, speaking in rapid-fire Spanish, a taunting tone to his voice.

Karl turned away in disgust and saw David.

"What is it?" David stopped a few feet from him, glancing at the man on the stretcher.

"One of the looters." They had discovered fairly quickly that morning that the mounds Jason and Karl had noticed before were the buildings of an additional site, and that one—a temple—had been partially excavated and looted. "He says—" Karl stopped and seemed at a loss for words, something that was rare and thus frightening.

"Tell me." David's hard gaze rested on the smug man on the stretcher, and he was gratified to see a flicker of fear in the man's eyes.

"He says—"

"Hey, your friend. He's dead!" The thief taunted David from his stretcher. "I shot him dead, and then the mountain came down and buried him!"

Before anyone could stop him, David was there, his hands around the man's neck. An official with a gun strapped to his belt uttered a few sharp syllables, and David was pulled back. The criminal laughed hysterically. The man in charge barked another order, and the stretcher was lifted and carried down the gully, back to the west.

The Mexican official spoke rapidly to the rest of his helpers, and people began to disperse, trudging along the arroyo.

"Hey! Where the hell are they going?"

"The sergeant says there is no use looking for his body; it will be buried beneath all this rubble."

"He's not dead."

Karl placed a hand on David's shoulder. "David, I know how hard this is, but—"

"He's not dead." David stared at the pile of rock and debris. "I feel it."

Karl shook his head. "David…"

David turned and started back along the ravine, watching for a place with enough purchase so that he could get back to the top. As he started clambering up the side, Karl hollered, "What are you doing?"

"I'm going to follow this ravine from up top. Past the slide."

"David, that's crazy."

David didn't bother to answer, simply kept moving.

"Shit." David heard the sound of shifting rock and dirt from below. "Wait for me."

At the top, David turned eastward, trudging along the top of the ravine.

Karl walked silently alongside him. David could tell he was just humoring him, unwilling to let him go off on his own. But David was certain that Jason wasn't dead. He knew the difference between wishful thinking and instinct, and his instincts were telling him that Jason was still alive. His instincts were never wrong.

Ten minutes later they were past the slide. David walked slowly now, peering down into the gulch, watching for any sign of life. He saw nothing but rocks, dirt, roots and an occasional puddle. An hour later, Karl stopped. "This is crazy, David. He's not down there. This canyon could run for miles. No telling how far we'd have to walk to find the end of it."

David had continued walking, and Karl hurried to catch up with him, grabbing his arm. "David. You have to stop. It's going to take us two hours to get back to camp, and—"

David stopped abruptly, pointing down into the canyon. "Look," he breathed.

Karl peered in the direction David pointed. Several feet down, there was a dark smear on a pale rock. "What is it?"

"I think it's blood." David studied the side of the canyon, but it was too steep to try and climb down. "Come on."

He continued walking along the cliff's edge, looking for a place to go down. Glancing ahead, he spotted a bright spot of light at the canyon's bottom. "What's that?"

Karl shaded his eyes and looked. "Don't know."

David started walking fast, keeping his eyes on what looked like a pale heap of rocks, then started running as the illusion resolved into a man, light glinting off the camera hanging from his neck. He was lying on his back, one limp arm draped over his face, the other tucked across his stomach, a dark stain coloring his shoulder. "Jason!"

David flung himself down the hill, heedless of the rocks and limbs that tore at him as he half-slid, half-crawled down to Jason's side. "Jason!" For a moment, he just stared, then his body flooded with relief as he saw Jason's chest move. He was breathing! Without thinking, he grabbed Jason by the shoulders and shook him.

Jason moaned. "Come on, Jason," David coaxed. "Open your eyes."

Jason's lips parted slightly.

"Here." David hadn't even realized that Karl had made it to the bottom. He handed David the canteen from around his neck. "Give him some water."

David's hands trembled as he fumbled with the lid, but he got it off and dribbled a little between Jason's lips. Jason choked and began coughing. David waited until the fit had passed and poured in a little more. This time Jason swallowed.

Behind him, David heard Karl yelling into his cell phone. "Yeah, probably about two miles from where we found that guy. And we'll have to winch him up. The sides are too steep to carry him. Okay."

Karl knelt beside David. "The medics are on their way. Mark's going to bring the winch and some extra rope. It's going to be a heck of a job, getting him up top."

"What about a 'copter?"

"By the time we get in touch with someone in town, locate a chopper, and get it out here, it'll be too dark. We're better off lifting him out now and carrying him back."

David nodded and returned his attention to Jason, offering him tiny dribbles of water every few minutes. The second that Jason opened his eyes was the most exultant moment in David's life. "Oh, God, man." He started to grab Jason's shoulders again, then realized what he was doing and settled for squeezing his thigh.

"I'm not dreaming, am I?" Jason croaked.

David shook his head, unable to speak past the lump in his throat.

Jason laughed weakly. "Good." He winced suddenly. "How long?"

"How long have you been gone?"

Jason shook his head. "No. How long 'til they come?" He closed his eyes.

"Jason? Don't check out on me." David turned to Karl. "How long do you think?"

"Well, thank God Carmen had talked the medics into hanging around a while longer. They were still at the camp. They'll be moving faster than we were. Maybe an hour and a half."

David made a face, but there was nothing he could do. He looked down at Jason. His eyes were closed, and he was frighteningly pale, but his chest was moving in a steady rhythm, for which David was supremely thankful.

Each minute seemed like an hour. Jason would open his eyes briefly and take water, but tired easily and lost consciousness so quickly sometimes that David held his breath each time Jason's eyes closed, until he was certain that Jason was still breathing. Finally, about an hour and fifteen minutes later, he and Karl heard voices up above.

"Hello down there!" Mark was waving at them from the top of the canyon. "Give us a few minutes to set up, and then we'll send the stretcher and medics down.

Karl gave him a thumbs-up, and Mark disappeared from view. A few minutes later, two ropes slithered over the canyon's edge, their ends dangling a couple of feet from the bottom. Then two sets of feet appeared, making their way down the cliff face, supporting a stretcher attached to two more ropes between them.

When they reached the bottom, they wasted no time stripping off Jason's shirt. With Karl and David's help, they managed to get him onto the stretcher without causing him too much pain. They quickly and efficiently cleaned and wrapped his wound. One of the medics picked up a thick blanket they'd brought down with them. "We'll start the IV up top. He's lost a lot of blood, probably has heat exhaustion. Here's what we're gonna do. The three of you will lift the stretcher so I can wrap this blanket around it. Then we'll fasten the straps. Hopefully, that will keep him stationary, keep his shoulder from jarring too badly on the way up."

David and Karl nodded and grabbed the sides of the stretcher near Jason's feet. The other medic grabbed the poles to either side of his head. "One, two, three." They lifted him smoothly, and the medic had him wrapped and strapped within minutes.

"Let's take him to the side." They carried the stretcher over to the cliff and the first medic hollered, "Winch it up *very* slowly." The four of them held the stretcher, carefully easing it up into a vertical position as the slack left the ropes. Jason moaned softly, but didn't wake. When the stretcher rested against the wall, one medic yelled, "Hold it!" He and his assistant fastened themselves to their ropes. "Okay, start hauling us up!"

The two men did their best to keep the stretcher away from the wall, but it was difficult going past a couple of rock shelves. David breathed a sigh of relief when all three men disappeared over the canyon's edge. A minute later, the ropes were lowered again. David and Karl had no belt lines, so they had to do some hard climbing, but it wasn't long until they were at the top.

Thankfully, someone had located Joy, who was holding Jason's right hand as the medics got the IV going. "That's it," said the one who appeared to be in charge in his only slightly accented English. "Let's go." The two medics, Mark, and another of Karl's team whose name David couldn't remember lifted the stretcher and started off at a brisk pace. David strode over to Joy and wrapped his arm around her shoulders. Wordlessly, they followed the stretcher back to camp.

* * *

David turned off the engine and climbed out of the van, hurrying around to the side to open the door for his passenger. As Jason stepped out, leaning heavily on him for support, he looked up at David's house. "Are you sure about this?" he asked for the twentieth time since David had picked him up at the hospital.

David pushed the door shut. "I'm sure. As a matter of fact…" He planted a chaste kiss square on Jason's mouth, cocked his head thoughtfully, grinned, then kissed him again, this time teasing with his tongue until Jason responded, shuddering slightly as he kissed David back. "I've never been more sure of anything."

He heard the front door open behind him and turned. A tawny-headed whirlwind bounded down the steps and embraced them both.

Jason kissed the top of Joy's head. "Um…sweetie? Could you please…?" He shifted his shoulder a bit, where her grip was crushing it.

Joy stepped back, biting her lip in consternation. "Oh, God, Jason. I'm sorry!"

He shook his head. "It's okay." He smiled, his eyes twinkling. "I'm glad to see you, too."

Joy smiled, but there were tears in her eyes. "I thought we'd lost you."

Jason pulled her close with his good arm. The three of them stood in a circle, all but Jason's bound right arm wrapped around each other's waists. "It's okay, baby." He glanced at the house, then looked into David's eyes. "We're home."

And David nodded, never once thinking about anyone but the two people in his arms as he walked with them up the steps into a house that was, finally, a home.

# STRENTH IN NUMBERS 3: BRANDED

# Prologue

"I'm just so frustrated," Brandy said. "I've gone out with…who knows, probably a hundred guys in the last six years, and not one of them was even worth a second date." She was exaggerating, of course, but not by much. And damn it, she was *lonely*.

"You dated a couple of guys for a while, if I'm not mistaken," Kendall reminded her.

"That was only because I gave up. I thought maybe if I stuck it out, one of them would grow on me." She made a face. "Didn't happen."

"Maybe you need to take a vacation," Kendall said. "The twins are in school all day now. I can start carrying more of the weight down at the shops."

"But we've got Art & Artifacts opening in just a few months, and—"

"I'll take care of it, Brandy." Kendall covered her best friend's hand with her own. "You've been running yourself ragged managing both Lady and Driftwood for Sutter and me, and getting ready for the opening. You deserve a break. You need to take some time away from work and decide what it is that you really want from a relationship."

*I want what* you *have*, Brandy thought. But not necessarily with two guys. She sighed. She was surrounded by people in loving, happy, committed unions, but they were unorthodox in that they were ménage-a-trois relationships. Despite the fact that it was supposed to be every woman's fantasy, Brandy just couldn't picture herself with two guys. But maybe she should try it. Hell, if David Campbell, who used to be the most angry, uptight, unhappy person in the world could do it, why shouldn't she? But then again, she shouldn't try something just because it had worked for Kendall and Joy. They were all great friends, but completely different in many ways.

"As a matter of fact..." Kendall rifled through the newspaper, fishing out the lifestyle section. She handed it to Brandy, pointing out the featured article. "Here's something you might enjoy. Maybe you should give it a try."

Brandy quickly scanned the article. A new company, E. M. Enterprises, was starting a cruise line out of Galveston. Their maiden voyage would be an eleven-day trip from Galveston to various ports-of-call, including Cozumel, Belize, Cristobal, Montego Bay, and the Grand Caymans. Brandy nodded thoughtfully. Eleven days on a cruise ship, basking under the sun, snorkeling, swimming—it sounded like heaven. "Maybe you're right."

"You know I am."

Brandy glanced at her watch. "Oh, shoot. Gotta run. Do you mind if I keep this?" She waggled the paper as she stood.

"Go ahead." Kendall walked Brandy to the front door. "I'll stop by the shop this afternoon after I pick up the twins."

Brandy nodded and dashed down the steps, waving goodbye as she turned out of the driveway in a spurt of sand and gravel.

## Chapter One: Unexpected Reception

Brandy sipped at a soda, watching the people around her. The cruise line had pulled out all the stops for this welcome reception, offering great food, fantastic music, and free drinks at all of the onboard clubs. Brandy sat in a comfy leather chair in a secluded corner, surveying the festivities. One of her favorite pastimes was people-watching, and there were certainly some curious couples coming along on this trip.

Wandering the ship this first night on board, she'd visited no less than seven clubs. Each one had a different style, featuring a different kind of music. She closed her eyes, losing herself in the deep bass thrum coming from the speakers. She'd chosen the angst-filled, throbbing beats of the alt club, Promises in the Dark, for this first night. She drifted with the lyrics, allowing a stranger's pain to begin to wash away the stress from the last few, hectic months.

As that song ended and another began, she felt the familiar sensation of being watched. Opening her eyes, she scanned the room.

An attractive couple lounged against the wall to her right. The man was tall, and muscular in a lean, athletic way. In the muted light, the only other features she could make out clearly were the brilliant blue eyes staring into hers.

A petite woman stood at his side. Her striking auburn hair, cut in a pageboy, gleamed as she turned her head to meet Brandy's inquisitive gaze. On anyone else, Brandy would have considered the haircut old-fashioned. On this woman, it was gorgeous...seductive. She followed the lazy curve of one dark copper strand to where it just brushed the bottom of the woman's full, red lips, and felt an unexpected tightening in her nipples.

Hell's bells! Embarrassed, she looked away. She could still feel them watching. Nervous, she nipped at her bottom lip. She'd never had that kind of reaction to a woman before. What the heck was going on?

Unable to stop herself, she glanced at them again. They seemed to have been waiting for exactly that. The man's bright gaze captured hers, held her captive as he lowered his head, brushing strong, narrow lips against his companion's luscious red ones.

Brandy's nipples began to flat-out tingle. She allowed her gaze to travel down, saw his hand sliding up across the woman's toned, red-clad belly to cup her breast. With one swift movement, he brushed the wisp of fabric covering her chest to the side, freeing one compact, pert breast.

Brandy gasped. The woman's eyes found hers. She smiled seductively as her companion teased her nipple between a thumb and forefinger.

Brandy tore her gaze away, searching the crowded room. No one else seemed to notice what was going on. As a matter of fact, there were quite a few risqué situations playing themselves out in dark corners.

Brandy sat up, toyed with her glass. She should get out, go back to her room. This was just a little too kinky for her. But, damn! She had mentioned to Kendall dating a lot of guys over the last six years, but the truth of the matter was, she'd pretty much quit dating about three years ago. She hadn't found it worth the trouble.

And now this. She shifted, crossing her legs, pressing her thighs tight against her now-throbbing clit. She hadn't been this horny in ages. She'd never thought of herself as a voyeur, but...just one more peek.

She looked up, saw them watching her. They both smiled. The woman glanced down, drawing Brandy's attention to the place where her slender fingers slipped beneath her companion's waistband. He continued to watch Brandy as he lowered his head, his mouth closing on the woman's exposed nipple as she licked her lips, her bold gaze traveling the length of Brandy's body.

Brandy took a deep breath, a surge of hot desire enveloping every place the woman's gaze rested. She set her glass down, drew fingers tipped by cool, glistening condensation along her neckline, thinking that would cool her off.

Instead, she found her hand drifting down to toy lightly with one prominent nipple as she watched the dark-haired man suckle. His gaze flicked to her hand. Opening his mouth, he mimicked her finger's movements with his tongue while his companion closed her eyes and murmured something.

Brandy couldn't look away, couldn't stop. They unearthed such a fire in her belly, such burning need. She leaned back into the deep chair, turned slightly, and drew one leg up. No one else would be able to see her actions, but *they* would. Sliding one hand beneath her skirt, she pushed her panties aside and slipped two trembling fingers into her saturated pussy.

The man moved, whispering into his companion's ear. She turned and stood in front of him, leaning back against him, and they both watched Brandy. Even as she fingered her pussy, she couldn't believe she was doing it. The woman was playing with her own nipples, staring at the place where Brandy's hand disappeared beneath her skirt.

The man reached down, placing his hands on the woman's firm, rounded buttocks. He walked his fingers like spiders, sliding the lower half of her dress up in the back. The red-haired beauty grinned at Brandy as her companion unzipped his pants. She leaned forward, and the man's hands held her waist. They turned slightly, allowing Brandy a brief glimpse of his long, rigid cock before it disappeared between the woman's bronzed, shapely thighs.

Oh, damn! Brandy pressed her legs together tight around her wrist, fingers buried deep inside her, riveted by the performance. Their hot, hungry gazes never left her. The man let the skirt fall. The woman straightened slightly, reaching back to cup his buttocks, drawing him tightly against her.

Brandy no longer registered anyone else but them. The fingers in her pussy twisted and writhed. Her entire body was one tightly wound thread that threatened to break at the slightest touch. In the back of her mind, she was shocked at her own behavior, but she couldn't look away. Didn't want to. She caught her bottom lip between her teeth as she felt her climax building.

The couple's eyes bore into hers—calculating, measuring, weighing. Brandy found that she was holding her breath, as though waiting for their judgment. Her climax wavered, held at bay by their careful scrutiny. Just when she thought she wouldn't be able to take it any longer, their features softened. They smiled.

Brandy gasped, arched. She broke out in a sweat as her climax peaked and ebbed, peaked and ebbed. The woman's eyes glazed. She arched. The man grasped her shoulders, pressing her down tight against him, and Brandy watched in fascination as they trembled with their own pleasure.

Moments later, they were straightening their clothes. Abruptly aware of her surroundings again, Brandy did the same. She picked up her watered-down soda and drained it in one gulp. Took a deep, calming breath.

She glanced toward them again. To her horror, the couple was heading her way. Brandy stood, pushing through the crowd. Once on the companionway, she had to use every ounce of control she possessed to keep from running.

She closed her stateroom door behind her with a sigh of relief. Brushing back wisps of pale blond hair that had escaped her French braid, she made her way through the dark into the small bathroom and turned on the light, staring at herself in the mirror.

What had come over her?

Hands trembling, she turned on the water, splashed the cold liquid over her face, her chest. Grabbing a towel, she rubbed herself dry as she stepped over to the bed and collapsed back against it.

Obviously, Kendall had been right. Brandy had definitely needed a vacation. Actually, it looked like what she needed was a good fucking!

The problem was, who was going to do the fucking?

She turned onto her side, staring into the dark. She pictured two pairs of eyes—one bright, bright blue, the other the tawny green-gold of a tiger's eyes—boring into her, filling her with a heat, a need, she hadn't felt in a long time. She moaned, her pussy flooding with juices as she imagined the handsome cock she'd glimpsed, buried between her thighs.

And the woman… Brandy sighed, shifted restlessly again. She'd never, ever, been even remotely attracted to a woman. And yet this one had made her horny with a look. Her traitorous nipples tightened once more as she pictured those bright red lips. How would it feel to have those lips touching hers? To have that beautiful, bow-shaped mouth close around her—

Shit! Brandy flung herself off the bed, started pacing the little room. It was just a voyeuristic encounter in a dark club. A game. She might never even see the couple again, given how big the ship was.

Was that a hint of disappointment she felt?

No, it couldn't be.

But their image wouldn't leave her mind.

Could this be it? What was missing from her life? No, that was crazy.

But...what was wrong with finding a man *and* a woman attractive? Her body flushed with wicked desire as she remembered the way they had looked at her. They'd *both* been coming on to her, that was for sure. And what was wrong with that? If she could accept Kendall's marriage to Josh and Sutter, and Joy's relationship with David and Jason, wasn't it a little hypocritical to frown on the idea of two *women* and a man?

Feeling suddenly stifled, Brandy slipped out of her clothes. Standing there, naked, she ran her hands over her body. She thought back on the men she'd dated over the years, the women she'd known, and felt nothing. No one else had ever turned her on with a glance, made her feel the way she had felt in that club.

Closing her eyes, she saw again a set of piercing blue eyes that watched her over a wealth of silky auburn hair. A soft, shapely thigh wrapped around a lean, jeans-clad leg. The fire in her belly flared. She touched herself. Stroked her pussy the way she imagined *he* might. Wet her finger and touched her nipples, imagining it was the woman's tongue.

Damn, she needed to come again so badly. She fingered her G-spot, rubbed her clit frantically. Even with their image in her mind, with their hungry eyes watching, she couldn't manage it.

Frustrated, she finally gave up, snapping on the bedside light. Rummaging in the drawer, she pulled out one of the books she'd brought along. It was going to be a long, lonely night.

## Chapter Two: Strange Company

Brandy searched until she found a secluded sundeck, a small one isolated from the others, toward the back of the boat. Delighted to find herself alone, she lay back in the deck chair, closing her eyes and sighing contentedly. She'd enjoyed chatting with her tablemates at breakfast, but sometimes she needed a little space.

The meal had been awesome, with more food laid out than Brandy had ever seen in one place in her life. She had heard that about these cruises—that the food was to die for. She'd have to be careful, or she'd get back to Galveston ten pounds heavier.

As she'd suspected, she had yet to run into the anonymous couple from the night before. For that, she was thankful.

Wasn't she?

Her belly felt cold for a moment and she opened her eyes. "Do you mind?" A tall, lean, darkly tanned man with laughing blue eyes pointed at the chair to her left.

Brandy's voice froze in her throat as she recognized him.

He raised his eyebrows. "If this seat's taken..." There seemed a world of meaning behind those simple words.

She should say yes. She wanted to say yes. Didn't she?

Nope. She wanted to say no, I was saving it for you. She wanted to say, what was that last night? She wanted to say, could you *please* fuck me? Now? Instead, she settled for "Go ahead."

The stranger turned and stretched out on the lounger. He exuded confidence and moved with the liquid grace of a jungle cat. Brandy studied him surreptitiously. He was older than she'd thought. In the light of day, a touch of gray glinted in his short-cropped, light brown hair. Forty, maybe? But he was in damn good shape. Through lowered lashes, she admired his narrow hips, his well-defined thigh and calf muscles.

"May I join you?" A deep, slightly husky voice with a musical lilt startled Brandy. She looked up into hazel eyes dotted with flecks of green. There was a hint of accent to the words. French, maybe? Without waiting for an answer, the woman sat down in the chair to Brandy's right and held out her hand. "Hi. I'm Madeleine, but you can call me Lin."

Brandy hesitated for a moment. This wasn't a chance encounter. These people had sought her out. If she picked up her bag and left, then this would be over before it started. That's probably what she should do.

The woman waited, she and her partner watching Brandy patiently with their unusual, mesmerizing eyes. Like a match to dry tinder, their presence fanned the heat in her groin.

Brandy took a deep, unsteady breath. Held out her hand. Listened to herself say, in a strangely breathless voice, "It's nice to meet you. I'm Brandy Mitchell."

Their smiles were like twin suns, burning their way into her soul. Her heart skipped a beat. She stared at Lin's smooth hand in hers.

The woman held on for just a moment longer than necessary, then let go with obvious reluctance. Her fingers grazed Brandy's palm lightly—sending a shiver up her spine—as she pulled away. She gestured toward the man in the lounger. "This is my husband, Eric Brogan."

"That's right," Brandy said, striving to keep her voice light and friendly. "I remember seeing you two together at the party last night."

Oh. My. God. Heat rushed to her cheeks as she realized what she had just said. Frantically, she reached for her beach bag. "Here. I'll move so you two can sit together."

"Oh, no." Madeleine reached out and grasped Brandy's arm to stop her from rising. The tips of her fingernails inadvertently, or perhaps purposely, brushed across Brandy's nipple. Brandy felt a very different kind of flush rising in her chest at the contact. "You stay right there," Madeleine purred. She exchanged a glance and a small smile with her husband. "We're fine."

Brandy had no idea what to do next. They seemed to be waiting for something, but she didn't know what it was they wanted her to do. Actually, she had an idea, but she wasn't sure she was ready yet. She imagined saying, "Your cabin or mine?" but the words just wouldn't come. Her brain kept telling her to get up and walk away, but her body wanted to stay and see what would develop. Disgusted with herself, she settled for a noncommittal, "Okay, if you're sure." Lying back against the lounger, she closed her eyes, wondering what she would do if they made the next move.

She didn't have long to wait. As she lay there, she could almost feel the tension building in the air—like the electric potential that gathered just before a lightning storm. Without opening her eyes, Brandy sensed that both her companions were watching her as they had the night before, their gazes raking her body. She shifted nervously, her nipples hardening into rounded pebbles that strained against her bikini top.

A cool touch on her neck nearly made her jump out of her skin. She opened her eyes to find Lin's hazel ones only inches from hers. "You're so fair. You're getting a little pink. I thought you might want some sunscreen." Her lotion-slathered hand slid smoothly down Brandy's neck.

Brandy swallowed hard, working to keep her breathing slow and measured. She gazed into those hazel eyes as the woman's hands smoothed the cool lotion over her chest. Distracted by movement, she looked up to find Eric kneeling by her side.

Squirting lotion into his hands, he smiled. "I'll do your legs."

Brandy's heart was stuck in her throat. Lin's touch stoked the fire in her belly, and her breath fluttered in her chest at the look in Eric's eyes. They hesitated for a moment, as though waiting for her to protest. When she said nothing, they carried on, as though it were the most natural thing in the world.

She was both startled and excited by her body's strong responses. Appalled at her willingness to let it continue, and yet intrigued by the fierce attraction she felt to them both. Wondering what it would be like to be loved by them.

She looked from Eric to Lin and back again. Lin's palms were cool and soft on her chest; Eric's warm and rough on her calves. He worked his way up to her thighs, kneading them softly. Lin described soothing circles on Brandy's heated flesh.

Moisture gathered between her legs. Her nipples ached. Madeleine's gaze flickered, resting on the taut peaks evident beneath the thin material of Brandy's swimsuit. She licked her lips, ran her French-manicured nails over the swell of Brandy's breasts, along the edge of the cream-colored swim top.

Eric's fingers were toying with the elastic of her bikini bottoms. She tensed, and they both looked up. For a long moment, the three of them seemed suspended in time. Eric and Lin watched her intently. Waiting. They seemed to see so deep, reawakening dark desires she had relegated to the depths, hiding them even from herself.

She burned for them. Yearned for their touch.

As though sensing her desire, Lin slipped her hand beneath the top. Ran her lotion-slicked fingers over Brandy's nipple.

Brandy sighed. Spread her legs.

Eric grinned. Pushing aside the fabric at her crotch, he buried one long, strong finger inside her.

Lin tugged at her nipples, plucking them like ripe strawberries.

Brandy moaned, arched into the caress. Eric leaned in, claiming her mouth with his. He was rough, bruising her lips. She sighed. Opened her mouth, let her tongue dance with his.

"*Ma chère*," Lin whispered. "I knew you were for us." Her deft fingers moved to Brandy's neck, releasing the catch so that her ivory breasts spilled out into the sunlight.

Eric dragged his lips from hers. Brandy opened her mouth to protest the loss, but then her nipples were inside their hot, hungry mouths and the protest turned into a startled exclamation of pleasure. Eric was eager, relentless, sucking so hard that her nipple throbbed with mingled pain and arousal. Lin's delicate tongue circled Brandy's other nipple rapidly, flicking across the swollen peak ever so lightly. "Oh, God." Brandy arched into them, reached out and grasped their heads, pressing their mouths tightly against her. Eric's short, coarse thatch tickled her palm, while Lin's silken strands slipped through her fingers like molten copper.

Her pussy clenched as Eric's finger wiggled inside her. Brandy moaned, thrust her hips. His other hand crept beneath her, cradling the small of her back as he roughly forced another finger inside her tight pussy.

It had been a long time since anything larger than Brandy's slender digits had touched that place. She whimpered as her pussy stretched, yet each painful thrust pushed her closer to the edge of oblivion. It hurt, and yet she found herself grinding her hips, urging him on.

Which seemed to excite them both immensely.

The quality of Lin's touch changed. She caught one throbbing nipple between her teeth and tugged. Brandy yelped, startled. Again, it hurt...but it also made her pussy throb deliciously. Lin let go. She was watching her, looking worried. "Please." Brandy's voice trembled. She thrust out her breast. "Don't stop."

Lin lowered her head slowly, grinning when Brandy made a soft, impatient sound. She trapped the swollen bud between her teeth, pulled and worried it like a puppy with a toy, while Brandy gasped with pleasure.

Eric grasped her other breast, holding it tight, pinching just below the peak so that it stood up, tingling and buzzing, while his tongue danced across the tip. Brandy moaned, unable to speak, to think, drowning in their touch.

Lin's hand crept between her legs. Brandy trembled with anticipation. "Yes," she breathed. She thrust out her hips when the redhead hesitated a moment longer. "Touch me. Please."

Lin worked her slippery finger in alongside the two Eric had buried within. "Oh, God! Oh, yes," Brandy moaned. They breathed hard, milking her nipples fiercely as their joined fingers plunged into her again and again. Her eager body writhed beneath their rough, demanding touch. Each stinging penetration, each smarting pinch and nibble, drove her higher and higher, until Eric covered her mouth with his, swallowing her frenzied cry as she writhed, plunging over the edge into ecstasy.

He drank her joy roughly; then Lin's plump lips replaced his, breathing Brandy's fitful sighs as the last shudders faded.

When they moved away, she felt abandoned.

Their fingers slid from between her legs. She whimpered fretfully. Her nipples were purple, throbbing. Her pussy stung...and it all felt so *good*. The tension of weeks...no, years, had drained from her body, leaving her more relaxed than she ever remembered.

Until the reality of the situation hit her.

At some point, Lin had taken off her own swim top. Now, she traced damp circles around her pale golden nipples with Brandy's juices. Eric had pushed down his trunks. A drop of pre-ejaculate gleamed at the tip of his cock, shivering in the sunlight.

Brandy felt a desperate hunger. She wanted to taste Lin's inviting nipple, drink Eric's cock. Then laughter drifted up to them from one of the causeways below the sundeck.

Brandy abruptly registered the fact that they were all half-naked, in broad daylight, on the upper deck of a cruise ship where just about anyone could show up at any time.

Lin was leaning in, offering her one perfect, peach-ripe breast. Brandy longed to take a bite, but panic was setting in. She pushed the woman away, tugged up her top, and tried to fasten it with shaking hands.

The couple shared a look. Within seconds, they were covered again. Calm, cool, and collected. Brandy, however, still couldn't seem to get her damn top fastened. Eric reached over and grasped her wrists gently, stilling her anxious movements. "It's okay," he said soothingly.

Brandy pushed him away. Covered her face in her hands. Her cheeks burned, and to her dismay, she felt tears threatening.

"Let me." Lin reached over and fastened her top. "Did we hurt you?" she asked softly.

Brandy shook her head. "No. Yes. I mean…hell, I don't know what I mean."

She could feel them, sitting to either side of her. Radiating concern and dismay. She finally let her hands drop and faced them. "I don't know what to say." She looked away. "I know everyone says this, but I'm not—"

"Usually like that." Eric watched her the way an equestrian would a horse he thought was about to bolt—wanting to reach out, but wary, in case he spooked her. "We know."

"We're not usually like that, either," Lin offered. Then she laughed. "Actually, we *are* rather demanding lovers. But we don't usually approach someone we like in quite this fashion. It's just..." She leaned forward, touched Brandy's arm. "When we first saw you yesterday, waving goodbye to your...sister?"

"Kendall," Brandy murmured. "She's my best friend."

"You took our breath away." She ran her hand along Brandy's arm. "So beautiful. So vibrant."

"Like a magnet," Eric said. "Drawing us all over the ship in your wake."

To Brandy's disbelief, Lin's touch on her arm was making her nipples hard again. She pulled her arm away. "That's quite a line," she observed sharply.

Lin started. She looked genuinely hurt. "Didn't you enjoy it, Brandy? Just a little?"

She looked away. She *had* enjoyed it. A lot.

In her heart of hearts, she felt an incredible longing. She was attracted to them. Both of them. She'd like to spend the rest of the cruise getting to know them. But, despite her usual open-mindedness, she was really struggling with the way Lin, especially, made her feel. It was hypocritical, she knew.

Brandy searched their eyes. Were they sincere, or was this just some kind of game they played?

She clasped her hands tight in her lap. "I'm sorry. I don't think I can do this."

"Is it me?" Lin whispered.

They stared at each other, the hot sun beating down on them.

Brandy pictured herself getting up. Leaving. Spending the rest of the cruise on her own. "I've never felt this way before."

She couldn't bring herself to look at them any longer, yearning to touch them and yet struggling to understand her own feelings. She stared out over the ocean. "I've never, *never* been attracted to a woman before. I have friends that are in multiple-partner relationships, so that part isn't strange to me; but their lovers are men. So...yes, the fact that you're a woman...it's disconcerting."

Lin sat back, gripping the arms of her chair. "I see." She sat silently for a moment. Brandy could feel Eric's anger on her behalf. He stood abruptly and held out his hand.

Lin grasped it, allowed him to pull her up. Brandy looked up, inadvertently meeting their gazes.

She saw hurt. Disappointment. The most surprising thing, though, was the way that knowledge made her heart ache.

It didn't make any sense. She'd just *met* them!

They turned away.

Took a step. And another.

They were going to walk out of her life and never come back. That idea bothered her more than she ever could have imagined. "Wait!"

Their steps faltered.

"I thought about you all night," she confessed in a rush. "I couldn't sleep. I was even disappointed, when I didn't see either of you at breakfast this morning."

They stopped. Eric looked back. "Why are you telling us this?" he asked tersely.

"I... I don't want you to go."

He shook his head. Looked away.

"Please." She drew her knees up, wrapping her arms around them. Pressed against her thighs, her sore nipples ached deliciously. "I… I did enjoy it," she whispered, her cheeks hot.

Lin turned. "What does that mean, Brandy?"

She made herself stand. Walk over to them. "It means…don't give up on me." She looked into Lin's tawny tiger-eyes. "I came on this cruise to try and figure out what's missing from my life."

Eric turned, as well. His piercing blue eyes seemed to see right down to her core. She shivered. "Do you think we can help you with that?"

She couldn't believe she was doing this. But moments earlier, she'd felt as though the world were ending. Now, she felt as though it was just beginning. She decided to let her heart lead, instead of her head.

Reaching out, she took one of Eric's calloused hands, Lin's soft ones, in each of hers. It felt natural. Right. She stepped back toward the chairs. "Come sun with me. Let's talk." They resisted, but she could feel them wavering. "I'm sorry I hurt you," she whispered. "I was only trying to be honest. And I'm being honest now, when I say… I don't know where this is going, but I can't stand the thought of not finding out."

She took another step. This time, they moved with her.

They sat as before, on either side of her. For a little while, it was uncomfortable. Brandy made herself talk, commenting on breakfast, on the welcome reception the night before.

She asked them about the tattoo she had seen on their backs as they walked away. A blue-black panther and orange-and-black-striped tiger, one above each hip—facing one another, their paws upraised and almost touching in the middle.

"That's our totem," Lin said. "Eric is the panther. I'm the tiger."

Brandy laughed. "It's so funny—I've been thinking you two remind me of jungle cats since I first saw you!"

Slowly, the quality of tension changed. Discomfort vanished, to be replaced by the quivering ultra-awareness that had caught her so off-guard from the beginning.

It simmered, beneath the surface, while they chatted about inconsequential things until the intercom called them to lunch.

## Chapter Three: Hot and Bothered

After lunch, Lin and Eric reluctantly informed her that they had business to attend to in their cabin. "It's kind of a working vacation for us," Lin explained, sharing a secretive glance with her husband.

They were walking with Brandy toward her stateroom. She tried to cover her disappointment. "No problem," she said lightly. "I'll see you guys later." She stopped in front of her cabin. "This is me." She turned to unlock the door.

"Wait." Eric grasped her shoulders and turned her back to face them. There was something in his eyes—like a jungle cat, trying to break free. Brandy's heart beat like a hummingbird's. "Don't make plans with anyone." He leaned in. "You're ours." His mouth covered hers, his tongue invading her, his lips bruising. Just when Brandy thought her legs would melt, he let her go, looked into her eyes. "Right?"

"Yes," she gasped. "I mean, all right."

Madeleine stepped close. "Nine days," she murmured, her hazel eyes simmering with desire, her accent very pronounced.

"And we're going to spend every one of them helping you discover what's missing from your life." Her elegant hand stroked Brandy's crotch through her suit. "Yes?"

Brandy was transfixed by the sight of those luscious lips so close to hers. "Yes," she breathed.

Lin smiled. Stuck out her tongue and traced Brandy's feverish, bruised lips. Brandy's breath faltered. She opened her mouth, touched her tongue to Lin's.

The hand at her crotch clenched, pinched Brandy's clit tight between two fingernails. Tugged, moving it in slow, sensuous circles. Brandy gasped. Lin deepened the kiss, her tongue investigating every part of Brandy's mouth.

Brandy moaned. She wrapped one leg around Lin's firm thigh, hot spirals of desire corkscrewing through her belly with each twinge of her captive clit. She thrust against Lin's hand, sucked her tongue. She tasted so good, felt so right.

Lin groaned. Pulled away. "You are like a drug," she murmured, her voice thick. She gave Brandy's clit one last, painfully arousing twist. "We must go." She put her arm around Eric's waist.

"We'll see you at dinner," Eric promised. "We're at the same table tonight."

Brandy nodded, not trusting her voice.

They smiled—predatory, possessive. A panther and a tigress who had just cornered their prey. And God help her, she had no intention of trying to escape.

They walked away, sauntering sensuously down the corridor as she watched them go.

Once inside her room, the doubts began almost immediately.

What the hell was she doing? They had to be playing with her. They were a worldly couple, quite metropolitan. Brandy had heard stories about swingers who trolled these types of cruises, looking for individuals or couples to join them in their games.

Pacing, she argued with herself. So what? Male or female, individuals or couples, there would be no guarantees from *anyone* she met on this trip. This was a vacation. If she just so happened to want to spend her time with a couple, rather than a male individual, no biggie.

Right?

And if that couple just so happened to fuck her brains out in the process, there was nothing wrong with that.

Right?

She sat on the bed and forced herself to look at the situation realistically. The bottom line was, if she had met two men and felt this way about them, she wouldn't have questioned it at all. She would have had her fun, and gone on, none the worse for wear.

It was stupid to drive herself crazy just because Madeleine was involved. Finding herself attracted to a woman was unexpected, but hell, Brandy prided herself on being nonjudgmental. On accepting people for what they were, not what society thought they should be. Josh and Sutter's relationship with Kendall, David and Jason's with Joy—they weren't strictly heterosexual, she knew. Kendall had told her flat-out that Josh and Sutter were every bit as sexually attracted to each other as they were to Kendall, and that it was an incredible turn-on. It hadn't bothered Brandy at all to know they thought of each other that way. And she was the one who had helped Kendall to uncover David's long-ago affair with Jason, and that hadn't bothered her, either. So, why should she judge herself and Madeleine any differently?

Brandy took a long, shuddering breath and made a decision. For the next nine days, she was theirs. She wasn't going to question it, wasn't going to spend hours trying to figure out why she felt the way she did. She was going to go with the flow, relax, let the world carry her along for a while, instead of carrying the world on *her* shoulders.

Feeling better, she stood and walked over to the tiny closet. First she'd pick out something sexy to wear to dinner. Then she'd take a shower and relax on the bed with her book, maybe even take a nap. She grinned impishly at her reflection in the narrow mirror on the closet door. She had a feeling she just might need the rest.

* * *

Brandy paused outside the dining room, experiencing an unfamiliar mixture of anticipation and trepidation. She smoothed her tight black dress, a clingy knit that zipped up the front. An asymmetrical brass heart dangled from the zipper. She tugged it down a bit, exposing just a little more cleavage. It felt wonderful and strange to have someone she wanted to look sexy for. *Two* someones. Taking a deep breath, she walked in.

Lin and Eric were already at the table, chatting amicably with another couple.

They looked so natural together, so normal, that despite her intentions, Brandy felt a twinge of doubt again.

Eric glanced up. Did a double-take.

He whispered in Lin's ear. She looked up, and doubt scattered to the four winds in the face of their admiration. Their welcoming smiles were like ambrosia to Brandy's hungry heart.

Eric stood, pulling out a chair next to him. "Everyone, I'd like you to meet Brandy Mitchell," he said as she sat down.

There was a confused chorus of voices saying hello, introducing themselves. One of the younger men, obviously unattached, told her how beautiful she looked. Brandy, acutely aware of Lin and Eric's possessive observation, thanked him casually, careful not to offer any encouragement.

Dinner was pleasant, with lots of talk about how the cruise had been so far, what everyone's plans were at the first port of call. Brandy enjoyed it, but she couldn't help wishing that she had Lin and Eric all to herself.

Finally, the dessert course was brought. Conversation wound down as people finished up, began drifting away. Lin and Eric stood, held out their hands. "Come on."

Brandy reached out. They pulled her up, led her into the ship. "Where are we going?"

Lin flashed a VIP card. "We've been invited to the captain's private club."

The place proved to be *very* private. Very intimate. A small dance floor glowed with muted blue and green lights. People swayed—kissing, touching intimately, oblivious to everyone around them. Tables dotted the room in small, separate groupings, wreathed in shadows.

Eric took their drink orders and headed for the bar while Brandy and Lin found a place to sit.

"So, what do you do, Brandy?" Lin asked after Eric had returned with their drinks.

"I manage a couple of shops in Galveston."

"That sounds interesting. Tell us about it," Eric said.

"Well, one is called Lady of the Myths. My boss, Kendall Reed-Campbell, is an artist. She makes a lot of the pieces. Specializing in mythical creatures, of course, especially those associated with the sea. Plus we carry the regular tourist inventory. Seashells. T-shirts." She took a sip of her Mai Tai, warming to her subject. "The other is her husband's. Hand-carved wood of all types—display pieces and collectibles, cabinets, furniture, moldings and banisters. You name it, Sutter makes it. He's an incredible woodworker." She sipped her drink again, feeling a bit flushed and knowing the liquor was making her gush, but too relaxed to care. "You should see the house he helped to build. It's incredible."

"Sounds like you really like what you're doing," Lin commented.

"Oh, I do. I *love* it, actually." She laughed. "I went to college intending to become an English professor. But I went to work for Kendall at the end of my junior year, and the rest is history." She finished the rest of her drink and signaled the waiter, intending to order another. Then she hesitated. She didn't drink very often—she was already feeling a little tipsy. Did she really want to go into this with a muddled head?

No, she decided. When he came over, she ordered a plain soda, then continued. "I manage both shops now, and we're getting ready to roll out a new place this summer." The waiter brought Brandy's soda and she took a quick sip.

"What kind of a place?" Lin asked, leaning forward over the table.

She was wearing a red dress. Brandy had always thought redheads couldn't wear that color. But Lin's hair was a rich, deep auburn, her skin a pale gold. On her, red looked…extremely enticing. The neckline dipped so low, in the greenish-blue light from the dance floor, Brandy could make out just a hint of areole peeking above the edge on both breasts. Warmth suffused her chest, her nipples tightening. She forced her eyes away.

They were staring at her. Waiting. She struggled to recall Lin's question. "Ummm…oh! The new place. Art & Artifacts. It's upscale. More of a gallery slash fine art venue. We want to showcase local talent. I've got a great bunch of artists lined up—sculptors, painters. And we're importing some more expensive, more exotic pieces. I've been gearing up for this for the last two years."

Eric smiled at Brandy's enthusiasm. "Stuffy English professor turned exotic art dealer, huh?"

Brandy laughed. "That about sums it up, I guess. But I'm still into academia. I have a gift for languages, so I've continued to study those."

Madeleine raised her eyebrows. "Oh? *Parce que, pour moi, tu es une des plus belles femmes que j'ai jamais connues.*" Her voice was a breathy purr.

Brandy did, indeed, speak French. Her cheeks grew hot and she picked up her glass, drinking deeply to hide her confusion. *Because, for me, you are one of the most beautiful women I have ever known.* It felt so strange to have a woman complimenting her in that way, looking at her as though she were the dessert course in a five-star restaurant.

She searched her mind for something to say that wasn't totally inane. "*Merci beaucoup*," she managed "*Et que faites-vous?*"

Lin clapped her hands in delight. "Wonderful! You really do know the language. I'm impressed." She took a sip of her soda, then answered. "I'm in marketing and public relations, and Eric is an entrepreneur."

"Marketing?" Brandy set her glass down. "I think you'd be good at that. You're very bold." She gasped and covered her mouth with her hand. "I'm sorry, I didn't mean to say that."

"That's quite all right." Madeleine's eyes bore into hers. "You're absolutely correct." She moved a hand across the swell of one breast, pushing the fabric of her dress just low enough to reveal one swollen nipple. Brandy licked her lips nervously as Lin's white-tipped fingernail grazed the dark peak.

"Would you like to touch?" Lin murmured.

Brandy glanced at the silhouettes moving in the semi-darkness surrounding them.

"Trust me," Lin whispered. "No one will care."

Brandy's own breasts were throbbing, not just the nipples, but each entire globe. As if from a great distance, she watched herself reach out. Press the tips of her fingers against the prominent peak. Lin's eyes closed. Brandy stroked the dark bud, felt it swell even further, standing out sharply.

Eric's hand found her zipper, tugged it down an inch more. His fingers slipped beneath the fabric, stroked one aching breast. She caught her lip between her teeth to keep from moaning.

Lin captured her hand. Stood up, lithe and graceful. "May we have this dance?"

Eric was there, pulling out her chair. Brandy stood, reached for her zipper.

Eric grasped her wrist. "Leave it."

Brandy glanced around the room again.

Everywhere she looked, people were touching. Stroking. One man looked right at her as his hand crept beneath his partner's skirt, registering nothing, his eyes glazed with passion.

Eric and Lin pushed her gently, herding her into a dark corner of the dance floor.

Eric stood close behind her. Brandy could feel the heat of him through the thin material of her dress. Madeleine swayed in front, her eyes dark and sultry. Her full lips gleamed, and green-blue light outlined the orb of her exposed breast.

Lightheaded with desire, Brandy pulled her zipper down to her navel and brushed the gaping fabric aside.

Eric put his arms around her from behind. His hands grasped her hips, pressed them back against him. She could feel his cock, a hard bulge at her back. He moved his hips, and hers with them, in slow, grinding arcs.

Brandy moaned. Raising her arms, reaching back over her head, she laced her fingers around his neck. He pressed his lips into the curve of hers, the tip of his tongue teasing her flesh.

Madeleine moved close. Looked into Brandy's eyes as she covered one breast with her cool, smooth hand. She squeezed the nipple, rolling it between her thumb and forefinger.

Brandy arched into her touch.

Lin smiled. Brought her lips close, her breath hot on the tingling peak.

Brandy waited, breathless. Lin licked her lips, a hairsbreadth from the buzzing nipple. "Please," Brandy whispered.

"What do you want, *ma chère?*" Lin teased.

Brandy saw the jungle cat in those hazel eyes. Pacing, pacing. Waiting to be unleashed.

A flood of desire ripped through her. She knew what her tiger wanted.

"Bite me," she begged, and meant it. Literally.

Lin's eyes widened. Her breath quickened. She reached up, tugged the rest of her neckline down so that her other breast was exposed. One hand slipped behind Brandy's back, holding her while the other pinched just below her left nipple, making the peak stand out. She caught it between her teeth. Bit it.

Brandy gasped, her pussy gushing.

With his free hand, Eric tugged up the back of her dress. Slipped his hand beneath her hose, her panties. His fingers slithered between her cheeks, seeking her pussy.

She moaned. Let go of his neck. Clutched the back of Lin's dress.

His fingers found her slit, glided between her slick folds.

Brandy whimpered fitfully. She was no longer aware of the club, the music, the people around them. There was nothing else. Nothing but their touch.

Eric's mouth closed on the tender flesh of her neck. Sucking. Sucking.

The tiger at her breast fed hungrily—nibbling, nipping, drawing her teeth across the sensitive bud.

Tremors wracked her body. She wrapped one leg around Lin's golden thigh.

Eric's fingers danced in her pussy.

Lin's teeth caught her bud. Held it tight, pain and pleasure mingling, becoming one.

Brandy gasped. Bucked frantically, riding Lin's thigh. She would have screamed in ecstasy, but Lin's mouth covered hers, capturing the sound before it could escape.

They supported her until the trembling passed. When her legs could support her, they let her go.

She looked around, embarrassed. A couple of guys seated at a nearby table were grinning. One of them held up a hand, making a circle with his thumb and forefinger, mouthing the word "awesome."

Brandy felt the heat flare in her cheeks. With trembling fingers, she tugged up her zipper, smoothed down her skirt.

Lin tucked her breasts back inside her dress, watching enigmatically.

Eric was still standing behind her. He tucked a stray strand of her pale hair behind her ear. Whispered, "It's up to you, Brandy. Where do we go from here?"

It had been one of the most incredible experiences she'd ever had, and it wasn't enough. She wanted his cock inside her. Wanted to touch them the way they'd touched her. Wanted to find out what it was like to suck Lin's nipple, bury fingers in her pussy. "I want…" She shook her head, shocked by her own needs.

Lin leaned in close. "What?" Eric's breath tickled her ear.

"Come to my cabin," she whispered tremulously.

"*Ma chère*," Lin breathed.

"*Allons*," Eric said. *Let's go*. They each took a hand, leading her urgently and unerringly to her room.

Brandy's hands trembled as she went to unlock the door, and she dropped the key.

Eric picked it up and fit it into the lock, and a moment later Brandy was flipping on the light. She blushed as he moved the Do Not Disturb hanger to the outside handle, then shut and locked the door.

Then they were pushing her back toward the bed. The edge of the mattress hit the back of her knee, and she fell across it.

Eric tugged her zipper down until it stopped, about six inches above the hemline. Looking into her eyes, he grasped the fabric to either side of it. His muscles clenched. Brandy swallowed hard. He was a hell of a lot stronger than his lean body implied. He grinned hungrily. Pulled.

The fabric parted.

Heart pounding, Brandy slipped her arms out of the sleeves.

He cupped her breasts with his hands, pressed his lips against hers. Lin knelt between his legs, at her feet. She tugged the straps of Brandy's shoes down. Slipped them off. Ran her hands over the silky hose, up Brandy's thighs, stroked her bushy mound through the fabric.

"Why do you wear so many clothes?" Lin murmured.

Eric lifted his mouth.

"I-I don't know," she stammered.

Lin's finger pressed into her. Eric straddled her, unzipping his pants as he reclaimed her mouth roughly.

Lin climbed up onto the bed beside them. Forced panties, hose, and finger inside her.

Brandy gasped, spreading her legs wide. Wriggled as the fabric stretched, as Lin forced her finger deeper and deeper.

Eric grasped her nipples—kneading, pinching. His tongue raped her mouth. Her lips were bruised, throbbing. She moaned. He drew back, impaled her with his stormy blue eyes. "Nothing," he demanded. "For the rest of this trip. Nothing between you and your clothes."

Brandy swallowed. Nodded.

"Say it," he growled.

"I-I won't wear anything under my clothes!"

Eric grinned and swung his leg back. Stood up and shoved his pants down, kicking them into a corner.

"Such a hot, tight pussy," Lin whispered. "Show it to me. Show me, Brandy."

She slid off the bed and crouched between Brandy's legs.

Brandy fumbled with the waist of her hose, pushed them off, and her panties with them.

"*Show* me," Lin purred.

She parted her legs. Waited.

Lin shook her head. "No, *ma chère*." She grasped Brandy's calves. Stood.

Looking into Brandy's eyes, she guided Brandy's legs up onto the bed. Pushed her knees down against the coverlet roughly. Grabbed Brandy's hands and pressed them to either side of her swollen labia, pushing them apart. She licked her lips hungrily. "I said, *show* me." Her tongue sank into Brandy's pussy.

"Oh, God!" Brandy pressed her thighs down against the bed, scrabbled frantically with her fingers to expose even more of her pussy to Lin's hungry mouth.

Lin laughed throatily, sending wicked vibrations through Brandy's crotch. "Oh, God, yes."

Eric's fingers closed on her clit. He pushed back the folds that covered the reddened swell. Bent over and flicked his tongue across it.

Brandy's pussy convulsed.

Lin withdrew, sat watching. "Oh, yes." She murmured. "So beautiful." She slipped two fingers between the folds. "Come for me, *ma chère*. I want to see. I want to watch you come."

Brandy's pussy convulsed again at Lin's erotic words.

Eric milked her clit as he sucked.

Brandy moaned. Writhed. Cried out as Lin's fingers pressed into her sweet spot. "What's this?" Lin asked. She crooked her fingers again and again, stroking rapidly.

"Oh, God!" Brandy gasped. Arched. Moaned wildly. She tried to buck, but Eric's hands held her hips, kept her still. Her pussy flooded with juices. "Yes, Lin. Yes!"

Pleasure slammed through her belly. Her pussy sucked frantically at the fingers buried inside it. "*Ah, oui, bebe. Suce-moi,*" Lin whispered. *Oh, yes, baby. Suck me.*

Eric raised his head. Tilted it so that he could watch, too. "Oh, baby," he breathed. "I wish you could see it. How horny you are. How much you want it."

It was too much. The way they talked, the way they watched. Another climax swept over her before the first one even finished.

Lin's tongue glided in alongside her fingers. Brandy arched again. Opened her mouth to scream, but Eric's hand covered it. "Easy, baby," he whispered in her ear. "Easy does it."

Brandy shuddered uncontrollably, thrashed against Lin's mouth. "That's it, baby," he murmured. "That's it. Let it out."

Finally, the climax ebbed.

Eric moved his hand from her mouth. Lin climbed up onto the bed. Brandy couldn't look at them. She closed her eyes, felt tears seeping out.

"What's wrong, *belle?*" Lin asked.

Brandy shook her head.

"Tell us," she murmured. Their hands stroked her belly lightly.

Brandy had never been so scared. They created such a heat in her. Such need. Everything she did with them was so intense. "I… I don't understand why…I…want you so much. How you can…" She shuddered.

"Make you feel so good?" Eric asked.

Lin nodded.

"Trust me, *belle*. We know what you need." Lin's lips brushed Brandy's earlobe as she swept two fingers across Brandy's lip. "Taste me," she whispered. "Taste *you*."

Brandy opened her mouth. Madeleine's salty fingers brushed across her tongue. Brandy whimpered, closed her mouth. Sucked her essence from them. Searched out the tiny reservoirs of thick cream gathered beneath the tips of Lin's perfect manicure with her tongue and swallowed them down.

Their lips found her nipples, kissed them lightly. Brandy moaned, sucked harder. Lin laughed. "You want more?"

Brandy nodded.

Their hands slid across her quivering belly. Two fingers eased slowly, gently, into her slit. Brandy moaned, arched, pussy spasming. They swept their fingers round and round, then brought them to her lips.

Brandy licked, sucked...ate herself from their fingers. She reached out, ran her hand along Eric's waist, sought Madeline's damp crotch with her fingers. They caught her hands, pushed them gently away. "Please," Brandy moaned. "I want to touch you."

"In due time," Eric murmured.

Their fingers sank into her cunt once more. Moving slowly, sensuously, in and out, while their tongues danced across her breasts, her belly, her bush, to caress her clit again. Together.

Brandy couldn't take it. With a sharp cry, she arched. Brought her thighs together, forcing them to relinquish her clit.

Lin's voice in her ear. "Wait, Brandy."

Eric. "Open your legs, baby. Let us see again."

Eager hands, forcing her legs apart. Entwined fingers, deep inside her, caressing, fondling. Brandy arched again, cried out, clutched at the bed as spasm after spasm rocked her body.

"Mmmm, yes," Madeleine purred. "Look at it, Eric. I told you her pussy would be beautiful."

Brandy whimpered, bucked.

"That's it," Eric whispered. "Fuck us, baby." His voice trembled. "Suck us again with that perfect pussy."

Brandy thrust one last, desperate time and was lost, riding a relentless wave of sensation that knocked the breath from her.

"Yes, baby. Yes!" Her lovers stroked her thighs. Used their hands to gather her pussy tight around their fingers while she milked them over and over.

Brandy collapsed against the bed, gasping for breath. Eric and Lin eased their fingers from inside her and joined her on the bed. Brandy opened her eyes, stared at the ceiling. "Oh, God."

"Are you all right?" Eric asked.

"No," she said. She remembered Lin's words from earlier in the day. "*I'm* not the drug; you are. And I'm already an addict."

They chuckled, and wrapped their arms around her.

They thought she was being funny, but she was totally serious. When she was with them, all restraint seemed to fly out the window. She thought she might do just about anything for them, if they asked her, and she'd known them less than twenty-four hours. It was frightening.

She wished she knew how it felt for them. They seemed to be enjoying themselves, but they were so much more in control than she was. If this was just a game for them, she could wind up being seriously hurt in the long run.

But she didn't send them away.

She rested for a while, lying between them, savoring their presence. Eventually, she sat up. Scooted off the bed and turned to face them. Reaching behind her, she pulled the elastic band from her braid.

They watched, reclining like cats after a kill. And she wanted to sate them.

She drew her long braid over her shoulder. Pulled her fingers between the strands, gasping softly as they brushed across her breast.

Eric shifted restlessly. Lin drew her own fingers across her chest, pausing to play with a nipple as she watched.

Brandy worked her pale blond hair loose, shook the gossamer strands out so that they flowed across her breasts, her belly, her buttocks. Untamed, her hair reached the middle of her thighs.

"So beautiful," Eric whispered hoarsely.

She stepped forward. Climbed onto the bed and sat between them, facing them. She eyed them both, then bent over Eric, letting her hair fall like a curtain around them. "May I kiss you?" she whispered.

Eric nodded, speechless for the first time since she'd met him. She pressed her lips to his, ran her tongue along their muted, masculine curves. Planted tiny kisses at their corners, then across his cheek and along the strong line of his jaw, down his neck to just above his Adam's apple. He swallowed, hard, and Brandy was glad her hair hid her look of triumph. She sat up, allowed her gaze to travel to his stiff shaft. "Can I touch now?"

He nodded. Brandy ran her fingers over his straining erection.

He groaned and caught her hand in his. Sat up and pushed her back against the bed. "I'm sorry, baby," he said. "I can't wait any longer."

Brandy parted her legs. He slipped his ripe head between her throbbing lips, slipped it out. Slipped it in again, just burying the tip.

Brandy caught her bottom lip in her teeth. Started to thrust against him. He drew back. "No, baby," he whispered. "This time we're taking it slow. Slow and easy."

He rocked his hips shallowly, barely penetrating her pussy with each thrust. Brandy heard herself making inarticulate, needy sounds. Protesting. Begging. Eric persisted, his gaze locked on hers.

The pressure built slowly, so slowly that Brandy didn't know it was there until she felt her body shudder, her pussy clench. Eric's eyes glazed with satisfaction. He buried himself all the way with one slow, smooth motion. Her belly clenched, her pussy grasping his thick member again and again as she climaxed, his hot seed warming her soul.

It was over too soon. Brandy moaned in disappointment as he climbed from between her legs. Then she remembered Madeleine and sat up shakily.

Lin was lying on her side, stretched out on the bed, watching them. Brandy reached out, brushed her fingers across one of the hard pebbles outlined by Madeleine's dress. She looked into those hazel eyes, dreaming of jungles and lazy sex on a hot afternoon. She caressed Lin's shoulders, pushed her straps down over her arms. Grasped the neckline and drew the clinging fabric down along her body, until it slipped off and dropped off the edge of the bed to the floor.

She was naked beneath, her copper bush glittering in the room's light. Brandy touched the silky curls, drew her fingertips through them. Madeleine sighed, parted her legs, her gaze never leaving Brandy's face.

She reached down and parted her curls. Exposed her pale clit.

Brandy drew the tip of one finger delicately across it. Madeleine shivered. Her response sent a spiral of heat through Brandy's groin.

Brandy moved, knelt between Madeleine's legs. Rubbing Lin's clit in a circular motion, she felt it swell beneath her touch. Lin's eyes closed, her hips pressing up against Brandy's fingers. Her wet slit gleamed invitingly.

Brandy slid the tip of one finger inside. Lin arched, driving her finger deeper. Her pussy clenched, and Brandy's spasmed in response. She grinned in delight, pressed another finger into that warm, wet cavern.

It was different, touching another woman's body. She had to listen, to watch, to know what Lin felt. She didn't know Lin's body the way she knew her own. She had to explore. Investigate.

In the past, the thought of touching another woman would have made her cold, turned her off. With Lin, the thought had caused her pussy to throb, set her nipples aching. Actually doing it was driving her wild. Each unexpected spasm of her lover's pussy on her questing fingers sent a bolt of desire shooting through her, each soft moan was a reward she wanted to earn again and again.

She searched with those fingers. Searched for that magic place. When Lin gasped and arched into her, she felt a surge of triumph.

Slowly, eagerly, she massaged. Tickled. Rubbed. Madeleine writhed, moaning, her pussy clenching erratically.

Her cheeks flushed. A fine sheen appeared on her body. Instinctively, Brandy moved her fingers faster and faster. When Madeleine gasped and held her breath, Brandy intuitively buried her fingers as deep as they would go, slowing her rhythm but pressing *hard.*

Madeleine's legs came together, her thighs closing on Brandy's forearm, squeezing. She thrust, over and over, crying out inarticulately in French.

Her pussy wrung Brandy's fingers, each spasm a fierce, desperate embrace. Brandy gasped, felt an answering heat in her groin.

Madeleine thrust out a hand, grasping, seeking. Brandy parted her legs, guided Lin's fingers into her convulsing pussy.

Writhing, moaning, they came together.

When it was over, Lin pushed up onto her elbows, stared down at Brandy with laughing eyes. "Does the idea of two women still bother you?"

"Yes." She wiggled her still-buried fingers, thrilled to see Madeleine's eyes glaze with desire. "It's definitely got me bothered." She leaned forward, dragging her tongue through the tart juices seeping from between her fingers.

"Hot," she whispered.

She covered Lin's clit with her mouth, sucked lightly for a moment, then let go. "And bothered," she purred.

Lin laughed. "We've created a monster!" She shifted, easing Brandy's fingers from her pussy. She patted the bed between her and Eric. "Come here."

Brandy moved, reclining on the bed between them. Eric reached out and turned off the light. A wave of exhaustion washed over her. "Thank you," she murmured sleepily.

"Thank *you,*" they replied simultaneously, sounding amused.

Brandy wanted to stay awake, to cuddle, but sleep beckoned and she tumbled into its embrace.

## Chapter Four: Her Lovers' Arms

Brandy woke in a place she hadn't expected to be.

Her lovers' arms.

It was a warm, safe, delicious place. She savored the unexpected pleasure. She'd thought they would be gone when she awoke.

It was so very nice to be wrong.

She sighed contentedly. Opened her eyes to find Eric watching her indulgently.

He smiled. "Good morning."

Brandy stretched, grinned. "'Morning."

He cupped her chin. Kissed her. She could still taste herself on his lips. On hers.

Madeleine stirred against her back. Her hand crept around Brandy's waist. Brandy covered that hand with hers, entwined her fingers with Lin's.

Lin propped herself up on one arm. Pushed Brandy's pale hair aside and kissed the rapidly beating pulse in her neck.

"'Morning, love," she murmured.

"You stayed," Brandy whispered huskily.

Madeleine smiled. "Did you think we wouldn't?"

"I didn't know."

Eric grasped a handful of her hair, tickled her belly with it. "Didn't we promise to spend every possible moment with you?"

"We never break a promise," Lin purred.

Brandy stretched luxuriously.

"I'm hungry," Eric announced.

"Me, too," Brandy said, then laughed as her stomach rumbled.

"Then let's get going," Lin urged. "Cozumel is glorious. We don't want to miss it."

They left, promising to meet Brandy in the dining room after they freshened up. Brandy took a quick shower, then put on her bikini and pulled a pair of shorts and a t-shirt on over it. Grabbing a bag, she tossed in a couple of towels and a change of clothes for dinner. Her hair needed a good brushing, but that would take too long. She tied a bandana around it. That would have to do. She tugged on a pair of socks and sneakers, and headed out.

They took the day trip out to Tulum to visit the Mayan temples. It was a wonderful experience, as it turned out that Madeleine was also a closet archaeologist, very knowledgeable about the ancient ruins, and acted as Eric and Brandy's own private tour guide. Brandy had learned a lot, too, researching ancient art for Kendall's new venture, and they had lively discussions about the architecture and intricate designs.

Afterward, they stopped at Xel-Ha, swimming and snorkeling in the lagoon and eating dinner at one of the five restaurants.

Returning to the ship just before seven, they relaxed together in the bar. Brandy embarrassed herself by nodding off, lulled by her drink and the quiet hum of conversation. She started when Eric touched her shoulder. Blushed. "I'm sorry," she stammered. "I guess all the unaccustomed activity is getting to me."

"Don't worry about it."

"I'm so busy at home, but it's a different kind of rush. Paperwork, phone calls, back and forth between the shops. It's more of a mental exercise."

Lin nodded sympathetically. "I know exactly what you mean." She glanced at her watch. "Besides, it's nearly ten; are we ready to call it a night?"

"Ten? Really?" The evening had passed so pleasantly, Brandy hadn't even realized it was that late.

Eric stretched and nodded. "I'm ready." He stood, crooked his elbows. "Shall we?"

Brandy stood, snaked her hand through one arm. Lin took the other.

Brandy managed to unlock the door herself this time. Eric and Lin hesitated at the threshold. She looked at them. Grinned impishly. "We *are* going to fuck again, aren't we?"

Their eyes flashed. They stepped inside. Brandy shut the door and locked it, tossing her key on the nightstand and dropping her bag to the floor. Eric stepped up behind her.

She'd left the closet door open that morning. Eric's eyes met hers in the mirror as he began unbuttoning the navy blouse she'd changed into for dinner. He smiled when the fabric parted, revealing her firm, bare breasts.

Lin knelt on the floor, then grasped the waistband of her loose skirt and slipped it down over her hips. She smiled, too, when she saw that Brandy had absolutely nothing on underneath. "Where are your panties?" she murmured teasingly.

"You told me not to wear them."

"And that was important to you?"

"Yes," Brandy whispered.

"Good girl," Eric murmured in her ear.

Lin stood, slipped out of her sundress.

Eric pulled off his pants, his shirt. Tossed them in a corner.

Lin picked up the brush from the nightstand and sat on the bed. "Come here."

Brandy climbed onto the bed, sat in front of her. Lin untied the bandana. Starting at the bottom, she ran the brush through Brandy's hair.

It took an hour, the two of them alternating, for Lin and Eric to brush all the tangles out of her pale mane. Lin's deft hands caught it up, held it, worked it into a neat French braid. She held out a hand. Eric raised his eyebrows questioningly. Brandy pointed toward the bathroom. "There's one by the sink."

He came back, handed Lin the elastic band, which she quickly wrapped around the tail of the braid. She rested her hands on Brandy's shoulders, drew them down along her arms, sending shivers through her spine. She grasped her wrists, brought them around behind her. Brandy waited breathlessly.

Eric picked up the bandana. Looked into Brandy's eyes as he reached behind her, tying her wrists together. Brandy drew in a shaky breath as he grasped her legs, guided her until she sat Indian-style, with her pussy bared.

Lin's hand came up, holding the brush. Turning it, she drew the stiff bristles across Brandy's nipples.

Brandy's breathing quickened. Lin brushed them again. And again.

It tingled at first. Then they grew very sensitive, starting to pulse painfully. Brandy moaned.

"Do you want me to stop?" Lin whispered. Brandy shook her head.

Eric toyed with his cock, his eyes locked on the tips of Brandy's reddened nipples.

Lin brushed harder. Faster. Brandy gasped, thrusting out her breasts. Leaning into the exquisite torture.

Her nipples stung. Burned. Sent bolts of fire spiraling into her groin. She moaned, shivering as a spasm wracked her body.

Eric reached out, took the brush from Lin's hand. Then turned it and thrust the handle into Brandy's pussy.

She arched. Lin grabbed her braid, forced Brandy back, over her bent knee.

Eric pumped the brush in and out—rapid, rough. Brandy gasped. Cried out softly.

"It's what you want tonight, isn't it, Brandy?" Lin said huskily. "What you need? Fast and hard?"

"Yes!" Brandy sobbed. "God, yes!"

Lin's teeth closed on her nipple. Brandy cried out her name. Eric buried the brush deep inside her. Grabbed her clit. Squeezed. Twisted.

She opened her mouth. "Don't scream," Lin warned.

She was reduced to uttering soft, animalistic cries as alternating storms of fire and ice wracked her body. It was one of the most amazing orgasms she'd ever experienced.

"Oh, God," she sobbed when it was over.

"Too rough?" Eric asked.

Brandy stared at him in disbelief. "God, no." She took a deep breath, shuddered. "You both make me feel so good." She smiled, closing her eyes. "You keep fucking me like that, and I'm your slave forever."

She didn't see the pregnant glance the couple shared.

She opened her eyes when Lin turned her gently to untie the bandana. Brandy brought her arms around, rolled her shoulders. "All right?" Lin asked.

"I'm fine."

Lin turned out the light and the three of them cuddled, caressing each other softly in the dark.

## Chapter Five: Alone in a Crowd

Belize, Cristobal, and Montego Bay passed in a blur. They spent every day together. The three of them had so much in common—similar musical likes and dislikes, similar political views. Common interests. It was as though they had been together all their lives. Brandy was pleased to find that sex wasn't the only thing tying them together. Some nights, they didn't touch each other at all, simply holding on to one another as they drifted off.

She found out that Eric's parents were both French, but he had been born and raised in the states. Madeleine had lived in France all her life, until they met when Eric was on a hiking vacation his senior year in college. Which explained why Eric spoke French, but only rarely, and had no trace of an accent, while Madeleine spoke French often—and why she spoke it more frequently and with a thicker accent when she was upset. Or aroused.

She discovered they lived in Galveston, as well.

It was good news, and bad. Brandy felt something growing inside, a feeling of contentment, of belonging. She very strongly suspected she was falling in love, and she dreaded the trip's end. Dreaded finding out they didn't feel the same. If they had lived somewhere else, somewhere far away, it would have been easier to part at the end of the trip. Now, if they didn't want to see her...she pushed those thoughts away. Whatever happened, nothing would erase the glory of these days—the sense of joy she felt, the memories they made.

The last port of call before returning to Galveston was Georgetown, Grand Cayman. The three of them pored over brochures at breakfast as they tried to decide for certain what they were going to do.

"I vote for Stingray City," Eric said. "There's nothing better than swimming with a bunch of mantas."

"Have you been there before?" Brandy asked.

Eric looked embarrassed. "Uh, no. I've just heard that."

"Oh." Brandy read the brochure again. "Well, that's fine with me. What do you think, Lin?"

Lin nodded. She'd been unusually quiet the last couple of days and seemed to be in the same mood this morning. Brandy wondered if she was dreading the end of the trip, as well.

They returned to their rooms to change into swimsuits. Brandy pulled on a lightweight sundress over hers and slipped on some sandals, then grabbed her bag. Together, they met with another couple that were visiting the same location and went ashore. They caught a taxi and chatted amiably as they rode along, Eric and Brandy providing the bulk of the conversation.

When they arrived, Eric and Brandy opted for sunbathing and swimming first, Madeleine trailing along with them. Brandy searched out a sunny spot, instinctively heading away from the couples with children, settling down among people who were so wrapped up in each other that they were oblivious to anyone else. She stretched out on a towel, Lin and Eric to either side.

Feeling mischievous, she sat up and rummaged in her bag for her sunscreen. Eric was lying on his stomach. She squirted a trail of lotion down his back. Eric grunted and opened his eyes, glancing back at her. "Hey!"

Lin opened her eyes. Brandy winked at her. "You look like you're burning." Brandy explained innocently. "I thought you might need some sunscreen."

Madeleine laughed, a rich, throaty chuckle.

Eric grinned. "I see. Carry on, then."

Brandy rubbed the pale cream into his dark skin. He really was magnificent. Their days at sea had deepened his tan, and he positively radiated health and vitality. She knew now that her first guess had been correct. He was forty, yet he was healthier and younger-looking than many men *her* age. Sexy. Sensuous.

Finished with his back, she applied lotion to his thighs. Ran her hands up under his trunks and massaged his firm butt. Moisture gathered between her legs as she ran her hands over the taut muscles.

"Mmmm. That feels good."

She rubbed the lotion in, shocking herself by running her hands between his cheeks, cupping his balls in a public place, in broad daylight. She shivered with desire. Pictured herself pushing his trunks down, taking one of the enticing globes in her mouth. She shook her head. *Down, girl.* These two definitely brought out the minx in her. She glanced around. No one was watching. No one cared.

She sat back, dried her hands on her towel.

Madeleine watched her, a hand shading her eyes. "Are you going to do me?" she asked.

Brandy grinned. "Definitely." She squirted a mound of lotion into her hand and started with Lin's legs, massaging her calves and thighs, becoming increasingly aroused as her hands approached the bottom of Lin's suit, unable to turn her gaze away from the coppery strands that peeked out from beneath the fabric at the woman's crotch. Brandy stopped short of the skimpy bottom, finding herself breathing hard, her cheeks flushed.

She scooted up toward Lin's head. Holding the bottle a few inches above her chest, she drew a pattern of milky white dots across the swell of her breasts. Setting the bottle aside, Brandy reached out and ran her hands through the lotion, up under Lin's chin, mesmerized by the woman's hypnotic tiger eyes. Brandy began scribing slow circles across Lin's chest, moving lower and lower, until her fingers were massaging the round upper swells and her palms were grazing the tips of Lin's swollen nipples through the fabric of her suit. Lin drew in a deep breath, those nipples pressing into Brandy's hands. Brandy swallowed as she trailed her fingers across them, awed at how large the swollen protrusions were. She glanced over at Eric, found him watching intently, a wide grin on his face.

Lin reached up and grabbed her hand, standing with one graceful movement. "Let's go swimming."

Brandy followed them into the water. Whenever they did something like this, it always amazed her that no one seemed to notice, that all the other vacationers remained oblivious to their actions, their arousal. But as she looked around, she realized they were all caught up in their own private worlds, whether with lovers or children or their own secret daydreams.

As the water covered their shoulders, Lin caught both Brandy's hands in hers and brought them up to the lower band of her swim top. Brandy worked the tips of her fingers under the fabric, sliding them up until she felt Lin's hard nipples and captured them between her middle and index fingers. Lin gasped, nodding as Brandy pressed her fingers together, then released. Pressed, then released.

Brandy sighed, leaning into Eric as he stepped behind her, his hands slipping beneath her own suit, his calloused fingers scratching roughly across her ripe peaks.

Lin's hand slipped between Brandy's legs, stroked her through her swimsuit. Brandy stared into those hazel-green eyes, letting Lin see how much she wanted them.

Beneath the waves, Eric pushed her bottoms down and placed his cock between her cheeks, like a hot dog in a bun. Brandy squirmed, wriggling against him. He thrust repeatedly, running his cock up and down between those buns, creating a tantalizing heat around her anus that threatened to melt her from the waist down.

Lin's fingers massaged her clit. Brandy reached out, pushed the crotch of Lin's swimsuit aside, and thrust her middle finger into Lin's pussy.

Lin gasped, arched. Her fingers grasped Brandy's clit. Milked her. Brandy bit her lip, holding back a cry.

Eric grasped her butt, pressing her cheeks tight against him as he thrust. Brandy wriggled her hand, found Lin's hot spot, and fingered-fucked her until they both came, pussies clenching fiercely. Her cheeks compressed against the stiff cock between them as she convulsed, and warmth blossomed across her lower back as Eric's seed spilled into the water.

His hand tightened painfully on her buttocks until his climax passed. He let go, drifting back in the water. Brandy and Lin shuddered one last time, let each other go. Brandy pulled up her bottoms, checked her top to make sure nothing was out of place.

She looked around. No one watched. No one pointed.

They floated on their backs, drifting, basking in the sun and the afterglow. Eventually, Eric herded them out of the water, took them over to Stingray City, where they fed the beautiful creatures from their own hands, watching as they sailed effortlessly through the water.

They didn't make love that night. Just held onto each other like drowning sailors. A bubble of dread bobbed and danced in Brandy's stomach. How was she ever going to let them go?

## Chapter Six: Just About Anything

The last two days of the trip were on open water, heading back toward Galveston. The trio spent the first day doing all the shipboard activities they hadn't tried yet—shuffleboard, water polo, dominoes. They chatted with other vacationers about their experiences, ate a light dinner, and spent the evening in Brandy's room, she and Lin reading a book together while Eric flipped through a magazine.

"We can't stay tonight," Eric said when Brandy stretched and yawned, announcing she was tired.

She froze. There were only two nights left. They weren't going to spend them together?

Lin rested a placating hand on her shoulder. "We've been neglecting our business. There are things we have to take care of before we get back."

Brandy shrugged, feigning unconcern. "It's all right. I understand."

Lin sighed. "We'll be busy tomorrow, too."

Brandy scooted off the bed, blinking back tears. So. It was just as she'd thought. This was a game for them. Not something they took seriously. Not something that might last once they got back to Galveston. "No problem." She walked over to the door, fumbled with the knob.

Eric's arms wrapped around her from behind. "I know what you're thinking, and you're wrong."

Brandy shook her head. "I'm not thinking anything."

"You are." He turned her around to face them.

Lin stood beside him, her arm around his waist. "We have something very important to discuss with you, but it has to wait."

"What is it?"

"It has to wait," Lin insisted.

"Tomorrow night," Eric promised. "Have dinner with us, and afterwards...we'll talk."

That tiny bubble of fear was now a hot-air balloon that threatened to swallow Brandy up and carry her away over dark waters. Still, they were going to an awful lot of trouble to try and calm her, if all they wanted was to call it quits.

"All right," she said. "I'll see you tomorrow."

She hadn't realized how tense they both were until they relaxed. "Good." Eric rested his forehead against hers. Brought her hand up to his lips and kissed it. "'Night, love."

He opened the door and stepped around her. Lin planted a soft kiss on her cheek. "Tomorrow, *ma chère*."

Brandy shut the door behind them, mulling over this new development.

They'd been too serious. Whatever was coming couldn't possibly be good.

* * *

They'd meant what they said. Brandy didn't see them at all the next morning. She spent the entire day wandering the ship aimlessly, unable to concentrate on anything, looking for them around every corner. Finally, she fled, hibernating in her room until it was time for dinner.

She dressed with trepidation, debating whether or not to wear undergarments. In the end, she left them off. Even when the three of them were just sitting on deck, passing the time platonically, Eric or Lin's glance would sometimes rest on her breasts, her crotch. They would smile, meet her eyes, their gazes heavy with the secret knowledge of her nakedness. It made them happy.

Brandy thought she might do just about anything to make them happy.

Dinner was a noisy, raucous affair. The captain's table rang with laughter and toasts. Brandy sat to Lin's left, trying to enjoy it, but her stomach was in knots, and she felt only relief when Eric and Lin finally stood.

She joined them, said her goodbyes.

They walked to either side of her, arms around her waist, as they headed for her cabin.

Once inside, Brandy sat on the edge of the bed. Waited.

For the first time since she'd met them, they seemed nervous. Uncertain.

"Please," she rasped. "Just say it."

When they did speak, their words were nothing she ever would have expected.

"You know we're a little different from other couples."

Brandy snorted. "Uh, yeah. I kinda had that figured out."

"We're Dominants, Brandy. As in, Dominants and submissives."

Her brain heard the words, but couldn't quite believe them. She waited for more.

"You know what that means, right?" Eric asked.

"Not really."

Lin sighed, sat on the floor. Eric claimed the tiny chair next to the bed.

"BDSM," Lin said. "You know what that is, right?"

Brandy started to nod her head, changed it to a shake. "Not really. I mean, people use the word. I've heard it. But do I know what it really means?" She shrugged. "Huh-uh." She brought her legs up onto the bed, hugged her knees. "You're starting to worry me, though."

Lin took a deep breath. "Okay." She reached into the purse she was carrying. Brandy had a moment to wonder what the heck she was doing with a purse—she never carried one. She brought out a sheaf of papers, held them in her hands while she talked. "Simplistic definitions, then. B, D. Bondage and discipline. You know what bondage is." She looked at Brandy.

"That one, I know."

"Discipline. That's two-fold, really. It's self-discipline, as in training yourself to act in certain ways. To react in certain ways. To follow the rules."

"And it's punishment." Eric's voice was deep and husky. "When those rules are broken."

Brandy's pulse pounded in her ears. What were they getting at?

"D, S. Dominance and submission." Lin said. "Submission, that's giving up control. Of yourself, or of certain aspects of your life. It's something that has to be worked out, between you and the person or persons that dominate you."

"Dominance is…well, lots of people have the wrong idea. It's not just controlling another person. It's taking on their burdens, their worries. Making their wants and needs—their welfare—your own. We do the same thing for our submissives as they do for us—just in a different way. Domination is a way of…releasing a person to feel." She struggled for clarity. "You were so tense when we met you. So burdened. We felt that. We sensed that you needed what we have to give, whether you knew it or not. To unburden yourself. To…open your soul to passion. Love."

"Do you understand? Or are you just thinking this is a load of crap?" Eric interjected

"I-I don't know."

He sighed. "S and M," he continued. "Sadism. Masochism. Simply put, sadism is one person's enjoyment of another's pain. Masochism is—"

"The enjoyment of one's own pain." Brandy finished for him. She swallowed hard. "Like us. Like what we do, sometimes, when we're together."

Eric nodded.

"In our case…" Lin broke off, mumbled to herself in French. The thickness of her accent was a measure of how much this meant to her. She went on. “In our case, the S also stands for sodomy.”

Brandy’s little bubble lodged itself in her throat. “What?”

“Anal penetration,” Eric provided roughly. “We both enjoy it. Doing it. To others.”

Brandy drew in a shaky breath. “Oh.” Was that what this was all about? They were asking her to have that kind of sex with them? “I… I don’t know how I feel about that.”

Lin nodded. “That’s one of the reasons we needed to talk.” She looked at Eric. “Eric and I are a Dominant couple. That means we’re both Dominants.” She turned back to Brandy. “We belong to a group in Galveston, a dungeon. We meet submissives there. Play with them. Sometimes it lasts a while, but never too long. We haven’t met the right person.”

Eric leaned forward. “Until now.”

Brandy couldn’t swallow past that lump in her throat. “I’m not sure I understand where all this is going.”

Lin looked down at the papers in her hand. “We… I can’t tell you how much you’ve come to mean to us in the past few days.” Her accent was so thick, Brandy had a hard time making out the words. “This is a contract. It’s a document that states the kinds of things we would expect from you, if you wanted to continue this relationship when we get home. There are places in here where you tell us what you expect, as well. What your limits are. For example, for us the anal sex is non-negotiable. If that’s not something you could participate in, then—”

Anger flared in Brandy’s chest. “Let me get this straight. You want to *hire* me? As some sort of freaking sex slave?”

Spots of red appeared on Lin’s cheeks. “No!”

Eric stood, towering over her. "Brandy. Dominance and submission is a radical lifestyle, one that shouldn't be embraced if both parties aren't clear on exactly what's involved. We're trying to tell you that we really like you. A lot. But there are things you need to know, things you have to consider, and the contract helps spell them out.

That doused her rage. "You still want to see me?" she whispered. "After we get home?" Relief flooded her, but it was tempered by confusion and wariness.

"Yes."

"But this is the kind of couple we are," Lin explained. "The kind of relationship we have to have."

Eric squatted by the bed. "We've only been *playing* at dominance and submission on this trip, baby. We didn't want to frighten you away. If this relationship continues once we're back in Galveston, it's a whole new ballgame."

Lin stood. Handed her the papers. "You should read these. Think about it."

Eric tapped the pile. "Our address is in there. If you haven't decided by tomorrow morning, you can call."

Brandy shook her head. Closed her eyes. Her mind whirled. "I-I need some time."

"Of course."

Brandy opened her eyes. Eric moved as though to embrace her, but Lin touched his arm. Shook her head. He backed away. "There's no time limit, Brandy," he said.

"We're willing to wait," Lin added.

Brandy nodded. They hesitated a moment longer, then turned and went out, shutting the door carefully behind them.

Brandy stared at the floor. She was so relieved that they still wanted to see her…but what had she gotten herself into?

She shivered. Looked down at the papers in her hand. Began to read.

## Chapter Seven: Their Little Secret

*Someone was nibbling on her ear, whispering sweet endearments in French. Brandy shifted restlessly, felt their breath on her neck. A rush of warmth swept through her body, and she moaned. She needed something, but she wasn't quite sure what that something was. Maybe the questing fingers in her pussy. Brandy moaned again. Yes, that was it…*

*"Kiss me,* ma chère,*" Madeleine whispered. A tongue teased her lips. Brandy opened her mouth. "That's it,* mon amour.*" Their tongues danced together intimately. Madeleine's teeth were so smooth, her breath fresh and sweet. Brandy sighed, opening her legs, moving into the woman's touch. "Oh, yes, my love," Madeleine breathed. Brandy gasped as Madeleine fingers found her sweet spot. "Is that it, my love?" Brandy gasped again as Madeleine probed, thrusting her hips eagerly. "Oh, yes," Madeleine whispered against her lips. "That's it, isn't it?"*

*A masculine touch. Eric's mouth on her breast. Brandy rocked her hips frantically. Eric's hand slid down her belly, joining Madeleine's between her legs. He pushed another finger into her, stretching her, hurting her. But it felt good. A breathless sob escaped her. "Come for us, Brandy," Madeleine whispered. "I want to feel your pussy tightening on my fingers."*

*"Do it, Brandy," Eric forced their fingers deeper. Brandy gasped and arched. "Come now!"*

*Brandy tossed her head from side to side, moaning. She tried, but she couldn't do what he wanted. He chuckled. "I know what you need," he said.*

*"We know what you need," Lin echoed.*

*Their fingers slid from her pussy. Snaked their way between the cheeks of her ass. Eric lay across her stomach, immobilizing her, as he and Lin thrust deep inside her—*

Brandy woke abruptly, covered in sweat. Every part of her body ached for their touch, and yet that last image. She shivered. Glanced at the clock.

Five a.m. She'd only been asleep for twenty minutes.

To hell with it. She climbed out of bed, went into the bathroom, and started a shower, as hot as she could stand it.

Standing under the rushing water, she remembered thinking the day before that she would do anything to please Eric and Lin.

Anything.

The contract hadn't been as bad as she'd thought. Actually, it had excluded a lot of things that she'd never even thought about. Like golden showers. Or knife play.

She shivered. Who the hell would enjoy knife play?

But some things concerned her. The anal sex, for one. She wasn't a prude, but that was one thing she'd never wanted to try. In her mind, anal sex was for bad guys. Guys who wanted to hurt the woman they were with.

Well, that was part of it, wasn't it?

She groaned. Rubbed her tired eyes. That was another thing that bothered her. The idea that pain turned her on. She'd let Eric and Lin pinch her nipples until they were purple. Fuck her with a brush. The pain was never too much. They seemed to know instinctively exactly what she needed, how much she could take.

And she enjoyed it. Hell, if she was honest with herself, each experience left her craving even more.

Maybe that's what was so scary. Would they honor the boundaries? Reading through the contract last night, Brandy had come to what was, for her, a stunning realization. The boundaries were as much for her as for them. In the grip of a passion like she'd experienced on this trip, she really might be tempted to try anything. Something like this could escalate into…she shook her head. What?

She still hadn't decided what to do. She thought she might love them, but she wasn't sure. It was all so new, so different. At home, in the midst of her normal life, would she regret the things she'd done on this trip?

Could she live with that kind of intensity on a permanent basis?

The water was getting cold. Brandy turned it off. Stepped out and dried herself briskly. She might as well finish packing. There was no way she was going to be able to go back to sleep.

When the ship pulled into port, most of her fellow travelers had gathered in the ballroom. Brandy stood on the fringes of the crowd, searching for Eric and Madeleine, yet scared to death she might actually find them. What would she say?

The captain stepped up to the mike and cleared his throat. "On behalf of E. M. Enterprises, I'd like to thank you for taking this maiden voyage." He gestured to his right. "And now the owners themselves would like to say a word or two."

Brandy heard a rushing in her ears as Eric and Madeleine Brogan stepped up onto the platform and moved as one to the mike. *E. M. Enterprises. Eric and Madeleine.* A confused murmur rippled through the crowd. She listened in disbelief as Madeleine spoke. "Eric and I want to thank you all for giving this little venture of ours a try." She smiled. "And we'd like to apologize for pulling the wool over your eyes. We wanted to take the trip this first time the same way you did. Figure out what worked and what didn't. Have a chance to hear your uncensored opinions. And in return for acting as an unknowing focus group, we'll be refunding all of you three hundred dollars of the cost of your cruise. The checks will be in the mail next week." A cheer went up. "Thank you again, and if you enjoyed the cruise, please be sure to let your friends know." Madeleine smiled her dazzling smile, and the crowd pressed forward, eager to rub elbows with the owners.

Brandy turned and pushed her way through the crush, tears nearly blinding her. So much of what they were asking of her depended on trust. How could they have kept this from her? How could she trust them, now?

* * *

Brandy leaned against the counter, staring out at the people passing by on the boardwalk. The girl they had hired to cashier at Lady had called in sick, so Brandy was filling in for her until three, when Kendall would be back from the field trip she'd gone on with the kids' kindergarten class. Sutter was going to close the shop then and take the kids home so Kendall could work until closing. It was so slow today, though, they probably could have closed and been just fine. Brandy sighed, thinking about all the things she needed to be doing.

As always whenever she was idle, her thoughts turned to Eric and Madeleine.

Knowing that they were E. M. Enterprises had explained a lot of things. Why their table assignments had never changed, as others had. The permanent VIP pass to the captain's private club. Maybe even the type of people that frequented the club. Bold about their sexuality, oblivious to the kinds of things Eric and Lin had done to her.

However, despite her sense of betrayal, she couldn't seem to rid herself of thoughts of them. She woke up in the middle of the night, expecting their warm hands upon her skin, and met only the chill breath of her air conditioning. Saw their faces, heard their voices, like ghosts, whenever her mind wasn't occupied. Groaning, Brandy pushed back from the counter and began pacing the floor. It was too damn slow today. Not enough to keep her busy. She definitely had to get a hobby. Maybe cross-stitching.

She looked up as the bell on the door jangled.

"Auntie B!" The twins ran up and threw their arms around her legs.

"Hey, monsters!" She grinned, hugged them tight. "How was the field trip?"

"Cool!" Race pronounced.

Kendall sat on the stool behind the counter. "How's it been?"

"Kind of slow." Tuesdays were notoriously slow, though, so it wasn't anything either of them would worry about.

Kendall nodded. "You going to stay and keep me company?"

Brandy started to say yes, then stopped. No, she decided on the spur of the moment. "Not today. I've got an errand to run."

Kendall looked at her quizzically, no doubt catching the odd note of strain in her voice. Good friend that she was, she sensed Brandy wasn't ready to talk about it, and didn't press for an explanation. "Okay. I'll see to you tomorrow, then?"

"Sure." Brandy grabbed her purse and keys and gave Kendall a hug. "Come on, kiddoes. Give Auntie B a goodbye kiss!"

After two sloppy kisses, she headed out the door and climbed into her car.

She pulled the contract out of her purse. Stared at the address. She'd memorized it a dozen times in the past few weeks, but now that she'd decided to make the next move, it flitted out of her head. Her resolve wavered. Should she or shouldn't she?

The ache in her head made the decision for her. She was a mess. Had been ever since they got back. It was time to either end it or jump in. She started the car and headed down to the wharfs.

The building that housed their offices was relatively new, bright and shining among the older buildings that surrounded it. Brandy stepped out of her car and locked it, staring up and the façade. She almost climbed back into the vehicle and drove away, but a persistent voice kept telling her to go on and get it over with. She walked across the parking lot and opened the door, welcoming the air conditioning as she stepped out of the hot July sun. Walking over to the elevators, she found the listing. Once in the car, she punched the button for the eighth floor and fidgeted nervously as the elevator climbed.

When it stopped, she stepped out and walked across a plush carpet to a set of tinted glass doors. Pushing them open, she stepped inside and approached the receptionist, who looked up at her questioningly.

Brandy cleared her throat. "Um, I don't have an appointment. But if you could just tell Eric or Madeleine—I mean, Mr. or Mrs. Brogan, that Brandy Mitchell is here, I—"

One of the doors behind the receptionist opened and a familiar melodious voice greeted her. "Brandy! What a surprise." Madeleine glided over to the receptionist. "Melanie, would you be so kind as to hold my calls for fifteen minutes?"

The secretary nodded, and Madeleine gestured for Brandy to follow her. Brandy looked around the office with curiosity as the door snicked shut behind her. Elegantly furnished in gleaming mahogany and jewel-toned fabrics, it was darkly provocative, like the woman now sitting behind the desk.

"Have a seat."

Brandy sat on the edge of a plump chair upholstered in soft, supple leather. She and Madeleine stared at each other for a moment, Brandy at a loss for words.

"What can I do for you?" Madeleine's calm expression revealed nothing. Brandy might almost be a client or a business associate Lin was meeting for the first time.

Swallowing hard, Brandy wondered just how bad a mistake she was making. Madeleine didn't seem to have missed her at all.

She twisted the bracelet on her wrist—a nervous habit. "I-I just wanted to…to see you."

"Have you signed the contract?"

Brandy did a double-take. "No, I—"

"Have you torn it up?"

"No!"

Madeleine stood gracefully and walked around the desk, leaning against it in front of Brandy. "Spread your legs," she said.

Brandy's jaw dropped. "What?"

"Spread your legs, Brandy. Now."

Brandy's legs jumped apart, seeming to have a will of their own. Madeleine squatted and lifted the edge of Brandy's skirt, peeking underneath. She shook her head and stood. "We told you never to wear anything under your clothes, Brandy. Come back tomorrow—without the panties and bra—and we'll talk." She turned and made her way back around the desk.

"You can't possibly be—"

"Have you *read* the contract?"

"Yes, but—"

"Then you know what's expected." Madeleine pressed a button on her phone. "Melanie, can you please send in my three-thirty now?" She released the button and met Brandy's gaze coolly.

Brandy grabbed her purse and stood, shaking in disbelief and anger. “How *dare* you?”

“This isn’t a game.” Madeleine sat down. “We told you how it would be. Spelled it out in black and white.” Brandy heard the door opening behind her. “There’s no sense investing our time and effort in a relationship that isn’t going to work.” Madeleine’s gaze never wavered. “Either tear up the contract, or sign it and follow the rules.”

Brandy stalked out of the office, pushing roughly past Melanie and the man standing just outside the door, waiting to come in. There was absolutely *no way* she was signing that contract now. No way.

## Chapter Eight: Undiscovered Country

And that's what she kept telling herself the next day. Every time she found herself watching the clock. Every time thoughts of Eric and Lin insinuated themselves into her mind. She tried to concentrate on the packing list before her, to match it up with the items she had just unloaded. But her eyes strayed back to the clock. Madeleine had said to come back today. It was four o'clock now. Their offices closed at five.

Brandy kept telling herself she could do this, she could stay away. Miss the deadline and tear up the contract.

And there was no doubt in her mind that what Lin had given her was a deadline, despite the fact that they'd told her on the boat that there was no time limit. Still, she couldn't expect them to wait forever.

Her body wasn't helping. Her pussy throbbed relentlessly as the minute hand crept forward. She closed her eyes, but that was even worse, her mind showing her images of Eric and Madeleine on the cruise—Madeleine's body swaying gracefully as she danced for Brandy, one naked breast gleaming. Eric grinning up at her as he rubbed lotion onto her thighs.

She *couldn't* do it. Brandy tossed the list down on her desk and stood. She checked to make sure the office door was closed, then reached beneath her short leather skirt. She pulled off her panties and stuffed them into her purse. Unbuttoning her blouse, she slipped off her bra and tucked that into her purse as well. She grabbed her keys and headed out the door. "I've gotta run," she called out in the direction of the shop proper, not waiting for Kendall's reply.

It was ten minutes before five when Brandy walked into the office. Melanie looked up from her computer screen. "You can go on in. She's expecting you."

At that, Brandy almost turned around and walked out. Was she really that transparent, that Lin was so sure she would come?

Ah, well, what did it matter? She *had* come.

Taking a deep breath, she crossed the room and opened the door, closing it softly behind her as she faced the woman behind the desk.

Madeleine looked up. "Brandy. I'm glad you came."

She walked over and sat down in the chair.

Madeleine eyed the naked, dark peaks visible through Brandy's white silk shirt. "What's it to be?" she asked softly, as though she didn't already know.

Brandy swallowed. Opened her purse. Took out the contract. "Do you have a pen?"

Madeleine's eyes blazed. With desire. Triumph. Relief. Brandy was gratified to see that she hadn't been so sure, after all. She held out a pen.

Brandy took it and shuffled through the papers. Signed the last page with a trembling hand.

"Are there any modifications we should be aware of?" Madeleine asked.

Brandy shook her head.

Madeleine stood, and Brandy waited breathlessly as the redhead walked around the desk. Without being told, Brandy parted her legs. Madeleine knelt beside her, reaching up under the skirt and feathering her fingers across Brandy's damp curls. "I missed you, *ma chère*. Missed your sweet pussy."

Brandy sighed softly as two fingers entered her, deftly finding her sweet spot. She closed her eyes. Madeleine's hand stilled. "No, Brandy. Look at me." Brandy opened her eyes. "You come into this with your eyes wide open, *ma belle*. No hiding." Brandy swallowed and nodded. Madeleine's fingers moved, and Brandy gasped, biting her lip as the pressure built inside her. She scooted closer to the edge of the seat, eyes locked on Madeleine's sultry gaze.

Madeleine played her like an instrument, brought her zooming to the top of a cliff, balanced on the peak. Her lips twitched, and she stopped.

"Oh, please," Brandy whispered. Smiling, Madeleine brought her to fruition with one quick stroke, and Brandy cried out, bucking wildly.

When it was over, Madeleine pulled out her fingers, brought them to Brandy's lips.

Brandy opened her mouth and surrounded Madeleine's slender fingers, licking her sticky juices from each digit. Madeleine breathed in sharply as Brandy began sucking gently.

"That's enough, *ma belle*, or you'll have me fucking you again on the desk."

Brandy raised her eyebrows. "What's wrong with that?"

Madeleine shook her head. Stood. "Friday night. Eight o'clock at the Four Horsemen. We'll have dinner, discuss some specifics. Begin the relationship properly." She smiled. "Eric's going to be very pleased."

Brandy stood. Realized she'd forgotten her purse and bent over to pick it up.

"Oh, my," Madeleine breathed. She pushed Brandy's skirt up to her waist, ran her hands over her buttocks. Her thumbs parted them, and Brandy flushed, knowing she was staring at the tight pucker. "I can't wait to play with *this*," she purred.

Brandy's immediate instinct was to stand and pull her skirt down. Madeleine had mentioned one of the things she was most apprehensive about. But her contract said that when she was alone with them, they controlled her every movement. And she had just signed it.

Time to start following the rules.

She waited. Madeleine sighed. "Eric's away on business. It's not right to play without him. Not until he knows." She pushed Brandy's skirt down. Patted her butt. "You may go now."

Brandy stood. Madeleine walked her to the door. Kissed her, long and deep.

Brandy's legs were trembling when she walked out, relieved to find that the secretary was gone, so there was no one to see her leave in such disarray.

## Chapter Nine: The Pleasure of Pain

The rest of the week dragged. Working with her in the office on Thursday night, frustrated by the third incorrect batch total in a row, even Kendall remarked on her obvious preoccupation.

"I'm sorry," Brandy said. "I met someone on the cruise." She took a deep breath. "Two someones, actually."

Kendall raised her eyebrows. Grinned. "Brothers?"

Brandy shook her head. Stared down at the tally sheet. "A couple. Eric and Madeleine Brogan."

"Brandy! That's wonderful!"

Brandy glanced up. "It is?"

Kendall appeared confused. "Isn't it?"

"Well," Brandy toyed with the papers in her hands. "Me…and another woman. I never would have pictured it." She eyed Kendall anxiously. "This isn't going to change our friendship, is it?"

Kendall looked shocked. "What, like I'm going to think you want to jump my bones all of a sudden?" She laughed. "You know better than that." She grabbed Brandy's hands, held them tight. "I want what's right for *you*. Do you love them?"

"Well…" She found herself reluctant to tell Kendall how she felt. It was still so new. She was afraid if she said the words aloud, the whole thing might vanish in a puff of smoke. "I like them a lot."

"So…is everything okay? I mean, you've been pretty distracted the last couple of days."

"It is now. It took me a while to come to terms with it."

"That's understandable. I went through that when I realized how I felt about Josh and Sutter." She grinned. "I'm a little more impetuous than you are, though. I don't think I worried about it so much."

"It's different for you, anyway. Two men is every woman's fantasy. It's acceptable, somewhat."

Kendall shrugged. "I'm not saying it's going to be easy. But it will be a lot more so if you're not dealing with your own doubts."

Brandy nodded. "I know. And I think I've come to terms with it. It's just… I'm so nervous." She couldn't quite bring herself to tell Kendall exactly what kind of relationship this was. Not yet, anyway. "We're meeting tomorrow night for dinner. Our first official date, in a way."

Kendall smiled. "I know it'll be great." She squeezed Brandy's hands, picked up the batch sheet. "Look, why don't I finish this up? You go home, get some rest. Take tomorrow off."

Brandy hesitated for a moment, then sighed. There was no way she was going to get anything productive done until tomorrow night was out of the way. "Okay." She grabbed her stuff and headed out the door. "Thanks, Kendall."

"No problem."

* * *

At three o'clock on Friday afternoon, Brandy took a deep breath and dialed E.M. Enterprises. "This is Brandy Mitchell. May I speak to Madeleine or Eric, please?" There was a faint click as she was transferred, and then Eric's rich tones.

"Brandy?"

"Eric. Hi!"

"Hi, yourself." He was quiet for a moment. "I was very happy to hear about your decision. We missed you."

"I missed you, too." She fidgeted with the phone cord.

"Is something wrong?"

"No! I just…is there something specific I should wear tonight?" *Or not wear.*

There was a brief silence, then, "I'd like to see that short leather skirt you wore for Madeleine. Do you have any tops that zip?"

Brandy thought for a moment. "I have a leather vest that—"

"That will do. The leather vest and the skirt." A note of warning crept into his voice. "Absolutely nothing else."

"Nothing?" Brandy squeaked. "But the vest isn't meant to be—"

"Nothing," Eric said firmly.

"All right." Brandy couldn't think of anything else to say. "So, I'll see you tonight."

"You certainly will," Eric replied, a hint of amusement in his voice.

Five hours later, Brandy walked into the restaurant right on the stroke of eight. She had been afraid to show up early. Madeleine had said eight o'clock, and Brandy had decided to take everything she and Eric said literally until she discovered whether there was ever any wiggle room. And of course, she hadn't dared show up late.

Eric and Madeleine were waiting for her at a secluded table on the balcony overlooking the main dining area. Brandy felt extremely self-conscious making her way to the table, feeling everyone's eyes on the tight leather skirt and the skimpy leather vest. She prayed they couldn't tell she didn't have anything on underneath them.

Eric stood and pulled out a chair. Brandy slipped into the seat.

Eric sat down and turned to her. "What are you wearing under those clothes?"

Brandy met his gaze. "Nothing, Eric."

Eric smiled. "I'm very pleased. However, there are always small things that are not spelled out in the contract." He raised a finger. "One. When we are in public, addressing us by our first names is acceptable, but when we're alone, you will refer to us as Master and Mistress. Understood?"

Brandy nodded.

Madeleine leaned forward. "Two. When we are…enjoying ourselves in public, or anyplace where we might be overheard, you must not cry out, no matter what we may do to you."

Brandy tilted her head in question.

"For example, the other day in my office, when you so obligingly shared your sweet pussy with me, you cried out. That is not acceptable."

Brandy sat up a little straighter. Swallowed. "I-I'm sorry, ma'am."

"Your punishment will be mild. However, you *will* be disciplined."

Brandy felt a tiny finger of ice creeping up her spine. It was easy to push the punishment portion of the relationship to the back of her mind, but now... "Still, you've pleased us very much, demonstrating how eager you are to do this right. By calling and asking how to dress, and by following those instructions to the letter." Her appreciative gaze raked over Brandy's body, until her pussy burned like a hot coal.

Eric dangled a small velvet bag in front of her. "So, we brought you a gift."

"A gift? Sir?"

Eric nodded. "Come with me."

Brandy stood and followed Eric down to the main floor and out to the bathrooms. When he pushed open the door to the men's room, she balked. "But...Eric, I can't go in there!"

Eric frowned. "But you will. Yes?"

Brandy subsided in the face of his displeasure. Nodded.

Once inside, Eric opened the bag and dumped its contents into his hand. "Unzip your vest."

Brandy did as she was told, glancing at the door nervously. Eric reached out and fastened something cold and very tight onto her right nipple. Looking down, Brandy saw a gold ring with a spring, pinching her nipple tightly, dangling from it. It didn't hurt at the moment, but she knew it would begin to sting as the evening wore on.

Eric fastened another ring to her left nipple and then with one sudden movement lifted her onto the countertop. He pushed her legs apart at the exact moment someone pushed open the bathroom door. The newcomer's mouth dropped open, eyeing them in surprise as he took in Brandy's bared breasts. "Way to go, man!"

Eric smiled. Watched Brandy. Her cheeks burned as the man did his business and left, grinning the whole time.

When he was gone, Eric pushed Brandy's skirt up above her waist and made her spread her legs wide. He rubbed her clit until it swelled. Then, squeezing the flesh beneath it to make it stand out, he fastened another of the rings to it. *That* stung. Brandy started to cry out, then remember Madeleine's warning and bit her lip to hold it back. Eric noticed and nodded approvingly. As he set her back on the floor, he whispered in her ear. "You're doing very well, Brandy. I can't tell you how happy we are to have you back with us."

That small bit of praise suffused Brandy with joy. The pain in her clit subsided. Eric reached out and zipped up her vest, then straightened her skirt. He took her hand and led her back to their table.

"Do you like your gifts?" Lin asked after they sat down.

"Very much, Lin," Brandy replied. "Thank you."

"Let me see."

Brandy's eyes widened. "Pardon?" Exhibitionism had been one of their listed preferences, but doing that on a cruise ship they owned was one thing. In a darkened club or under the surface of the water. In the bathroom. But here in the dining area? Granted, the lights were muted, and her back was to the rest of the room, but—

"Show me, Brandy," Madeleine insisted.

Brandy closed her eyes. Took a deep breath. Opened them. "Yes, Lin." She reached up, pulled down the ring attached to her zipper.

Eric reached over, brushing the flaps aside.

"Oh, yes," Madeleine breathed. "Very nice."

Eric put his finger through the nearest ring. Tugged. Brandy breathed in sharply as pain shot through her nipple, down into her belly. Her pussy clenched in response.

Eric let go. Pulled up her zipper.

"I ordered for all of us. Is that all right?" Madeleine asked.

Brandy nodded, not trusting her voice.

The waiter brought their drinks: iced tea for Lin and Brandy, draft beer for Eric. Brandy took a long drink from her glass.

Madeleine had ordered lasagna. Brandy waited while they started eating, not sure whether to ask permission to begin. Madeleine stopped. "For the purposes of dining out, you always have our permission to eat as soon as your meal arrives."

"Thank you." She began to eat, feeling stiff and self-conscious.

Eric set down his fork. "Brandy." His voice was deep. Concerned. "Relax, baby." He cupped her chin, made her look at him. "We want this to be wonderful for you. I hate seeing you wound so tight."

Brandy lowered her lashes. "I'm sorry. I'm just so afraid I'll make a mistake."

"You'll make mistakes," he pointed out gently. "So will we. It happens in any relationship. We'll learn from them and move on."

Brandy took a deep breath. Nodded. Eric studied her a moment more, then nodded as though satisfied.

She turned back to her plate. Took a few bites. Every time she moved, the leather vest brushed across her already tingling nipples, making them ache. And her clit was hot. Throbbing.

Madeleine's eyes met hers. The woman's lips parted in a simmering, sensuous smile.

Brandy started at a touch between her knees.

Madeleine watched her. Urged her legs apart with her foot. Brandy leaned back, scooted her butt to the very edge of the seat and spread her legs.

Lin's toes brushed over her clit. Brandy gasped. The contact sent a searing burst of pain and pleasure through her, flooding her with heat from the waist down.

Eric held out his hand. Brandy grasped it, squeezed tight as Lin worked a toe through the ring and tugged. It was all Brandy could do to keep from crying out.

Madeleine's eyes glittered. She tossed down her napkin. Looked at Eric. "I'm full," she said. "Are you ready to go?"

"Definitely."

Lin tugged on the ring again. "Brandy? Ready?"

"Yes, please," Brandy replied in a strangled tone.

Lin eased her toe from inside the ring. Brandy took a deep breath, breathed out slowly.

"Let's go." Lin stood. Brandy followed them out of the restaurant.

* * *

Their home was located in a very private, very exclusive residential area. They gave Brandy a quick tour of the ground floor. “It’s beautiful, Eric, Lin,” she said when they had returned to the foyer.

“Here, we are Master and Mistress,” Eric reminded her.

Brandy looked at the floor. “Yes, Master.”

Lin cupped her chin, drew her head up. “No lowering your eyes. We do expect you to do as you’re told, as you’ll be trained, but you’re *not* a slave. You’re an equal partner in this relationship. You must always look us in the eye.”

“Yes, Mistress.” Brandy found it incredibly difficult *not* to lower her eyes, but she managed it.

“Good.”

They took her hands, led her through a small door in Eric’s study, down a steep flight of steps. At the bottom was another door. This one, Lin unlocked with a key hung from the chain around her neck. She turned to Brandy. “This room, you never enter clothed.”

“Yes, Mistress.” Brandy’s hands shook as she unzipped her vest, let it drop to the floor, and shimmied out of her skirt.

Lin nodded. Pushed the door open and waved Brandy inside.

The room was filled with strange implements. Cages. Manacles. Oddly shaped couches and seats she couldn’t begin to imagine a use for. In a glass-faced cabinet, bright steel implements gleamed. For the first time, it hit her how very little she knew about this lifestyle. Reading about it on paper and facing the reality were two very different things.

She started trembling, and couldn't stop.

"Brandy!" Lin and Eric came to her, wrapped their arms around her.

"It's okay, baby," Eric murmured. "We'll take it slow, all the way, and we'll never do anything that hurts you."

She knew he meant a kind of pain she didn't want. Something outside of her limits. Still, she was no longer sure her limits approached anything like what they might want from her.

"Brandy," Lin whispered. "It's going to be all right, I promise."

They held her until the trembling subsided. When they stepped away, she blinked back tears, ashamed, but she gazed into their eyes, remembered not to look down. "I'm sorry, Mistress. Master."

"It's all right," Lin assured her.

"But there is the matter of your punishment. Not for this, but for crying out the other day, and for the tiny mistakes in address," Eric said.

Brandy felt another round of trembling coming on, but clenched her fists and refused to give in to it. "I understand, Master."

Eric led her over to a bench, made her lie back against it. He took her arms, pulled them back, under the bench, and fastened them in place with leather straps.

Lin did the same with her legs, fastening leather straps around her ankles, then pulling them up and back, watching until Brandy winced involuntarily. She nodded and did something that locked them in place.

Eric swung a bar out over her. It snapped into position with a clang. Brandy swallowed, tried hard not to let her apprehension show. Two chains hung from the bar, with two rather wicked-looking clamps swinging from the end.

Lin grabbed a chain. Pressed open the clamp. Eric squeezed her breast, making her nipple with its golden circle stand out prominently. Lin placed the clamp just below it. Let it close. Brandy gasped, but didn't cry out. Frowning, Lin reached out, turned a knob on its side.

The clamp tightened. Brandy gasped again. Lin turned the knob again. Brandy cried out, throbbing bursts of pain coursing through her. Lin nodded.

Eric did the same with her right breast. Understanding that he was going to tighten it as Lin had, until it hurt enough to make her cry out, she was tempted to fake pain with the first adjustment. But something inside wouldn't allow her to do that. Faking would be quitting before she even started. She thought back to that first day on the ship. To the incredible release of pressure she'd felt after that first, erotically painful sexual encounter.

It was happening now, even. She'd been wound tight this week. Worried. Stressing over them, over the gallery opening. As her left breast throbbed, and Eric tightened the second clamp on her right breast, the tension was already beginning to drain away. When he tightened it a third time, she squealed involuntarily.

He quirked an eyebrow, stepped away. Swung a second arm out over her waist. Lin brushed her dark blond, curly mound aside, exposing her clit, and slipped off the little ring, placing it on a tray near the bench.

Brandy moaned, a thousand pins and needles piercing her sensitive clit as blood and feeling rushed back to that area.

Lin squeezed just beneath it. The clamp closed on it. It hurt immediately. She whimpered. Eric tightened the knob just a bit, watching her face.

She yelped.

They stood. Pulled the chains up, placing one of the links on each chain over a hook on the bar, so that there was no slack in them.

Brandy moaned. Continuous bolts of pain coursed through her nipples, her breasts. Her clit began to throb in time with her heartbeat, feeling as though it was on fire.

Lin surveyed her with a look of satisfaction. "Fifteen minutes of continuous silence," she announced. "That's the price of removal."

Eric pointed toward the ceiling, where Brandy saw for the first time a series of speakers, microphones, and cameras. "I've set up quite a system. We'll be listening upstairs. Watching. When you've been silent for fifteen consecutive minutes, we'll let you out." He grinned. "Then, the real fun begins."

He and Lin turned, walked out of the room arm in arm.

Brandy gritted her teeth. She could do this. She could stand the pain for fifteen minutes.

Couldn't she?

There was a clock on the wall. She resisted the urge to watch it. She turned her head. The glass cabinet stood against the wall to her right, so she began studying its contents.

Bad idea. The first object that jumped out at her was a metal instrument with a serrated wheel attached to it. The second looked like a rounded vent brush, but it was made of stainless steel, and the short "bristles" were stiff wires. She turned away quickly.

Which jostled her shoulders, which shook her breasts, which pulled against the clamps, which caused her to cry out.

Shit.

She closed her eyes.

That was worse, because then, all she had was the pain. It thrummed through her, like some great beast's heartbeat.

Brandy whimpered.

Her clit burned. She shifted, trying to create slack in the lines.

Screamed as the chain at her groin pulled even tighter.

*This* was "mild" punishment?

"Get the hell down here!" She screamed. Everything was so delicately poised, even speaking jostled her tortured clit, bringing tears to her eyes. "Let me out, damn it! I changed my mind!"

No one came. Brandy sobbed, each shake sending a fresh wave of pain through her nipples. She screamed inarticulately. Screamed again. Drew in great, sobbing breaths and screamed again.

And again.

And felt tension draining from her trussed limbs. She shrugged her shoulders, wiggled her hips, let the tears flow with each fresh pang, and felt tension ebb.

She screamed again, long and loud.

Laughed.

Laughed again when she realized that even *that* hurt.

She was becoming hysterical. That wouldn't do.

She subsided. Lay still. Closed her eyes.

She had a safeword. A word she'd never use in casual conversation. If she said it now, they would come, and this would all be over. Brandy breathed in, slow and deep. She felt a twinge with each rise and fall of her chest.

Moisture gathered between her legs.

She wiggled her hips ever so slightly, fanning the fire in her clit.

Pictured Eric and Lin tracing slow circles around that fire with cubes of ice.

Moaned with desire.

Uh-oh. That wouldn't do. They hadn't said no *screaming* for fifteen minutes, they just said "silence."

Her shoulders were beginning to ache. Her thigh muscles, stretched taut, were beginning to hurt as well.

She drew in a shaky breath, prepared to scream again.

Found she didn't need to.

The pain was a punishment, but it was also a release. Eric and Lin were right. In her normal life, Brandy was a control freak, taking on more and more. Relying only on herself to get things done. She didn't trust anyone, even Kendall, to get things right. Had to do it all herself.

Eric and Lin were forcing her to trust them. Forcing her to give up control.

They did know what she needed.

She settled in. Embraced the pain.

When she heard the door open, she was proud. She had come through her first punishment.

When they released her clit, Eric swallowed her cries with kisses.

When they loosed her nipples, Lin laved them with her tongue, warm and soothing.

They had changed their clothes while they were gone. Eric wore tight-fitting, black-dyed jeans laced at the crotch with a leather thong. Lin wore nothing but a pair of red heels. She itched to touch them. To have them touch her.

They unfastened her wrists and ankles and massaged her arms and legs until the pins and needles faded away.

Brandy glanced at the clock. An hour had passed.

An hour!

She frowned, disappointed. She thought she'd done better.

Lin noticed her expression. "Hey. You did good."

"Really, Mistress?"

Lin gave her calf one last squeeze. "Really."

"Thank you," Brandy said, startled at the amount of pleasure this small bit of praise gave her.

Eric leaned back against the wall. "It's not too late to change your mind."

Brandy searched his face, looking for disappointment. Afraid he was the one changing his mind.

"I'm just making sure. It's difficult to accurately describe what actually goes on between a Dominant and a sub on paper. Someone like you, who's never had the experience..." He cleared his throat. "I just need to know, now that you've seen what it's like, that this relationship is still something you want."

Brandy slid off the bench, knelt on the floor before him. She didn't think about it—just did it. It seemed right. "It is, Master. Very much so."

Eric stared down at her, several emotions flickering across his face. Pride. Pleasure. Admiration. And that animal strength, that barely restrained jungle cat, pacing behind those eyes.

"Time to play," he murmured in a dangerous voice.

He held out his hand, drew her up from the floor.

"What scares you the most about this, Brandy?" he asked softly, as he and Lin led her toward the middle of the room.

"I would have said punishment, Master, until tonight."

"And now?"

She hesitated.

"Quickly, Brandy," Lin prompted.

"Yes, Mistress." She hated to say it. Hated to remind them of it. "It's...the anal sex, Master. I'm sorry. I've just...never..." She stopped, at a loss for words.

Lin's eyes glittered dangerously. "It's always best to face our fears. Isn't it, Brandy?"

Brandy swallowed. "Yes, Mistress," she whispered.

They halted before something resembling a gynecologist's chair, except instead of stirrups, there were a pair of upright bars at the sides from which jutted two handles with a furry sleeve over them. Without being told, Brandy climbed up onto the chair and lay back.

Eric fastened a wide, padded belt around her middle. Lin pulled her hands up over her head, strapped them in place. Eric looked at her, pushing her legs out and back, nodding toward the furry handles.

Brandy understood. With Eric's guidance, she managed to hook her knees over the handles. He reached out and pressed a button on the chair's side.

It tilted, raising Brandy to about a sixty-five-degree angle.

Her ass slipped to the chair's edge. Her pussy gleamed wetly, cold in the air-conditioned room.

She felt horribly exposed. Vulnerable.

To her surprise, Lin placed a small pillow under her head. Then she realized what was happening, and felt twin spots of fire in her cheeks.

She had a bird's eye view of her pussy. Could probably even see the tight pucker between her cheeks, if they parted them for her.

Whatever they were planning to do to her, they wanted her to watch.

Eric had moved to the sink. Lin walked over to the intimidating glass cabinet and took out a tray, but Brandy couldn't see what was on it. She pulled up a short bench, positioned it at the foot of the table. She looked up at Brandy. "Eyes wide open, love."

"Yes, Mistress."

Lin set the tray to the side.

Eric returned with a tub of soapy water and a large sponge. He sat beside Lin and swished the sponge through the water, then reached up and brushed it across Brandy's swollen clit.

Brandy drew breath with a sharp hiss. God, it hurt! She wanted to close her eyes, hide from the discomfort, but they were watching her. Besides, as he stroked and rubbed, the pain curled through her body. Made her sore nipples ache. Filled her with a familiar, aching need.

Her pussy spasmed. Eric cocked an eyebrow, pressed the soapy sponge hard against her clit.

It was so incredibly difficult not to close her eyes! She wanted to. Wanted to close her eyes and concentrate on everything she was feeling.

"Talk to us, Brandy," Lin purred. She reached out, added her own pressure to the weight of Eric's hand on her crotch.

"Oh! It feels…so good, Mistress," she moaned.

Their hands moved the sponge down, to her slit. Their fingers worked together, tucking it inside of her.

Brandy moaned again. They pulled it out. Tucked it in again. Pulled it out. Her pussy spasmed uncontrollably.

"Oh, Brandy." Lin leaned forward, kissed her plump labia. "Your pussy's so beautiful." She ran a fingernail around the edge of the cleft. Brandy's muscles clenched, milky juices seeping from the furrow. "Mmmm. I love watching it. Seeing how we make you feel." She scooped up a milky glob with her fingernail. Brought it to her mouth. Licked it off while Brandy watched.

Brandy moaned, her vision cloudy with desire.

Eric soaked the sponge again, brought it up, swept it across the pale globes of her cheeks. Ran it up and down between them. It felt good—warm and wet. Her anus clenched erratically.

He reversed the sponge, pressed it against her butt-cheek and rubbed vigorously.

This other side was rough, bristly, like a scouring pad. He rubbed both cheeks in a circular motion, until her pearly skin glowed red, then set the sponge aside. He and Lin feathered their fingers over the sensitive skin.

"Oh!" Brandy licked her lips. The tips of their fingers—Lin's cool and smooth, Eric's warm and a bit rough—trailed fire across the abused skin. But that was nothing compared to the blaze each stroke lit in her belly. "Oh, God!"

"You like this, baby?" Eric asked.

"Oh, yes, Master. Yes." Brandy wanted to arch, writhe. But the pillow kept her head focused downward, her midriff was caught in the padded belt, and her hands were strapped above her. She couldn't move into their touch. Couldn't look away, either.

Which was making her even hornier. Seeing the way her own body responded to them—it was an aphrodisiac.

Lin winked at Eric. Held her fingers a scant inch away from Brandy's tender skin. They watched her. Waited.

Brandy groaned. "Please, Mistress."

Lin feigned confusion. "You'll have to be more specific, *ma chère*."

"Please...Mistress," she begged haltingly. "Please...touch me."

Lin's fingers fluttered against her flesh.

"Oh!"

"What, Brandy?" Lin prompted.

She felt herself blushing. It had always been hard for her, to talk about her body. To tell her partners what she wanted, what felt good. Lin waited, fingers poised for another pass. "It-it feels so good, Mistress."

Lin stroked. Brandy shivered.

Eric reached out, traced a lazy figure eight on her other cheek. "What feels good, Brandy?"

She trembled with need. "Your…your touch, Master. Both of you. Your fingers."

"How do they feel?"

Her voice shook. "Like fire, Master."

"And what does that do to you?"

"It…" Her face burned, almost as hot as the fire in her gut, but she pressed on. "It makes me tingle."

Lin's long, lazy stroke nearly drove her wild. "Where, *ma chère?*"

Brandy hesitated. Lin stroked again. "Where?"

Eric started another figure eight. "Tell us, baby. Tell us what it does to you."

Brandy moaned. "It makes my…pussy…burn, Mistress." She drew in a shaky breath. "Master. Every touch…it's like…a flame, curling from your fingers…into my pussy." They were stroking her continuously now. Watching, rapt, as her body shook. "My…clit…tingles. Throbs." She sobbed. "Please."

"What do you want, Brandy?" Lin whispered.

"Fuck me…please, Mistress…fuck me."

The heat in Lin's eyes took Brandy's breath away. She reached down, picked something up from the tray. It was a plastic bottle. She took off the lid, pushed a length of narrow plastic tubing over the bottle's applicator.

She squeezed. A glistening drop of oil formed at the tip of the tube, then oozed down its side.

Brandy could feel the pulse in her neck racing. Lin set the bottle down, reached into a slotted cardboard box. Pulled out a pair of surgical gloves.

She looked at Brandy, her gaze deep and dark with desire as she fitted the gloves on her hands, smoothed them over her fingers. Brandy swallowed. Tried to ignore the pounding of her heart.

Lin picked up the bottle and squeezed it again, rubbing oil over the length of tubing. She looked up, reached out, and snaked the tube into Brandy's ass.

Brandy gasped, more from surprise than from anything else. The tube was so narrow that she barely felt it.

Lin smiled, squeezing the bottle slowly.

Warmth flooded her ass. Brandy took in a slow, shuddering breath. Felt her butt clench.

Eric smiled. "I think she likes it, love. Look at the way she's sucking." He looked up at Brandy. "Do you see, baby? Do you see how your body likes sucking our straw?"

She did. Her anus convulsed again. Her voice shook as she said, "Yes, Master. I see."

Lin licked her lips. Squeezed again, hard and fast. Brandy moaned as the warm fluid rushed in, seeping out from around the tube inside her. "How does it feel, Brandy?"

"Like… I'm sorry, Mistress. I don't know. It's nothing I ever expected. Very pleasant."

Lin chuckled, wiggled the bottle so that the tube inside her jiggled. "Just pleasant?"

Brandy gasped, tiny fingers of arousal writhing through her abdomen. "No, Mistress." She didn't care any more about embarrassing herself. She would tell them anything. Beg if they wanted her to. Just so long as they kept up this sweet torture. "It's making me so horny!" A shudder wracked her body.

Eric reached out, ran a finger through the oil dribbling down her crack. Shivered. "Me, too, baby."

Brandy shook her head as Lin pulled the tube out, whimpered in protest. "Don't worry, *ma belle*. We're nowhere near finished." She squirted oil into her gloved hands, coating them generously. Brandy closed her eyes briefly, anticipating what was coming. She wanted this. Wanted it as much for them as for herself. Seeing how much they wanted it was making it even more of a turn-on for her, and yet she was scared.

Eric pinched her bottom. Hard. Brandy yelped, opened her eyes. "I'm sorry, Master!"

He pinched her again. Brandy bit her lip to keep from crying out. She deserved it. They'd told her not to close her eyes. Her silence apparently pleased him, because he nodded and caressed her buttock once, gently.

Lin stood. She leaned into Brandy. Caressed her bottom with her oiled fingers. Massaged her anus.

"Oh!" The touch was so unexpectedly erotic. Her anus contracted in unison with her spasming cunt. "Oh, Mistress!"

Lin teased the opening with her little finger. Paused. "Perhaps we should wait."

Eric grinned. Nodded. "We might be going a little fast," he agreed.

"No! Please. Mistress, Master."

"Please, what?" Eric asked innocently.

"Please! I want to feel...your fingers...in my ass."

In one swift movement, Lin's finger was buried. "Oh, God!"

Lin wiggled her hand back and forth, twisting the finger inside her. Brandy arched her shoulders. "Oh, God. Yes!" The smallest of Lin's fingers had slipped in easily, comfortably. There was no pain—only pleasure. Curling tendrils of warming sensation made their way to her belly, her pussy, her clit. "Yes, Mistress."

Lin tilted her hand, pressing toward the outer rim. Moved it around and around, stretching the tight pucker. Even that didn't hurt. It was only pressure, and it meant the tip of Lin's sheathed fingernail circled round and round inside her, sending shocks of pure delight running up her spine. Brandy moaned.

"Talk to us, Brandy," Eric reminded in a sharp tone.

Brandy felt a wave of disappointment with herself. She wanted to please them, so much. "Oh, Mistress. Thank you. You feel so good in my ass."

Lin pulled her finger out, thrust the next one in. "I'm going to fuck you with every finger on my hand," she promised. "And then Eric's going to fuck you with every finger on his hand." She pushed the finger in deep, stroked like she was petting a cat. "And then, we're going to fuck you for real."

It was too much. Brandy cried out, shoulders arching, as her body vibrated with delight. Having Lin inside her ass—something to squeeze, something to hold on to—it felt so good. And even more important, Lin's breath came in ragged gasps. Her eyes glowed with pleasure. That knowledge—that her Mistress was pleased, even aroused—took her over the edge. She tossed her head back and forth, tried to buck, as wave after wave of pleasure slammed through her.

In the midst of it, Lin pulled her ring finger out. Pushed in her long, strong middle finger. Thrust it in deep, so deep, driving Brandy's climax to an even higher level. Brandy couldn't help it. She had to close her eyes, pressing her head back against the pillow as every bone in her body seemed to melt.

Her eyes flew open at the sharp slap on her butt. "That's twice now," Eric noted. "You'll have to be punished."

"Yes, Master. I'm sorry, Master." Brandy shuddered as the last of her orgasm faded. "Please forgive me."

Lin switched fingers yet again. Each penetration was becoming more and more forceful, creating a little more pressure, more discomfort. This time, instead of burying it and leaving it submerged while she stroked and twisted, she drove her finger in and out, again and again.

Brandy caught her bottom lip with her teeth. This time, it hurt. Each time Lin had penetrated her before, burying her finger and leaving it, the initial discomfort had faded. Her body had been able to adjust to the width of that finger. This time, with her plunging in and out so quickly, it had no memory. Her anus contracted tight again with each withdrawal, stretched painfully with each new thrust. A tiny squeak escaped her with one particularly vigorous invasion.

"Does it hurt?"

"Yes, Mistress."

"But I'm not going to stop."

"No, Mistress."

"Because you don't want me to, do you?"

"Please, no, Mistress."

"As a matter of fact…"

Brandy hissed in shock as Lin's thumb plunged into her ass. Sobbed, even while she was screaming, "Yes, Mistress. Oh, God, yes!" Lin pumped in and out quickly. Prickles of heat, pain, and pleasure danced through her ass, her tummy, an erotic symphony about to reach its crescendo.

And then it was gone, and Brandy was sobbing with frustrated desire. Eric stood. His hands were gloved now, and glistening with oil. Without warning or preamble, he drove his own thumb into her ass. Brandy screamed. Eric wrapped his arm around Lin's waist, fondled her breast as they watched Brandy writhe. Watched his thumb plumb her ass.

Lin's hands went to his waist and untied the leather thong, pulling it from the grommets, so that his engorged cock sprang out.

Brandy experienced an unanticipated sense of disappointment when he replaced his thumb with his little finger. It was much more comfortable, much less painful.

And she was beginning to realize what they had recognized from the start. That she needed the pain. Pain stripped away her inhibitions, released her tension. Freed her mind of the constant, endless worrying over this shipment, that artist. Developed a narrow focus in her—a focus on her body, on how she was reacting, that deeply intensified her pleasure.

"Please, Master," she moaned.

He raised his eyebrows in question.

"Please...h-h—" She had difficulty saying what she wanted to say—what she *needed* to say. The conservative side of her brain balked. She pushed at the unwelcome restraint. "Please, h-hurt me."

Eric and Lin both froze. "What did you say?" Eric asked quietly.

"Please, Master. Please. Hurt me."

Lust and pleasure seemed to radiate from them. And pride. Pride in *her*. Their eyes gleamed with the predatory, voracious glitter that always reminded her of jungle cats. Lin stepped away as Eric withdrew his little finger.

Brandy's breath hissed from her as he pushed his forefinger and middle finger in at once, forcefully, painfully. She groaned.

Lin was holding the bottle over his cock now, coating him with lubricant. Brandy hissed again as Eric parted his fingers slightly, turning and turning them, reaming her ass. The pain was a bellows, fanning the hot coals of desire into a blazing inferno of desperate need. "Yes, yes," she heard herself croak. "You know. You've always known."

Eric groaned. Pulled out his fingers. Grabbed her thighs with his strong hands. Pressed the tip of his cock against her. Hesitated. "We said we'd take it slow, baby, but...this is going to hurt," he said, his voice husky. "Really hurt."

"I know," Brandy whispered. "I can take it, Master." Her voice gathered strength. "Please, Master. I want that huge cock in my ass."

He gasped, his grip on her thighs tightening painfully. Thrust. Her body resisted, the tight orifice screaming with pain. Brandy screamed with it, worrying in the back of her mind that it might make him stop.

Then she realized, as his punishing grip tightened, as he pushed harder and harder, animal lust in his eyes, that stopping wasn't going to be an option. He pushed deeper and deeper, despite her screams. Maybe *because* of them. The dark beast, the jaguar, had been unleashed. And this time, it wasn't going to stop.

His breathing quickened. His eyes locked on hers, and she was drowning in their blue depths as he plunged into her faster and faster. She screamed and screamed, releasing tension, stress, doubt. Moving them out of her way, so that she became intensely aware of other things. Things like the long, luxurious stroke that sent pleasure smoldering through her as the head of his cock furrowed her ass. The way his eyes seemed to be memorizing every line of her face—adoring, proud, possessive.

Brandy shivered, arching her shoulders, clenching her hands. She watched his thick cock, gleaming with oil, pushing in and out of her. Her body clung to him each time he drew back, releasing him only reluctantly. Her clit throbbed in response to this image. Gazing into his eyes again, she saw how pleased he was. How utterly happy.

She moaned, felt herself tumbling inward, every molecule of her focused on giving him pleasure. She squeezed her ass as tight as she could.

He gasped, thrust erratically. Brandy smiled through her tears, tightening those muscles over and over. "Yes, Master," she whispered. "Yes. I want your seed in my ass."

Lin grabbed her breasts, squeezing hard, pulling them out, pinching the nipples with her strong nails. Brandy and Eric gasped at the same time, arching. "Thank you, Mistress!" Brandy cried as Eric's cock pulsed inside her. "Thank you, thank you," she whispered, and then her voice failed as her ass spasmed, closing again and again on the thick cock packed inside it, driving his seed into her. And Brandy watched. Watched her ass milk his cock until his essence seeped out from where their flesh met, until he shuddered as the last of his climax faded.

Brandy whimpered. His orgasm was fading, but she remained suspended just below the peak, striving for that ultimate release. And she knew why. She had to have them both. They completed her. Made her whole.

"Mistress!"

Lin pinched her nipples, the tips of her nails biting into the skin. "Yes, yes," Brandy whimpered. "Please, Mistress. Hurt me." Lin's hazel eyes, so like a tiger's, drew her in. "I need you, Mistress," Brandy whispered. "I need you, too."

Lin made a sound like a purr and a growl rolled into one. Drew her tongue along the flesh between Brandy's breasts as she milked them mercilessly. Brandy made constant, inarticulate sounds of pleasure, unable to contain herself.

Eric slowly withdrew, grinning at Lin. "Your turn." He pressed the button that controlled Brandy's chair, lowering it back to horizontal.

Brandy stared, confused. Disappointed. Lin laughed at the look on her face. She drew a finger along Brandy's slit, then slapped her clit, making her gasp. "Don't worry, *ma chère*. We're just going to do it a little bit differently, you and I."

She stepped over to the wall, reaching for something hanging there, while Eric set Brandy free from the chair. He had to support her for several moments, as the muscles in her thighs protested the unaccustomed positions they'd been forced into. Then he led her to yet another contraption.

They certainly did like their toys.

Then again, so did she. Brandy giggled.

Eric gave her a questioning look.

"I like your toys, Master," she explained.

The beast flared again in his eyes. "That's good, baby," he said in a dangerous tone. He had one arm around her waist. With his free hand, he grabbed her braid, tugged it until she was arched back, one plump nipple pointing at the sky. "Because you'll be getting to know them." He caught her nipple in his mouth, scraped his teeth roughly across the swollen bud, then let go, swinging her back up to meet his gaze. "Quite intimately."

Brandy shivered at the dark promise in those eyes.

He turned her to face the device. The near side was shaped sort of like a sawhorse. Without being told, she straddled it.

Eric stood beside her. A smooth, rounded knob jutted up just in front of her. He made her scoot up, eyeing her position. When he was satisfied, he nodded, gesturing toward the front.

Brandy leaned forward. Her breasts fit neatly into two holes. She turned her head to the right, rested her cheek against the padded surface, facing the mirror on the wall beside them. He fastened the ubiquitous belt around her waist, pulling it tight. As always, it was about immobilization. Submission.

And Brandy was fast discovering that she was fine with that. It was exciting, not knowing exactly what was coming next. Having no control. Already, her heart rate was climbing again, her body flushing with renewed heat.

She felt her clit swelling, pressing against the cool metal mound beneath it.

"Close your eyes," Eric said, "Just until we tell you to open them."

She nodded. Closed her eyes.

She heard Lin's heels clicking on the floor as she walked up to the horse. She looped something rough and scratchy across Brandy's shoulder blades. Wrapped it around her and the bench several times, pulling it taut as she went, binding her breasts tightly. Then she lifted Brandy's feet, guided them into stirrups. She repositioned them, shortening the length, pulling them forward, then buckling Brandy's ankles in place. Brandy lay quietly. She was experiencing a strange sense of calm, a meditative state. A place where she was no longer Brandy.

She was an amalgam. Her body no longer belonged to her. She was an extension of the Mistress. The Master. Theirs to do with as they wished.

"Open your eyes, *ma belle*," Lin prompted.

Brandy opened her eyes. Lin stepped to her rear. The state of calm vanished abruptly. In the mirror, she could see the harness Lin was wearing, the huge dildo it held gleaming with oil. In the background, she saw Eric lounging in a deep leather chair, watching. She stared at Lin in the mirror, her gaze wide. "Mistress," she murmured, her voice trembling. Pleading. "I can't take that!"

"But you can, *ma chère*," Lin purred. Her eyes flashed darkly. The beast was close to the surface, gathering itself for the feast. "You will."

A tear tracked its way across the bridge of Brandy's nose. "Yes, Mistress."

Lin stroked the pale globes of her cheeks. "We can end this now, Brandy," she murmured, her accent thick. Brandy had to listen hard. "You can walk away from all of it. Or you can use your safeword, and we can do something else. Something less...intimidating."

She said it casually, as though it meant nothing. But Brandy could hear the desire, thick and hot, beneath the words. Laced with excitement, anxiety, hope.

Something less intimidating.

Something less than what her Mistress wanted. Needed.

"No, Mistress," Brandy said, hearing her voice as though from very far away. "I'm yours, Mistress. Take me, please. Take me."

Even before she finished speaking, Lin's slender, surprisingly strong hands were on her hips, the tip of the dildo pressing against her anus. It was long—longer than Eric's cock, and thicker. Much thicker.

Lin pressed into her very, very slowly. Brandy winced, bit her lip. Lin closed her eyes and shuddered. Brandy knew instinctively that she was fighting to maintain control. To truly keep it to a level Brandy could handle. This certain knowledge filled her with a warmth she couldn't name, couldn't place. It was so different, something she'd felt only fleetingly, and only since she'd met these two.

"Please, Mistress," she whispered. She took a deep breath, letting it out slowly, relaxing her body completely. Lin opened her eyes.

Brandy urged the tiger. "Fast and hard, Mistress. Please."

In the mirror, Eric sat up, stroking his cock, his gaze riveted to the place where flesh met rubber-sheathed metal.

Lin's gaze held hers. Her hips moved slightly. Brandy winced, caught her lip in her teeth again, but didn't look away. Lin looked down, watching with obvious delight as Brandy's flesh stretched around her toy.

Brandy watched, too, in the mirror. Watched as her Mistress's tool eased into her, bit by bit. She whimpered with pain, moaned with desire. It was oddly erotic, watching the huge surrogate cock disappear inside her, attached to one of the most beautifully compact females she'd ever met.

Her blood thrummed. Her pussy gushed, filling the room with the scent of her desire. Lin's nostrils flared. With a moan, she bucked abruptly, shoving the dildo in a full inch.

Pleasure and pain blossomed. Brandy screamed. Lin panted, drove her hips forward.

Brandy screamed and sobbed as the metal knob, warmed now by the heat of her body, rolled over her clit. Pain, heat, pressure, pleasure, swirled within her. It seemed that not only her nipples swelled, but her breasts, the ropes that bound her biting into tender flesh. "Oh, Mistress, please, please," she moaned. "It feels so good."

Lin lost control, driving the dildo hard and fast, until the suede harness touched Brandy's ass. Brandy screamed herself hoarse, but felt a sense of triumph. She had done it. Her anus burned like fire, but her ass was full of Lin-by-proxy. Her Mistress. Whose face in the mirror was astonished, ecstatic. Glowing.

Eric was standing now, walking toward them, his hand caressing his rigid cock. He came around the table, stood by Brandy's head, stroking as he watched.

Lin drew back slowly, plunged in again. Coming faster and faster, each thrust pounded Brandy's clit into the knob, made the ropes bite into her breasts. She shivered like a guitar string. Each thrust, each stroke, was a finger, plucking her, sending mini-orgasms rippling through her.

Lin laughed—a wild, vibrant sound. Eric grabbed Brandy's braid, held her head up as he pushed on the bench below her cheek.

It swung down on hinges just beneath her shoulders. Even before he stepped up, her mouth was open, ready. He shoved himself into her, thrusting in unison with his wife.

She was a lake. A puddle of desire and need, and Lin and Eric were raindrops, plunging into her again and again, until the three of them froze, poised like ice above a raging inferno.

The ice shattered. Lin screamed, bucking frantically. Eric buried himself against the back of Brandy's throat.

They carried her with them, waves of bliss crashing through her.

Eric's seed swirled down her throat. She could feel Lin's body, shuddering, pressed up tight against her ass.

They were a part of her. There was nothing missing any longer.

She went from a state of nothing but feeling to feeling nothing at all, wrapped in a haze of ultimate satisfaction. She was vaguely aware of her bonds being released. Of Eric picking her up, as though she weighed nothing, and carrying her up the stairs. He entered a spacious bedroom, the walls painted a midnight blue, with a massive bed covered in a purple velvet so dark it was almost black.

"Pretty," she murmured.

Eric chuckled.

He walked through, into a bathroom dominated by a huge Jacuzzi tub. He held her, waiting while Lin undressed and stepped into the steamy water. Brandy wondered briefly how the water could still be so hot, because they must have prepared it while she was being disciplined.

Then he squatted, and Lin eased her from his arms, into the tub.

Her clit, crotch, and ass stung, but the discomfort faded quickly, replaced by warmth and exhaustion.

Without thinking, she rested her head on Lin's shoulder.

Lin put an arm around her, brushed damp wisps of hair back from her cheeks. Eric slipped into the water beside them.

"You were wonderful, Brandy."

She felt a glow of pride at his praise. "Was I, Master?"

Lin caressed her shoulder. "Perfect, *ma chère*."

"So strong," Eric said.

"So brave," Lin whispered.

"I..." She shouldn't be, after all they had done—all she had let them do—but she felt shy, all of the sudden. She lowered her eyes. "I only want to please you, Mistress. Master."

A tremor went through the arm Lin had wrapped around her. "Oh, you do, *ma chère*." She and Eric looked at each other, their faces glowing. "You do."

They washed her gently, taking special care with her overly sensitive areas. It was loving and romantic without being erotic, something that touched her heart. She felt a sudden pang of apprehension.

She was falling head over heels for these two. How long would it last? What would she do when it was over?

But she was too tired, and their ministrations too relaxing, to worry for long. By the time they had half-carried her from the tub, dried her off with a big, fluffy towel, and guided her to the big bed, she was barely coherent. Eric helped her up onto the bed, scooting her into the middle. He and Lin climbed in, lying to either side of her. “Nice bed,” she murmured.

“Even better, now,” Eric agreed, grinning down at her.

Brandy smiled drowsily, and sleep overtook her.

## Chapter Ten: Second Thoughts

She woke the next morning cold and alone. She reached down to pull up the covers and groaned as the muscles in her arms screamed in protest.

"Good morning, *ma chère*," Lin said, coming into the room with a platter loaded with breakfast. Eric followed her, a few other oddments in his hands.

Lin set the platter on the bedside table. Eyed Brandy shrewdly. "How do you feel?"

"I hurt." She said it matter-of-factly, without malice. She didn't blame them.

She blamed herself.

It was true that she hadn't been completely prepared for everything that had happened that night—hadn't known what to expect, really, despite the contract—but it had all been her choice. She had begged them to touch her. To hurt her. In the light of day, it made her blush to remember how she had begged them to ram themselves up her ass. She looked away, unable to meet their eyes.

Eric sat on the bed. "Not having second thoughts, are we?"

Brandy shrugged. "It's… I don't know." She shifted, suddenly uncomfortable with her nakedness. She reached for the covers again, despite her protesting body.

Eric caught her hand. Pushed the covers back even from where they rested across her calves, baring her completely. Brandy glared at him. She started to sit up.

Lin put an arm across her shoulders, pushed her back against the bed. Sat down beside her. "What bothers you the most, Brandy? The things we did to you? Me? What?"

Brandy looked away. Images flashed through her mind, and they had nothing to do with Lin and Eric. It was all her—crying for them, begging for their touch, getting hot and bothered at the thought of being hurt. "It's…it's me." She glanced up, and she could see in Lin's eyes that she had known that would be her answer.

Eric swung his legs up onto the bed, lounged on one arm, facing her. "You think it's wrong." It wasn't a question. "For you to like what we did last night."

Brandy nodded. Eric reached out and stroked her cheek. "What about this? Is this all right to like?"

Brandy frowned. "Yes, of course."

Lin leaned over, pressed a kiss to the corner of her mouth. "And this?"

Brandy swallowed. Nodded.

Lin quirked an eyebrow. "Even though I'm a woman?"

Brandy nodded again.

Eric chuckled. Cupped one of her breasts, teasing the nipple gently with his thumb. "And this?"

"Yes," Brandy sighed.

He sat up abruptly. Took his hand away "Why?"

Brandy stared at him. "What do you mean?"

"Why is that okay, and not what we did last night?"

Brandy shrugged, stared at the ceiling, the walls. Anything but their frustrated faces.

"Because it doesn't hurt?" Eric asked softly.

She sighed. "Yes. Because it doesn't hurt." She shook her head. "I was…" She stopped. Swallowed. Forced herself to say the word. "Begging…for things… I don't feel right about, now."

"So, it's not all right for us to give you what you want," Lin said. "What you need."

Brandy took a deep breath. This was so much harder than she had thought it would be. "I just…wonder…if we could have a more traditional relationship."

Eric's shoulders slumped. Lin's expression became stony. "That would satisfy you."

Brandy nodded. "I think so."

Lin leaned over her abruptly, graceful as a cat, looking deep into Brandy's eyes. "Has it ever…in the past? Satisfied you?"

Brandy closed her eyes. Didn't answer. She couldn't say yes, because it wasn't true. But she didn't want to admit it.

The bed shivered. When she opened her eyes, they were standing. "I'll get your clothes," Eric said.

She looked from one to the other. "Are you…are you saying it's over? You're not even going to give it a chance?"

"Brandy—" Eric's voice broke. "You're the one not giving it a chance." Lin walked around the bed. Put her arm around him.

"What Eric's trying to say is that we've looked a long time for someone like you. Someone who seemed so right." She was speaking calmly, but Brandy sensed a maelstrom of emotions behind that bright gaze. "Someone we could love in our own, unique way. We even thought—" She broke off, looking away. Then continued softly. "For the first time, we thought there might be a soulmate for us...someone we would consider spending the rest of our lives with. A person who might feel the same way."

She squared her shoulders. "This is who we are, Brandy. We can't change. Not even for you."

Brandy sat up, wincing. "But you want me to."

Eric's eyes flashed angrily. "No. We never asked you to change, Brandy. We only gave you a chance to be the person you really are, deep inside." He shrugged. "But millions of people go through life with masks on. Why should you be any different?"

He turned and strode from the room. Lin stared at her for a moment longer, then followed him.

## Chapter Eleven: Behind the Mask

Brandy paid the cab driver and headed for the stairs behind Lady of the Myths. Wincing with each step, she hobbled her way up to the small apartment above the shop that she rented from Kendall. She let herself in, shut the door, leaned back against it, and began to cry.

If she'd done the right thing, why did she feel so miserable?

When she managed to get herself under control, she pushed away from the door. In the kitchen, she opened a cabinet, took out a bottle, and shook two extra-strength pain relievers into her hand. She dry-swallowed them, then made her way into the bedroom, where she stripped and pulled on a nightgown, then slipped into bed.

Two hours later, the insistent ringing of the telephone woke her up. She hesitated briefly before answering. She didn't know if she could handle talking to Eric or Lin right now. Gingerly, she lifted the receiver. She definitely needed to get one of those phones that identified callers' numbers.

"Brandy?" It was Kendall. Brandy sighed, flooded with a mixture of relief and disappointment.

"Yeah," she mumbled. "What's up?"

"I just called to see how your date went."

Brandy lay back against the pillow. "Awful."

"Oh, Brandy. I'm sorry." Kendall was quiet for several moments. "Do you want to talk about it?"

She started to pour out the whole story, to ask Kendall what she thought, but when she opened her mouth, nothing came out.

"Brandy?" Kendall asked after a couple of minutes.

Brandy sighed. She usually told Kendall everything. After all, she was her best friend. But this was something she needed to work out on her own. "You know, Kendall, I don't think I do. I think this is something I need to handle by myself."

"Okay." She could almost see Kendall frowning, worried. "If you need me, you know where I am."

"Sure I do." Brandy twirled the phone cord around her finger. "Kendall?"

"Yeah?"

"Thanks." Kendall was the best kind of friend—one who knew when to push for details, and when to step back.

"You're welcome. See you at work Monday?"

"I'll be there."

Brandy hung up. Her stomach growled. She crawled out of bed. Felt a wave of gratitude as she was able to walk with a minimum of pain. Her heart might be broken, but at least the painkillers were working.

* * *

On Sunday, she spent the afternoon online. She told herself she was only going to check out the news, and maybe buy a couple of e-books to read. But after an hour, she finally typed in the letters BDSM and clicked search.

There were so many sites, she didn't know where to start. She finally settled on a webring that, from the introduction on the portal page, seemed to be geared toward someone like herself. A newcomer who wanted to know more about the lifestyle, and the people who engaged in it.

Several hours later, she shut off the computer, her mind churning. She had skimmed over the information for Dominants, just to get a feel for the different styles and attitudes. But what had captured her attention, kept her riveted for hours, were the pages and pages written by subs. One essay, in particular, stuck in her head. The writer had used their sub name—apparently, some Dom/sub relationships included using different names from those they presented to the outside world—so she didn't know if the author was a man or a woman, but the person's observations had struck a major chord with her.

fullmoon—subs who used them usually didn't capitalize their sub names—had described something called "sub space." A place where tension and anxiety melted away, where a sub became something both less and more than usual. Less, because they were completely subsumed by their Dom—melding, blending, until they didn't know where they ended and that person began. But more, too, because that subsumption—that submission—released them. Took them to a place, as never before, where the only thing that mattered was another person's needs. And in meeting those needs, they cleared their minds of the clutter of daily living, opening themselves to deep emotions that otherwise never made it past all the white noise.

She'd been there. Friday night, with Lin and Eric. In sub space.

As she read more, she thought she might be gaining a glimmer of understanding about someone she'd never known very well.

Herself.

At first, it surprised her to read message after message from subs who described themselves as control freaks. Not all, of course, but a good number of subs appeared to be people who normally took charge, told others what to do, made the difficult decisions in their public lives—and were submissives, some even going so far as to call themselves slaves, in private.

But, in a weird sort of way, it made sense.

When she looked at herself, for example. She had taken on managing both Kendall's shop and Sutter's, and she had been the one to push for the new venue—a more upscale, artsy place that would cater to the fine arts crowd. And when Kendall and Sutter had tried to do things to help her, she had turned them away, until she was doing it all. She'd always been like that, taking on more and more responsibility, because she liked to stay busy and was proud of her abilities.

And her personal relationships had reflected that. She'd always been the one to decide where to go, what to do, whether or not there would be any sex that night. Who drove, who paid, when the relationship would end.

She had always thought she functioned best under pressure.

And maybe that was true, in the business world. But privately, there had always been something missing. The men in her life had always deferred to her. Even her father, for whom she'd basically been the executive secretary after her mother died when she was twelve—reminding him of appointments, balancing his checkbook, deciding where and when they would go on vacation and what they would do.

It was exhilarating and exhausting at the same time. She'd never been able to relax. She seemed to always be worrying about what was left to be done, what she had to take care of next.

It was different with Lin and Eric. From the beginning, they had approached her boldly, with confidence. Taken charge of the relationship.

Work hard, play hard. That was the old adage. But Brandy had never played much. Maybe it took a little more for some people to let go. She'd always felt like she was doing for others, when she took on projects, responsibilities. Now, she was beginning to suspect she'd been doing it all for herself, for some inner demon that was always looking for the next challenge, the next triumph.

For such a person, it might take a different kind of relationship—something others might consider extreme—to break past that barrier of self-reliance. To allow them to open up and share their deepest emotions with another.

But was this all truth? Or did it just sound good—modern psycho-babble the Dom/sub culture could use to legitimize its excesses. After all, even the worst criminals could usually come up with some explanation for their behavior that validated their actions, at least to themselves.

Brandy rubbed her tired eyes. She just didn't know.

## Chapter Twelve: Her Proper Place

Everything was different now.

Brandy worked her butt off every day, trying to blot Lin and Eric from her mind, but she couldn't stop thinking about them. She kept remembering the expressions on their faces when they'd parted. The disappointment, the frustration. The blankness—where once she'd witnessed joy and a secret hope for the future.

Her physical pangs were nothing compared to the aching of her heart.

On Friday evening, while she and Kendall were going over the last of the preparations for next month's opening of the new venture, she glanced up and caught Kendall staring at her, her eyes moist.

"What's wrong?" she asked.

"It hurts, to see you so lonely."

Brandy forced a laugh. "What do you mean? I haven't had a minute alone this week, there's been so much going on, except when I fall into bed at night. And my best friend's been keeping me company."

Kendall fixed her with a knowing gaze, until Brandy finally had to look away. It occurred to her for the first time that even though she considered Kendall her best friend, she'd always been waiting, in the back of her mind, for the woman to abandon her—for Sutter and Josh, for the twins, for a bigger, better business opportunity. Was that why she'd pushed the new studio? To keep from losing Kendall?

Had she always been this way? Holding people at arm's length while at the same time she tried to ensure they wouldn't disappear from her life?

The question rushed out of her before she could stop it. "Kendall? I always think of you as my best friend, but...do you think of me that way? I mean, have I been a good friend to you?"

Kendall looked like a deer caught in headlights.

"Be honest, Kendall. I want the truth."

Kendall nodded. "Okay, then. I've always felt a...distance between us." She took a deep breath, as though what she said next was going to hurt. "To be honest, I've tried not to get too attached, because I wasn't sure you were going to stick around."

Tears sprang to Brandy's eyes. "Really? That's ironic, because I've just come to the conclusion that the main reason I suggested this new partnership was because I didn't want to lose you, and this was one sure way to keep you in my life."

"Really?" To her horror, Kendall, who never let things get her down, started sobbing.

"I'm sorry," Brandy wailed. "I don't know what it is...ever since my mother died, I've felt like I have to be totally self-reliant. I just...I want to keep people leaning on me, but I'm afraid to let them get too close."

Kendall smiled as she wiped tears from her eyes. "It's okay. I'm crying because I'm happy."

"What?" Brandy choked out between her own sobs. "Why?"

"Because you just told me, in your own way, that you care."

Brandy smiled, tasting salty tears. "I did, didn't I?"

Kendall nodded.

"You *are* my best friend," Brandy confessed, "Even though I've been too stupid to let you know how much that means to me. I... I'd do anything for you, Kendall. I hope we can start over again."

Kendall shook her head. "We don't have to. I might have intended to stay emotionally detached, but I haven't. Don't you know that?"

Brandy felt strange. It took her a minute to decide what the feeling was. She nodded slowly. "I do." She stared into Kendall's eyes. "You love me, don't you? I mean, really love me. Like a sister."

Kendall laughed. "Like a best friend."

"I love you, too," Brandy said, in a tone full of wonder.

"You sound surprised."

"I am. It just hit me. I've been wondering what's missing from my life, when it isn't what's missing. It's what *I'm* missing. The things I already have that I'm too busy, or too scared, to see. I've always considered you a good friend, but I never actually understood that I love you."

They stared at each other for a long moment, and then Brandy stood abruptly. "Kendall, I think I've made a terrible mistake."

Kendall waved her toward the door. "Go ahead, and good luck."

Brandy felt fresh tears coming on and blinked them back. "I'll tell you all about it later. I promise."

Kendall smiled. "I'll be here."

Brandy grabbed her keys and rushed up to her apartment. Inside, she tugged off her clothes and took a quick shower. She dried off, then unplaited her braid and brushed out her hair, so that it fell in soft waves against her bare skin.

She pulled on an old jacket of her father's.

He had been a large man. The jacket was about four sizes too big for her, hanging halfway to her knees.

In other words, it was perfect.

She zipped it up. Folded the sleeves so that they didn't hang six inches past her fingertips.

She slipped on a pair of sandals, tossed a t-shirt and a denim miniskirt into a bag, and grabbed her purse.

Thirty minutes later, she was telling a security guard her name. He scanned a clipboard. "I'm sorry. You're not on their guest list. I'll have to call in."

Brandy nodded. He punched a number into a cell-phone and waited. "Sir, I have a Brandy Mitchell here. She's not on your list." He listened for a moment, then punched another button. The gate swung open. "Go on in."

"Thank you."

Brandy drove through the gate, down wide streets with magnificent houses set on three-acre lots. Her apprehension mounted as she pulled down the Brogans' long drive. In the circular driveway, she stopped, frowning. There were several cars parked along its curve. Her heart pounded. It had never occurred to her that they might not be alone. She considered leaving, but she couldn't stomach the thought of allowing one more day to pass without speaking to them. She took a deep breath to calm her nerves and gathered her things. She walked up the steps and rang the doorbell.

The door opened, and a stranger greeted her. "Come in, please, Miss Mitchell." He was a tall, well-groomed man, fiftyish, with graying hair, dressed in khaki pants and a white, short-sleeved golf shirt. "Wait here a moment, please."

Brandy fidgeted while she waited. She wondered how many people were here, whether she was making another big mistake. She began to doubt her ability to carry on with the plan.

When she saw them, however, her reservations melted away. A flood of emotion had her swallowing past a huge lump in her throat.

The man who had answered the door had returned with them and stood unobtrusively to the side.

Their expressions were carefully neutral. "What is it, Brandy?" Lin asked.

Hearing Lin's voice almost brought tears to her eyes. With renewed resolve, and despite the stranger's presence, Brandy unzipped her oversized jacket and let it fall to the floor. She knelt, clasping her hands behind her back, knees about a foot apart, shoulders back and chest thrust out, as she'd seen pictured and described on the web sites. It seemed second nature to bow her head and avoid their eyes while she apologized, but they had told her to look them in the eyes, always. So she did. "I made a mistake."

They stared at her silently.

"I'm sorry. I was...overwhelmed, but I understand now." Their faces remained impassive, and she swallowed nervously. "I... understand myself. What I am. What I need." She searched their faces for any hint of acceptance.

There was no change, but they weren't sending her away. They were waiting, with their man looking on silently. What should she say?

"Please, Master, Mistress." She looked into their beautiful, dangerous eyes. "I..." Damn. Why was this so hard?

Because she might get hurt, that's why—and she wasn't talking about any physical pain. She made herself say what was in her heart. "I think I'm falling in love with you."

No response.

Her thoughts raced frantically. "And...you were right, both of you, about what's inside me. I need what you give me. I... I need to be a submissive. *Your* submissive." Was that a flicker of approval she saw in Lin's eyes? She forged on. "Please forgive me for questioning your wisdom, Master, Mistress. I see now that you have always done what is best for me."

It was, definitely. Even Eric was beginning to look less stony. "Please. I know I must be punished, but I hope... I hope you'll give me another chance to be yours."

Eric looked down at Lin. They seemed to communicate silently for a moment, then Lin turned to their silent observer. "Edward, will you please inform Mrs. Sanchez that there will be one more for dinner tonight?"

"Of course, Mrs. Brogan." Edward turned and headed for the kitchen.

They turned back to her. Lin glanced up at Eric.

"Your punishment begins immediately." He bent and picked up her bag, purse, and the jacket. "You will wear no clothing for the remainder of the weekend. You will accompany us to the dining room, and eat at our table, but you will neither speak nor be spoken to, touch nor be touched."

Brandy swallowed. "Yes, Master."

"After dinner, you will remain by our sides, either standing a pace behind us, or positioned at our feet, as you are now."

"Yes, Master."

They turned and strode toward the dining room. Brandy quickly stood and followed, a pace behind them. Eric paused to give her belongings to Edward, murmuring quietly. Edward nodded and disappeared down the hall. Lin opened the dining room door and led them in.

Brandy's steps faltered as they entered the room. Seated around the long table were over a dozen people, Dominants and subs, all staring at her curiously. Eric stepped up to the single empty chair and pulled it out. "This is our sub, Brandy." As a chorus of hellos and welcomes started, he held up a hand and shook his head. "Brandy is in training, and she is currently being punished." The room became intimidatingly silent. To her surprise, it was the subs that glared at her the most. "She is not to be spoken to or touched, or acknowledged in any way." Heads around the table nodded.

Brandy swallowed and slipped into the seat. All around her, conversation began again.

In a room full of people, she was bereft. Alone.

She wasn't even seated near Eric and Lin. She was between two others, a Dominant to her left—a svelte woman dressed in a figure-hugging red leather pantsuit, with a male sub sitting at her feet, also dressed in red leather pants, but with the crotch cut out and a rather painful-looking harness fastened around his balls. Brandy looked away.

To her right was a sub—a willowy brunette wearing a sheer catsuit. She had a collar around her neck, with a leash attached, which was in turn fastened to a wristband on the man sitting beside her.

They all avoided her gaze, acting as if she didn't exist.

She didn't know what to do. Eric had said to eat, but she couldn't ask for permission, because she wasn't supposed to speak. Lin had told her in the restaurant that she always had permission to eat as soon as her food arrived, but she had specified "for the purposes of dining out."

To her relief, the question was settled by Edward, who brought a plate piled high with meat and potatoes and set it before her, then poured her a glass of tea. She started to thank him, but then remembered the edict, and said nothing. She felt guilty, but she thought she saw a flash of understanding in his eyes. It made her feel a little better.

But only a little. It was astonishing, how difficult it was to sit in a room full of people and be ignored. She felt especially upset when Lin or Eric spoke. The rich timbre of their voices seemed to strike a nerve in her, making her vibrate with shame and longing whenever they spoke. She forced herself to eat a decent portion of her meal, since she had no idea what else her punishment might entail, but it was a relief when Edward came and whisked her plate away.

Lin and Eric stood, leading their guests into a room Brandy had glimpsed only briefly during her tour a week earlier. Dark paneling, leather everywhere. She thought of it as the leather room.

Had it only been a week? It seemed like a lifetime.

Eric and Lin sat in leather chairs near a decorative fireplace filled with candles. Brandy hastened to kneel at their feet, between the two chairs.

The low murmur of conversation filled the room. Edward entered with an older lady—plump, with dark hair and laughing eyes—who she assumed was Mrs. Sanchez. They passed out desserts—an assortment of brownies, candied nuts, and lemon squares—and took drink orders. This time, Brandy was not offered anything.

As the evening wore on, it became harder and harder to maintain her composure. The willowy brunette was sitting on the arm of her Master's chair. Her sheer black catsuit was crotchless, and his fingers probed her pussy as he talked to the Dom sitting across from him. The sub's eyes were closed, and she stroked her Dom's arm, her lips curved in a smile of pure pleasure.

Brandy had never imagined she would want to be touched that way in a place where she could be observed, even openly admired, by so many others. Now, her pussy wept, and she found herself wishing that Eric or Lin would touch her. Show these people that they cared. That she belonged to them.

Red Leather's sub sat massaging her feet. Every now and then she would look down and whisper a word of praise, and his face would light up.

Two men sat on the couch. Their sub, dressed in a cut-out bra and a black velvet miniskirt, sat Indian-style on the floor between them. Whenever the one man spoke, she would finger her pussy. When the other one talked, she would gather one of her large breasts in her hand and bring it to her mouth to suckle. They both glanced at her frequently, as though checking to make sure she was doing so. Brandy got the impression that she was in training, as well.

The other two subs in the room knelt at attention, as she did, speaking only when spoken to. She found herself staring at one. A huge, well-muscled black man, he was extremely handsome. He seemed a strong, self-possessed person, but he knelt, collared, between two medium-height, medium-built, not particularly attractive males—one black, one white—and appeared perfectly content. They included him in their conversation often, and when they did, his face positively glowed.

She felt her lips trembling, a tear tracking its way down her cheek. The dark man's eyes met hers briefly, flashed with sympathy and interest, but then he looked away.

When people finally began to stir, mentioning the time, her legs were trembling, her thighs and calves aching. She had vacillated between states of calm and silent sobbing several times, and now she was emotionally numb.

When Lin and Eric stood, it was a relief to stand with them, to stretch her cramped muscles. She trailed them to the door, stood a pace behind them as they hugged and kissed their guests, saying goodbye.

They shut the door. Lin spoke to Edward for a moment, then she and Eric walked toward the bedroom. Brandy followed.

They ignored her completely. Lin shucked her form-fitting, navy blue gown, letting the fabric pool at Brandy's feet, and padded barefoot into the bathroom. Eric took off his slacks, shirt, and undergarments and stepped through the doorway. Brandy moved to follow, but he shut the door in her face.

Brandy stood there, tears threatening again. She heard a door open behind her and glanced back. Edward came in, carrying a bundle. He unrolled a thin foam pad, put a thick sleeping bag on top of it, and placed a pillow in the center.

She stepped to the side when the bathroom door opened. They strode past her and climbed into the bed. Lin reached out and turned off the light.

Brandy made her way blindly to the sleeping bag, squirming into it awkwardly. It was so close to the bed that, even after her eyes had adjusted to the dark, she couldn't see them.

But she could hear. The whisper of sheets against skin. Their low murmurs, quiet kisses.

Whispers. Rapid breathing. The moist sounds of sex.

She finally let the tears fall, face buried in her pillow as they carried each other away, without her.

* * *

When she woke in the morning, they were gone. She searched the house, unable to believe they had really left, but found only Edward and Mrs. Sanchez. Edward was on the back patio, rolling up a length of hose, and nodded almost imperceptibly as he glimpsed her walking past the French doors. In the kitchen, Mrs. Sanchez raised a dark eyebrow when she appeared, then turned back to the pasta she was rinsing in the sink.

It wasn't until later, when she was sitting in the library, trying to read a book and failing miserably, that she realized her nudity had ceased to be an issue for her. She hadn't thought about it a single time the night before, in front of all those people. She was so focused on her feelings for Lin and Eric that everything else was irrelevant.

She wasn't sure if that was good or bad.

Around two, she wandered into the kitchen. Mrs. Sanchez had disappeared down the hall with a laundry basket. Brandy opened the refrigerator and pulled out some lunch meat and mayonnaise. She made herself a sandwich. Restless, she wandered into the dining room. The French doors were open, letting in a warm breeze. She stepped outside, looking around the yard.

They had fenced in about two acres. With the high privacy fencing and the nearest houses too far away to be able to see her even from their second story windows, she felt safe enough to lie in a lounge chair, letting the warm sun caress her while she ate.

She'd never sunbathed in the nude before. The warmth and her relatively sleepless night caught up with her, and soon she was dozing.

When she finally roused herself, she found that someone, probably Edward, had set up a large umbrella. It was a good thing, too, because if he hadn't she probably would have burned to a crisp.

Brandy stood and stretched, then headed back into the house. She heard the noise of a television coming from the den and went in, to find Eric sitting on a couch, his attention divided between the evening news and the newspaper in his hand.

Brandy walked over and knelt at his feet. Facing him, so she could see his face. She was hoping for some kind of acknowledgment, even brief eye contact, but it was as if she didn't exist.

She had been scared to death of what her punishment might be this time, envisioning all kinds of painful discipline. The reality was much worse than anything she had imagined.

Her heart ached. She longed for a touch, a word, anything that would show they still cared. There was nothing. Lin came in and joined Eric on the couch, both of them ignoring her completely. The only thought she had to comfort her was that they would have sent her away if they weren't willing to give her another chance.

When dinner was ready, she found a place set for herself as well, and ate in melancholy silence as they chatted about their day. Afterward, they went into the den again, and Brandy knelt between them as they watched movies. Her legs were trembling and her shoulders cramping, but she gritted her teeth and sat through it, determined not to fail them again.

She lay on her pallet again that night, listening dry-eyed as they made love. It didn't hurt any less, but it was a part of her punishment, and she was resigned to accepting it.

The next day, she was their silent shadow. They ate breakfast, then walked down to the pool and swam laps. Brandy sat on the pool's edge, watching them, remembering the day at Stingray City, when they'd made love amongst strangers unaware.

It was almost more than she could take. She was tempted to run into the house, try to find her clothes, and leave. But she couldn't.

When they had finished, they climbed out of the pool, naked bodies glistening in the morning light. Brandy followed a pace behind, as always, as they went into the house. They made for the leather room, with its dark red walls and the candle-bearing fireplace. Eric switched on the sound system and sat on the couch. Lin curled up with a book, her head in his lap.

Brandy knelt before them, hoping again for some sign of forgiveness. As she watched, Lin drew up one leg, reached down to part her swollen lips, and began sliding one long, slender finger in and out of her pussy.

The rich, musky scent of her sex filled Brandy's lungs. Her body flushed with heat. Lin set the book aside, moaning as she pressed her finger deeper and deeper.

Eric, who had been resting back against the couch with his eyes closed, opened them. He smiled down at Lin, reached out, and covered her hand, his own finger joining hers.

Brandy trembled, bit back a sob. Lin smiled up at him, rubbing the back of her head against his cock. He smiled, caught her hair in his hand, and rubbed it up and down his engorged length.

They stood. Inches from her face, Lin's hand caressed his cock. She wrapped her far leg around his thigh, which meant Brandy had a perfect view of his fingers plunging into her over and over.

Tears ran like ice down her hot cheeks. Hearing it at night and being forced to watch and not participate were two very different things. She wanted to close her eyes and shut it out, but again, her desire to prove her commitment to becoming their sub was stronger than her need to avoid humiliation. She waited it out, didn't try to hide how much it hurt.

When they had finished, they turned to her. Reached for her. She thought they were finally going to touch her, but no. Their hands traced the curves of her breasts, her hips, scant inches from her skin. She quivered like a tuning fork. And then they went away. Just turned and walked out. Brandy knelt where she was, tears drying on her face, staring at the empty couch.

Edward found her there, later. The muscles in her legs and arms had gone from trembling to burning to numb. He placed a blanket and pillow on the couch, waited for her to crawl up onto it. Brandy ignored him. She was nothing without Eric and Lin. An empty shell, waiting to be filled.

Edward appeared concerned, but finally shrugged and walked out.

She stayed that way all night, listening to the house creak and moan around her. To the hissing of air through the vents, the faint helicopter sound of the ceiling fan. At some point, she fell asleep, eyes wide open. Still on her knees but totally unaware of her surroundings.

A sharp pain between her legs brought awareness rushing back. Brandy's eyes focused on Lin's face. She and Eric were sitting on the couch in front of her.

Lin's fingers were tangled in her bush, and she tugged again, hard.

Relief flooded through her, and her legs shook, almost folded. With iron control, she kept herself upright.

"We don't like all this hair," Eric said. "It needs to be gone."

"Yes," Lin purred. "I want you to feel my tongue when I lick you."

Brandy's heart skipped a beat. They were speaking to her again. Touching her. Strong emotion made her voice thick. "Yes, Master, Mistress," she said. "Should I take care of that now?"

Eric shook his head. "No. We have something special planned."

"Yes, Master."

"Turn around and bend over," Lin instructed.

Brandy complied without hesitation.

Eric's finger massaged oil into her anus. Brandy shivered with anticipation. When penetration came, it wasn't what she'd expected. She winced as something short and thick was shoved inside her ass. "Stand up."

She stood. Her legs felt like rubber, her muscles twitching spasmodically. Something hard bit into the inside curves of her cheeks. Her ass throbbed, tightening involuntarily on the toy buried inside. "Go to our bedroom and wash up," Lin said. "But do not remove the plug. There is clothing laid out on the bed for you. Put it on and wait by the bed, in the ready position, for one hour. When it is time, come to this room, and lay across this bench." She beckoned. "Come here."

Brandy walked over, calves twinging, the butt plug wiggling in her ass. The bench was long and narrow. The end toward her was a little lower than waist height, and the rest of the bench declined, so that the far end was only inches from the floor. Lin showed her, with a touch here, a murmur there, to place her feet on the platforms to either side, slipping them into straps so far apart that she was squatting, her pussy exposed. Then, she was to bend and lie along the bench, her head lower than the rest of her body, her ass high in the air. There were handles to either side of the lower end for her to grasp. When Lin was satisfied with her placement, she nodded. "Exactly like that." She helped Brandy to extricate herself and grinned. "We're having a little get-together this afternoon, and you, *ma chère*, are the party favor."

Brandy had no idea what that might entail, but she no longer cared. Her only desire was to make them happy. "Yes, Mistress."

Lin's eyes gleamed with satisfaction. Eric slapped her rump. "Get going, then." He caught her arm as she started away. "Oh, and Brandy, you absolutely must not allow yourself to come."

Brandy swallowed hard. Good God, what were they planning? "Yes, Master." She walked quickly to the bedroom, feeling their eyes on her, wincing a bit. Her legs were beginning to feel better, but the plug was quite large and stretching her continuously.

She followed their instructions to the letter, washing and then kneeling by the bed. She watched the digital clock on the dresser for exactly one hour, nervous and happy and apprehensive and excited all at once and trying not to think about it because it made her stomach tie up in knots. Then she made her way to the leather room.

Her steps faltered for just a moment when she saw people in there—many of the same ones from Friday night's dinner. But…this was what Eric and Lin wanted, so she squared her shoulders and walked in, ignoring the others as she went to her place and assumed the proper position.

There was a fur-lined oval at the bottom of the bench, into which her face fit perfectly. She lay there, hands on the bars, staring at the floor.

For quite some time, nothing happened. She was just another piece of furniture, as far as she could tell. However, eventually, a fingernail traced the furrow of her ass, stopping when it reached the plug. Even though she had suspected what was in store, that first touch made her jerk involuntarily.

A throaty laugh. "A little jumpy, isn't she, Eric?" she heard a woman's voice ask.

"She's new, Dana."

The tip of a nail circled around and around the plug. Brandy shivered. "It's rather a turn-on, actually," the woman murmured. She grasped the plug, pulled it out.

Brandy moaned.

"Mmmm." The woman's finger teased her anus. "Vocal, too. I like that."

Lin's voice joined them, and Brandy was thrilled to hear desire thickening her accent. "We do, too." She stroked Brandy's cheeks. "Don't we, Brandy?"

Brandy didn't know quite what to say. They'd never told her that before. "I-I'm sorry, Mistress. I didn't know that." She waited apprehensively, unsure whether not knowing was a punishable offense.

The plug invaded her ass abruptly. In and out, in and out. Brandy moaned with each new penetration. "Now you do, yes?"

"Yes, Mistress," Brandy whispered. "Oh, yes."

Another voice spoke. They were beginning to gather around her—like a child or a pet. Or an *hors d'oeurvres* table.

"You have yourselves a fine pussy, there." A finger plunged into her, searched until she gasped and moaned. "Oh, yes," the man murmured as her cunt clenched. "A fine pussy."

"Help yourself," she heard Eric say. A second finger joined the first, probing that magic spot.

Eric knelt beside her, his gaze dark. "Do you know how much it turns us on, baby? To watch people touch you?"

Before she could answer, someone took her toes in their mouth, sucking gently, running their tongue between each one. "Oh, God!" Brandy cried. Him, she could see. It was one of the two men, the ones whose sub was the beautiful, ebony giant.

"Shall I stop them, baby?" She turned her head so that she could see Eric. His hand caressed the bulge at his crotch.

"I'm yours, Master," she said, her voice trembling. "If their touching me gives you pleasure, it is my only wish."

He wrapped his hand around her head, kissed her hard.

"Ivory, come taste," someone said, and the fingers were gone, replaced by a dainty, flickering tongue that scooped Brandy's juices from her pussy. Another tongue traveled along her crack, back and forth. The butt plug was removed, and the tongue stopped briefly to tease her anus. She moaned loudly.

Eric sat back, watching.

She trembled with the effort of holding back her climax. Shivered and moaned, hands tightening on the bars, fighting her arousal.

The tiny tongue in her pussy disappeared, replaced again by a man's thick, fat fingers. The man sucking her toes looked up. "Donatello, would you like to play?"

Oh, God. She remembered Donatello, the strapping black man with the enormous cock.

"Yes, Master." She heard the giant's deep voice, pictured his gleaming black body. He'd worn black, body-hugging leather the last time, its glossy surface reflecting the candlelight, which had accented the curve of the huge erection trapped within.

Her pussy spasmed, and the man fingering her chuckled. "Tom, I think she likes your Donatello."

Everyone moved back, though the fingers buried inside her withdrew slowly, reluctantly. There was a breathless quality to the room now, as though they were all watching.

Which, of course, they were.

She should feel ashamed. Instead, she was horny as hell, eager for the next touch.

Two hands, large and calloused, caressed her cheeks. Oil dripped across them, slid down her crack. She could see Donatello's bare feet. His thumbs massaged and caressed, pulling at the edges of her anus.

"Oh, God," she moaned.

Her breath hissed in as he pressed into her, stretching her, working both thumbs beyond her rim. Her anus convulsed, tightening around them.

Donatello groaned, pressing up against her, his cock moving up and down between her cheeks.

She heard a startled gasp. She thought it might be the woman who had first touched her. Dana. "Oh, my God. Can she take him?" She seemed concerned, and yet there was a tight thread of excitement in her tone.

Lin's voice rang with pride. "Oh, yes, she'll take him." She squatted by the bench, tugging gently on Brandy's braid until she lifted her head and looked at her. "Won't you, *ma chère?*"

"Yes, Mistress," Brandy whispered throatily. "Whatever you ask, Mistress."

Lin's eyes flashed with that dark and dangerous something that was always hidden beneath the surface. "Look at it, Brandy."

Brandy looked back and up. Donatello's cock jutted above her cheeks, thick and hard, as big as the surrogate Lin had used on her that first day. She licked her lips. "Yes, Mistress." There was an underlying thread of eagerness to her own words, as well, that shouldn't have surprised her, but did. "I can take it."

Lin nodded, and Donatello pushed his cock between his thumbs, slipping them out as he penetrated her.

Lin still held her braid, making her watch. Brandy gasped and caught her lower lip between her teeth as pain and pleasure tickled her abdomen.

"Fast and hard," Eric prompted, eyes riveted to her face. "That's how we like it. Right, Brandy?"

Her gaze was fastened on the massive cock. Donatello was frozen, his stomach muscles clenched tight, his breathing rapid and ragged. Brandy took a deep breath. Allowed her gaze to travel up that rock-hard body, to meet the burning, eager eyes of her fellow sub. She licked her lips, smiling at the shiver that went through him. "Yes, Master. Fast. Hard."

He shoved, strong fingers digging into her hips, bruising her, as he drove himself deep. She screamed and arched. Registered briefly the arousal and awe in the faces of their audience. The woman who had touched her first, the Domme in tight black pants and a poet's shirt, someone who hadn't been at the party on Friday, sat down hard on the couch. Another woman lay there, legs spread, fingers buried in her pussy. The Domme tugged the sub's fingers out, pushed her own in, her breath quickening as she watched them.

The Master with thick, fat fingers was unzipping his pants, his eyes riveted to the place where Donatello's cock disappeared inside her. He gestured, and a willowy girl dressed in a sheer negligee, a collar around her neck, knelt and took him in her mouth, her own eyes watching Brandy and Donatello as eagerly as her Master's.

Tom and the other man who was Donatello's Master stood behind him, their hands caressing his chest, running along the part of his cock not buried. He shivered and closed his eyes.

He had only a third of his massive length buried inside her, and she was determined to take it all. "Deeper," she whispered.

She tightened her grip on the bars, heard him gasp when she pushed herself back as he thrust, embracing the penetration. He moaned, and Brandy sobbed with pleasure, her ass throbbing as it stretched to accommodate his thick middle portion, her pussy dripping.

All around her, subs were stroking and touching their Masters, being stroked and touched by them. Brandy felt a pang, wondering when Lin and Eric would touch her again. Make her come.

Eric glanced over, caught her eye. "Oh, Master," she whispered. "He's so big!"

She sensed the animal stirring within him. "He is, baby."

"Please, Master," she begged. "Make him hurry!"

His eyes flared. He looked up at Tom and the other master. They nodded. Tom reached into the slit at his crotch, pulled out his cock.

Brandy stared, disbelieving. Despite his average-sized body, his cock was massive, as thick as Donatello's, almost as long. He winked at her as he pushed on Donatello's shoulders, making him hunch down over her. The other master squirted liquid on Tom's cock, oiled Donatello's ass. Lin let go of her braid. "Down, Brandy," she murmured.

Brandy complied reluctantly. She understood, now, why Lin and Eric liked to watch. It was titillating, arousing, added to the sense of power. She was trembling uncontrollably now, fighting an imminent orgasm.

Donatello roared, and she knew Tom must have penetrated him. Her ass exploded with pain as he plunged into her, and she arched, pushing up on the bars, tossing her head back and forth as she fought her pussy's desire to clench and clench and never stop.

She glanced back. Donatello's eyes were closed, his face a mask of bliss. He withdrew, even as Tom did, and plunged in again as his Master thrust into him, fucking her as his Master fucked him.

Lin and Eric's eyes lit up each time Donatello penetrated her fully. She pushed up again and again, meeting him thrust for thrust, taking all of him for their sake.

His movements quickened, his breathing ragged, as he pounded into her again and again, creating friction and heat that made it harder and harder to control her responses. She sobbed. "Please, Mistress," she murmured.

"What is it, Brandy?" Lin asked.

"I have to come, Mistress. Please, let me come."

"No." Eric's voice, firm and final. "Not yet, Brandy."

She groaned. Pressed her face into the oval. "I can't do it, Master," she whispered.

"You can," Eric insisted.

A basso, sobbing groan. A deep, desperate thrust. Donatello imbedded himself inside her, and Brandy gasped hoarsely, repeatedly, each throb of his cock stretching her ass as his seed spilled into her, as he pumped and pumped his hips, an Amazonian giant bellowing "Yes, Master, yes!" as Tom groaned and froze, obviously joining the big man in release.

Brandy screamed hoarsely, not from pain, but from the pressure of holding back her own release. "Mistress, Master, please!"

They stroked her back. "Not yet, Brandy. Not yet."

She bit her lip, squeezed the bars tight.

Donatello gasped, fingers tightening on her hips spasmodically, and then he was sighing. He let go, brushed his fingers across her lower back lightly. "Thank you, Master Tom, Master Jonathan, for letting me play." He sighed again, hands tracing circles on Brandy's back. "Thank you, Master Eric, Mistress Lin, for sharing."

All around, voices joined in, adding their appreciation, their approval. Brandy was suffused with a warm glow. Donatello removed himself from her gently. Eric and Lin helped her to stand, turning her to face a sea of admiring gazes.

She looked down, cheeks burning.

Jonathan laughed. "Still a bit shy, eh?"

Eric embraced her from behind, rolling her nipples between his fingers. "Not for long, right, baby?"

Brandy moaned, pushing back the orgasm that threatened with each stroke. "Whatever you wish, Master."

He laughed, delighted. "That's right!"

Lin knelt in front of her. Leaned in and breathed on her clit. "Oh, please," Brandy moaned. "Please, Mistress. I can't take it."

"Not yet," Eric whispered in her ear as Lin's mouth closed on her clit.

Brandy arched.

Jonathan turned to Donatello, who was on all fours, waiting. He was another man whose looks belied his sexuality, Brandy thought, as he unveiled yet another unexpectedly large cock, slipping it between Donatello's cheeks. The sub moaned, arching.

So many well-endowed men. Eric. Short, scrawny Tom. Fat-fingers—whose name she still hadn't heard. Donatello. Every man in the room, as a matter of fact. It occurred to her that this would be a natural lifestyle for anyone so well-hung, because painful sex would be inherent in any relationship with them, at least for most women. How nice it must be, to have a partner that embraced that pain, made it their own. She felt proud to have been chosen, to have proven herself worthy of the challenge.

She rested her head back against Eric, gave herself up to Lin's facile tongue. Watched the sub in crotchless jeans rub her clit as she ate her Mistress's pussy. Watched Fat-fingers take his sub from behind, her juices glistening as he stroked in and out, slowly. She watched them all, leading each other toward ecstasy, freezing as they reached their peak, then gasping and trembling as they plunged over, one by one, and relaxed, smiling and sated.

Lin sucked her clit relentlessly. Brandy tossed her head, hands clenched. “Please, Mistress, please!”

Lin shook her head, tickling Brandy’s bush with her nose, flicking her tongue over the tip of her engorged clit one more time before she stood. She looked around. The room was still, Dominants and subs lounging in satisfied silence.

Lin walked across to the overstuffed leather chairs she and Eric had occupied on Friday night. This time, there was a low coffee table between them. Eric sat in the other chair, gestured to Brandy. She climbed onto the table and lay back. Lin reached over and parted her legs, pressing her knees down until they almost touched the table, placing the bottoms of her feet together so that she was open wide for them.

Lin picked up the remote and clicked the television on. All around them, conversation started up again. It was a normal Sunday afternoon gathering. Except for the strange attire. And the people kneeling at their Dom or Domme’s feet.

Lin’s finger slid into Brandy’s pussy as she turned to the woman in the poet’s shirt and asked her how business was going. Eric talked football scores and next year’s profits with Tom and Jonathan.

Lin’s fingers danced inside her, and Brandy grasped the edges of the table. They were going to drive her mad!

The afternoon dragged on and on. Sometimes she only had Lin’s fingers inside her, sometimes just Eric’s. Sometimes it was both of them, stroking and stroking, teasing her sweet spot. Glancing at her in warning when it seemed she might not be able to wait any longer. Each time, she managed to push the climax back. They even finger-fucked her during dinner, which consisted of sandwiches and chips brought around by Edward, one of them feeding her while the other one kept her constantly stimulated.

At some point, she lost all sense of her self. She was nothing but the feel of their fingers in her pussy, suspended in a twilight zone of sensation, forever poised just below the moment of release.

When the sensation disappeared, it was a shock. Brandy gasped, struggling to breathe, trying to understand why she felt so bereft. Eric and Lin were standing above her, holding out their hands. She took them, let them help her off the table. Followed and stood a pace behind them as they said goodbye to their friends.

"Edward?"

He appeared, a bundle Brandy couldn't identify in his arms. "Here, Mrs. Brogan."

He led the way to the bedroom. Inside, he opened the door and walked over to the closet, from which he pulled out a stepstool and carried it to one corner of the room. He stepped up onto it, fastening a series of ropes and pulleys into sturdy metal rings set into the ceiling. He stepped down and returned the stool to the closet.

"Thank you, Edward."

"You're welcome, Mrs. Brogan, Mr. Brogan. Good night." He turned and walked from the room, shutting the door quietly behind him.

Lin turned and took Brandy's hands in hers, backing up toward the corner. "Brandy," she purred. "Sweet Brandy."

She felt tears threatening again, at the look in Lin's eyes, the promise in her voice. In the back of her mind, she'd been so afraid that they were just playing with her. Wanting revenge. That when the weekend was over, they would laugh at her audacity, then send her out of their lives for good.

But Lin was happy, glowing. She stopped in front of the strange harness dangling from the ceiling. She reached up and drew down the zipper of her clingy knit dress. "Take it off, Brandy."

She reached out. Grasped the gaping fabric and pushed it back, her knuckles brushing across Lin's swollen nipples. That familiar fire flared in her gut. She knelt, drawing the fabric down with her, letting her own nipples glide along Lin's thighs. The coppery curls of her bush beckoned, and Brandy leaned close, inhaling the perfume of her Mistress's arousal.

Lin clutched at her shoulders. Pulled her up and turned her around. Eric was waiting, and Brandy reached out, carefully undid each button of his loose silk shirt and pushed it from his shoulders. She pulled the leather cord at his crotch, unlacing it, slowly revealing his swollen member. She knelt, working the tight pants down past his hips, her cheek brushing against his cock.

He groaned. Grabbed her braid and pulled her onto her feet. "You showed incredible restraint today, baby."

"Thank you, Master." Brandy thought for a moment. "If it pleased you, Master."

Lin leaned against her back, the hard pebbles of her nipples pressing into Brandy's flesh. "You've pleased us quite well, *ma chère*."

It was so stupid to cry, but she couldn't hold the tears back any longer. "Thank you, Mistress," she sobbed. "I-I'm so sorry, about everything. I—"

"Hush, baby." Eric wrapped her in his arms. "It's done. You're back, and we're never letting go."

Brandy snuggled into him, wiggled her butt against Lin's mound. It was so strange, to be sobbing and horny at the same time. Lin let go, walking over to the dresser. She rummaged in a drawer, pulled out something Brandy recognized. A shiver went through her as Lin positioned a dildo in the harness, strapped it around her hips.

Eric began strapping her into the thing hanging from the ceiling. Two wide straps went around her upper thighs, another around her waist. The fourth looped up under her arms, across her upper chest and shoulder blades. He pulled other straps, adjusted a tension ring, and when he let go, she was hung suspended, legs slightly bent, raw pussy exposed. Eric grinned and moved behind her.

Lin returned, holding slender silver chains in her hands. She stood in front of Brandy, looped one around her right breast. It was like a lariat, with a clasp through which she pulled the free ends of the chain, tightening it on Brandy's nipple until the dark bud stood out, prominent and purple. Brandy moaned, flickers of desire coursing through her. Lin smiled, roped the other nipple, pulled the chain tight. The ends dangled, swinging against her ribcage, each tickle having the delectable effect of making her nipples tingle wildly.

Lin knelt. "Mmmm. That pretty pussy." She slipped a finger inside, then two, watching Brandy's face. Brandy arched, setting herself swinging, groaning as Lin's fingers slipped out.

Eric captured her waist. Held her still while Lin pushed one, then two, then three fingers deep inside her, twisting and wriggling, stretching and probing. Bringing her to the brink of ecstasy over and over, but once again forbidding her to come. Brandy moaned and writhed, begged them to let her come. Eric tilted her back. Used his strong hands to press her nipples toward the center of her chest, so close together that he could cover them both with his mouth.

"Oh, God!" Brandy held onto the straps above her shoulders.

"Not yet," Eric warned.

His hand slid down, one of his fingers teasing the sore pucker between her cheeks. "Oh!" Brandy wriggled, hoping he would push it inside her.

Lin stood, fingers still buried below Brandy's bush. Her tongue joined Eric's, darting and dancing across her aching nipples. "Oh, God. Please, please," Brandy pleaded.

"Not yet." Eric stood back. Lin removed her fingers, coated Brandy's nipples with her juices, and began lapping it off hungrily. Brandy made tiny, desperate noises in the back of her throat, unable to speak.

Eric's hand slid between her cheeks, lubed her anus generously. Lin pulled her forward, positioning the tip of the dildo at the mouth of her pussy. Eric's cock slipped between her cheeks, bumping against the swollen opening there. "Oh, yes," she breathed. "Yes."

Brandy whimpered as Eric eased into her "Oh, God. It hurts!" He let her rest a moment, pushed a little more. She gasped and cried out with each tiny gain, swollen from Donatello's ministrations, but she wouldn't ask him to stop. She wanted him so much. Needed him.

After what seemed an eternity, he was there, his cock completely sheathed by her ass. Lin rocked her hips forward, driving the dildo into her pussy.

Brandy arched and groaned, shaking with need. They grasped the harness and started rocking her gently, back and forth. Pussy, ass. Pussy, ass. Pussy. Ass. She writhed. Begged. "Please, please."

"What is it, Brandy?" Lin asked.

"Please, Mistress," Brandy begged. "I need to be fucked." She licked her lips. "Hard and fast," she whispered, "Just the way we like it."

Lin looked at Eric. He nodded. They caught her waist, held her still, and plunged into her together. Brandy gasped, clutching the harness. Their cocks dueled inside her, trapping her flesh between them, driving her up, up, up.

She trembled on the verge of release, never quite tumbling over. It went on and on, until she was thrashing and moaning, whimpering fitfully.

Lin and Eric shared a look. Leaned forward. Whispered in her ears, "Now."

Brandy gasped. Arched. Felt pleasure roar through her, spinning like a twister, tying her stomach in knots and then exploding out along her limbs, until her fingertips and toes were numb. "Oh, God," she whispered when she could speak. "Oh, God. Thank you."

They took her again and again, all through the night, until she hung between them, limp and exhausted, and Eric took her down and carried her to the bed, to drown in darkness.

## Chapter Thirteen: Belonging

Leaving them to go to work the next day was pure agony. She wanted to beg them to let her stay, but she didn't. She was afraid her sudden, consuming need for them would be too much. Smothering. She held her emotions in check and left in what she hoped was a dignified manner.

Their contract called for her to be theirs, completely, from eight o'clock on Friday night until the same time on Monday morning.

Though Brandy had thought the week would drag, it seemed like no time until Thursday night was there and she was trying to decide what to pack for the weekend. As she chose her outfits, a thought entered her head.

She hopped into the car and drove to a store she had noticed before, but never shopped in. She purchased a medium-sized butt plug and took it home.

After her shower, she lubed the plug and slid it into her ass, wincing. She was still quite sore from the weekend before.

She lay in bed, unable to keep from tightening her ass on the plug, which made her pussy throb. She closed her eyes and began rubbing her clit.

The phone rang. She reached out lazily, still rubbing her clit with her left hand, and picked up the phone with her right.

"Hi, Brandy." Eric's voice sent prickles running down her spine.

She wondered what she was supposed to call him when they were on the phone. She settled for Master, since she was alone. "Yes, Master?"

"You may call me Eric, on the phone."

"Oh, but I'm alone," she said. "And I like calling you Master."

He chuckled. "In that case, call me Master."

Brandy sighed, rubbing her clit frantically. "Yes, Master." Just the sound of his voice was making her horny.

Lin's voice purred over the line. "What are you doing, Brandy?"

"Just lying in bed, Mistress," Brandy murmured.

"Is that all? You're not...touching yourself?"

Brandy blushed. How had they known? "I—yes, Mistress, I am. I-I'm playing with my clit." She rubbed it even faster, even more aroused by the act of talking about it.

"Mmmmm," Eric murmured. "Are you wet, baby?"

"Yes, Master," she moaned. "Would you...would you like to hear?"

Two quick gasps. "Yes," Eric barked.

Brandy held the phone between her legs, swirling her fingers in and out of her pussy, letting them hear the moist, sucking sounds. She brought the phone back to her ear. "Did you hear, Master? Mistress?"

They were breathing hard now. "Yes, baby, we heard." There was a pause, during which she thought she could hear them kissing, and was suddenly jealous. She should be there. With them.

"Brandy," Lin breathed, "Will you play with your pussy for me?"

Brandy gasped, then plunged her fingers back inside her pussy. "Yes, Mistress."

"All night?" Eric asked.

"Yes," Brandy whispered, "Oh, yes."

"But no climax," Lin murmured.

Brandy moaned. "Please, not again."

"Yes," Lin insisted. "Who does your pussy belong to?"

Brandy moaned again, fingers dancing. "You," she whispered.

"Who?" Eric prompted.

"My pussy belongs to Master Eric and Mistress Lin," she said, louder.

"And who decides when it's okay for you to come?" Lin said.

"You do," Brandy answered. "Mistress Lin and Master Eric decide when it's okay for me to come."

"Very good," Lin purred. "Goodnight now, *ma chère*."

"Mistress… I could come over tonight, for just a little while."

Eric's voice was amused, and pleased. "No, baby. Tomorrow."

Brandy groaned in frustration, but said, "Yes, Master."

"Play with your pussy for us, baby," he said. "We'll be hearing you, in our dreams."

And then she was listening to the dial tone, while her fingers stroked and stroked, just like theirs had, keeping her wired taut, yet just this edge of satisfaction. She had no idea when she finally fell asleep.

The next day passed in a blur. The new gallery was opening in just a week, and Brandy whirled through the afternoon in a frenzy of last-minute details. It was a relief to say goodnight to Kendall and head up to her apartment.

She took off her clothes, pulled on a very short, very tight red knit skirt. Pulled on a white lace camisole. Her nipples thrust out, dark skin peeking through the lacy fabric. She hoped they would like it.

She slipped on a pair of sandals and dashed down the stairs to her car.

Ben, Friday evening's gate guard, waved her through like an old friend.

The front door was standing open when she arrived. She walked in, saw no one. Headed for the leather room. No one there, either. She set her bag on one of the couches. Heard a laugh and a splash out back.

She headed for the pool. Eric and Lin saw her, swam over to the side. She kicked off her sandals and sat on the edge, legs dangling in the cool water.

"Hey, baby," Eric said. "How was your week?"

"Hectic," Brandy admitted. "We have the opening next Wednesday, and it's amazing how many little problems are cropping up at the last minute. Which reminds me, did you get your invitations?"

"We did," Lin said. "We'll be there."

Brandy smiled, "Good. I—"

They both reached up and grabbed an arm, pulling her into the pool. She came up sputtering and laughing. She chased them, trading dunkings and dares until they were all exhausted.

Brandy lounged on the steps in the shallows. Eric swam up to her, put his hands to either side of her on the top step and kissed her. He lowered his head, caught one pert nipple in his teeth, sucking lightly through the lace.

Dusk had fallen while they played, and at just that moment, the spotlights around the pool came on. Eric let go, looked down at her body in the bright light. "I like your top," he growled.

"Thank you, Master," Brandy said breathlessly.

Lin had joined them, leaning on one elbow at Brandy's side, watching them both. Her hand moved cross Brandy's stomach, tugged her skirt up. "I don't know," she teased. "I think it's still too much clothes. I prefer you naked." She rubbed Brandy's clit. "Did you play with yourself last night, Brandy?"

"Yes, Mistress," she confirmed.

"All night?"

"Until I fell asleep, Mistress."

"And when was that?" Eric asked, his tongue teasing her nipple again through the lace.

Brandy sighed with pleasure. "I'm sorry, Master. I'm not sure. It was very late."

Lin stood up and held out her hand. Brandy allowed herself to be drawn up. Followed her Mistress over to a blanket on the grass. Lin sat cross-legged on the checkered quilt. Brandy knelt at attention beside her.

Edward materialized out of nowhere, with fried chicken, potato salad, and lemonade for everyone. Eric walked over. He sat next to Brandy, gave her an odd look. Without warning, he reached and pulled out her butt plug. "What is this?" he asked, and he didn't sound happy.

Brandy swallowed. "I-I've been very sore this week, Master. Last night, I thought…it might be wise to…prepare myself for you. I… I thought you'd be happy."

He tossed the thing away, shaking his head. "No, no, no, baby."

Brandy shivered, though the August night was stifling. "Please forgive me, Master. I thought—"

"You're forgiven, Brandy, this one time. I won't punish you, because some initiative is good, like your actions last Friday, when you came to us again. You showed you had done some research, that you were committed to making things right again."

"But your body belongs to us now." He leaned in close, his breath hot on her lips as he looked into her eyes. "You don't even touch yourself unless we give you permission, *ma belle*. You understand?"

"Yes, Master."

"And you agree, yes?" Lin added.

"Yes, Mistress."

Eric's hands cupped her buttocks. His lips brushed hers as he spoke. "We've been enjoying *this*," he said, squeezing her ass for emphasis. "But these things must be carefully managed." His tongue slipped past her lips, tasted her. "We want you to stay tight, baby."

"Yes, Master," Brandy whispered against his lips. "I understand. Nothing like this will ever happen again."

"Good." He turned away and picked up his plate. "Bon appetite." He smiled.

Brandy allowed herself a quick sigh of relief. They chatted easily over their picnic supper. Lin was very pleased with the way the cruise line was performing so far. "It's still early," she mused. "But every cruise through the middle of next year is sold out, as of yesterday."

Brandy raised her lemonade. "Cheers!"

Lin chuckled throatily, clicked her glass against Brandy's. "Cheers." She tilted her head and drank.

The spotlights outlined every curve of Lin's body, reflected darkly from her strawberry-hued areole. Brandy caught herself several times during dinner, watching a tiny drop of water that quivered at the tip of one ripe nipple. Glancing down at the shadow between Lin's legs.

Lin caught her looking. She set her plate aside. Leaning back on her elbows, she drew her legs up and parted them. "Come here."

Brandy set her own plate aside, vaguely aware that Edward came and took them away, and Eric's as well, while she moved between Lin's legs. Her Mistress's eyes gleamed. "Is there something you'd like for dessert, Brandy?" she teased.

Brandy licked her lips. "May I, Mistress?"

Lin smiled voraciously. "I insist."

Brandy knelt. Reached out and parted Lin's copper curls to expose her plump clit.

She licked the little bud experimentally. Felt a thrill of satisfaction as her Mistress's hands tightened on the blanket. She covered it with her mouth, flicked her tongue across the sensitive peak over and over.

Lin moaned. Her sweet, musky odor surrounded them. Brandy inhaled deeply. She felt herself growing aroused, her nipples tingling. Her pussy throbbed. She let her tongue slide down to the edge of Lin's damp slit.

Her Mistress groaned, thrusting her hips. Brandy dipped her tongue between those lips.

Her juices were thick, tart. Every time Brandy breathed her scent, it felt like her breasts swelled a bit more, growing taut, twinging with need. She delved deeper.

Lin's cunt spasmed, tightening around her tongue. Brandy shivered. It was an incredible feeling, and desire washed over her in waves. She felt a heady rush with every whimper, each tiny moan.

Brandy wrapped her arms around Lin's thighs, buried her mouth in Lin's crotch. She caught a tender fold between her lips, sucking experimentally.

Lin moaned. Her hands found Brandy's head, held her as Lin thrust against her. Brandy sucked harder. Lin moaned and thrashed.

Brandy brought her hands to either side of her mouth. Used her fingers to spread Lin's labia, pushing them back, back, so that she could see the woman's red folds, trace each valley and ridge with the tip of her tongue. "*Ma chère, mi amour,*" Lin whispered.

Brandy started as Eric's head slid between her legs and he pulled her hips down to meet him. As she captured tiny folds of Lin's pussy in her mouth and suckled, he buried his tongue inside her, twisting and turning, sending spasms through her. She moaned loudly, and Lin bucked against her, lapsing into French. "*Mon dieu! Tu me rends sauvage.*" *My God! You're driving me wild.*

Her cunt spasmed, and Brandy buried her tongue deep, felt Lin's pussy flex and ripple against it. "*Oui,* Brandy, *oui. Fais-moi venir.*" *Yes, Brandy, yes. Make me come.*

Her own body shivered in response. She felt Lin tense as her tongue swept across one particular fold. She paused, pressed the tip of her tongue against it over and over. "*Mon dieu!*" Lin arched, her hands trapping Brandy's head against her as her pussy tightened spasmodically. Fresh, thick juices coated Brandy's tongue.

She licked greedily as her own pussy convulsed. Pressed her hips down, Eric's tongue flicking rapidly in and out of her pussy. She breathed in sharply through her nose, kept her tongue buried as she and Lin trembled in unison.

When it had passed, Lin drew her up, kissed her. "*Mon dieu,*" she whispered. "*Votre langue.*" *My God, your tongue.* "You are wonderful, *ma beauté.*"

Brandy caught Lin's lower lip between her teeth. Sucked—tasting salt, lemons, and the tangy residue of Lin's cunt. "Mistress. *J'aime ta saveur sur ma langue,*" she murmured. *I love the taste of you on my tongue.*

Lin held her tight, pressed her back against the blanket as she explored Brandy's mouth, her tongue eager, demanding.

Eric joined them, planting rough kisses on her abdomen, dipping his tongue into her belly button. Brandy moaned. She could lay there forever, wrapped in their arms, with nothing but their kisses to sustain her.

But Lin drew back. Brandy whimpered, reached out for her. "Come," Lin said. She and Eric rose, heading for the house, and Brandy followed.

Lin took the steps to the dungeon. Brandy remembered just before her Mistress unlocked the door that they had said she must always be naked in that room, and hastily wriggled out of her wet clothes. Eric nodded approval.

They guided her to a low table, made her lie back against it. There were stirrups for her feet, which she set in place without being told. Eric walked over to the sink/kitchen area. He picked up a small crock pot, playing out a long extension cord behind him as he carried it over and set it between himself and Lin on the bench at the table's foot.

Lin ran her fingers through Brandy's bush. Combed it up, held it as she snipped just below her fingers with a pair of scissors. Brandy watched as Lin continued, cutting all the hair at her crotch to about an inch long.

Eric raised one hand. He held a smooth metal dildo. Pushed it into her pussy.

She wanted to press that shiny dildo deep inside her, but she waited. Her pussy belonged to them. They would tell her what to do.

Lin held up a strip of linen, dipped it into the pot. Pressed the warm strip over the outer edge of Brandy's bush.

Brandy watched as the clear, warm wax hardened to milky opacity. Lin grasped the top edge of the strip. "Ready, *ma chère?*"

They were going to do it themselves. Take off her hair.

She gripped the sides of the table. Nodded.

Lin pulled the strip off.

It was like a thousand tiny needles, all piercing her at once. Brandy screamed. Eric began moving the dildo in and out of her pussy. She whimpered, pain and pleasure vying for her attention.

Lin readied another strip, placed it on Brandy's crotch, closer to her weeping slit. Brandy watched with a mixture of apprehension and anticipation as the wax hardened.

Lin grasped the edge. Brandy steeled herself. The strip came away. She screamed.

Eric turned on the vibrator. Brandy's scream became a moan, as pain and pleasure mingled, flooding her groin with hot need.

Lin placed the last strip for that side, pressing it close to her slit. "Oh, God," Brandy moaned.

"Shall I stop, *ma chère?*" Lin asked, as if Brandy had that choice. But she knew what they wanted, so there was no choice.

"No, Mistress," Brandy said. "Please. I want what you want."

"I want your pussy bare. Naked, the way I like *you*. I want nothing between us, *ma chère*."

"Yes, Mistress," Brandy whispered. "Please don't stop."

Lin grasped the strip. Pulled. Pain exploded at the edge of her pussy. Brandy writhed. Eric turned the vibrator up a notch, pressed his thumb against her clit, allowing the vibrations to travel through his hand to the sensitive nub.

Brandy moaned and bucked. Eric allowed her a moment's pleasure, then turned the vibrator off. "Other side," he murmured.

This time, Lin held the dildo while he placed the strips. Their gazes grew wilder and wilder with each raw scream she let out. When the final strip came away, Lin turned the vibrator to its highest setting. Pushed it deep inside Brandy. Stepped between her legs and pressed her pubic bone against it, holding it in place while Brandy thrashed. "Not yet, love," she murmured.

Brandy moaned and gasped. Eric pinched her nipples, drew them out, milking her. Brandy made inarticulate sounds in the back of her throat. Pleaded with them to let her come. "Not yet," Lin said, watching her face.

She thrashed and writhed. Her nipples ached, seeming swollen to the point of bursting. Her clit thrummed, vibrations from the toy buzzing through her pelvis. They kept her there, on the verge of ecstasy, for what seemed an eternity. Finally, Eric whispered in her ear. "Now, baby."

She came instantly, her mouth open in a silent scream of rapture.

When it had passed, she still quivered. They were training her, she knew. Training her body to respond only to them. Reinforcing the equation—pain equals pleasure. Tutoring her body to submit to them in all things—even to the point of whether or not to give in to a climax.

And she couldn't get enough.

Lin pulled the dildo from her pussy. Ran a hand over her red, raw flesh. "Oh!" Brandy shivered. It was so different, to have Lin's fingers glide over that part of her body, smooth flesh against smooth flesh. Lin bent and pressed a kiss to the bare skin to either side of her clit. "Oh, Mistress. It feels so good!"

Eric grabbed her hands and pulled them up over her head, holding them together and tying a strap around her wrists. He pulled the wide belt hanging from the table up and over her stomach, buckling her in.

He headed for the cabinet, came back carrying two leather floggers. He handed one to Lin. They shook them out. Eric looked her in the eye. "Don't scream," he said.

Brandy swallowed. Nodded. Eric raised his hand.

The flogger caught the inside of her thigh, stinging the tender flesh. Brandy bit her lip, kept silent. He brought it down again. Brandy jerked but didn't cry out.

They traded stroke after stroke, moving the blows closer and closer to her pussy, raising welts on her already sensitive flesh.

A leather strip snapped against her clit. She gasped, almost cried out. Again and again, the leather strips bit into her pussy, stung her clit.

But she was no longer fighting the urge to scream. Instead, her clit, red and plump, stung with desire. Her pussy ached with need. She watched for each blow, raising her hips to meet them.

Eric's eyes gleamed. "Oh, yes, baby. That's it."

Brandy moaned, rocked her head back and forth. Eric turned his flogger, stepped in close. He leaned over her, slipped his arm under her, and held her tight as he pushed the polished wooden handle, worn smooth with use, deep inside her. "Master, yes!" Brandy hissed.

Lin peppered her clit with blows. "Yes, Mistress. Yes!"

Eric plumbed her pussy again and again.

"Yes. Oh, God, yes!" Brandy screamed.

Lin snapped the flogger against her clit over and over. "Come for me, Brandy!"

Her body exploded in white-hot ecstasy. Eric pulled out the flogger, rammed his cock into her, his seed spilling as her pussy milked him dry.

And that was the order of her life for the next few months. She worked her butt off during the week. Drove out to the house on Friday night. Told them about her week. Learned about theirs. Then they took her to the dungeon and made her scream until the tension was gone, for all of them. Sometimes, they spent the rest of the weekend in normal pursuits—swimming, playing backgammon. Sitting together in the den, Lin and Brandy working a crossword while Eric watched television.

And sometimes they fucked her relentlessly, surfacing only long enough to eat, then plunging back in again, until she was raw and exhausted and still begged for more.

She began to feel melancholy, experiencing a desperate ache she couldn't seem to get rid of. It came as a shock when she was talking to Kendall one night and figured out what it was.

"It just…it hurts all the time," she was saying. She and Kendall had grown closer than ever. She now knew everything about Brandy's relationship. "And I don't understand why, because I'm happier than I've ever been."

"Is it your job?" Kendall asked. "Do you think you need a change?"

Brandy shook her head.

"Well, is it something to do with Eric and Lin?"

Brandy shook her head again. "No. Everything's wonderful. Every day, I thank God I went back."

Kendall frowned. "Are you sure? Your tone is...you sound strained."

"Do I?" Brandy shrugged. "I don't know why." Her voice became thick, hoarse. "I love them so much."

"Ahhh. So *that's* it."

Brandy stared at her. "I said that, didn't I?"

Kendall nodded.

"I love them."

She nodded again.

"What am I going to do?"

"Well, how do you feel about...the arrangement?"

"You mean the contract?"

"I mean with the whole thing. Only seeing them on weekends, maybe a quick word on the phone during the week, that sort of thing."

"Oh." Brandy frowned. "Honestly, I hate it." She closed her eyes. "I feel like a shell during the week. An automaton, going through the motions. I just... I miss them so much."

"Maybe you need to talk to them about that."

"What do you mean?"

Kendall shrugged. "Maybe it's time to move this relationship to the next level."

"You mean…like, moving in with them?"

"I don't know, Brandy. Is that what you want?"

"I… I'm not sure. That might be it." She sighed. "I keep waiting for the other shoe to drop. For the day I walk in and they tell me it's over."

"Is that what you think is going to happen, Brandy? I had gotten the impression, from things you've told me, that they might be looking for something more meaningful. Something permanent. Have you told them how you feel?"

"No. I…every time I try, my throat closes up on me. I'm afraid I'll…scare them away. What if they don't want what I want? I'd rather have them for three more months like this, than lose them now because they don't feel the way I do."

"Oh, Brandy." Kendall hugged her friend. "What if they're just as worried as you are? What if, in a month or so, they start drawing away, because you've never made your feelings clear and they decide they have to let you go?"

Brandy stared, horrified by the idea. "Oh, God. Do you think they might?"

"I don't know. I just know someone has to make the first move, and since you balked in the beginning, they may be even more reluctant than you are to press the issue."

Brandy nodded thoughtfully.

"You wanted this, Brandy, and you went after it, despite the inherent difficulties of the situation. If there's one thing I've learned, it's that happiness doesn't just fall into your lap. You have to go out and grab it, no matter what the rest of the world thinks. Do what's right for you, Brandy."

## Chapter Fourteen: Renegotiation

The Wednesday night gate guard didn't know her, but her name was on the list, so he waved her on through. Brandy drove up to the house feeling lost and a little frightened, but determined to find out exactly where this was going.

She stepped out of the car, adjusted her skirt and vest. She was wearing the same leather skirt and vest she'd worn that first night so long ago. She had the nipple rings on, and the clit clamp, and everything tingled deliciously as she walked up the steps and rang the bell.

Edward was surprised to see her. "Miss Mitchell, we weren't expecting you, were we?"

"No, Edward. Are the Master and Mistress in?" It was second nature to her to refer to them this way now.

"Yes. If you'll wait one moment?" His tone was apologetic. Brandy nodded.

Eric and Lin appeared a moment later, looking worried. "Brandy. Is something wrong?"

She shook her head, a knot lodging itself in her throat. “No…ummmm, could we talk?”

They shared a look. Didn’t even reprimand her for leaving off the Master and Mistress, which she didn’t feel right addressing to them directly until she knew how the evening was going to end. “Sure,” Eric said. “Come on.”

She followed him into the den. Sat on the couch, while they took two of the chairs, staring at her intently. She swallowed, her throat suddenly dry.

Edward glided silently into the room, carrying three tall ice-waters. Brandy took one gratefully, wondering how the man always seemed to know exactly what everyone in the house needed. She sipped hers, waiting for him to leave the room, then set it on the coffee table. “I want to…renegotiate the terms of our contract.”

“Renegotiate?” Eric leaned forward. Lin stayed back, watching her closely.

“Yes. I…I’m not content with things the way they are.”

“Not content.” Eric’s jaw clenched.

She knew what he was thinking, and hastened to reassure him. “Please. I… I miss you both so much when we’re apart.” Her voice faded to a whisper, and she took another sip of water. “I… God, I’m so afraid to say this.”

Lin was leaning forward now, an expectant look on her face.

“If…if this is just a fling for the two of you, I’m willing to continue as long as you want me. I’d rather have you every weekend for six months than not have you at all, but…” They were watching her intently. “What I’m trying to say is… I… I want to be with you. All the time." It felt so good to say it. She looked up. "I love you."

Lin's eyes were gleaming with unshed tears.

"I love you," she said again.

Eric stood and walked to the mantel. Brandy's heart dropped like a stone. Lin was crying, Eric had turned away. Everything was falling apart.

He came back and knelt on the floor between them. He held up a rectangular box, covered in red velvet. Lin placed her hand on his, opened it with him.

Inside, a necklace gleamed on white cotton. Three entwined hearts, in tri-color gold. The thick one on the right, with the greenish cast, she immediately associated with Eric. A matching one on the left, with a rosy cast, was Lin. And there in the middle, joining them—joined *by* them—a smaller heart, in pale gold.

Hers.

"*Resterez-vous avec nous?*" they asked her softly. *Will you stay with us?*

"*Pour toujours*," she whispered. Forever.

Eric's eyes were bright, and Brandy was astonished to see a tear making its slow way down his cheek. She reached out, caught it on her finger. He captured her hand, brought the finger to his lips, sucked the tear from it. Brandy stood and turned, pulling her braid out of the way. Eric placed the necklace around her neck, and Lin fastened the clasp. Brandy let her braid fall, the weight of their promise comfortable and comforting at her chest.

They laced their fingers through hers, drew her with them down the hall, into the bedroom. Exclaimed in delight as they undressed her, playing with the jewelry on her nipples, her clit. They gave her what she needed, over and over, long into the night.

* * *

Eric was watching her, elbow cocked, head propped up by his hand, when she woke the next morning. "Did you sleep well?"

Brandy stretched and sighed. "Mmm. Yes." She grinned impishly. "Yes, Master."

Lin stirred beside her, snaked an arm around her waist. "Good morning, *ma belle*."

Brandy clasped her hand, brought it to her lips. "Morning, Mistress."

Lin sighed. Rolled over and straddled her, pressing her shoulders into the pillow. Her damp curls tickled Brandy's pelvis. "Mmm." Lin rocked her hips, rubbing her clit against Brandy's, making her pulse race. "It's so nice to wake up to you."

"Yes, Mistress," Brandy breathed. "So nice."

Lin leaned in, kissed her softly by the ear. "I'm going to fuck you, *ma chère*."

"Thank you, Mistress," Brandy whispered.

Lin laughed, scooted off the bed and headed for the dresser.

Eric pressed his feverish erection against her hip.

Brandy sat up, straddled him. Eased down, sheathing him with her wet folds. She clenched her muscles, tightening her pussy on his hard length. He groaned, started to thrust. She put a hand on his chest. "Wait."

She reached behind and unplaited her long braid, combing her hair out. Leaned forward so that it fell around them like a curtain.

She moved, sliding up and down on his shaft, her eyes never leaving his. Faster and faster, breathing hard, moaning, watching his eyes until they clouded and she shoved herself down on him, hard, clenching again and again, wringing him dry as she arched and moaned.

As the last of his seed filled her, he shuddered. "God, baby." He reached out, caressing her cheek with a trembling hand. "I can't believe how you make me feel."

She pressed her cheek into his hand. "Master." The word itself was a caress.

She sat up, flung her hair back. Eased herself off of him. Madeleine was lying on the bed beside them, watching. She started to sit up, but Brandy touched her arm. "Please, Mistress," Brandy murmured, straddling her. "May I?"

Lin raised her eyebrows. Nodded. Brandy closed them off from the world with her pale curtain. Looked into her tiger eyes as she eased onto the dildo.

She leaned in close, let the tips of her nipples drag across Lin's chest as she rode. Her Mistress gasped, arched. Caught one of Brandy's nipples in her mouth, nibbling.

Brandy moaned.

Lin spread her legs. Brandy wondered why. Ignored it, riding her faster and faster.

Then Eric's thumb invaded her ass.

She glanced back. He was watching them avidly, two of his fingers buried in Lin's pussy, while his thumb wriggled inside *her.* She gasped, rocked her hips feverishly. Lin moaned and bucked, driving the dildo deep. Brandy sat up abruptly. Froze, arching back, as Lin's fingers milked her nipples and Eric's free hand pinched her clit, and the heat of her climax burned her to ashes once again.

"*Mon dieu,*" Lin exclaimed as they all fell back against the bed.

"That was fantastic," Eric murmured.

"You both make me so horny," Brandy whispered.

"What are we going to do?" Eric asked. He sat up. Looked at Lin.

She turned to Brandy. "Are you serious about this, *ma chère?*"

"Serious about what?" Brandy asked.

"We want you with us, twenty-four hours a day. You would still have some autonomy, of course. Enough to function in the business world. I'd prefer to have you at the offices with us, but if not, then you must ride with us in the morning, meet us for lunch, and ride home with us in the afternoon."

"I'll have to talk to Kendall. So much of what I do now could be handled remotely if Josh hooked me into the computer systems. I'd have to spend…maybe one day a week actually visiting the shops, making sure everything is okay."

"Do it," Eric said.

"Yes, Master."

## Chapter Fifteen: The Ultimate Surrender

It took her a week and a half to arrange everything. She was going to continue paying Kendall for the lease on the apartment above the shop, until they could find a renter. She rented a small trailer and was able to take all her things to Eric and Lin's in one trip. Kendall, Josh, Sutter, and the twins helped her move and spent that afternoon lounging in the pool, getting to know her new family.

"I like them," Kendall said while they were making their goodbyes at the door. "Are you happy?"

Brandy felt like her whole body must be glowing. "I am, Kendall. Thank you so much for giving me that nudge."

Kendall shrugged. "Hey, that's what friends are for."

Eric and Lin seemed oddly subdued after they left. She waited, sensing that they would tell her what was bothering them before long.

After dinner, she sat cross-legged on the floor at their feet while Lin undid her braid and spread the pale locks across their laps. She and Eric began brushing, and Brandy rested her head against Eric's knee. She had her eyes closed, almost dozing, when Lin spoke. "Brandy, Eric and I need to talk to you."

She took a deep breath and sat up, turning to face them. "Yes, Mistress?"

Lin's gaze rested on one pert breast. Sighing, she leaned forward, pulled Brandy's hair over her shoulder to cover it. Grinned wryly. "Too distracting."

Brandy felt a flush of pleasure.

"We wanted to know…it never occurred to us to ask…how you feel about kids."

This was the last thing Brandy had expected to hear. "I… I'm sorry, Mistress. What do you mean?"

Eric leaned forward, his expression earnest. "I'm forty, Brandy. And Lin's thirty-five. We made a conscious decision when we first got married not to have children."

Brandy eyed them warily. "O-kaay."

"What he's trying to say is…you're only twenty-eight. You've never been married. We want this relationship to be permanent, but if you want children…"

Brandy gasped. She had been so wrapped up in the relationship, and it had been so long since she'd had a sexual partner, that it had never occurred to her to ask Eric to use a condom. Or to go to her gynecologist and get back on the pill.

Eric must have suspected what she was thinking, because he squeezed her shoulder. "It's okay, Brandy, I've had a vasectomy." He glanced at Lin. "We're not doing this very well. That's what we wanted you to know. Seeing you with the twins today, it made us think. It wouldn't be right to move forward with this relationship if you didn't know that Lin and I don't want children."

"Our lifestyle is so different," Lin started to explain. "We didn't think it was fair to—"

Brandy was shaking her head. Smiling. "You don't have to explain. It's all right."

Lin seemed astonished. "Really?"

Brandy nodded. "Actually, I'm relieved. I love the twins, and next to the two of you and Kendall, they're the most important people in my life, but I've never really been good with kids." She laughed. "I'm too much of a control freak." Even knowing everything she now knew about herself, and submission and dominance, it seemed strange to call herself a controlling person to them. "Every time a friend is late because their child couldn't find their shoes, or a meeting gets canceled because that person is home with a sick kid, I realize that if I had a child, I would drive myself to distraction trying to control every little thing. Besides..." She reached up, pushed her hair back behind her shoulders. "Now that I've found you, I don't want to share."

Eric growled, tangled his hand in her hair, and pulled her up to lay across them. "Are you sure about this, baby?"

She picked up the brushes, held them out. "Could we do *this* if there were children in the house?"

She spread her legs and arched, and Eric brushed her nipples, and Lin brushed the bare skin surrounding her pussy, until she was red and swollen and begging them to fuck her. And they did, hard and fast and completely.

* * *

She had decided to make Monday her day to make the rounds of the shops. Coming off an entire weekend with her soulmates, she felt it would be less difficult to be apart from them. They had made arrangements to meet for lunch at a restaurant close to the wharfs so that Lin and Eric could stay for as close to an hour as possible. She had teased them about putting a time limit on it, saying they were the bosses, couldn't they do what they wanted?

Lin had groaned. "If we did what we wanted, *ma chère*, we would lock ourselves in this house with you forever, and the world could end and we'd never know it."

Brandy smiled, remembering the comment as she drove to the restaurant that first Monday. She still couldn't fathom how much they seemed to need her…want her. She felt the same way, and it was still scary at times, that intensity. She couldn't imagine what she would do if she ever lost them, how she would survive.

Eric stood when she came in, letting her slide into the circular booth to sit between them. They ordered, and shared the events of their day so far. She drew her legs up onto the seat, sitting cross-legged, her short skirt crawling up, but her bare pussy hidden from the other patrons by the long tablecloth. Throughout the meal, they reached out periodically, stroking her clit, slipping a finger into her cunt. By meal's end, she was flushed and desperately horny. After their waiter brought the bill, Lin leaned close. "Now," she whispered.

Brandy stiffened, pressed her lips together to prevent the sharp cry that struggled to escape as her pussy convulsed.

She remained rigid, flushed, as Eric paid the waiter. As the boy walked away, her orgasm faded, and she let out her breath with a long, slow hiss. "*Bonne fille*," Eric murmured.

She walked back to her car in a warm afterglow. Her body belonged to them completely now. They had spent hours—entire weekends—stimulating her to the point of orgasm, only to force her to hold back until they gave permission.

Now she spent every day in a subliminal state of arousal. They could make her come with a single touch. A single word. She sighed contentedly. She couldn't wait for the next day, her first with them at work.

* * *

Lin laid out a conservative business suit for her to wear to the office the next day, sans undergarments as always. She rode to work with them, sitting between them, so excited and happy to be with them that her pussy wept copiously, dampening her skirt, filling the car with her musk. Eric quirked an eyebrow. "Are you horny, baby?"

"Very, Master," she admitted.

He looked over at Lin, who waggled her eyebrows. "We're going to have to do something about that when we get to work, aren't we, husband?"

He reached out, clasped her hand. "Definitely, wife."

Brandy squirmed at the promise, her pussy flooding with fresh juices as their clasped hands rested in her lap.

When they arrived, she scooted across the seat and followed Eric to the elevator. Lin walked a little behind her. As they got on the elevator, she patted Brandy's rump where the skirt was damp. "This won't do, *ma chère*. I think tomorrow, you must ride with your skirt pulled up, so that your wet pussy doesn't mark it."

"Yes, Mistress," Brandy said, secretly thrilled to know that she would ride to work with them the next day with her bare pussy exposed. They might be tempted to touch her. Fuck her on the way to work. She felt her nipples hardening, rubbing against the heavy suit jacket through the thin fabric of her blouse.

Melanie, their secretary, gave her a curious look as the three of them marched past her desk and into Lin's office. As soon as the door had shut, Eric pushed Brandy up against it, hiked her skirt up over her hips. He stroked her pussy. "Oh, baby," he growled "You're so wet."

Lin reached around him from behind, unfastening his pants. Brandy pushed them down, freeing his cock. He locked the door, swung her around, and stretched her out on the carpet.

Lin reached back and unzipped her own skirt, letting it slide to the floor. Brandy felt a surge of lust as she realized Lin was naked beneath her clothes, as well.

Eric knelt between her legs. Lin straddled her, facing him, knees to either side of Brandy's shoulders, her curly bush just inches from Brandy's face. "Oh, yes, Mistress," Brandy whispered very, very softly, grasping Lin's waist and guiding that red, weeping cunt onto her questing tongue as Eric slid his cock into her pussy.

Eric and Lin embraced above her, locked in a passionate kiss as their hips rocked. Brandy wanted to moan, to tell Lin how wonderful she tasted and Eric how perfect his cock felt inside her. But Melanie was in the next room, and she had to stay silent. The realization seemed to increase her desire tenfold, and she gasped, arching.

Eric looked down at her over Lin's shoulder as her pussy clenched. "Oh, baby, that was quick," he said softly.

Lin's pussy tightened abruptly. "You want to come already?" she murmured.

Her pussy milked Brandy's tongue, sending spirals of delight down to her clit. Brandy buried her tongue even deeper. Tried to nod.

"All right, my love."

Brandy arched. Grasping Lin's waist, she burrowed her tongue as deep as she could while they came in unison, pussies clenching, Eric's hot seed flooding her womb.

Lin shivered, stood up shakily and looked down at Brandy. "Oh, yes, *ma chère*. We're going to like this very much."

Eric eased himself out of her. Brandy sat up. Picked up Lin's skirt and held it as her Mistress turned, stepping into it so that Brandy could draw it up over her hips and zip it.

Then she turned and helped Eric into his pants, remained kneeling as he zipped them. He held out a hand and helped her up, held it clasped in his as he walked over to a door in the back corner of the office.

"This will be your room," he said, opening the door. "It was originally meant to be a sort of executive lounge, where Lin and I could come to relax for a moment or two during a rough day." He grinned. "I think it's going to work beyond our wildest dreams."

Brandy stepped inside. It was done in the sensual, dark colors Eric and Lin preferred, midnight blue and purple-black velvet. There was a desk with a computer, a couch, a small bathroom tucked in one corner. There was even a narrow bed, up against one wall. "It's beautiful, Master. Mistress. Thank you."

Eric smiled. "Lin, could you sit at the desk?"

Lin nodded, smiled knowingly.

"I want to show you something." He turned and walked back to Lin's desk, waving for Brandy to follow. He opened a wide drawer in the middle of the left-hand side.

There were nine small screens, all showing Brandy's room from different angles. Eric pressed a button, zooming in on Lin's crotch. "Oh, my," she breathed. Her pussy gushed at the thought of them sitting at their desks, able to watch her at all times.

Eric shut the drawer. "I have one, as well." He walked back into the room. Pointed. "That door leads to my office."

Lin came around from behind the desk. "Your friend Josh was very helpful," she purred. "He wired the whole setup, installed your office software on the computer. You're hooked directly into the computer systems of all three shops."

"It's all wonderful, Mistress. Master. Thank you so much."

"Now, for the rules."

Brandy knelt on the floor in the submissive position, waiting.

"Any time you are in this room, the clothes come off," Eric stated.

"Yes, Master."

"If we call you on the intercom, and do not state specifically that you should dress before you come out, you will come to us naked," Lin continued.

"Yes, Mistress."

Eric walked over to a built-in cabinet, opened the door. "I've brought a few toys." He grinned. "Throughout the day, we may be calling you, giving you various…tasks to perform. You are to do so immediately, without question, and continue until you are told to stop."

Brandy shivered deliciously. "Yes, Master."

"And never, ever, come without permission."

"Yes, Mistress."

"There may be other things that come up, as we explore this new arrangement. As always, your unquestioning obedience will be required," Lin concluded.

"Yes, Mistress."

"Now, take off those clothes."

Brandy stood and stripped, then resumed the position. "We have no special instructions for you at this moment," Lin said. "We'll share lunch with you in this room at one."

"Yes, Mistress."

They turned and went to their respective offices, closing the door behind them. Brandy wandered around the room. Behind the other door of the built-in, there was a television and sound system, with a DVD player and remote control. She ran a finger over the stack of DVDs on the shelf below it. There were copies of her favorite movies, which made her smile, and some she'd never seen but had mentioned wanting to. And there were a few with handwritten labels. "Brandy's First Punishment." "The Day She Came Back." "The Party." "The Swing."

She shook her head. It couldn't be! She picked up the first one. Turned on the television and settled the DVD in the player. Pressed play.

Her own likeness sprang from the screen. She was trussed to the punishment table on that first night. Her breasts were stretched taut, her nipples purple above the metal clamps. She could even see her clit, huge and swollen, trapped in its own tight clamp. She took a shaky breath, stepped back until she felt the couch against her legs. Sat down. She watched herself scream, cry, grow flushed with desire.

Brandy moaned softly and drew her legs up onto the couch. She slipped a finger into her pussy, wishing she had her clit clamp and nipple rings with her.

The phone rang, and she groaned. Stood up and walked over to the desk, picking up the receiver.

"Are you enjoying the movie?" Eric teased.

Brandy rubbed her clit, still watching the screen. "Yes, Master."

"We forgot something. Keep the phone with you at all times." He chuckled. "It was a shame for you to have to get up to answer it when you were having so much fun."

Brandy leaned against the desk, knees weak. "Yes, Master. Please, Master, may I come?" She rubbed her clit frantically.

"Mmmm…no." Brandy groaned. "No, I think I want you to wait."

She could hear the smug satisfaction in his voice, and she couldn't even work up any resentment. The whole setup was so erotic, she couldn't imagine what it was going to be like. To be here every day, at their beck and call, to fuck and be fucked.

"Yes, Master," she choked out.

"Carry on," he said, voice filled with amusement. Brandy sighed as the dial tone sounded.

She hung up. Carried the phone with her to the couch. Then stood, going back to the cabinet. She took out the first disk and put in the one labeled "The Party."

There she was, her ass in the air, her legs spread wide. She watched the female Domme, Dana, draw a finger between her crack, tug the butt plug from her ass.

Watched the waif-like Ivory lick her pussy, while Master Tom sucked her toes and Fat-fingers, who she now knew was Master Sam but simply couldn't think of in any other way, explore her anus with his pinky. "Oh, God," she whispered. She lay back on the couch, slid her thumb into her pussy. Longed to slip a finger into her ass, but after the butt-plug incident, Eric and Lin had forbidden her to touch that part of her body without their permission.

The phone buzzed. She picked it up, held it to her ear. "Go over to the…let's see…we'll call it our tool cabinet," Lin murmured.

Brandy stood, walked over, and opened the door. "On the bottom shelf, there's a pink device." Brandy picked it up, carried it with her to the couch.

"I want you to use it, *ma belle*." Lin's voice deepened. "But you *absolument* must not allow yourself to come, understood?"

Brandy made a sound of frustration. "Yes, Mistress."

"I'll be watching," Lin purred.

That set Brandy's nipples tingling. She hung up the phone and set it aside. Studied the toy. It was a vibrator, but like nothing she'd ever used, or had used on her, before. The central rod was a thick, ribbed cock. Jutting out from one side was a dolphin-shaped appendage, which she knew from seeing them in magazines was meant to be used for clitoral stimulation. Opposite that, there was another attachment shaped like the head and beak of a hummingbird. "Oh, no," she moaned, but her body was saying, oh yeah!

She looked for the cameras, spotted one mounted just to the right of the television, inside the cabinet. She positioned herself on the couch so the camera aimed right at her pussy. On the screen, Donatello was now standing behind her, oiling her ass. Brandy moaned, working the central shaft into her pussy. When it was buried, she shifted it slightly so that the nose of the dolphin and the tip of the hummingbird's beak seated themselves in their proper places.

She took a deep breath, watching as—on the screen—she begged Eric to make Donatello hurry. Gasped as she watched Tom's huge erection pierce the big man's ass, then move with him as he roared and buried himself inside her. She pressed a button on the pink toy.

"Oh, God!" The tip of the cock vibrated, but the shaft turned, the ribs along its length massaging her pussy. "Oh!" The dolphin wiggled back and forth, rubbing her clit with its nose. And the bird—it pecked and pecked, its beak penetrating her anus, shallow and rapid. She arched, pressed the toy deeper, biting her lip as she screamed on-screen, the way she couldn't in this little room.

The doors to Eric and Lin's offices opened and shut. Lin's hands stroked down her breasts from behind, capturing her nipples. Brandy held her breath, desperately holding off her release. Eric took off his pants. Knelt in front of her. Took away the toy.

Lin leaned in over her, pulled her ass cheeks apart. Brandy gasped as Eric pressed the tip of his cock against her anus. They hadn't taken her this way since the incident with the plug—a sort of unacknowledged punishment, she'd always thought. Lin grasped her hands, brought them down and made her hold herself open for him. She picked up the dildo. "Open your mouth," she said as one hand twisted and pinched Brandy's nipples.

She opened her mouth. Lin slid the dildo in as far as she could take it. "Can't have you crying out, love." Brandy swallowed, tasting her own salty sex on the shaft.

Eric trembled with need. He dipped his fingers in her pussy, coated his cock with her juices. Brandy bit down on the plastic shaft as he grunted, thrusting hard. She arched, moaned around the toy. Lin swung a leg over the couch. Sat beside her, slipping her fingers into Brandy's pussy as Eric's cock plunged deeper and deeper.

Her Mistress's fingers pleasured them both. Found Brandy's sweet spot and pressed it, over and over. Stroked Eric's shaft through her tissues, as he plunged in and out. Brandy moaned again, reaching out to touch Lin's bush.

Lin let go of the dildo, guided Brandy's fingers deep inside, along with two of her own. Brandy whimpered softly, deep in her throat, lips wrapped tightly around the toy.

"Now," Lin and Eric gasped at the same time.

Brandy arched. Lin's pussy milked her fingers, while her own cunt sucked at Lin's. Eric's cock pulsed in her ass. She moaned and moaned, the sound muted by the thick plastic cock, until the pleasure faded to a warm glow in her belly.

Lin reached up and took the toy from her mouth. Brandy eyed it appreciatively. "Mistress, that is…very pleasing," Brandy murmured. "Thank you."

"No, *ma chère*. Thank *you*." Lin pulled their fingers from her cunt, held Brandy's up to her mouth, licking her own juices from each digit.

Brandy's breasts tingled. "Oh, Mistress," she breathed.

Lin laughed with delight. "Oh, Eric. I think our baby's horny again!"

Eric eased himself from her ass. Took her hand and guided her thumb into her pussy. "Is that right, baby? Do you want to come again?"

"If it pleases you, Master," Brandy managed to choke out.

He lowered his head, took her middle finger in his mouth while she stroked her thumb in and out of her pussy. He let go, pressed the finger against her still-throbbing anus. "Oh, Master! May I?"

He nodded, and Brandy buried her finger eagerly. "Oh, God!" She didn't even have time to savor it, for she had their permission, and her body responded to that knowledge immediately, a fierce orgasm rocketing through her. "Oh, God. Oh, God." It was so hard to keep her voice down! Lin solved the problem by covering her mouth, capturing her cries with her tongue.

She slept after they left, curled up on the couch in a cocoon of sexual satisfaction.

## Chapter Sixteen: Branded

Life was perfect.

Brandy sighed and stretched in the sun, lying naked on a lounger in the backyard. It had been six weeks since she rearranged that life so that she could dedicate it almost entirely to her Master and Mistress, and she had absolutely no regrets.

The thing was, every time she thought nothing could be better, her Doms found a way to surprise her.

She heard their voices, wafting out to her from the dining room. They'd had to run an errand earlier. It was a mark of her training and the trust between them that she never questioned where they went, what they did, when they were without her. She shaded her eyes and looked toward the house.

Lin and Eric were walking toward her, a stranger between them. She felt a surge of love. Lin was radiant in a pale pink blouse, her snow-white shorts setting off her tanned legs nicely. Eric was tall and handsome in his khaki shirt and shorts, lean and athletic, and she thought again how he looked like someone ten years younger.

They stepped up onto the deck and crossed over to the lounger, smiling down at her. "Brandy, we'd like you to meet Bryan."

Brandy stood, totally unselfconscious now about her nakedness. Bryan didn't seem taken aback, either, and she assumed he was part of the culture. She held out her hand. "Nice to meet you."

He grasped it longer than was necessary. His eyes caressed her body, resting for a few moments on her tanned breasts, eyebrows lifting as he took in her bare pubic mound. Her nipples swelled under his scrutiny. "Wow."

"We told you she was exquisite."

He nodded. "Congratulations," he said to her. "Permanent relationships are a rare gift, and your Master and Mistress are the best." He let go of her hand.

She knelt, assuming the submissive position. "I know, sir. I cherish their presence, every day."

He nodded, looking down at her with hungry eyes. He was about Lin's age, handsome in a surfer dude sort of way. His expression made her nipples tingle. Brandy's hand strayed to her clit. Her Master and Mistress had told her never to hold back. If she felt aroused, she was to express that arousal immediately—in a discreet manner when they were in public, of course. More openly when they were at home or in the privacy of the office. Since nearly everything they said or did turned her on, she now spent the majority of her time in a heightened state of arousal, spurred by self-stimulation.

She rubbed her clit in slow circles. Bryan's eyes followed her movements, darkening with desire.

"She likes you," Lin murmured. "That will work out nicely, yes?"

"Yes," the man breathed.

"Brandy."

"Yes, Mistress?" She continued to stimulate herself, because she did not have permission to stop.

"Bryan is the man who did our tattoos. Look!" She and Eric turned together, pulling their shirttails up.

There was a new addition. On each of their backs, balanced on the upraised paws of the panther and tiger, was an elaborate, colorful butterfly. She reached out and feathered her fingers across it. "They're beautiful," she whispered.

Lin turned. "It's you, Brandy."

Eric nodded. "You were a chrysalis when we met you, wrapped in questions and doubts, and now you've blossomed into something so beautiful and tender, we can hardly stand to be away from you."

"And now it's your turn, Brandy. We want our mark on you. Our brand."

"Yes, Mistress," Brandy breathed. "Oh, yes. Thank you, Mistress. Thank you, Master."

"Bryan is a very good friend of ours, baby." Eric tilted her head up, looked into her eyes. "He's offered to do this at a large discount, if we let him play with you. Would you like that?"

Brandy trembled. Only once since the party had they allowed someone else to touch her as they watched, and the lovemaking afterward…fierce. Phenomenal. It was worth it to her for that reason alone. "Yes, Master," she said. "I'd like to be played with."

Bryan's erection strained against his zipper. "Oh, hell," he said. "Can we please get started?"

Eric grinned. "Come on."

He led them down to the dungeon. Bryan stripped out of his clothes. He was very muscular, yet another well-endowed male. Brandy licked her lips hungrily, fingering her pussy.

He walked over to a high bench, set the large case he was carrying on a table beside it, and opened it. Brandy caught a brief glimpse of inks and needles before Eric guided her onto the bench in front of him.

It was the one from her day as a party favor, but Eric had adjusted the legs, so that she was horizontal, rather than leaning with her head almost to the floor. He had her bend over it, then placed her feet into their places, so that her legs were spread wide. She rested her face in the oval. "I can't strap you in, because it would be in his way, so you mustn't move," Eric warned her.

"Yes, Master."

Lin had brought over a power strip, into which Bryan was plugging various implements. "We're starting from scratch here," he said, "So this is going to take a while." He looked at Eric. "Do you want this done in two sessions...maybe three?"

Eric and Lin both shook their heads. "Finish it today."

Brandy glanced back. Bryan looked skeptical, and she also suspected he was disappointed he wasn't going to get more than one session with her.

She turned back to the oval, squirmed against the device. It was frustrating, because she wanted to touch herself, but her breasts were trapped against the bench, and her pussy was too far to reach.

"That could take a few hours. Can she take it?"

Brandy smiled as they answered. "She can take it."

She figured he probably shrugged. "You're the bosses."

She heard him stand. His hands grasped her hips, drew her back to the very edge of the bench. His fingers brushed across her sex.

"She likes to have her ass played with," Lin said in a stage whisper, and Brandy could almost feel Bryan's desire ramp up.

He sank several fingers on his left hand into her pussy. Leaned into her. Pressed something against her back with his right.

Brandy gasped, clenching her pussy as tiny, exquisite prickles made their way slowly across her lower back. She moaned, tightening on his fingers again. He wiggled them. "Mmmm. She does like it."

Eric brought his lips close to her ear. "You have our permission to come whenever you want."

Her pussy spasmed immediately. Brandy clutched the bench, pressing her pelvis into it, hard, to keep from moving.

"Oh, hell," Bryan said, his voice shaky. His right hand faltered as she milked his fingers. "Oh, yeah."

The spasms passed. Bryan slipped his thumb inside her, swirled it around. Then he buried his two middle fingers within, teased her crack with his wet thumb.

"Here," Lin murmured. Her smooth hands grasped Brandy's cheeks, pulled them apart. Bryan grunted wordless thanks, thrusting his thumb inside her.

"Oh, yes," she breathed. "That feels so good, Bryan." She tightened her anus over and over, rapidly. "I like your thumb in my ass."

Bryan groaned. He leaned into her again, moving his thumb in slow circles inside her as he pressed the needle to her back.

Brandy moaned. He kept it up for a long time, torturing her back exquisitely while his fingers and thumb moved expertly, bringing her to the brink of pleasure again and again, only to ease off, withholding her release.

Brandy whimpered nearly continuously, begging, sensing the pleasure it gave him. "Please, Bryan. Oh, please. Let me come. Let me come."

Finally, he set the device aside. Leaning on her, he rested his elbow on her lower back as he pulled one cheek aside with his left hand so that he could watch. He slipped his fingers out of her pussy, drove his thumb into her again and again. "Oh, yes. Oh, yes!" Brandy cried. She arched, reaching back to grasp his wrist, shove him even deeper. "God, yes, Bryan. Yes!"

"Holy shit!" Bryan's cock spurted as she came, coating his abdomen. Stray droplets splattered her thigh. He groaned in disappointment.

Brandy panted. When the shudders passed, she looked back at him. Whispered hoarsely, "It's all right, Bryan. Put it inside me. I'll make it hard again."

He stared at her in disbelief, then shook his head as though coming out of a daze. He eased his thumb out, washed his hands in the soapy tub Lin had set beside him.

He dried them. Brandy rested her head in the oval again. He stepped up between her legs. "Wait." Eric's strong hands parted her lips. Bryan tucked his limp cock inside her pussy.

There was a brief pause while he changed inks and tips. Then the needles were pricking her again, driving tiny corkscrews of need into her pussy. She tightened around him.

His breathing quickened. The slow, wonderful torture continued. Brandy gasped repeatedly, tightening her pussy erratically against his cock.

He moaned, but his hand never faltered. She felt him twitch inside her. "Oh, yes, Bryan," she murmured. "I love your cock. I want it inside me, this time. I want to feel you come."

He moaned again, his cock thickening, his breathing fast and shallow. She waited patiently. Waited, waited, until he was ripe and ready inside her. Then she waited some more, until she sensed he was just about finished with that portion of the design. "And after that," she whispered, "I want to make you hard again, so I can drink your seed."

His hand froze. He bucked once, twice, a third time, and then warmth filled her as her pussy sucked him greedily. She felt him shiver against her. "God, Eric, Lin. She's pure gold."

Brandy turned her head to look at them. They were naked now. Lin sat in Eric's lap, facing them, watching, his cock buried in her pussy. His finger massaged her clit as she toyed with her nipples. They didn't bother to answer.

Brandy licked her lips. Bryan switched out inks and tips, went to work on her back again.

As Brandy watched, Lin worked her legs, raising and lowering herself on Eric's cock. Brandy caught a glimpse of its rigid length, gleaming with juices.

She moaned, licking her lips. They fucked, slowly and deliberately, knowing she was watching, and when their climax was imminent and they mouthed the word “now” at her, she came along with them, moaning, legs trembling, pressing her clit hard against the table’s edge.

Bryan was hard again, too, and finished with that color. He harvested her juices, coating his cock. He pressed the engorged tip against her anus. Hesitated. “Do you mind, Eric? Lin?”

Lin stood and sauntered over to the table. Caressed Brandy’s cheeks lovingly. “I don’t know. Brandy, do we mind?” She parted her cheeks, teased the reddish pucker with her nail.

“Whatever you wish, Mistress,” Brandy answered shakily.

Lin’s hands held her open, as Bryan’s cock, a nice size, but not nearly so big as Eric’s, pressed into her. She sighed contentedly. “Mmmm.”

His cock twitched, but he didn’t come. He started on her back again.

His ardor was less urgent now, more patient. He worked on her back for a long time, occasionally withdrawing his cock from her ass and then sheathing himself again, slowly and deliberately, seeming determined to savor her this time.

Which Brandy could appreciate, but it was really making her horny. And she had permission to come as often as she could. If Eric and Lin were touching her, speaking to her, she would probably be exhausted by her climaxes by now. But Bryan wasn’t them. She needed more. She moaned continuously, whispering his name.

Finally, finally, he set his tool aside once more. Grabbed her cheeks and massaged the area closest to his cock with his thumbs while he penetrated her again and again, each stroke long and lazy. Brandy gasped and rocked back, pressing her ass into him. He groaned, began bucking frantically. "Yes, yes!" Brandy screamed. "Fuck my ass, Bryan!"

His cock exploded, flooding her ass. Brandy's breath came in ragged gasps as her anus compressed repeatedly, emptying him inside her.

Bryan sat down hard on the bench when it was over. "Damn." He laughed. "My hands are shaking. I need a minute."

"Take your time." Eric stepped up to Brandy, drew a slow circle around the design on her back. "It's going to be beautiful, baby."

Lin joined him, drawing soft pictures around her shoulder blades. Brandy sighed contentedly, just enjoying their touch, their presence.

Shortly, Bryan indicated he was ready.

An hour later, he was finally finished. He and Eric helped Brandy down from the table.

"How much do we owe you?" Eric asked.

Bryan shook his head. "It's free, man."

"Are you sure?"

Bryan looked at Brandy. "Definitely."

She pouted. "But you never let me drink you, and I promised I would. Won't you let me do this one small thing to thank you?" Lin and Eric radiated approval.

He froze, then set down the paints he was putting up. "Ummm…sure. If you insist."

Brandy knelt before him. "Oh, I do," she purred. She soaped up a sponge, washed his cock thoroughly, happy to see that she had no trouble making him hard again. Damned if these

Dom/sub culture people didn't have more stamina than anyone she knew!

She took him in her mouth, sucking and licking, cupping his balls and teasing them gently. He groaned, wrapping his hand around her head and pushing into her.

Eric and Lin fondled themselves, breathing hard, watching.

She took him deeper, pressing up against his shaft with the back of her tongue, humming deep in her throat. "Oh, shit. Not yet!" he moaned, but he was already pulsing, and Brandy drank him down.

Afterward, he drew in a long, shuddering breath. "Thank you."

Brandy smiled "You're welcome."

Bryan finished gathering his things, dressed, and gave them instructions on caring for her back, handing her a tube of antibiotic ointment to use to help prevent infection.

"We'll walk you out," Lin said. "Back in a minute, love." They disappeared out the door, up the stairs.

Brandy stood in front of the mirror wall, looking at the tattoo over her shoulder.

She was branded.

Theirs. Forever.

Eric and Lin returned, their arms snaking around her waist, whispering, "Do you know what you need?"

Brandy smiled. Eyed them possessively in the mirror. "No, but you do."

As they pulled her to them, she thought again that nothing could ever be any better.

And they showed her what she needed, proving over and over that she was wrong.

With them, there would always be something better.

## Rachel Bo

Rachel Bo is an award-winning author currently published in several genres. On the weekends, she works as a Clinical Laboratory Scientist. During the week, Rachel writes and rides herd on her handsome husband, two wonderful daughters, a rabbit, a snake and several remarkably hardy goldfish.

You can always find Rachel on the Internet at http://webpages.charter.net/rachelbo/ or e-mail her at rachbo03@yahoo.com.

Turn the page for an exciting preview of

WOLF-BOUND: BEASTS IN THE LABYRINTH

By Rachel Bo

Now available in e-book format from Loose Id®

At a club called the Blue Moon, Johnathan scooted into one of the semicircular booths lining the back wall, and Tara and Jake slid in beside him. She couldn't help thinking of herself as the meat in a very unusual sandwich as their eyes roamed her body, caressing each curve and peak like a familiar lover. Cheeks hot, she looked away.

"Tara." Jake's voice, rich and smooth as molasses, oozed into her every pore, imbuing her with desire, flooding her pussy with sticky warmth. Their animal nature, the rich, sensual vitality of them, tugged at her body with a strength and allure that was overwhelming—like a dark, dangerous pool that she nevertheless yearned to jump into, knowing she might drown. "What brings you to New Orleans?"

She shrugged, looking back and forth between them, unable to drink in enough of their dark, shaggy hair, their swoon-inducing eyes. "It's my birthday. Well, it will be in a couple more days. St. Patrick's Day."

Jake chuckled. "An Irish lass born on St. Patrick's Day? What are the odds?"

Tara laughed, too. "I know. You wouldn't believe how many kids accused me of making that up when I was young. Anyway, I decided to take a week off around my birthday this year. A friend of mine had been to New Orleans a few years ago, and it sounded like such fun that I've wanted to visit ever since. So here I am. Kind of a birthday present to myself."

Johnathan watched her intently. "No...significant other back home?"

Tara squirmed, unaccountably shy now that it came down to particulars. "Why?"

Johnathan smiled, a big, toothy grin that sent shivers to her groin. "Because if there isn't, we don't have to feel guilty about seducing you."

Tara swallowed hard. "Is that what you're doing?"

Johnathan flicked a glance toward his brother. Tara turned her head, and sank in the quicksand of Jacob's deep, penetrating gaze. "I don't know, Tara." His hand closed on her knee, slid up beneath her skirt. Her heart pounded as he pressed his fingers against her panties. "You're so wet." His fingers teased at the elastic.

"Can we?" Johnathan whispered in her right ear. "Can we fuck you, Tara?"

There were very few patrons in the dark bar on this Tuesday night, and the few that were there paid no attention to the people around them. A blues singer played the piano softly. Her rich, husky voice throbbed with the pain of longing, echoing Tara's need. Moaning, she parted her legs. With a growl, Jacob pushed aside her panties and slipped a finger inside her. Unable to face those piercing eyes any longer, Tara closed hers, laying her head back against the booth's padded plastic.

Johnathan's hand crept between her thighs, one finger joining his brother's inside her. Oblivious to the world, Tara tossed her head, moaning softly, repeatedly, as their fingers dipped and glided among her slick folds. Heat and pleasure blossomed in her groin. Reaching out, she grasped their shoulders as she began to rock her hips.

Responding to her urgency, their fingers wriggled faster and faster, until Tara arched and held her breath as sheer pleasure twisted her up like a child on a swing, then released her in a wild, spinning rush that left her reeling and gasping for breath, hanging on to them for balance.

Tara opened her eyes. "Oh, God."

Jacob chuckled. "How was it?"

Tara pulled him roughly toward her and kissed him, sliding her tongue over his sharp, gleaming teeth. Johnathan's breath warmed her neck. Growling softly, he nipped her, then ran his tongue tantalizingly across the tender flesh.

Tara tore herself away from Jacob's lips to gasp, "More."

~ * ~

"The sequel to *Twice Blessed* from *Rated: X-mas, Beasts in the Labyrinth* is packed with sexuality that jumps off the page, drawing me into the passionate encounters between Johnathan, Tara, and Jacob."

—Francesca Haynes, *Just Erotic Romance Reviews*

"*Wolf-Bound: Beasts in the Labyrinth* is a keeper. This book comes highly recommended for fans of erotica who enjoy a little something extra."

—Tammy, *Love Romances*

NOW AVAILABLE In Print
From Loose Id®

ROMANCE AT THE EDGE: In Other Worlds
MaryJanice Davidson, Angela Knight and Camille Anthony

CHARMING THE SNAKE
MaryJanice Davidson, Camille Anthony and Melissa Schroeder

HARD CANDY
Angela Knight, Morgan Hawke and Sheri Gilmore

TAKING CHARGE
Stephanie Vaughan and Lena Austin

THE SYNDICATE: VOLUMES 1 & 2
Jules Jones & Alex Woolgrave

AVAILABLE FROM YOUR FAVORITE BOOKSELLER!
Publisher's Note: All titles published in print by Loose Id® have been previously released in e-book format.

Check out these other titles, also available in print

From Loose Id®

WHY ME?

Treva Harte

THE PRENDARIAN CHRONICLES

Doreen DeSalvo

SHE BLINDED ME WITH SCIENCE FICTION

Kally Jo Surbeck

FOR THE LOVE OF…

Kally Jo Surbeck



Publisher's Note: All titles published in print by Loose Id® have been previously released in e-book format.

Printed in the United States
47743LVS00003BA/2

9 781596 322011